Davenport Dunn
A Man Of Our Day
Vol. I

By

Charles Lever

Double 9
BOOKS

Davenport Dunn
A Man Of Our Day
Vol. I
by Charles Lever

ISBN: 978-93-61152-33-7
Published by

DOUBLE 9 BOOKS

2/13-B, Ansari Road
Daryaganj, New Delhi – 110002
info@double9books.com
www.double9books.com
Tel. 011-40042856

ABOUT THE AUTHOR

Lever and Boyle earned pocket money by singing their own ballads in Dublin's streets and engaging in a variety of other pranks, which Lever dramatized in his novels O'Malley, Con Cregan, and Lord Kilgobbin. In 1833, he married his first love, Catherine Baker, and in February 1837, after a number of experiences, he began publishing The Confessions of Harry Lorrequer in the newly created Dublin University Magazine. In 1833, he married his first love, Catherine Baker, and in February 1837, after a number of experiences, he began publishing The Confessions of Harry Lorrequer in the newly created Dublin University Magazine. During the previous seven years, popular taste had turned toward the "service novel," examples of which include Frank Mildmay (1829) by Frederick Marryat, Tom Cringle's Log (1829) by Michael Scott, The Subaltern (1825) by George Robert Gleig, Cyril Thornton (1827) by Thomas Hamilton, Stories of Waterloo (1833) by William Hamilton Maxwell, Ben Brace (1840) by Frederick Chamier, and The Bivouac (1837), also by Maxwell. Lever had met the genre's nominal founder, William Hamilton Maxwell.

CONTENTS

CHAPTER I
HYDROPATHIC ACQUAINTANCES

We are at Como, on the lake—that spot so beloved of opera dancers—the day-dream of prima donnas—the Elysium of retired barytones! And with what reason should this be the Paradise of all who have lived and sighed, and warbled and pirouetted, within the charmed circle of the footlights? The crystal waters mirroring every cliff and crag with intense distinctness; the vegetation variegated to the very verge of extravagance; orange-trees overloaded with fruit; arbutus only too much bespangled with red berries; villas, more coquettish than ever scene-painter conceived, with vistas of rooms within, all redolent of luxury; terraces, and statues, and vases, and fountains, and marble balconies, steeped in a thousand balmy odours, make up a picture which well may fascinate those whose ideal of beauty is formed of such gorgeous groupings. There is something of unreality in the brilliant colouring and variety of the scene suggesting the notion, that at any moment the tenor may emerge, velvet mantle and all, from the copse before you; or a prima donna, in all the dishevelment of her back hair, rush madly to your feet. There is not a portal from which an angry father may not issue; not a shady walk that might not be trod by an incensed basso!

The rustic bridges seem made for the tiny feet of short-petticoated damsels, daintily tripping, with white-napkin covered baskets, to soft music; and every bench appears but waiting for that wearied old peasant, in blue stockings, a staff, and a leather belt, that has vented his tiresomeness in the same spot for the last half century. Who wonders, if the distracted Princess of "the scene" should love a picture that recalls the most enthusiastic triumphs of her success? Why should not the retired "Feri" like to wander at will through a more enchanting garden than ever she pirouetted in?

Conspicuous amongst the places where these stage-like elements abound is the Villa d'Este; situated in a little bay, with two jutting promontories to guard it, the ground offers every possible variety of surface and elevation. From the very edge of the calm lake, terrace rises above terrace, clad with all that is rich and beautiful in vegetation; rocks, and waterfalls, and ruins, and statues abound. Everything that money could buy, and bad taste suggest, are there heaped with a profusion that is actually confounding. Every stone stair leads to some new surprise; every table-land opens some fresh and astonishing prospect. Incongruous, inharmonious, tea-gardenish as it is, there is still a charm in the spot which no efforts of the vilest taste seem able to eradicate. The vines *will* cluster in graceful groupings; the oranges *will* glow in gorgeous contrast to their dark mantle of leaves; water *will* leap with its own spontaneous gladness, and fall in diamond showers over a grassy carpet no emerald ever rivalled; and, more than all, the beautiful lake itself *will* reflect the picture, with such softened effects of light and shadow, that all the perversions of human ingenuity are totally lost in the transmission.

This same Villa d'Este was once the scene of a sad drama; but it is not to this era in its history we desire now to direct our reader's attention, but to a period much later, when no longer the home of an exiled Princess, or the retreat where shame and sorrow abandoned themselves to every excess, its changed fortune had converted it into an establishment for the water cure!

The prevailing zeal of our day is to simplify everything, even to things which will not admit of simplicity. What with our local athenæums, our mechanics' institutes, our lecturing lords and discoursing baronets, we have done a great deal. Science has been popularised, remote geographies made familiar, complex machinery explained, mysterious inscriptions rendered intelligible. How could it be expected that in the general enthusiasm for useful knowledge medicine should escape, or that its secrets should be exempt from a scrutiny that has spared nothing? Hence have sprung up those various sects in the curative art which, professing to treat rationally and openly what hitherto has been shrouded in mysticism and deception, have multiplied themselves into grape cures, milk cures, and water cures, and Heaven knows how many other strange devices "to cheat the ills that flesh is heir to."

We are not going to quarrel with any of these new religions; we forgive them much for the simple service they have done, in withdrawing their followers from the confined air, the laborious life, the dreary toil, or the drearier dissipation of cities, to the fresh and invigorating breezes, the cheerful quietude, and the simple pleasures of a country existence.

We care little for the regimen or the ritual, be it lentils or asses' milk, Tyrol grapes, or pure water, so that it be administered on the breezy mountain side, or in the healthful air of some lofty "Plateau" away from the cares, the ambitions, the strife, and the jar-rings of the active world, with no seductions of dissipation, neither the prolonged stimulants, nor the late hours of fashion.

It was a good thought, too, to press the picturesque into the service of health, and show the world what benefits may flow, even to nerves and muscles, from elevated thoughts and refined pleasures. All this is, however, purely digressionary, since we are more concerned with the social than the medical aspects of Hydropathy, and so we come back at once to Como. The sun has just risen, on a fresh morning in autumn, over the tall mountain east of the lake, making the whole western shore, where the Villa d'Este stands, all a-glitter with his rays. Every rock, and crag, and promontory are picked out with a sharp distinctness, every window is a-blaze, and streams of light shoot into many a grove and copse, as though glad to pierce their way into cool spots where the noonday sun himself can never enter. On the opposite shore, a dim and mysterious shadow wraps every object, faint outlines of tower and palace loom through the darkness, and a strange hazy depth encloses the whole scene. Such is the stillness, however, that the opening of a casement, or the plash of a stone in the water, is heard across the lake, and voices come from the mysterious gloom with an effect almost preternaturally striking.

On a terrace high up above the lake, sheltered with leafy fig-trees and prickly pears, there walks a gentleman, sniffing the morning air, and evidently bent on inhaling health at every pore.

Nothing in his appearance indicates the invalid; every gesture, as he moves, rather displays a conscious sense of health and vigour. Somewhat above the middle size, compactly but not heavily built, it is very difficult to guess his years; for though his hair and the large whiskers which meet beneath his chin are perfectly white, his clear blue eyes and regular teeth show no signs of age. Singularly enough, it is his dress that gives the clue to this mystery. His tightly-fitting frock, his bell-shaped hat, and his shapely trousers, all tell of a fashion antecedent to our loosely-hanging vestments and uncared-for garments; for the Viscount Lackington was a lord in waiting to the "First Gentleman" in Europe at a time when Paletots were unknown, and Jim Crows had not been imagined.

Early as was the hour, his dress was perfect in all its details, and the accurate folds of his immaculate cravat, and the spotless brilliancy of his boots, would have done credit to Bond-street in days when Bond-street cherished such glories. Let our modern critics sneer as they will at the dandyism of that day, the gentleman of the time was a very distinctive individual, and, in the subdued colour of his habiliments, their studious simplicity, and, above all, their unvarying uniformity, utterly defied all the attempts of spurious imitators.

Our story opens only a few years back, and Lord Lackington was then one of the very few who perpetuated the traditions in costume of that celebrated period; but he did so with such unerring accuracy, that men actually wondered where those marvellously shaped hats were made, or how those creaseless coats were ever fashioned. Even to the perfume of his handkerchief, the faintest and most evanescent of odours, all were mysteries that none could penetrate.

As he surveyed the landscape through his double eye-glass, he smiled graciously and blandly, and gently inclined his head, as though to say, "Very prettily done, water and mountains. I'm quite satisfied with you, trees; you please me very much indeed! Trickle away little fountain—the picture is the better for it." His Lordship had soon, however, other objects to engage his attention than the inanimate constituents of the scene. The spot which he had selected for his point of view was usually traversed, in their morning walks, by the other residents of the "Cure," and this circumstance permitted him to receive the homage of such early risers as were fain to couple with their pursuit of health the recognition of a great man.

Like poverty, hydropathy makes us acquainted with strange associates. The present establishment was too recently formed to have acquired any very distinctive celebrity, but it was sufficiently crowded. There was a great number of third-rate Italians from the Lombard towns and cities, a sprinkling of inferior French, a few English, a stray American or so, and an Irish family, on their way to Italy, sojourning here rather for economy than health, and fancying that they were acquiring habits and manners that would serve them through their winter's campaign.

The first figure which emerged upon the plateau was that of a man swathed in great-coat, cap, and worsted wrappers, that it was difficult to guess what he could be. He came forward at a shambling trot, and was about to pass on without looking aside, when Lord Lackington called out, "Ah! Spicer, have you got off that eleven pounds yet?" "No, my Lord, but very near it. I'm seven stone ten, and at seven eight I'm all right."

"Push along, then, and don't lose your training,' said his Lordship, dismissing him with a bland wave of the hand. And the other made an attempt at a salutation, and passed on.

"Madame la Marquise, your servant. You ascend these mountain steeps like a chamois!"

This compliment was addressed to a little, very fat old lady, who came snorting along like a grampus.

"Benedetto Dottore!" cried she. "He will have it that I must go up to the stone cross yonder every morning before breakfast, and I know I shall burst a blood-vessel yet in the attempt."

A chair, with a mass of horse-clothing and furs, surmounted by a little yellow wizened face, was next borne by, to which Lord Lackington bowed courteously, saying, "Your Excellency improves at every hour."

His Excellency gave a brief nod and a little faint smile, swallowed a mouthful from a silver flask presented by his servant, and disappeared.

"Ah! the fair syren sisters! what a charming vision!" said his Lordship, as two bright-cheeked, laughing-eyed girls bounced upon the terrace in all the high-hearted enjoyment of good health and good spirits.

"Molly, for shame!" cried what seemed the elder, a damsel of about nineteen, as the younger, holding out her dress with both hands, performed a kind of minuet curtsey to the Viscount, to which he responded with a bow that might have done credit to Versailles.

"Perfectly done—grace and elegance itself. The foot a little—a very little more in advance."

"Just because you want to look at it," cried she, laughing. "Molly, Molly!" exclaimed the other, rebukingly. "Let him deny it if he can, Lucy," retorted she. "But here's papa."

And as she spoke, a square-built, short, florid man, fanning his bald head with a straw hat, puffed his way forward.

"My Lord, I'm your most obaydient!" said he, with a very unmistakably Irish enunciation. "O'Reilly, I'm delighted to see you. These charming girls of yours have just put me in good humour with the whole creation. What a lovely spot this is; how beautiful!"

Though his Lordship's arm and outstretched hand directed attention to the scenery, his eyes never wandered from the pretty features of the laughing girl beside him.

"It's like Banthry!" said Mr. O'Reilly—"it's the very ditto of Banthry."

"Indeed!" exclaimed my Lord, still pursuing his scrutiny.

"Only Banthry's bigger and wider. Indeed, I may say finer."

"Nothing, in *my* estimation, can exceed this!" said his Lordship, with a distinctive smile, addressed to the young lady.

"I'm glad you think so," said she, with a merry laugh. And then, with a pirouette, she sprang up the steep steps on the rocky path before her, and disappeared, her sister as quickly following, leaving Mr. O'Reilly alone with his Lordship.

"What heaps of money she laid out here," exclaimed O'Reilly, as he looked at the labyrinth of mad ruins, and rustic bridges, and hanging gardens on every side of him.

"Large sums—very large indeed!" said my Lord, whose thoughts were evidently on some other track.

"Pure waste—nothing else; the place never could pay. Vines and fig-trees, indeed—I'd rather see a crop of oats.".

"I have a weakness for the picturesque, I must own," said my Lord, as his eye still followed the retreating figures of the girls.

"Well, I like a waterfall; and, indeed, I like a summer-house myself," said O'Reilly, as though confessing to a similar trait on his own part.

"This is the first time you have been abroad, O'Reilly?" said his Lordship, to turn the subject of the conversation.

"Yes, my Lord, my first, and, with God's blessing, my last, too! When I lost Mrs. O'Reilly, two years ago, of a complaint that beat all the doctors—"

"Ah, yes, you mentioned that to me; very singular indeed!"

"For it wasn't in the heart itself, my Lord, but in the bag that houlds it."

"Oh yes, I remember the explanation perfectly; so you thought you'd just come abroad for a little distraction."

"Distraction indeed! 'tis the very word for it," broke in Mr. O'Reilly, eagerly. "My head is bewildered between the lingo and the money, and they keep telling me, 'You'll get used to it, papa, darling—you'll be quite at home yet.' But how is that ever possible?"

"Still, for your charming girls' sake," said my Lord, caressing his whiskers and adjusting his neckcloth, as if for immediate captivation—"or their sake, O'Reilly, you've done perfectly right!"

"Well, I'm glad your Lordship says so. 'Tis nobody ought to know better!" said he, with a heavy sigh.

"They really deserve every cultivation. All the advantages that—that—that sort of thing can bestow!"

And his Lordship smiled benignly, as though offering his own aid to the educational system.

"What they said to me was this," said O'Reilly, dropping his voice to a tone of the most confiding secrecy: "'Don't be keeping them down here in Mary's Abbey, but take them where they'll see life. You can give them forty thousand pounds between them, Tim O'Reilly, and with that and their own good looks—-'"

"Beauty, O'Reilly—-downright loveliness," broke in my Lord.

"Well, indeed, they are handsome," said O'Reilly, with an honest satisfaction, "and that's exactly why I thought the advice was good. 'Take them abroad,' they said; 'take them into Germany and Italy—but more especially Italy'—for they say there's nothing like Italy for finishing young ladies."

"That is certainly the general impression!" said his Lordship with the barest imaginable motion of his nether lip.

"And here we are, but where we're going afterwards, and what well do when we're there, that thief of a Courier we have may know, but I don't."

"So that you gave up business, O'Reilly, and resigned yourself freely to a life of ease," said my Lord, with a smile that seemed to approve the project.

"Yes, indeed, my Lord; but whether it's to be a life of pleasure, I don't know. I was in the provision trade thirty-eight years, and do you know I miss the pigs greatly."

"Every man has a hankering of that sort. Old cosmopolite as I am, I have every now and then my longing for that window at Brookes's, and that snug dinner-room at Boodle's."

"Yes, my Lord," said O'Reilly, who hadn't the faintest conception whether these localities were not situated in China.

"Ah, Twining, never thought to see you here," called out his Lordship to a singularly tall man, who came forward with such awkward contortions of legs and arms, as actually to suggest the notion that he was struggling against somebody. Mr. O'Reilly modestly stole away while the friends were shaking hands, and we take the same opportunity to, present the new arrival to our reader.

Mr. Adderley Twining was a gentleman of good family and very large fortune, whose especial pleasure it was to pass off to the world for a gay, light-hearted, careless creature, of small means, and most lavish liberality. To be, in fact, perpetually struggling between a most generous temperament and a narrow purse. His cordiality was extreme, his politeness unbounded; and as he was most profuse in his pledges for the present and his promises for the future, he attained to a degree of popularity which to his own estimation was immense. This was, in fact, the one sole self-deception of his very crafty nature, and the belief that he was a universal favourite was the solitary mistake of this shrewd intelligence. Although a married man, there was so constantly some "difficulty" or other—these were his own words—about Lady Grace, that they seldom were seen together; but he spoke of her when absent in terms of the most fervent affection, but whose health, or spirits, or tastes, or engagements unhappily denied her the happiness of travelling along with him. Whenever it chanced that they were together, he scarcely mentioned her.

"And what breeze of fortune has wafted you here, Twining?" said his Lordship, delighted to chance upon a native of his own world.

"Health, my Lord,—health," said he, with one of his ready laughs, as though everything he said or thought had some comic side in it that amused him, "and a touch of economy too, my Lord."

"What humbug all that is, Twining. Who the deuce is so well off as yourself?" said Lord Lackington, with all that peculiar bitterness with which an embarrassed man listens to the grumblings of a wealthy one.

"Only too happy, my Lord—rejoiced if you were right. Capital news for me, eh?—excellent news!" And he slapped his lean legs with his long thin fingers, and laughed immoderately.

"Come, come, we all know that—besides a devilish good thing of your own—you got the Wrexley estate, and old Poole's Dorsetshire property. Hang me if I ever open a newspaper without reading that you are somebody's residuary legatee."

"I assure you, solemnly, my Lord, I am actually hard up, pressed for money, downright inconvenienced." And he laughed again, as though it were uncommonly droll.

"Stuff—nonsense!" said my Lord, angrily, for he really was losing temper; and to change the topic he curtly asked, "And where do you mean to pass the winter?"

"In Florence, my Lord, or Naples. We have a little den in both places."

The "den" in Florence was a sumptuous palace on the Arno. Its brother at Naples was a royal villa near Posilippo.

"Why not Rome? Lady Lackington and myself mean to try Rome."

"Ah, all very well for you, my Lord, but for people of small fortune—"

There was that in the expression of his Lordship's face that told Twining this vein might be followed too far, and so he stopped in time, and laughed away pleasantly.

"Spicer tells me," resumed Lord Lackington, "that Florence is quite deserted; nothing but a kind of second and third rate set of people go there. Is that so?"

"Excellent people, capital society, great fun!" said Twining, in a burst of merriment.

"Spicer calls them 'Snobs,' and he ought to know."

"So he ought indeed, my Lord—no one better. Admirably observed, and very just."

"He's in training again for that race that never comes off," said his Lordship. "The first time I ever saw him—it was at Leamington—and he was performing the same farce, with hot baths and blankets, and jotting down imaginary bets in a small note-book."

"How good—capital! Your Lordship has him perfectly—you know him thoroughly—great fun! Spicer, excellent creature!"

"How those fellows live is a great mystery to me. You chance upon them everywhere, in Baden or Aix in summer, in Paris or Vienna during the winter. Now, if they were amusing rogues, like that fellow I met at your house in Hampshire—"

"Oh, Stockley, my Lord; rare fellow, quite a genius!" laughed Twining.

"Just so—Stockley; one would have them just to help over the boredom of a country house; but this creature Spicer is as devoid of amusing gifts, as tiresome, and as worn out, as if he owned ten thousand a year."

"How good, by Jove!" cried Twining, in ecstasy. And he slapped his gaunt limbs and threw his long arms wildly about in a transport of delight.

"And who are here, Twining—any of our set?" "Not a soul, my Lord; the place isn't known yet, that's the reason I came here—so quiet and so cheap, make your own terms with them.

"Good fun—excellent!"

"*I* came to meet a man of business," said his Lordship, with a strong emphasis on the pronoun. "He couldn't prolong his journey farther south, and so we agreed to rendezvous here."

"I have a little affair also to transact—a mere trifle, a nothing, in fact— with a lawyer, who promises to meet me here by the end of the month, so that we have just time to take our baths, drink the waters, and all that sort of thing, while we are waiting."

And he rubbed his hands, and laughed away again.

"What a boon for my wife to learn that Lady Grace is here! She was getting so hipped with the place—not so much the place as the odious people—that I suspect she'd have left me to wait for Dunn all alone."

"Dunn! Dunn! not Davenport Dunn?" exclaimed Twining.

"The very man—do you know him?"

"To be sure, he's the fellow I'm waiting for. Capital fun, isn't it?"

And he slapped his legs again, while he repeated the name of Dunn over and over again.

"I want to know something about this same Mr. Dunn," said Lord Lackington, confidentially.

"So do I; like it of all things," cried Twining. "Clever fellow-wonderful fellow—up to everything—acquainted with everybody. Great fun!"

"He occupies a very distinguished position in Ireland, I fancy," said his Lordship, with such a marked stress on the locality as to show that such did not constitute an imperial reputation.

"Yes, yes, man of the day there; do what he likes; very popular— immensely popular!" said Twining, as he laughed on.

"So that you know no more of him than his public repute—-no more than I know myself," said his Lordship.

"Not so much as your Lordship, I'm certain," said Twining, as though it would have been unbecoming in him to do so; "in fact, my business transactions are such mere nothings, that it's quite a kindness on his part to undertake them—trifles, no more!"

And Twining almost hugged himself in the ecstasy which his last words suggested.

"*Mine*," said Lord Lackington, haughtily, "are of consequence enough to fetch him hither—a good thousand miles away from England; but he is pretty certain of its being well worth his while, to come."

"Quite convinced of that—could swear it," said Twining, eagerly.

"Here are a mob of insufferable bores," said his Lordship, testily, as a number of people were heard approaching, for somehow—it is not easy to say exactly why—he had got into a train of thought that scorned to worry him, and was not disposed to meet strangers; and so, with a brief gesture of good-by to Twining, he turned into a path and disappeared.

Twining looked after him for a second or two, and then slapping his legs, he muttered, pleasantly, "What fun!" and took the road towards the house.

CHAPTER II
HOW TWO "FINE LADIES" PASS THE MORNING

In a room of moderate size, whose furniture was partly composed of bygone finery and some articles of modern comfort—a kind of compromise between a Royal residence and a Hydropathic establishment—sat two ladies at an open window, which looked out upon a small terrace above the lake. The view before them could scarcely have been surpassed in Europe. Enclosed, as in a frame, between the snow-clad Alps and the wooded mountains of the Brianca, lay the lake, its shores one succession of beautiful villas, whose gardens descended to the very water. Although the sun was high, the great mountains threw the shadows half way across the lake; and in the dim depth of shade, tower and crag, battlement and precipice, were strangely intermixed, giving to the picture a mysterious grandeur that contrasted strongly with the bright reality of the opposite shore, where fruit and flowers, gay tapestries from casements, and floating banners, added colour to the scene.

Large white-sailed boats stole peacefully along, loaded, half-mast high, with water-melons and garden stores; the golden produce glittering in the sun, and glowing in the scarcely rippled water beneath them, while the low chant of the boatmen floated softly and lazily through the air—meet sounds in a scene where all seemed steeped in a voluptuous repose.

The two ladies whom we have mentioned were not impassioned spectators of the scene. Whenever their eyes ranged over it, no new brilliancy awoke in them, no higher colour tinged their cheek. One was somewhat advanced in life, but with many traces of beauty, and an air which denoted a lifelong habit of homage and deference.

There was that in her easy, lounging attitude, and the splendour of her dress, which seemed to intimate that Lady Lackington would still be graceful, and even extravagant, though there were none to admire the grace or be dazzled by the costliness. Her companion, though several years younger, looked, from the effects of delicate health and a suffering disposition, almost of her own age. She, too, was handsome; but it was a beauty which so much depended on tint and colour, that her days of indisposition left her almost bereft of good looks. All about her, her low, soft voice, her heavily raised eyelids, her fair and blue-veined hands, the very carriage of her head, pensively thrown forwards, were so many protestations of one who asked for sympathy and compassion; and who, whether with reason or without, firmly believed herself the most unhappy creature in existence.

If there was no great similarity of disposition to unite them, there was a bond fully as strong. They were both English of the same order, both born and bred up in a ritual that dictates its own notions of good or bad, of right and wrong, of well-bred and vulgar, of riches and poverty. Given any person in society, or any one event of their lives, and these two ladies' opinion upon either would have been certain to harmonise and agree. The world for them had but one aspect; for the simple reason, that they had always seen it from the one same point of view. They had not often met; they had seen very little of each other for years; but the freemasonry of class supplied all the place of affection, and they were as fond and as confiding as though they were sisters.

"I must say," said the Viscountess, in a tone full of reprobation, "that is shocking—actually shameful; and, in *your* place, I'd not endure it!"

"I have become so habituated to sorrow," sighed Lady Grace

"That you will sink under it at last, my dear, if this man's cruelties be not put an end to. You really must allow me to speak to Lackington."

"It wouldn't be of the slightest service, I assure you. In the first place, he is so plausible, he'd persuade any one that there was nothing to complain of, that he lived up to his fortune, that his means were actually crippled; and secondly, he'd give such pledges for the future, such promises, that it would be downright rudeness to throw a doubt on their sincerity."

"Why did you marry him, my dear?" said Lady Lackington, with a little sigh.

"I married him to vex Ridout; we had a quarrel at that *fête* at Chiswick, you remember, Tollertin's *fête*. Ridout was poor, and felt his poverty. I don't believe I treated his scruples quite fairly. I know I owned to him that I had no contempt for riches—that I thought Belgrave-square, and the Opera, and Diamonds, and a smart Equipage, all very commendable things: and Jack said, 'Then, there's your man. Twining has twenty thousand a year.' 'But, he has not asked me,' said I, laughing. Ridout turned away without a word. Half an hour later, Mr. Adderley Twining formally proposed for my hand, and was accepted."

"And Jack Ridout is now the Marquis of Allerton," said Lady Lackington.

"I know it!" said the other, bitterly.

"With nigh forty thousand a year."

"I know it!" cried she, again.

"And the handsomest house and the finest park in England."

The other burst into tears, and hid her face between her hands.

"There's a fate in these things, my dear," said Lady Lackington, with a slight paleness creeping over her cheek. "That's all we can say about them."

"What have you done with that sweet place in Hampshire?"

"Dingley? It is let to Lord Mauley."

"And you had a house in St. James's-square."

"It is Burridge's Hotel, now."

Lady Lackington fanned her swarthy face for some seconds, and then said, "And how did you come here?"

"We saw—that is, Twining saw—an advertisement of this new establishment in the *Galignani*. We had just arrived at Liége, when he discovered a vetturino returning to Milan with an empty carriage; he accordingly bargained with him to take us on here—I forget for what sum—so that we left our own carriage, and half my luggage, at the Pavilion Hotel, and set off on our three weeks' journey. We have been three weeks all but two days on the road! My maid of course refused to travel in this fashion, and went back to Paris. Courcel, his own man, rebelled too, which Twining, I must say, seemed overjoyed at, and gave him such a character for honesty in consequence, as he never could have hoped for; and so we came on, with George the footman, and a Belgian creature I picked up at the hotel, who, except to tear out my hair when she brushes it, and bruise me whenever she hooks a dress, has really no other gift under heaven."

"And you actually came all this way by vetturino?"

Lady Grace nodded a sad assent, and sighed deeply.

"What does he mean by it, my dear? The man must have some deep, insidious design in all this;—don't you think so?"

"I think to myself, sometimes," replied she, sorrowfully. And now their eyes met, and they remained looking steadily at each other for some seconds. Whatever Lady Grace's secret thoughts, or whatever the dark piercing orbs of her companion served to intimate, true is it that she blushed till her cheek became crimson; and as she arose, and walked out upon the terrace, her neck was a-flame with the emotion.

"He never married?" said Lady Lackington.

"No!" said Lady Grace, without turning her head. And there was a silence on both sides.

Oh dear! how much of the real story of our lives passes without expression—how much of the secret mechanism of our hearts moves without a sound in the machinery!

"Poor fellow!" said Lady Lackington, at last, "his lot is just as sad as your own. I mean," added she, "that he feels it so."

There was no answer, and she resumed. "Not but men generally treat these things lightly enough. They have their clubs, and their Houses of Parliament, and their shooting. Are you ill, dearest?" cried she, as Lady Grace tottered feebly back and sauk into a chair.

"No," said she, in a faint voice, "I'm only tired!" And there was an inexpressible melancholy in the tone as she spoke it.

"And I'm tired too!" said Lady Lackington, drearily. "There is a tyranny in the routine of these places quite insupportable—the hours, the discipline, the diet, and, worse than all, the dreadful people one meets with." Though Lady Grace did not seem very attentive, this was a theme the speaker loved to improve, and so she proceeded to discuss the house and its inhabitants in all freedom. French, Russians, and Italians—all were passed in review, and very smartly criticised, till she arrived at "those atrocious O'Reillys, that my Lord will persist in threatening to present to me. Now one knows horrid people when they are very rich, or very well versed in some speculation or other—mines, or railroads, or the like—and when their advice is so much actual money in your pocket—just, for instance, as my Lord knows that Mr. Davenport Dunn—"

"Oh! he's a great ally of Mr. Twining; at least, I have heard his name a hundred times in connexion with business matters."

"You never saw him?"

"No."

"Nor I, but once; but I confess to have some curiosity to know him. They tell me he can do anything he pleases with each House of Parliament, and has no inconsiderable influence in a sphere yet higher. It is quite certain that the old Duke of Wycombe's affairs were all set to rights by his agency, and Lady Muddleton's divorce bill was passed by his means."

The word "divorce" seemed to rally Lady Grace from her fit of musing, and she said, "Is that certain?"

"Julia herself says so, that's all. He got a bill, or an act, or clause, or whatever you call it, inserted, by which she succeeded in her suit, and she is now as free—as free——"

"As I am not!" broke in Lady Grace, with a sad effort at a smile.

"To be sure, there is a little scandal in the matter, too. They say that old Lord Brookdale was very 'soft' himself in that quarter."

"The Chancellor!" exclaimed Lady Grace.

"And why not, dear? You remember the old refrain, 'No age, no station'—what is it?—and the next line goes—'To sovereign beauty mankind bends the knee.' Julia is rather proud of the triumph herself; she says it is like a victory in China, where the danger is very little and the spoils considerable!"

"Mr. Spicer, my Lady," said a servant, entering, "wishes to know if your Ladyship will receive him."

"Not this morning; say I'm engaged at present Tell him—But perhaps you have no objection—shall we have him in?"

"Just as you please. I don't know him."

Lady Lackington whispered a word or two, and then added aloud, "And one always finds them 'useful,' my dear!"

Mr. Spicer, when denuded of top-coat, cap, and woollen wrapper, as we saw him last, was a slightly made man, middle-sized, and middle-aged, with an air sufficiently gentlemanlike to pass muster in any ordinary assemblage. To borrow an illustration from the pursuits he was versed in, he bore the same relation to a man of fashion that a "weed" does to a "winner of the Derby"—that is to say, to an uneducated eye, there would have seemed some resemblance; and just as the "weed" counterfeits the racer in a certain loose awkwardness of stride and an ungainly show of power, so did he appear to have certain characteristics of a class that he merely mixed with on sufferance, and imitated in some easy "externals." The language of any profession is, however, a great leveller; and whether the cant be of the "House," Westminster Hall, the College of Physicians, the Mess Table, or the "Turf," it is exceedingly difficult at first blush to distinguish the real practitioner from the mere pretender. Now, Spicer was what is called a Gentleman Rider, and he had all the slang of his craft, which is, more or less, the slang of men who move in a very different sphere.

As great landed proprietors of ambitious tendencies will bestow a qualification to sit in Parliament upon some man of towering abilities and small fortune, so did certain celebrities of the Turf confer a similar social qualification on Spicer; and by enabling him to "associate with the world," empower themselves to utilise his talents and make use of his capabilities. In this great Parliament of the Field, therefore, Spicer sat; and though for a very small and obscure borough, yet he had his place, and was "ready when wanted."

"How d'ye do, Spicer?" said Lady Lackington, arranging the folds of her dress as he came forward, and intimating by the action that he was not to delude himself into any expectation of touching her hand. "My Lord told me you were here."

Spicer bowed, and muttered, and looked, as though he were waiting to be formally presented to the other lady in company; but Lady Lackington had not the most remote intention of bestowing on him such a mark of recognition, and merely answered the mute appeal of his features by a dry "Won't you sit down?"

And Mr. Spicer did sit down, and of a verity his position denoted no excess of ease or enjoyment. It was not that he did not attempt to appear perfectly at home, that he did not assume an attitude of the very calmest self-possession, maybe he even passed somewhat the frontier of the lackadaisical territory he assumed, for he slapped his boot with his whip in a jaunty affectation of indifference.

"Pray, don't do that!" said Lady Lackington; "it worries one!"

He desisted, and a very awkward silence of some seconds ensued; at length she said, "There was something or other I wanted to ask you about; you can't help me to it, can you?"

"I'm afraid not, my Lady. Was it anything about sporting matters?"

"No, no; but now that you remind me, all that information you gave me about Glaucus was wrong, he came in 'a bad third.' My Lord laughed at me for losing my money on him, and said he was the worst horse of the lot."

"Very sorry to differ with his Lordship," said Spicer, deferentially, "but he was the favourite up to Tuesday evening, when Scott declared that he'd win with Big the Market. I then tried to get four to one on Flycatcher, to square your book, but the stable was nobbled."

"Did you ever hear such jargon, my dear?" said Lady Lackington. "You don't understand one syllable of it, I'm certain."

Spicer smirked and made a slight approach to a bow, as though even this reference to him would serve for an introduction; but Lady Grace met the advance with a haughty stare and a look, that said, as plainly as any words, "At your peril, Sir!"

"Well, one thing is certain!" said Lady Lackington, "nothing that you predicted turned out afterwards. Glaucus was beaten, and I lost my three hundred pounds—only fancy, dearest, three hundred pounds, with which one could do so many things! I wanted it in fifty ways, and I never contemplated leaving it with the legs at Newmarket."

"Not the legs, I assure you, my Lady—not the legs. I made your book with Colonel Stamford and Gore Middleton—"

"As if I cared who won it!" said she, haughtily.

"I never knew that you tempted fortune in this fashion!" said Lady Grace, languidly.

"I do so very rarely, my dear. I think Mining Shares are better, or Guatemala State Bonds. I realised very handsomely indeed upon them two years ago. To be sure it was Dunn that gave me the hint: he dined with us at the Hôtel de Windsor, and I asked him to pay a small sum for me to Hore's people, and when I counted the money out to him, he said, 'Why not buy in some of those Guanaxualo shares; they'll be up to—' I forget what he said—'before a month. Let Storr wait, and you'll pay him in full.' And he was quite right, aas I told you. I realised about eight hundred pounds on my venture."

"If Glaucus had won, my Lady—"

"Don't tell me what I should have gained," broke she in. "It only provokes one the more, and above all, Spicer, no more information, I detest 'information.' And now, what was it I had to say to you; really *your* memory would seem to be failing you completely. What could it be?"

"It couldn't be that roan filly——"

"Of course it couldn't. I really must endeavour to persuade you that my thoughts occasionally stray beyond the stable. By the way, you sold those grey carriage-horses for nothing. You always told me they were the handsomest pair in London, and yet you say I'm exceedingly lucky to get one hundred and eighty pounds for them."

"You forget, my Lady, that Bloomfield was a roarer——"

"Well, you really are in a tormenting mood this morning, Spicer. Just bethink you, now, if there's anything more you have to say, disagreeable and unpleasant, and say it at once; you have made lady Grace quite ill——"

"No, only tired!" sighed her friend, with a melancholy smile.

"Now I remember," cried Lady Lackington, "it was about that house at Florence. I don't think we shall pass any time there, but in case we should,

I should like that Zapponi palace, with the large terrace on the Arno, and there must be no one on the ground-floor, mind that; and I'll not give more than I gave formerly—perhaps not so much. But, above all, remember, that if we decide to go on to Rome, that I'm not bound to it in the least, and he must new-carpet that large drawing-room, and I must have the little boudoir hung in blue, with muslin over it, not pink. Pink is odious, except in a dressing-room. You will yourself look to the stables; they require considerable alteration, and there's something about the dining-room— what was it?—Lord Lackington will remember it. But perhaps I have given you as many directions as your head will bear."

"I almost think so too, my Lady," muttered he, with a half-dogged look.

"And be sure, Spicer, that we have that cook—Antoine—if we should want him. Don't let him take a place till we decide where we shall stop."

"You are aware that he insists on a hundred and fifty francs a month, and his wine."

"I should like to know what good you are, if I am to negotiate with these creatures myself!" said she, haughtily. "I must say, Lady Grace will suspect that I have rather overrated your little talents, Spicer." And Lady Grace gave a smile that might mean any amount of approval or depreciation required. "I shall not want that saddle now, and you must make that man take it back again."

"But I fear, my Lady——"

"There, don't be tiresome! What is that odious bell? Oh, it's the dinner of these creatures. You dine at the table d'hôte, I think, so pray don't let us keep you. You can drop in to-morrow. Let me see, about two, or half-past. Good-by—good-by."

And so Mr. Spicer retired. The bow Lady Grace vouchsafed being in reality addressed rather to one of the figures on her fan than to himself.

"One gets a habit of these kind of people," said Lady Lackington, as the door closed after him; "but really it is a bad habit."

"I think so too," said Lady Grace, languidly.

"To be sure, there are now and then occasions when you can't employ exactly a servant. There are petty negotiations which require a certain delicacy of treatment, and there, they are useful. Besides," said she, with a half-sneering laugh, "there's a fashion in them, and, like Blenheim spaniels, every one must have one, and the smaller the better!"

"Monsignore Clifford my Lady, to know if you receive," said a servant, entering.

"Oh, certainly. I'm charmed, my dear Grace, to present to you the most agreeable man of all Rome. He is English, but 'went over,' as they call it, and is now high in the Pope's favour."

These words, hurriedly uttered as they were, had been scarcely spoken when the visitor entered the room. He was a tall, handsome man, of about five-and-thirty, dressed in deep black, and wearing a light blue ribbon across his white neckcloth. He advanced with all the ease of good breeding, and taking Lady Lackington's hand, he kissed the tips of her fingers with the polished grace of a courtier.

After a formal presentation to Lady Grace, he took a seat between the two ladies.

"I am come on, for *me*, a sad errand, my Lady," said he, in a voice of peculiar depth and sweetness, in which the very slightest trace of a foreign accent was detectable—"it is to say good-by!"

"You quite shock me, Monsignore. I always hoped you were here for our own time."

"I believed and wished it also, my Lady; but I have received a peremptory order to return to Rome. His Holiness desires to see me at once. There is some intention, I understand, of naming me as the Nuncio at Florence. Of course this is a secret as yet." And he turned to each of the ladies in succession.

"Oh, that would be charming—at least for any one happy enough to fix their residence there, and my friend Lady Grace is one of the fortunate."

Monsignore bowed in gratitude to the compliment, but contrived, as he bent his head, to throw a covert glance at his future neighbour, with the result of which he did not seem displeased.

"I must of course, then, send you back those interesting books, which I have only in part read?"

"By no means, my Lady; they are yours, if you will honour me by accepting them. If the subject did not forbid the epithet, I should call them trifles."

"Monsignore insists on my reading the 'Controversy,' dear Lady Grace; but how I am to continue my studies without his guidance———"

"We can correspond, my Lady," quickly broke in the other. "You can state to me whatever doubts—difficulties, perhaps, were, the better word— occur to you; I shall be but too happy and too proud to offer you the solution; and if my Lady Grace Twining would condescend to accept me in the same capacity—."

She bowed blandly, and he went on.

"There is a little tract here, by the Cardinal Balbi—'Flowers of St. Joseph' is the title. The style is simple but touching—'the invitation' scarcely to be resisted."

"I think you told me I should like the Cardinal personally," broke in Lady Lackington.

"His Eminence is charming, my Lady—such goodness, such gentleness, and so much of the very highest order of conversational agreeability."

"Monsignore is so polite as to promise us introductions at Rome," continued she, addressing Lady Grace, "and amongst those, too, who are never approached by our countrymen."

"The Alterini, the Fornisari, the Balbetti," proudly repeated Monsignore.

"All ultra-exclusives, you understand," whispered Lady Lacking-ton to her friend, "who wouldn't tolerate the English."

"How charming!" ejaculated Lady Grace, with a languid enthusiasm.

"The Roman nobility," continued Lady Lackington, "stands proudly forward, as the only society in Europe to which the travelling English cannot obtain access."

"They have other prejudices, my Lady—if I may so dare to call sentiments inspired by higher influences—than those which usually sway society. These prejudices are all in favour of such as regard our Church, if not with the devotion of true followers, at least with the respect and veneration that rightfully attach to the first-born of Christianity."

"Yes," said Lady Lackington, as, though not knowing very well to what, she gave her assent, and then added, "I own to you I have always experienced a sort of awe—a sense of—what shall I call it?"

"Devotion, my Lady," blandly murmured Monsignore, while his eyes were turned on her with a paraphrase of the sentiment.

"Just so. I have always felt it on entering one of your churches—the solemn stillness, the gloomy indistinctness, the softened tints, the swelling notes of the organ—you know what I mean."

"And when such emotions are etherialised, when, rising above material influences, they are associated with thoughts of what is alone thought-worthy, with hopes of what alone dignifies hope, imagine, then, the blessed beatitude, the heavenly ecstasy they inspire."

Monsignore had now warmed to his work, and very ingeniously sketched out the advantages of a creed that accommodated itself so beautifully to every temperament—that gave so much and yet exacted so little—that poisoned no pleasures—discouraged no indulgences—but left every enjoyment open with its price attached to it, just as objects are ticketed in a bazaar. He had much to say, too, of its soothing consolations—its devices to alleviate sorrow and cheat affliction—while such was its sympathy for poor suffering humanity, that even the very caprices of temper—the mere whims of fancied depression—were not deemed unworthy of its pious care.

It is doubtful whether these ladies would have accorded to a divine of their own persuasion the same degree of favour and attention that they now bestowed on Monsignore Clifford. Perhaps his manner in discussing certain belongings of his Church was more entertaining; perhaps, too—we hint it with deference—that there was something like a forbidden pleasure in thus trespassing into the domain of Rome. His light and playful style was, however, a fascination amply sufficient to account for the interest he excited. If he dwelt but passingly on the dogmas of his Church, he was eloquently diffuse on its millinery. Copes, stoles, and vestments he revelled in; and there was a picturesque splendour in his description of ceremonial that left the best-"effects" of the opera far behind. How gloriously, too, did he expatiate on the beauty of the Madonna, the costliness of her gems, and the brilliancy of her diadem! How incidentally did he display a rapturous veneration for loveliness, and a very pretty taste in dress! In a word, as they both confessed, "he was charming." There was a downy softness in his enthusiasm, a sense of repose even in his very insistence, peculiarly pleasant to those who like to have their sensations, like their perfumes, as weak and as faint as possible.

"There is a tact and delicacy about these men from which our people might take a lesson," said Lady Lackington, as the door closed after him.

"Very true," sighed Lady Grace; "ours are really dreadful."

CHAPTER III
A FATHER AND A DAUGHTER

A DREARY evening late in October, a cold thin rain falling, and a low wailing wind sighing through the headless branches of the trees in Merrion Square, made Dublin seem as sad-looking and deserted as need be. The principal inhabitants had not yet returned to their homes for the winter, and the houses wore that melancholy look of vacancy and desertion so strikingly depressing. One sound alone woke the echoes in that silence; it was a loud knocking at the door of a large and pretentious mansion in the middle of the north side of the square. Two persons had been standing at the door for a considerable time, and by every effort of knocker and bell endeavoring to obtain admittance. One of these was a tall, erect man of about fifty, whose appearance but too plainly indicated that most painful of all struggles between poverty and a certain pretension. White-seamed and threadbare as was his coat, he wore it buttoned to the top with a sort of military smartness, his shabby hat was set on with a kind of jaunty air, and his bushy whiskers, combed and frizzed out with care, seemed a species of protest against being thought as humble as certain details of dress might bespeak him. At his side stood a young girl, so like him that a mere glance proclaimed her to be his daughter; and although in her appearance, also, narrow means stood confessed, there was an unmistakable something in her calm, quiet features and her patient expression that declared she bore her lot with a noble and high-hearted courage.

"One trial more, Bella, and I 'll give it up," cried he, angrily, as, seizing the knocker, he shook the strong door with the rapping, while he jingled the bell with equal violence. "If they don't come now, it is because they 've seen who it is, or, maybe——"

"There, see, papa, there's a window opening above," said the girl, stepping out into the rain as she spoke.

"What d' ye mean,—do ye want to break in the door?" cried a harsh voice, as the wizened, hag-like face of a very dirty old woman appeared from the third story.

"I want to know if Mr. Davenport Dunn is at home," cried the man.

"He is not; he 's abroad,—in France."

"When is he expected back?" asked he again.

"Maybe in a week, maybe in three weeks."

"Have any letters come for Mr. Kellett—Captain Kel-lett?" said he, quickly correcting himself.

"No!"

And a bang of the window, as the head was withdrawn, finished the colloquy.

"That's pretty conclusive, any way, Bella," said he, with an attempt to laugh. "I suppose there's no use in staying here longer. Poor child," added he, as he watched her preparations against the storm, "you 'll be wet to the skin! I think we must take a car,—eh, Bella? I *will* take a car." And he put an emphasis on the word that sounded like a firm resolve.

"No, no, papa; neither of us ever feared rain."

"And, by George! it can't spoil our clothes, Bella," said he, laughing with a degree of jocularity that sounded astonishing, even to himself; for he quickly added, "But I *will* have a car; wait a moment here, under the porch, and I 'll get one."

And before she could interpose a word, he was off and away, at a speed that showed the vigor of a younger man.

"It won't do, Bella," he said, as he came back again; "there's only one fellow on the stand, and he 'll not go under half a crown. I pushed him hard for one-and-sixpence, but he 'd not hear of it, and so I thought—that was, I knew well—you would be angry with me."

"Of course, papa; it would be mere waste of money," said she, hastily. "An hour's walk,—at most, an hour and a half,—and there's an end of it And now let us set out, for it is growing late."

There were few in the street as they passed along; a stray creature or so, houseless and ragged, shuffled onward; an odd loiterer stood for shelter in an archway, or a chance passer-by, with ample coat and umbrella, seemed to defy the pelting storm, while cold and dripping they plodded along in silence.

"That's old Barrington's house, Bella," said he, as they passed a large and dreary-looking mansion at the corner of the square; "many's the pleasant evening I spent in it."

She muttered something, but inaudibly, and they went on as before.

"I wonder what 's going on here to-day. It was Sir Dyke Morris used to live here when I knew it" And he stopped at an open door, where a flood of light poured forth into the street "That's the Bishop of Derry, Bella, that's just gone in. There's a dinner-party there to-day," whispered he, as, half reluctant to go, he still peered into the hall.

She drew him gently forward, and he seemed to have fallen into a revery, as he muttered at intervals,—

"Great times—fine times—plenty of money—and fellows that knew how to spend it!"

Drearily plashing onward through wind and rain, their frail clothes soaked through, they seldom interchanged a word.

"Lord Drogheda lived there, Bella," said he, stopping short at the door of a splendidly illuminated hotel; "and I remember the time I was as free and welcome in it as in my own house. My head used to be full of the strange things that happened there once. Brown, and Barry Fox, and Tisdall, and the rest of us, were wild chaps! Faith, my darling, it was n't for Mr. Davenport Dunn I cared in those times, or the like of him. Davenport Dunn, indeed!"

"It is strange that he has not written to us," said the girl, in a low voice.

"Not a bit strange; it's small trouble he takes about us. I'll bet a five-pound note—I mean, I'll lay sixpence," said he, correcting himself with some confusion,—"that since he left this he never as much as bestowed a thought on us. When he got me that beggarly place in the Custom House, he thought he 'd done with me out and out. Sixty pounds a year! God be with the time I gave Peter Harris, the butler, just double the money!"

As they talked thus, they gained the outskirts of the city, and gradually left the lamps and the well-lighted shops behind. Their way now led along a dreary road by the sea-side, towards the little bathing-village of Clontarf, beyond which, in a sequestered spot called the Green Lanes, their humble home stood. It was a long and melancholy walk; the sorrowful sounds of the sea beating on the shingly strand mingling with the dreary plashing of the rain; while farther out, a continuous roar as the waves rolled over the "North Bull," added all the terrors of storm to the miseries of the night.

"The winter is setting in early," said Kellett "I think I never saw a severer night."

"A sad time for poor fellows out at sea!" said the girl, as she turned her head towards the dreary waste of cloud and water now commingled into one.

"'T is exactly like our own life, out there," cried he: "a little glimpse of light glimmering every now and then through the gloom, but yet not enough to cheer the heart and give courage; but all black darkness on every side."

"There will come a daybreak at last," said the girl, assuredly.

"Faith! I sometimes despair about it in our own case," said he, sighing drearily. "To think of what I was once, and what I am now! buffeted about and ill used by a set of scoundrels that I 'd not have suffered to sit down in my kitchen. Keep that rag of a shawl across your chest; you 'll be destroyed entirely, Bella."

"We'll soon be within shelter now, and nothing the worse for this weather, either of us," replied she, almost gayly. "Over and over again have you told me what severe seasons you have braved in the hunting-field; and, after all, papa, one can surely endure as much for duty as in pursuit of pleasure, — not to say that our little cottage never looks more homelike than after a night like this."

"It's snug enough for a thing of the kind," murmured he, half reluctantly.

"And Betty will have such a nice fire for us, and we shall be as comfortable and as happy as though it were a fine house, and we ourselves fine folk to live in it."

"The Kelletts of Kellett's Court, and no better blood in Ireland," said he, sternly. "It was in the same house my grandfather, Morgan Kellett, entertained the Duke of Portland, the Lord-Lieutenant of Ireland; and this day, as I stand here, there isn't a chap in the Castle-yard would touch his hat to me!"

"And what need have we of them, papa? Will not our pride of good blood teach us other lessons than repining? Can't we show the world that a gentleman born bears his altered fortunes with dignity?"

"Ye're right, Bella; that's the very thing they must acknowledge. There is n't a day passes that I don't make the clerks in the 'Long Room' feel the difference between us. 'No liberties, no familiarities, my lads,' I say, — 'keep your distance; for, though my coat is threadbare, and my hat none of the best, the man inside there is Paul Kellett of Kellett's Court.' And if they ask where that is, I say, 'Look at the Gazetteer,' — it's mighty few of them has their names there: 'Kellett's Court, the ancient seat of the Kellett family, was originally built by Strongbow, Earl of Pembroke.'"

"Well, here we are, papa, in a more humble home; but you'll see how cheery it will be."

And so saying, she pushed open a little wicket, and, passing through a small garden, gained the door of a little one-storied cottage, almost buried in honeysuckle.

"Yes, Betty, wet through!" said she, laughing, as the old woman held up her hands in horror; "but get papa his slippers and that warm dressing-gown, and I 'll be back in a minute."

"Arrah! why didn't you take a car for her?" said the old woman, with that familiarity which old and tried service warrants. "Sure the child will get her death from this!"

"She wouldn't let me; she insisted on walking on her feet."

"Ayeh, ayeh!" mattered the crone, as she placed his slippers on the fender, "sure ye oughtn't to mind her. She'd get a fever rather than cost you a shilling. Look at the shoes she's wearin'."

"By the good day! you'll drive me mad, clean mad!" cried he, savagely. "Don't you know in your heart that we have n't got it? Devil a rap farthing; that we're as poor as a church mouse; that if it wasn't for this beggarly place——"

"Now, Betty," cried the girl, entering,—"now for our tea, and that delicious potato-cake that I see browning there before the fire."

Poorly, even meanly dressed as she was, there was in her that gentle look, and graceful, quiet bearing that relieved the sombre aspect of a room which spoke but too plainly of narrow fortune; and as her father looked at her, the traces of recent displeasure passed from his face, and her eyes brightened up, while he said,—

"You bring a blessing with the very sound of your voice, darling." And he kissed her twice as he spoke.

"It is so comfortable to be here, and so snug," said she, seating herself at his side, "and to know that to-morrow is Sunday, and that we have our holiday, each of us. Come, papa, confess this little room and its bright fire are very cheery! And I have got a newspaper for you. I told Mrs. Hawksey there was nothing such a treat to you as a newspaper, and she gave me one."

"Ah! the 'Trumpet of Liberty,'" said he, opening it. "We'll have it after tea, Bella. Is there anything about our own county in it,—Cork, I mean?"

"I have not looked in it yet; but we 'll go through it honestly, papa, for I know how conscientious you are not to lose a paragraph."

"'T is that same makes a man agreeable in society. You know everything if you read the papers,—accidents and marriages, the rate of the money-market, the state of the crops, who is dining with the Queen, and who is skating on the Serpentine, who is ruined at Newmarket, and who drowned at sea, and then all about the play-houses and the wonderful panoramas; so that, let conversation turn how it will, you 're ready for it, and that 's the reason, Bella, you must go through every bit of it. It's like hunting, and the very field perhaps you don't try is just the one you 'd find a fox in!"

"Well, you 'll see. I 'll beat every cover for you!" said she, laughing; "and Mrs. Hawksey desires to have it back, for there is something about the Alderman having said or done—I don't know what or where."

"How I hate the very name of an Alderman!" said Kellett, peevishly; "regular vagabonds, with gilt coaches and red cloaks, running about prating of taxes and the pipe-water! The devil a thing I feel harder to bear in my poverty than to think you 're a visiting governess in an Alderman's family. Paul Kellett's daughter a visiting governess!"

"And very proud am I to be thought equal to the charge," said she, resolutely; "not to say how grateful to you for having enabled me to undertake it."

"Myself in the Customs is nothing; that I'd put up with. Many a reduced gentleman did the same. Sam Crozier was a marker at a billiard-table in Tralee, and Ennis Magrath was an overseer on the very road he used to drive his four-in-hand. 'Many a time,' says he, 'I cursed that fresh-broken stone, but I never thought I 'd be measuring it!' 'T is the Encumbered Court has brought us all down, Bella, and there's no disgrace in being ruined with thousands of others. Just begin with the sales of estates, and tell us who is next for sentence. God forgive me, but I feel a kind of pleasure in hearing that we 're all swamped together."

The girl smiled as though the remark were merely uttered in levity and deserved no more serious notice; but a faint sigh, which she could not repress, betrayed the sorrow with which she had heard it.

She opened the paper and glanced at its contents. They were as varied and multifarious as are usually to be found in weekly "channels of information." What struck her, however, most was the fact that, turn where she would, the name of Davenport Dunn was ever conspicuous. Sales of property displayed him as the chief creditor or petitioner; charities paraded him as the first among the benevolent; Joint-stock companies exhibited him as their managing director; mines, and railroads, and telegraph companies, harbor committees, and boards of all kinds, gave him the honors of large type; while in the fashionable intelligence from abroad, his arrivals and departures were duly chronicled, and a letter of our own correspondent from Venice communicated the details of a farewell dinner given him, with a "Lord" in the chair, by a number of those who had so frequently partaken of his splendid hospitalities while he resided in that city.

"Well—well—well!" said Kellett, with a pause between each exclamation, "this is more than I can bear. Old Jerry Dunn's son,—the brat of a boy I remember in the Charter' School! He used to be sent at Christmas time up to Ely Place, when my father was in town, to get five shillings for a Christmas-box; and I mind well the day he was asked to stay and dine with my sister Matty and myself, and he taught us a new game with six little bits of sticks; how we were to do something, I forget what,—but I know how it ended,—he won every sixpence we had. Matty had half a guinea in gold and some tenpenny pieces, and I had, I think, about fifteen shillings, and sorrow a rap he left us; and, worse still, I mortgaged my school maps, and got a severe thrashing for having lost them from Old White in Jervas Street; and poor Matty's doll was confiscated in the same way, and carried off with a debt of three-and-fourpence on her head. God forgive him, but he gave us a sorrowful night, for we cried till daybreak."

"And did you like him as a playfellow?" asked she.

"Now, that's the strangest thing of all," said Kellett, smiling. "Neither Matty nor myself liked him; but he got a kind of influence over us that was downright fascination. No matter what we thought of doing before he came, when he once set foot in the room everything followed his dictation. It was n't that he was overbearing or tyrannical in the least; just as little could you say that he was insinuating or nattering; but somehow, by a kind of instinct, we fell into his ways, and worked out all his suggestions just as if we were mere agents of his will. Resistance or opposition we never dreamed of while he was present; but after he was gone away, once or twice there came the thought that there was something very like slavery in all this submission, and we began to concert how we might throw off the yoke.

"'I won't play toll-bar any more,' said I, resolutely; 'all my pocket-money is sure to go before it is over.'

"'And I,' said Matty, 'won't have poor "Mopsy" tried for a murder again; every time she's hanged, some of the wax comes off her neck.'"

"We encouraged each other vigorously in these resolves; but before he was half an hour in the house 'Mopsy' had undergone the last sentence of the law, and I was insolvent."

"What a clever rogue he must have been!" said Bella, laughing.

"Was n't he clever!" exclaimed Kellett. "You could not say how,—nobody could say how,—but he saw everything the moment he came into a new place, and marked every one's face, and knew, besides, the impression he made on them, just as if he was familiar with them for years."

"Did you continue to associate with him as you grew up?" asked she.

"No; we only knew each other as children. There was a distressing thing—a very distressing thing—occurred one day; I'm sure to this very hour I think of it with sorrow and shame, for I can't believe he had any blame in it. We were playing in a room next my father's study, and running every now and then into the study; and there was an old-fashioned penknife—a family relic, with a long bloodstone handle—lying on the table; and when the play was over, and Davy, as we called him, had gone home, this was missing. There was a search made for it high and low, for my father set great value on it. It was his great-great-grandmother's, I believe; at all events, no one ever set eyes on it afterwards, and nothing would persuade my father but that Davy stole it! Of course he never told us that he thought so, but the servant did, and Matty and myself cried two nights and a day over it, and got really sick.

"I remember well; I was working by myself in the garden, Matty was ill and in bed, when I saw a tall old man, dressed like a country shopkeeper, shown into the back parlor, where my father was sitting. There was a bit of the window open, and I could hear that high words were passing between them, and, as I thought, my father getting the worst of it; for the old fellow kept repeating, 'You 'll rue it, Mister Kellett,—you 'll rue it yet!' And then my father said, 'Give him a good horsewhipping, Dunn; take my advice, and you 'll spare yourself some sorrow, and save him from even worse hereafter.' I 'll never forget the old fellow's face as he turned to leave the room. 'Davy will live to pay you off for this,' said he; 'and if *you* 're not to the fore, it will be your children, or your children's children, will have to 'quit the debt!'

"We never saw Davy from that hour; indeed, we were strictly forbidden ever to utter his name; and it was only when alone together, that Matty and I would venture to talk of him, and cry over—and many a time we did—the happy days when we had him for our playfellow. There was a species of martyrdom now, too, in his fate, that endeared him the more to our memories; every play he had invented, every spot he was fond of, every toy he liked, were hallowed to our minds like relics. At last poor Matty and I could bear it no longer, and we sat down and wrote a long letter to Davy, assuring him of our fullest confidence in his honor, and our broken-heartedness at separation from him. We inveighed stoutly against parental tyranny, and declared ourselves ready for open rebellion, if he, that was never deficient in a device, could only point out the road. We bribed a stable-boy, with all our conjoined resources of pocket-money, to convey the epistle, and it came back next morning to my father, enclosed in one from Davy himself, stating that he could never countenance acts of disobedience, or be any party to a system by which children should deceive their parents. I was sent off to a boarding-school the same week, and poor Matty committed to the charge of Miss Morse, a vinegar-faced old maid, that poisoned the eight best years of her life!"

"And when did you next hear of him?"

"Of Davy? Let me see; the next time I heard of him was when he attempted to enter college as a sizar, and failed. Somebody or other mentioned it at Kellett's Court, and said that old Dunn was half out of his mind, insisting that some injustice was dealt out to his son, and vowing he 'd get the member for somewhere to bring the matter before Parliament. Davy was wiser, however; he persuaded his father that, by agitating the question, they would only give notoriety to what, if left alone, would speedily be forgotten; and Davy was right I don't think there's three men now in the kingdom that remember one word about the sizarship, or, if they do, that would be influenced by it in any dealings they might have with Mr. Davenport Dunn."

"What career did he adopt after that?"

"He became a tutor, I think, in Lord Glengariff's family. There was some scandal about him there, —I forget it now, —and then he went off to America, and spent some years there, and in Jamaica, where he was employed as an overseer, I think; but I can't remember it all. My own knowledge of him next was seeing the name 'D. Dunn, solicitor,' on a neat brass-plate in Tralee, and hearing that he was a very acute fellow in election contests, and well up to dealing with the priests."

"And now he has made a large fortune?"

"I believe you well; he's the richest man in Ireland. There's scarce a county he has n't got property in. There's not a town, nor a borough, where he has n't some influence, and in every class, too, —gentry, clergy, shopkeepers, people: he has them all with him, and nobody seems to know how he does it."

"Pretty much, I suppose, as he used to manage Aunt Matty and yourself long ago," said she, laughingly.

"Well, indeed, I suppose so," said he, with a half sigh; "and if it be, all I can say is, they 'll be puzzled to find out his secret. He's the deepest fellow I ever heard or read of; for there he stands to-day, without name, family, blood, or station, higher than those that had them all, —able to do more than them; and, what's stranger still, thought more about in England than the best man amongst us."

"You have given me quite an interest about him, papa; tell me, what is he like?"

"He's as tall as myself, but not so strongly built; indeed, he's slightly round-shouldered; he is dark in the complexion, and has the blackest hair and whiskers I ever saw, and rather good-looking than otherwise,—a calm, cold, patient-looking face you'd call it; he speaks very little, but his voice is soft and low and deliberate, just like one that would n't throw away a word; and he never moves his hands or arms, but lets them hang down heavily at either side."

"And his eyes? Tell me of his eyes?"

"They 're big, black, sleepy-looking eyes, seldom looking up, and never growing a bit brighter by anything that he says or hears about him. Indeed, any one seeing him for the first time would say, 'There's a man whose thoughts are many a mile away; he is n't minding what's going on about him here.' But that is not the case; there is n't a look, a stir, nor a gesture that he does n't remark. There 's not a chair drawn closer to another, not a glance interchanged, that he has n't noticed; and I 've heard it said, 'Many would n't open a letter before him, he's so sure to guess the contents from just reading the countenance.'"

"The world is always prone to exaggerate such gifts," said she, calmly.

"So it may be, dear, but I don't fancy it could do so here. He's one of those men that, if he had been born to high station, would be a great politician or a great general. You see that, somehow, without any effort on his part, things come up just as he wished them. I believe, after all," said he, with a heavy sigh, "it's just luck! Whatever one man puts his hand to in this world goes on right and smoothly, and another has every mishap and misfortune that can befall him. He may strive, and toil, and fret his brains over it, but devil a good it is. If he is born to ill luck, it will stick to him."

"It's not a very cheery philosophy!" said she, gently.

"I suppose not, dear; but what is very cheery in this life, when you come to find it out? Is n't it nothing but disappointment and vexation?"

Partly to rally him out of this vein of depression, and partly from motives of curiosity, she once more adverted to Dunn, and asked how it happened that they crossed each other again in life.

"He's what they call 'carrying the sale' of Kellett's Court, my dear. You know we 're in the Encumbered Estates now; and Dunn represents Lord

Lackington and others that hold the mortgages over us. The property was up for sale in November, then in May last, and was taken down by Dunn's order. I never knew why. It was then, however, he got me this thing in the Revenue,—this beggarly place of sixty-five pounds a year; and told me, through his man Hanks,—for I never met himself about it,—that he 'd take care my interests were not overlooked. After that the Courts closed, and he went abroad; and that's all there's between us, or, indeed, likely to be between us; for he never wrote me as much as one line since he went away, nor noticed any one of my letters, though I sent him four, or, indeed, I believe, five."

"What a strange man this must be!" said she, musingly. "Is it supposed that he has formed any close attachments? Are his friends devoted to him?"

"Attachments,—friendships! faith, I'm inclined to think it's little time he'd waste on one or the other. Why, child, if what we hear be true, he goes through the work of ten men every day of his life."

"Is he married?" asked she, after a pause.

"No; there was some story about a disappointment he met early in life. When he was at Lord Glengariff's, I think, he fell in love with one of the daughters, or she with him,—I never knew it rightly,—but it ended in his being sent away; and they say he never got over it. Just as if Davenport Dunn was a likely man either to fall in love or cherish the memory of a first passion! I wish you saw him, Bella," said he, laughing, "and the notion would certainly amuse you."

"But still men of his stamp have felt—ay, and inspired—the strongest passions. I remember reading once—" "Reading, my darling,—reading is one thing, seeing or knowing is another. The fellows that write these things must invent what is n't likely,—what is nigh impossible,—or nobody would read it What we see of a man or woman in a book is just the exact reverse of what we 'll ever find in real life."

The girl could easily have replied to this assertion; indeed, the answer was almost on her lips, when she restrained herself, and, hanging down her head, fell into a musing fit.

CHAPTER IV
ONE WHO WOULD BE A "SHARP FELLOW"

One of the chief, perhaps the greatest, pleasures which Kellett's humble lot still secured him, was a long country walk of a Sunday in company with one who had been his friend in more prosperous times. A reduced gentleman like himself, Annesley Beecher could only go abroad on this one day in the week, and thus by the pressure of adverse fortune were they thrown more closely together.

Although by no means a favorite with Bella, she was far too considerate for her father, and too mindful of the few enjoyments that remained to him, ever to interpose her real opinion. She therefore limited herself to silence, as old Kellett would pronounce some glowing eulogy of his friend, calling him "good" and "amiable" and "kind-hearted," and extolling, as little short of miraculous, "the spirits he had, considering all he went through." But he would add, "He was always the same, and that's the reason everybody liked him,—everybody, that is, almost everybody!" And he would steal a sly glance at his daughter, half imploringly, as though to say, "How long are you to sit in that small minority?"

Whether the weather would permit of Beecher's coming out to see them, whether he 'd be able to "stay and take his bit of dinner with them," were subjects of as great anxiety to poor Kellett each succeeding Sunday morning as though there ever had been a solitary exception to the wished-for occurrence; and Bella would never destroy the pleasure of anticipation by the slightest hint that might impair the value he attached to the event.

"There's so many trying to get him," he would say; "they pester his life out with invitations,—the Chancellor and Lord Killybegs and the Bishop of Drumsna always asking him to name his day; but he 'd rather come out and take his bit of roast mutton with ourselves, and his glass of punch after it, than he 'd eat venison and drink claret with the best of them. There's not a table in Dublin, from the Castle down, that would n't be proud of his company; and why not?" He would pause after uttering a challenge of this sort; and then, as his daughter would show no signs of acceptance, he would mutter on, "A real gentleman born and bred, and how anybody can *mislike* him is more than I am really able to comprehend!"

These little grumblings, which never produced more than a smile from Bella, were a kind of weekly homily which poor Kellett liked to deliver, and he felt, when he had uttered it, as one who had paid a just tribute to worth and virtue.

"There's Beecher already, by Jove!" cried Kellett, as he sprang up from the breakfast-table to open the little wicket which the other was vainly endeavoring to unhasp. "How early he is!"

Let us take the opportunity to present him to our readers,—a duty the more imperative, since, to all outward semblance at least, he would appear little to warrant the flattering estimate his friend so lately bestowed upon him. About four or five-and-thirty, somewhat above the middle size, and with all the air and bearing of a man of fashion, Beecher had the gay, easy, light-hearted look of one with whom the world went habitually well; and when it did not, more was the shame of the said world! since a better, nobler, more generous fellow than himself never existed; and this *he* knew, however others might ungraciously hold an opposite opinion. There was not the slightest detail in his dress that could warrant the supposition of narrow fortune: his coat and his waistcoat, of one color and stuff, were faultless in make; the massive watch-chain that festooned across his chest in the last mode; his thick walking-boots the perfection of that compromise between strength and elegance so popular in our day; even to his cane, whose head was of massive gold, with his arms embossed,—all bespoke a certain affluence and abundance, the more assured from the absence of ostentation.

His hat was slightly, very slightly, set on one side,—a piece of "tigerism" pardonable, perhaps, as it displayed the rich brown curls of very silky hair, which he had disposed with consummate skill before his glass ere he issued forth. His large, full blue eyes, his handsome mouth, and a certain gentleness in his look generally, were what he himself would have called the "odds in his favor;" and very hard it would indeed have been at first sight to form an estimate in any way unfavorable to him. Bean Beecher, as he was called once, had been deemed the best-looking fellow about town, and when he entered the Life Guards, almost twenty years before the time we now present him, had been reckoned the handsomest man and best rider in the regiment. Brother of Lord Lackington, but not by the same mother, he had inaugurated that new school of dandyism which succeeded to the Brummell period, and sought fame and notoriety by splendor and extravagance rather than by the fastidious and personal elegance that characterized the former era. In this way Lord Lackington and his brother were constantly contrasted;

and although each had their followers, it was generally admitted that they were both regarded as admirable types of style and fashion. Boodle's would have preferred the Peer, the Guards' Club and all Tattersall's have voted for the Honorable Annesley Beecher.

Beecher started in life with all the advantages and disadvantages which attach to the position of a younger son of a noble family. On the one side he had good connections, a sure status in society, and easy admission into club life; on the other, lay the counterbalancing fact of the very slender fortune which usually falls to the lot of the younger born. The sum, in his case, barely sufficed to carry him through his minority, so that the day he came of age he had not a shilling in the world. Most men open their career in life with some one ambition or other in their hearts. Some aspire to military glory and the fame of a great general, some yearn after political eminence, and fashion to themselves the triumphs of successful statesmanship. There are lesser goals in the walks of the learned professions which have each their votaries; and sanguine spirits there are who found, in imagination, distant colonies beyond the sea, or lead lives of adventure in exploring unvisited and unknown regions. Annesley Beecher had no sympathy with any of these. The one great and absorbing wish of his heart was to be a "sharp fellow;" one who in all the dealings and traffic of life was sure to get the upper hand of his adversary, who in every trial where craft was the master, and in whatever situation wherein cunning performed a part, was certain to come out with the creditable reputation of being, "for a gentleman, the downiest cove to be met with anywhere."

This unhappy bent was owing to the circumstance of his being early thrown amongst men who, having nothing but their wits to depend upon, had turned these same wits to very discreditable purposes. He became, it is needless to say, their easy dupe; and when utterly bereft of the small patrimony which he once possessed, was admitted as an humble brother of the honorable guild who had despoiled him.

Men select their walk in life either from the consciousness of certain qualities likely to obtain success, or by some overweening admiration of those already eminent in it. It was this latter decided Beecher's taste. Never was there one who cherished such profound respect for a crafty fellow, for all other intellectual superiorities he could limit his esteem: for a rogue, his veneration was unbounded. From the man that invented a bubble company, to him who could turn the king at *écarté*—from the gifted individual who could puff up shares to an exorbitant value, to the no less fine intelligence that could "make everything safe on the Derby," he venerated them all. His early experiences had been unhappy ones, and so constantly had he found himself duped and "done" on every hand, that he ended by believing that honesty was a pure myth; the nearest approach to the quality being a certain kind of fidelity to one's "pall," as he would have called it, and an unwillingness to put "your own friend in the hole," while there were so many others available for that pleasant destiny. This little flickering flame of principle, this farthing candle of good feeling, was the solitary light that illuminated the gloom of his character.

He had joined the regiment Kellett formerly belonged to at Malta, a few weeks before the other had sold out, and having met accidentally in Ireland, they had renewed the acquaintance, stimulated by that strange sympathy which attracts to each other those whose narrow circumstances would seem, in some shape or other, the effects of a cruelty practised on them by the world. Kellett was rather flattered by the recognition of him who recalled the brighter hours of his life, while he entertained a kind of admiration for the worldly wit and cleverness of one who, in talk at least, was a match for the "shrewdest fellow going." Beecher liked the society of a man who thus looked up to him, and who could listen unweariedly to his innumerable plans for amassing wealth and fortune, all of which only needed some little preliminary aid—some miserable thousand or two to start with—to make them as "rich as Rothschild."

Never was there such a Tantalus view of life as he could picture,—stores of gold, mines of unbounded wealth,—immense stakes to be won here, *rouge et noir* banks to be broke there,—all actually craving to be appropriated, if one only had a little of that shining metal which, like the water thrown down in a pump, is the needful preliminary to securing a supply of the fluid afterwards.

The imaginative faculty plays a great part in the existence of the reduced gentleman! Kellett actually revelled in the gorgeous visions this friend could conjure up. There was that amount of plausibility in his reasonings that satisfied scruple as to practicability, and made him regard Beecher as the most extraordinary instance of a grand financial genius lost to the world,—a great Chancellor of the Exchequer born to devise budgets in obscurity!

Bella took a very different measure of him: she read him with all a woman's nicest appreciation, and knew him thoroughly; she saw, however, how much his society pleased her father, how their Sunday strolls together rallied him from the dreary depression the week was sure to leave behind it, and how these harmless visions of imaginary prosperity served to cheer the gloom of actual poverty. She, therefore, concealed so much as she could of her own opinion, and received Beecher as cordially as she was able.

"Ah, Paul, my boy, how goes it? Miss Kellett, how d'ye do?" said Beecher, with that easy air and pleasant smile that well became him. "I thought by starting early I should just catch you at breakfast, while I also took another hour out of my Sunday,—the one day the law mercifully bestows on such poor devils as myself,—ha, ha, ba!" And he laughed heartily, as though insolvency was as droll a thing as could be.

"You bear up well, anyhow, Beecher," said Kellett, admiringly.

"What's the odds so long as you're happy!" cried the other, gayly. "Never say die. They take it out in fifty per cent, but they can't work the oracle against our good spirits, eh, Kellett? The *mens sana in corpore*,—what d'ye call him, my lad?—that's the real thing."

"Indeed, I suppose it is!" said Kellett, not very clear as to what he concurred in.

"There are few fellows, let me tell you, would be as light-hearted as I am, with four writs and a judge's warrant hanging over them,—eh, Miss Bella, what do you say to that?" said Beecher.

She smiled half sadly and said nothing.

"Ask John Scott,—ask Bicknell Morris, or any of the 'Legs' you like,—if there's a man of them all ever bore up like me. 'Beecher's a bar of iron,' they 'll tell you; 'that fellow can bear any amount of hammering.' and maybe I have n't had it! And all Lackington's fault!"

"That's the worst of all!" said Kellett, who had listened to the same accusation in the self-same words at least a hundred times before.

"Lackington is the greatest fool going! He does n't see the advantage of pushing his family influence. He might have had me in for 'Mallow.' Grog Davis said to him one day, 'Look now, my Lord, Annesley is the best horse in your stable, if you 'd only stand to win on him, he is!' But Lackington would not hear of it. He thinks me a flat! You won't believe it, but he does!"

"Faith! he's wrong there," said Kellett, with all the emphasis of sincerity.

"I rather suspect he is, Master Kellett. I was trained in another school,—brought up amongst fellows would skin a cat, by Jove! What I say is, let A. B. have a chance,—just let him in once, and see if he won't do the thing!"

"Do you wish to be in Parliament, Mr. Beecher?" asked Bella, with a smile of half-repressed drollery.

"Of course I do. First, there's the protection,—no bad thing as times go; then it would be uncommon strange if I could n't 'tool the coach into the yard' safely. They 'd have to give me a devilish good thing. You 'd see what a thorn I 'd be in their sides. Ask Grog Davis what kind of fellow I am; he 'll tell you if I 'm easily put down. But Lackington is a fool; he can't see the road before him!"

"You reckon, then, on being a debater!" said she, quietly.

"A little of everything, Miss Bella," said he, laughing; "like the modern painters, not particular for a shade or two. I 'd not go wasting my time with that old Tory lot,—they're all worked ont, aged and weighted, as John Scott would call them—I'd go in with the young uns,—the Manchester two-year-olds, universal—what d'ye call it?—and vote by ballot. They 're the fellows have 'the tin,' by Jove! they have."

"Then I scarcely see how Lord Lackington would advance his family influence by promoting your views," said she, again.

"To be sure he would. It would be the safest hedge in the world for him. He 'd square his book by it, and stand to win, no matter what horse came in. Besides, why should they buy me, if I was n't against them? You don't nobble the horse in your own stable,—eh, Kellett, old boy?"

"You're a wonderful fellow, Beecher!" said Kellett, in a most honest admiration of his friend.

"If they'd only give me a chance, Paul,—just one chance!"

It was not very easy to see what blot in the game of life he purposed to himself to "hit" when he used this expression, "if they only give me a chance;" vague and indistinct as it was, still for many a year had it served him as a beacon of hope. A shadow vision of creditors "done," horses "nobbled," awkward testimonies "squared," a millenary period of bills easily discounted, with an indulgent Angel presiding over the Bankrupt Court,—these and like blessings doubtless all flitted before him as the fruits of that same "chance" which destiny held yet in store for him.

Hope is a generous fairy; she deigns to sit beside the humblest firesides,—she will linger even in the damp cell of the prison, or rest her wings on the wave-tossed raft of the shipwrecked, and in such mission is she thrice blessed! But by what strange caprice does she visit the hearts of men like this? Perhaps it is that the very spirit of her ministering is to despair of nothing.

We are by no means sure that our reader will take the same pleasure that Kellett did in Beecher's society, and therefore we shall spare him the narrative of their walk. They strolled along for hours, now by the shingly shore, on which the waves swept smoothly, now inland, through leafy lanes and narrow roads, freckled with patchy sunlight. The day was calm and still,—one of those solemn autumnal days which lend to scenery a something of sadness in their unvarying quiet. Although so near a great city, the roads were little travelled, and they sauntered for hours scarcely meeting any one.

Wherever the smoke rose above the tall beech-trees, wherever the ornamented porch of some lone cottage peeped through the copse, or the handsome entrance-gate proclaimed the well-to-do owner of some luxurious abode, Kellett would stop to tell who it was lived there,—the wealthy merchant, the affluent banker, the alderman or city dignitary, who had amassed his fortune by this or that pursuit. Through all his stories there ran the vein of depreciation, which the once landed proprietor cherished towards the men who were the "first of their name." He was sure to remember some trait of their humble beginnings in life,—how this one had come up barefooted to Dublin fifty years before; how that had held horses in the street for hire. It was strange, but scarcely one escaped some commentary of this kind; not that there was a spark of ill-nature in the man, but that he experienced a species of self-consolation in thinking that in all his narrow fortune he had claims of kindred and connection which none of them could compete with. Beecher's thoughts took, meanwhile, a different course; whenever not awakened to interest by some trait of their sharpness or cunning, to which he listened with avidity, he revelled in the idea of their wealth, as a thing of which they might be despoiled: "Wouldn't that fellow take shares in some impossible speculation?—Couldn't the other be induced to buy some thousand pounds' worth of valueless scrip?—Would this one kindly permit himself to 'be cleared out' at hazard?—Might that one be persuaded to lose a round sum at *écarté*?"

And thus did they view life, with widely different sympathies, it is true, but yet in a spirit that made them companionable to each other. One "grew his facts," like raw material which the other manufactured into those curious wares by which he amused his fancy. Poverty is a stronger bond than many believe it; when men begin to confess it to each other, they take something very like an oath of fidelity.

"By the way," said Beecher, as he bade his friend good night, "you told me you knew Dunn—Davenport Dunn?"

"To be sure I do,—know him well."

"Couldn't you introduce me to him? That's a fellow might be able to assist me. I 'm certain he could give me a chance; eh, Kellett?"

"Well; I expect him back in Ireland every day. I was asking after him no later than yesterday; but he's still away."

"When he comes back, however, you can mention me, of course; he'll know who I am."

"I'll do it with pleasure. Good-night, Beecher,—goodnight; and I hope"—this was soliloquy as he turned back towards the door,—"I hope Dunn will do more for you than he ever has for *me!* or, faith, it's not worth while to make the acquaintance."

Bella retired to her room early, and Kellett sat moodily alone by his fire. Like a great many other "embarrassed gentlemen," he was dragging on life amidst all the expedients of loans, bonds, and mortgages, when the bill for sale of the encumbered estates became the law of the land. What with the legal difficulties of dispossessing him, what with the changeful fortunes of a good harvest, or money a little more plentiful in the market, he might have gone on to the last in this fashion, and ended his days where he began them, in the old house of his fathers, when suddenly this new and unexpected stroke of legislation cut short all his resources at once, and left him actually a beggar on the world.

The panic created at the first moment by a law that seemed little short of confiscation, the large amount of landed property thus suddenly thrown into the market, the prejudice against Irish investment so strongly entertained by the moneyed classes in England, all tended vastly to depreciate the value of those estates which came first for sale; and many were sold at prices scarcely exceeding four or five years of their rental. An accidental disturbance in the neighborhood, some petty outrage in the locality, was enough to depreciate the value; and purchasers actually fancied themselves engaged in speculations so hazardous that nothing short of the most tempting advantages would requite them for their risk.

One of the very first estates for sale was Kellett's Court. The charges on the property were immense, the accumulated debts of three generations of spendthrifts; the first charge, however, was but comparatively small, and yet even this was not covered by the proceeds of the sale. A house that had cost nearly forty thousand pounds, standing on its own demesne, surrounded by an estate yielding upwards of three thousand a year, was knocked down for fifteen thousand four hundred pounds.

Kellett was advised to appeal against this sale on various grounds: he was in possession of an offer of more than double for the same property in times less prosperous; he could show a variety of grounds—surprise and others—to invalidate the ruinous contract; and it was then that he once again, after a whole life, found himself in contact with Davenport Dunn, the attorney for many parties whose interests were compromised in the sale. By no possible accident could the property be sold at such a price as would leave any surplus to himself; but he hoped, indeed he was told, that he would be favorably considered by those whose interest he was defending; and this last throw for fortune was now the subject of his dreary thoughts.

There was, too, another anxiety, and a nearer one, pressing on his heart. Kellett had a son,—a fine, frank, open-hearted young fellow, who had grown up to manhood, little dreaming that he would ever be called on to labor for his own support. The idle lounging habits of a country life had indisposed him to all study, so that even his effort to enter college was met by a failure, and he was turned back on the very threshold of the University. Jack Kellett went home, vowing he 'd nevermore trouble his head about Homer and Lucian, and he kept his word; he took to his gun and his pointers with renewed vigor, waiting until such time as he might obtain his gazette to a regiment on service. His father had succeeded in securing a promise of such an appointment, but, unhappily, the reply only arrived on the very week that Kellett's Court was sold, and an order from the Horse Guards to lodge the purchase-money of his commission came at the very hour when they were irretrievably ruined.

Jack disappeared the next morning, and the day following brought a letter, stating that he had enlisted in the "Rifles," and was off to the Crimea. Old Kellett concealed the sorrow that smote him for the loss of his boy, by affecting indignation at being thus deserted. So artfully did he dress up this self-deception that Bella was left in doubt as to whether or not some terrible scene had not occurred between the father and son before he left the house. In a tone that she never ventured to dispute, he forbade her to allude to Jack before him; and thus did he treasure up this grief for himself alone and his own lonely hours, cheating his sorrow by the ingenious devices of that constraint he was thus obliged to practise on himself. Like a vast number of men with whom the world has gone hardly, he liked to brood over his misfortunes, and magnify them to himself. In this way he opened a little bank of compassion that answered every draft he drew on it. Over and over to himself—like a miser revelling over his hoarded wealth—did he count all the hardships of his destiny. He loved thus to hug his misery in solitude, while he whispered to his heart, "You are a courageous fellow, Paul Kellett; there are not many who could carry your cheerful face, or walk with a head as high as you do to-day. The man that owned Kellett's Court, and was one of the first in his county, living in a poor cottage, with sixty pounds a year!—that's the test of what stuff a man's made of. Show me another man in Ireland could do it! Show me one that could meet the world as uncomplainingly, and all the while never cease to be what he was born,—a gentleman." This was the philosophy he practised; this the lesson he taught; this the paean he chanted in his own heart The various extremities to which he might—being anything other than what he was—have been tempted, the excesses he might have fallen into, the low associates he might have kept, the base habits he might have contracted, all the possible and impossible contingencies that might have befallen him, and all his difficulties therein, formed a little fiction world that he gloried to lose himself in contemplating.

It is not often that selfishness can take a form so blameless; nor is it always that self-deception can be so harmless. In this indulgence we now leave him.

CHAPTER V
THE WORLD'S CHANGES

While Mr. Davenport Dunn's residence was in Merrion Square, his house of business was in Henrietta Street,—one of those roomy old mansions which, before the days of the Union, lodged the aristocracy of Ireland, but which have now fallen into utter neglect and decay. Far more spacious in extent, and more ornate in decoration, than anything modern Dublin can boast, they remain, in their massive doors of dark mahogany, their richly stuccoed ceilings, and their handsome marble chimney-pieces, the last witnesses of a period when Dublin was a real metropolis.

From the spacious dinner-room below to the attics above, all this vast edifice was now converted into offices, and members of Mr. Dunn's staff were located even in the building at the rear, where the stables once had stood. Nothing can so briefly convey the varied occupations of his life as a glance at some of the inscriptions which figured on the different doors: "Inland Navigation Office," "Grand Munster Junction Drainage," "Compressed Fuel Company," "Reclaimed Lands," "Encumbered Estates," "Coast Fishery," "Copper and Cobalt Mining Association," "Refuge Harbor Company," "Slate and Marble Quarries," "Tyrawley and Erris Bank of Deposit," "Silver and Lead Mines." These were but a few of the innumerable "associations," "companies," and "industrial speculations" which denoted the cares and employments of that busy head. Indeed, the altered fortunes of that great mansion itself presented no bad type of the changed destinies of the land. Here, once, was the abode of only too splendid hospitality, of all that refined courtesy and polished manners could contribute to make society as fascinating as it was brilliant Here were wit and beauty, and a high, chivalrous tone of manners, blended, it is true, with wildest extravagance and a general levity of thought, that imparted to intercourse the glowing tints of an orgy; and in their stead were now the active signs of industry, all the means by which wealth is amassed and great fortunes acquired, every resource of the country explored, every natural advantage consulted and developed,—the mountains, the valleys, the rivers, the sea-coasts, the vast tracts of bog and moss, the various mines and quarries, the products once deemed valueless, the districts formerly abandoned as irreclaimable, all brought out into strong light, and all investigated in a spirit which hitherto had been unknown to Ireland. What a change was here, and what necessities must have been the fate of those who had so altered all their habits and modes of thought as to conform to a system so widely different from all they had hitherto followed! It was like re-colonizing an empire, so subversive were all the innovations of what had preceded them.

"Eh, Barton, we used to trip up these stairs more flippantly once on a time," said a very handsome old man, whose well-powdered hair and queue were rather novelties in modern appearance, to a feeble figure who, assisted by his servant, was slowly toiling his way upwards.

"How d' ye do, Glengariff?" said the other, with a weak smile. "So we used; and they were better days in every sense of the word."

"Not a doubt of it," said the other. "Is that your destination?" And he pointed to a door inscribed with the title "Encumbered Estates."

"Ay!" said Barton, sighing.

"It 's mine, too, I 'm sorry to say," cried Lord Glengariff; "as I suppose, erelong, it will be that of every country gentleman in the land!"

"We might have known it must come to this!" muttered the other, in a weak voice.

"I don't think so," broke in his Lordship, quickly. "I see no occasion at all for what amounts to an act of confiscation; why not give us time to settle with our creditors? Why not leave us to deal with our encumbrances in our own way? The whole thing is a regular political swindle, Barton; they wanted a new gentry that could be more easily managed than the old fellows, who had no station, no rank, but right ready to buy both one and the other by supporting—"

"Can I be of any service to your Lordship?" interrupted a very over-dressed and much-gold-chained man, of about forty, with a great development of chest, set off to advantage by a very pretentious waistcoat.

"Ah, Hankes! is Dunn come back yet?" asked Lord Glengariff.

"No, my Lord; we expect him on Saturday. The telegraph is dated St. Cloud, where he is stopping with the Emperor."

Glengariff gave Barton a slight pinch in the arm, and a look of intense meaning at the words.

"Nothing has been done in that matter of mine?" said Barton, feebly. "Jonas Barton is the name," added he, coloring at the necessity of announcing himself.

"Jonas Barton, of Curryglass House?"

"Yes, that's it."

"Sold yesterday, under the Court, sir—for, let me see—" And he opened a small memorandum-book. "Griffith's valuation," muttered he between his teeth, "was rather better than the Commissioner's,—yes, sir, they got a bargain of that property yesterday; it went for twenty-two thousand six hundred—"

"Great God, sir; the whole estate?"

"The whole estate; there is a tithe-rent charge—"

"There, there, don't you see he does not hear you?" said Lord Glengariff, angrily. "Have you no room where he can sit down for half an hour or so?" And so saying, he assisted the servant to carry the now lifeless form into a small chamber beside them. The sick man rallied soon, and as quickly remembered where he was.

"This is bad news, Glengariff," said he, with a sickly effort at a smile. "Have you heard who was the buyer?"

"No, no; what does it matter? Take my arm and get out of this place. Where are you stopping in town? Can I set you down?" said the other, in hurry and confusion.

"I'm with my son-in-law at Ely Place; he is to call for me here, so you can leave me, my dear friend, for I see you are impatient to get away."

Lord Glengariff pressed his hand cordially, and descended the stairs far more rapidly than he had mounted them.

"Lord Glengariff,—one word, my Lord," cried Mr. Hankes, hastening after him, and just catching him at the door.

"Not now, sir,—not now," said Lord Glengariff.

"I beg a thousand pardons, my Lord, but Mr. Dunn writes me peremptorily to say that it cannot be effected—"

"Not raise the money, did you say?" asked he, growing suddenly pale.

"Not in the manner he proposed, my Lord. If you will allow me to explain—"

"Come over to my hotel. I am at Bilton's," said Lord Glengariff. "Call on me there in an hour." And so saying, he got into his carriage and drove off.

In the large drawing-room of the hotel sat a lady working, and occasionally reading a book which lay open before her. She was tall and thin, finely featured, and though now entered upon that period of life when every line and every tint confess the ravage of time, was still handsome.

This was Lady Augusta Arden, Lord Glengariff's only unmarried daughter, the very type of her father in temperament as well as appearance.

"By George! it is confiscation. It is the inauguration of that Communism the French speak of," cried Lord Glengariff, as he entered the room. "There 's poor Barton of Curryglass, one of the oldest names in his county, sold out, and for nothing,—absolutely nothing. No man shall persuade me that this is just or equitable; no man shall tell me that the Legislature shall step in and decide at any moment how I am to deal with my creditors."

"I never heard of that Burton."

"I said Barton,—not Burton; a man whose estate used to be called five thousand a year," said he, angrily. "There he is now, turned out on the world. I verily believe he has n't a guinea left! And what is all this for? To raise up in the country a set of spurious gentry,—fellows that were never heard of, whose names are only known over shop-boards,—as if the people should be better treated or more kindly dealt with by them than by us, their natural protectors! By George! if Ireland should swarm with Davenport Dunns, I 'd call it a sorry exchange for the good blood she had lost in exterminating her old gentry."

"Has he come back?" asked Lady Augusta, as she bent her head more deeply over her work, and her cheeks grew a shade more red.

"No; he's dining with royalties, and driving about in princely carriages on the Continent Seeing what the pleasures of his intimacy have cost us here at home, I'd say that these great personages ought to look sharp, or, by George! he'll sell them out, as he has done us." He laughed a bitter laugh at his jest, but his daughter did not join in the emotion.

"I scarcely think it fair," said she, at length, "to connect Mr. Dunn with a legislation which he is only called upon to execute."

"With all my heart. Acquit him as much as you will; but, for my part, I feel very little tenderness for the hand that accomplishes the last functions of the law against me. These fellows have displayed a zeal and an alacrity in their work that shows how they relish the sport. After all," said he, after a pause, "this Dunn is neither better nor worse than the rest of them, and in one respect he has the advantage over them,—he has not forgotten himself quite so much as the others. To be sure, we knew him in his very humblest fortunes, Augusta; he was meek enough then."

She stooped to pick up her work, which had fallen, and her neck and face were crimson as she resumed it.

"Wonderful little anticipation had he then of the man he was to become one of these days. Do you know, Augusta, that they say he is actually worth two millions?—two millions!"

She never spoke; and after an interval Lord Glengariff burst out into a strange laugh.

"You 'd scarcely guess what I was laughing at, Augusta. I was just remembering the wretched hole he used to sleep in. It was a downright shame to put him there over the stable, but the cottage was under repair at the time, and there was no help for it. 'I can accommodate myself anywhere, my Lord,' he said. Egad, he has contrived to fulfil the prediction in a very different sense. Just fancy—two millions sterling!"

It was precisely what Lady Augusta was doing at the moment, though, perhaps, not quite in the spirit his Lordship suspected.

"Suppose even one half of it be true, with a million of money at command, what can't a man have nowadays?"

And so they both fell a-thinking of all that same great amount of riches could buy,—what of power, respect, rank, flattery, political influence, fine acquaintance, fine diamonds, and fine dinners.

"If he play his cards well, he might be a peer," thought my Lord.

"If he be as ambitious as he ought to be, he might aspire to a peer's daughter," was the lady's reflection.

"He has failed in my negotiation, however," said Lord Glengariff, peevishly; "at least, Hankes just told me that it can't be done. I detest that fellow Hankes. It shows great want of tact in Dunn having such a man in his employment,—a vulgar, self-sufficient, over-dressed fellow, who can't help being familiar out of his own self-satisfaction. Now, Dunn himself knows his place. Don't you think so?"

She muttered something not very intelligible, but which sounded like concurrence.

"Yes," he resumed, "Dunn does not forget himself,—at least, with me." And to judge from the carriage of his head as he spoke, and the air with which he earned the pinch of snuff to his nose, he had not yet despaired of seeing the world come back to the traditions which once had made it worth living in.

"I am willing to give him every credit for his propriety of conduct, Augusta," added he, in a still more lofty tone; "for we live in times when really wealth and worldly prosperity have more than their rightful supremacy, and such men as Dunn are made the marks of an adulation that is actually an outrage,—an outrage upon *us!*"

And the last little monosyllable was uttered with an emphasis of intense significance.

Just as his Lordship had rounded his peroration, the servant presented him with a small three-cornered note. He opened it and read,—

"My Lord,—I think the bearer of this, T. Driscoll, might possibly do what you wish for; and I send him, since I am sure that a personal interview with your Lordship would be more efficacious than any negotiation.

"By your Lordship's most obedient to command,

"Simpson Hankes."

"Is the person who brought this below?" asked Lord Glengariff.

"Yes, my Lord; he is waiting for the answer."

"Show him into my dressing-room."

Mr. Terence Driscoll was accordingly introduced into that sanctum; and while he employs his few spare moments in curious and critical examination of the various gold and silver objects which contribute to his Lordship's toilet, and wonderingly snuffs at essences and odors of whose existence he had never dreamed, let us take the opportunity of a little examination of himself. He was a short, fat old man, with a very round red face, whose jovial expression was rather heightened than marred by a tremendous squint; for the eyes kept in incessant play and movement, which intimated a restless drollery that his full, capacious mouth well responded to. In dress and general appearance he belonged to the class of the comfortable farmer, and his massive silver watch-chain and huge seal displayed a consciousness of his well-to-do condition in life.

"Are you Mr. Driscoll?" said Lord Glengariff, as he looked at the letter to prompt him to the name. "Pray take a seat!"

"Yes, my Lord, I'm that poor creature Terry Driscoll; the neighbors call me Tearin' Terry, but that's all past and gone, Heaven be praised! It was a fever I had, my Lord, and my rayson wandered, and I did many a thing that desthroyed me entirely; I tore up the lease of my house, I tore up Peter Driscoll's, my uncle's, will; ay, and worse than all, I tore up all my front teeth!"

And, in evidence of this feat of dentistry, Mr. Driscoll gave a grin that exposed his bare gums to view.

"Good heavens, how shocking!" exclaimed Lord Glen-gariff, though, not impossibly, the expression was extorted by the sight rather than the history of the calamity.

"Shocking indeed, my Lord,—that's the name for it!" said Terry, sighing; "but ye see I was n't compos when I did it. I thought they were a set of blackguards that I could n't root out of the land,—squatters that would n't pay sixpence, nor do a day's work. That was the delusion that was upon me!"

"I hold here a letter from Mr. Hankes," said his Lordship, pompously, and in a tone that was meant to recall Mr. Driscoll from the personal narrative he had entered upon with such evident self-satisfaction. "He mentions you as one likely—that is to say—one in a position—a person, in fact—"

"Yes, my Lord, yes," interrupted Terry, with a grin of unbounded acquiescence.

"And adds," continued his Lordship, "your desire to communicate personally with myself." The words were very few and not very remarkable, and yet Lord Glengariff contrived to throw into them an amount of significance really great. They seemed to say, "Bethink thee well, Terry Driscoll, of the good fortune that this day has befallen thee. Thy boldness has been crowned with success, and there thou sittest now, being the poor worm that thou art, in converse with one who wears a coronet."

And so, indeed, in all abject humility, did Mr. Driscoll appear to feel the situation. He drew his feet closer together, and stole his hands up the wide sleeves of his coat, as though endeavoring to diminish, as far as might be, his corporeal presence.

His Lordship saw that enough had been done for subjection, and blandly added, "And I could have no objection to the interview; none whatever."

"It's too good you are, my Lord; too good and too gracious to the like of me," said Terry, barely raising his eyes to throw a glance of mingled shame and drollery on his Lordship; "but I come by rayson of what Mr. Hankes tould me, that it was a trifle of a loan,—a small matter of money your Lordship was wantin' just at this moment."

"I prefer doing these kind of things through my solicitors. I know nothing of business, sir, absolutely nothing," said his Lordship, haughtily. "The present case, however, might form an exception. The sum I require is, as you justly remark, a mere trifle, and the occasion is not worthy of legal interference."

"Yes, my Lord," chimed in Driscoll, who had a most provoking habit of employing the affirmative in all situations.

"I suppose he mentioned to you the amount?" asked his Lordship, quickly.

"No, indeed, my Lord; all he said was, 'Terry,' says he, 'go over to Bilton's Hotel with this note, and ask for Lord Glengariff. He wants a little ready cash,' says he, 'and I tould him you 're a likely man to get it for him. It's too small a matter for us here,' says he, 'to be bothered about.'"

"He had n't the insolence to make use of these words towards *me!*" said Lord Glengariff, growing almost purple with passion.

"Faix, I 'm afeard he had, my Lord," said Terry, looking down; "but I 'm sure he never meant any harm in it; 't was only as much as to say, 'There, Terry, there 's something for *you*; you 're a poor strugglin' man, and are well plazed to turn a penny in a small way. If you can accommodate my Lord there,' says he, 'he 'll not forget it to you.'"

The conclusion of this speech was far more satisfactory to his Lordship than its commencement seemed to promise; and Lord Glengariff smiled half graciously as he said, "I 'm not in the habit of neglecting those who serve me."

"Yes, my Lord," said Driscoll, again.

"I may safely say that any influence I possess has always been exercised in favor of those who have been, so to say, supporters of my family."

Had his Lordship uttered a sentiment of the most exalted and self-denying import, he could not have assumed a prouder air than when he had finished these words. "And now, Mr. Driscoll, to business. I want five thousand pounds—"

A long, low whistle from Terry, as he threw up both his hands in the air, abruptly stopped his Lordship.

"What do you mean? Does the sum appear so tremendous, sir?"

"Five thousand! Where would I get it? Five thousand pounds? By the mortial man! your Lordship might as well ax me for five millions. I thought it was a hundred; or, maybe, a hundred and fifty; or, at the outside, two hundred pounds, just to take you over to London for what they call the sayson, or to cut a figure at Paris; but, five thousand! By my conscience, that's the price of an estate nowadays!"

"It is upon estated property I intend to raise this loan, sir," said his Lordship, angrily.

"Not Cushnacreena, my Lord?" asked Terry, eagerly.

"No, sir; that is secured by settlement."

"Nor Ballyrennin?"

"No; the townland of Ballyrennin is, in a manner, tied up."

"Tory's Mill, maybe?" inquired Terry, with more eagerness.

"Well, sir," said his Lordship, drawing himself up, "I must really make you my compliments upon the very accurate knowledge you appear to possess about my estate. Since what period, may I venture to ask, have you conceived this warm interest in my behalf?"

"The way of it was this, my Lord," said Driscoll, drawing his chair closer, and dropping his voice to a low, confidential tone. "After I had the fever,—the fever and ague I told you about,—I got up out of bed the poor crayture you see me, not able to think of anything, or do a hand's turn for myself, but just a burden on my friends or anybody that would keep me. Well, I tried all manner of ways to make myself useful, and I used to go errands here and there over the country for any one that wanted to know what land was to be sold, where there was a lot of good sheep, who had a drove of bullocks or a fancy bull; and, just getting into the habit of it, I larned a trifle of what was doing in the three counties, so that the people call me 'Terry's Almanack,'—that's the name they gave me, better than Tearin' Terry, anyhow! At all events, I got a taste for finding out the secrets of all the great families; and, to be sure, if I only had the memory, I'd know a great deal, but my head is like a cullender, and everything runs out as fast as you put it in. That's how it is, my Lord, and no lie in it." And Terry wiped his forehead and heaved a heavy sigh, like a man who had just accomplished a very arduous task.

"So, then, I begin to understand how Hankes sent you over here to me," said his Lordship.

"Yes, my Lord," muttered Terry, with a bow.

"I had been under the impression—the erroneous impression—that you were yourself prepared to advance this small sum."

"Me! Terry Driscoll lend five thousand pounds! Arrah, look at me, my Lord,—just take a glance at me, and you 'll see how likely it is I 'd have as many shillings! 'T was only by rayson of being always about—on the tramp, as they call it—that Mr. Hankes thought I could be of use to your Lordship. 'Go over,' says he, 'and just tell him who and what you are.' There it is now!"

Lord Glengariff made no reply, but slowly walked the room in deep meditation; a passing feeling of pity for the poor fellow before him had overcome any irritation his own disappointment had occasioned, and for the moment the bent of his mind was compassionate.

"Well, Driscoll," said he, at length, "I don't exactly see how you can serve me in this matter."

"Yes, my Lord," said Terry, with a pleasant leer of his restless eyes.

"I say I don't perceive that you can contribute in any way to the object I have in view," said his Lordship, half peevish at being, as he thought, misapprehended. "Hankes ought to have known as much himself."

"Yes, my Lord," chimed in Terry.

"And you may tell him so from *me*. He is totally unfitted for his situation, and I am only surprised that Dunn, shrewd fellow that he is, should have ever placed a man of this stamp in a position of such trust. The first requisite in such a man is to understand the deference he owes to *us*."

There was an emphasis on the last monosyllable that pretty clearly announced how little share Terry Driscoll enjoyed in this co-partnery.

"That because I have a momentary occasion for a small sum of ready money, he should send over to confer with me a half-witted—I mean a man only half recovered from a fever—a poor fellow still suffering from—"

"Yes, my Lord," interposed Terry, as he laid his hand on his forehead in token of the seat of his calamity.

"It is too gross,—it is outrageous,—but Dunn shall hear of it,—Dunn shall deal with this fellow when he comes back. I'm sorry for you, Driscoll,— very sorry indeed; it is a sad bereavement, and though you are not exactly a case for an asylum,—perhaps, indeed, you might have objections to an asylum—"

"Yes, my Lord."

"Well, in that case private friends are, I opine—private friends—and the kind sympathies of those who have known you—eh, don't you think so?"

"Yes, my Lord."

"That is the sensible view to take of it. I am glad you see it in this way. It shows that you really exercise a correct judgment,—a very wise discretion in your case,—and for a man in *your* situation—your *painful* situation—you see things in their true light."

"Yes, my Lord." And this time the eyes rolled with a most peculiar expression.

"If you should relapse, however,—if, say, former symptoms were to threaten again,—remember that I am on the committee, or a governor, or something or other, of one of these institutions, and I might be of use to you. Remember that, Driscoll." And with a wave of his hand his Lordship dismissed Terry, who, after a series of respectful obeisances, gained the door and disappeared.

CHAPTER VI
SYBELLA KELLETT

When change of fortune had reduced the Kelletts so low that Sybella was driven to become a daily governess, her hard fate had exacted from her about the very heaviest of all sacrifices. It was not, indeed, the life of unceasing toil,—dreary and monotonous as such toil is,—it was not the humility of a station for which the world affords not one solitary protection,—these were not what she dreaded; as little was it the jarring sense of dependence daily and hourly imposed. No, she had courage and a high determination to confront each and all of these. The great source of her suffering was in the loss of that calm and unbroken quiet to which the retired habits of a remote country-house had so long accustomed her. With scarcely anything which could be called a society near them, so reduced in means as to be unable to receive visitors at home, Kellett's Court had been for many years a lonely house. The days succeeded each other with such similarity that time was unfelt, seasons came and went, and years rolled on unconsciously. No sights nor sounds of the great world without invaded these retired precincts. Of the mighty events which convulsed the politics of states,—of the great issues that engaged men's minds throughout Europe,— they heard absolutely nothing. The passing story of some little incident of cottier life represented to them all that they had of news; and thus time glided noiselessly along, till they came to feel a sense of happiness in that same unbroken round of life.

They who have experienced the measured tread of a conventual existence—where the same incidents daily recur at the same periods, where no events from without obtrude, where the passions and the ambitions and cares of mankind have so little of reality to the mind that they fail to impress with any meaning—are well aware that in the peaceful calm of spirit thus acquired there is a sense of happiness, which is not the less real that it wears the semblance of seriousness, almost of sadness.

In all that pertained to a sombre monotony, Kellett's Court was a convent. The tall mountains to the back, the deep woods to the front, seemed barriers against the world without; and there was a silence and a stillness about the spot as though it were some lone island in a vast sea, where no voyagers ever touched, no traveller ever landed. This same isolation, strong in its own sense of security, was the charm of the place, investing it with a kind of romance, and imparting to Sybella's own life a something of storied interest. The very few books the house contained she had read and re-read till she knew them almost by heart. They were lives of voyagers,—hardy men of enterprise and daring, who had pushed their fortunes in far-away lands,—or else sketches of life and adventure in distant countries.

The annals of these sea-rovers were full of all the fascination of which gorgeous scenery and stirring incident form the charm. There were lands such as no painter's genius ever fancied, verdure and flowers of more than fairy brilliancy, gold and gems of splendor that rivalled Aladdin's cave, strange customs, and curious observances mingled with deeds of wildest daring, making up a succession of pictures wherein the mind alternated between the voluptuous repose of tropical enjoyment and the hair-breadth 'scapes of buccaneering existence. The great men whose genius planned, and whose courage achieved, these enterprises, formed for her a sort of hero-worship. Their rough virtues, their splendid hospitality, their lion-hearted defiance of danger, were strong appeals to her sympathy, while in their devoted loyalty she found a species of chivalry that elevated them in her esteem. Woman-like, too, she inclined to make success the true test of greatness, and glorified to herself those bold spirits who never halted nor turned aside when on their road to victory. The splendid self-dependence of such men as Drake and Dampier struck her as the noblest attribute of mankind; that resolute trust in their own stout hearts imparted to them a degree of interest almost devotional; and over and over did she bethink her what a glorious destiny it would have been to have had a life associated and bound up with some such man as one of these. The very contest and controversy his actions would have evoked, heightened the illusion, and there savored of heroism in sharing a fame that flung down its proud defiance to the world.

Estrangement from the world often imparts to the stories of the past, or even to the characters of fiction, a degree of interest which, by those engaged in the actual work of life, is only accorded to their friends or relatives; and thus, to this young girl in her isolation, such names as Raleigh and Cavendish—such characters as Cromwell, Lorenzo de' Medici, and Napoleon—stood forth before her in all the attributes of well-known individuals. To have so far soared above the ordinary accidents of life as to live in an atmosphere above all other men,—to have seen the world and its ways from an eminence that gave wider scope to vision and more play to speculation,—to have meditated over the destinies of mankind from the height of a station that gave control over their actions,—seemed so glorious a privilege that the blemishes and even the crimes of men so gifted were merged in the greatness of the mighty task they had imposed upon themselves; and thus was it that she claimed for these an exemption from the judgments that had visited less distinguished wrong-doers most heavily. "How can I, or such as I am, pronounce upon one like this man? What knowledge have I of the conflict waged within his deep intelligence? How can I fathom the ocean of his thoughts, or even guess at the difficulties that have opposed, the doubts that have beset him? I can but vaguely fashion to myself the end and object of his journey; how, then, shall I criticise the road by which he travels, the halts he makes, the devious turnings and windings he seems to fall into?" In such plausibilities she merged every scruple as to those she had deified to her own mind. "Their ways are not our ways," said she; "their natures are as little our natures."

From all the dreamland of these speculations was she suddenly and rudely brought to face the battle of life itself, an humble soldier in the ranks. No longer to dwell in secret converse with the mighty spirits who had swayed their fellow-men, she was now to enter upon that path of daily drudgery whose direst infliction was the contact with that work-o'-day world wherewith she had few sympathies.

Mrs. Hawkshaw had read her advertisement in a morning paper, and sent for her to call upon her. Now Mrs. Hawkshaw was an alderman's lady, who lived in a fine house, and had fine clothes and fine servants and fine plate, and everything, in short, fine about her but a fine husband, for he was a rough, homespun, good-natured sort of man, who cared little for anything save a stocking-factory he owned at Balbriggan, and the stormy incidents that usually shook the "livery" he belonged to.

There were six little Hawkshaws to be governed and geographied and catechised, and civilized in all the various forms by which untaught humanity is prepared for the future work of life; there were rudiments of variously colored knowledge to be imparted, habits instilled, and tempers controlled, by one who, though she brought to her task the most sincere desire to succeed, was yet deep in a world of her own thoughts,—far lost in the mazy intricacies of her own fancies. That poor Miss Kellett, therefore, should pass for a very simple-minded, good creature, quite unfit for her occupation, was natural enough; and that Mrs. Hawkshaw should "take her into training" was almost an equally natural consequence.

"She seems to be always like one in a dream, my dear," said Mrs. Hawkshaw to her husband. "The children do exactly as they please; they play all false, and she never corrects them; they draw landscapes in their copy-books, and she says, 'Very nicely done, darlings.'"

"Her misfortunes are preying upon her, perhaps."

"Misfortunes! why, they have been in poverty this many a year. My brother Terry tells me that the Kelletts had n't above two hundred a year, and that latterly they lost even this."

"Well, it is a come-down in the world, anyhow," said Hawkshaw, sighing, "and I must say she bears it well."

"If she only feels it as little as she appears to do everything else, the sacrifice doesn't cost her much," said the lady, tartly. "I told her she was to come here last Sunday and take charge of the children; she never came; and when I questioned her as to the reason, she only smiled and said, 'She never thought of it; in fact, she was too happy to be alone on that day to think of anything.' And here she comes now, nearly an hour late." And, as she spoke, a weary step ascended the steps to the door, and an uncertain, faltering hand raised the knocker.

"It is nigh eleven o'clock, Miss Kellett," said Mrs. Hawkshaw, as she met her on the stairs.

"Indeed—I am so sorry—I must have forgotten—I don't think I knew the hour," said the other, stammeringly.

"Your hour is ten, Miss Kellett."

"I think so."

"How is your father, Miss Kellett?" asked the alderman, abruptly, and not sorry to interpose at the juncture.

"He is well, sir, and seems very happy," said she, gratefully, while her eyes lighted up with pleasure.

"Give him my regards," said Hawkshaw, good-naturedly, and passed down the stairs; while his wife coldly added, —

"The children are waiting for you," and disappeared.

With what determined energy did she address herself now to her task,—how resolutely devote her whole mind to her duty. She read and heard and corrected and amended with all the intense anxiety of one eager to discharge her trust honestly and well. She did her very utmost to bring her faculties to bear upon every detail of her task; and it was only when one of the girls asked who was he whose name she had been writing over and over again in her copy-book, that she forgot her self-imposed restraint, and in a fervor of delight at the question, replied, "I 'll tell you, Mary, who Savonarola was."

In all the vigor of true narrative power, the especial gift of those minds where the play of fancy is only the adornment of the reasoning faculty, she gave a rapid sketch of the prophet priest, his zeal, his courage, and his martyrdom; with that captivating fascination which is the firstborn of true enthusiasm, she awakened their interest so deeply that they listened to all she said as to a romance whose hero had won their sympathies, and even dimly followed her as she told them that such men as this stood out from time to time in the world's history like great beacons blazing on a rocky eminence, to guide and warn their fellow-men. That in their own age characters of this stamp were either undervalued or actually depreciated and condemned, was but the common lot of humanity; their own great destinies raised them very often above the sympathies of ordinary life, and men caught eagerly at the blemishes of those so vastly greater than themselves,—hence all the disesteem they met with from contemporaries.

"And are there none like this now, Miss Bella?" asked one of the girls; "or is it that in our country such are not to be met with?"

"They are of every land and of every age; ay, and of every station! Country, time, birth have no prerogative. At one moment the great light of the earth has been the noblest born in his nation, at another a peasant,— miles apart in all the accidents of fortune, brothers by the stamp which makes genius a tie of family. To-morrow you shall hear of one, the noblest-hearted man in all England, and yet whose daily toil was the vulgar life of an exciseman. This great man's nature is known to us, teaching men a higher lesson than all that his genius has bequeathed us."

In the willingness with which they listened to her, Bella found fresh support for her enthusiasm. If, therefore, there was this solace to the irksome nature of her task, it rendered that task itself more and more wearisome and distasteful. Her round of duty led her amongst many who did not care for these things; some heard them with apathy, others with even mockery. How often does it happen in life that feelings which if freely expanded had spread themselves broadly over the objects of the world, become by repression compressed into principles!

This was the case with her; the more opposition thwarted, the more resolutely was she bent on carrying out her notions. All her reading tended to this direction, all her speculation, all her thought.

"There must be men amongst us even now," said she, "to whom this great prerogative of guidance is given; superior minds who feel the greatness of their mission, and, perhaps, know how necessary it is to veil their very ascendancy, that they may exercise it more safely and more widely. What concession may they not be making to vulgar prejudice, what submission to this or that ordinance of society? How many a devious path must they tread to reach that goal that the world will not let them strive for more directly; and, worse than all, through what a sea of misrepresentation, and even calumny, must they wade? How must they endure the odious imputations of selfishness, of pride, of hard-heartedness, nay, perhaps, of even crime? And all this without the recognition of as much as one who knows their purpose and acknowledges their desert."

CHAPTER VII
AN ARRIVAL AT MIDNIGHT

Night had just closed in over the Lake of Como; and if the character of the scene in daylight had been such as to suggest ideas of dramatic effect, still more was this the case as darkness wrapped the whole landscape, leaving the great Alps barely traceable against the starry sky, while faintly glimmering lights dotted the dark shores from villa and palace, and soft sounds of music floated lazily on the night air, only broken by the plashing stroke of some gondolier as he stole across the lake.

The Villa d'Este was a-glitter with light. The great saloon which opened on the water blazed with lamps; the terraces were illuminated with many-colored lanterns; solitary candles glimmered from the windows of many a lonely chamber; and even through the dark copses and leafy parterres some lamp twinkled, to show the path to those who preferred the scented night air to the crowded and brilliant assemblage within doors. The votaries of hydropathy are rarely victims of grave malady. They are generally either the exhausted sons and daughters of fashionable dissipation, the worn-out denizens of great cities, or the tired slaves of exciting professions,—the men of politics, of literature, or of law. To such as these, a life of easy indolence, the absence of all constraint, the freedom which comes of mixing with a society where not one face is known to them, are the chief charms; and, with that, the privilege of condescending to amusements and intimacies of which, in their more regular course of life, they had not even stooped to partake. To English people this latter element was no inconsiderable feature of pleasure. Strictly defined as all the ranks of society are in their own country,—marshalled in classes so rigidly that none may move out of the place to which birth has assigned him,—they feel a certain expansion in this novel liberty, perhaps the one sole new sensation of which their natures are susceptible. It was in the enjoyment of this freedom that a considerable party were now assembled in the great saloons of the villa. There were Russians and Austrians of high rank, conspicuous for their quiet and stately courtesy; a noisy Frenchman or two; a few pale, thoughtful-looking Italians, men whose noble foreheads seem to promise so much, but whose actual lives appear to evidence so little; a crowd of Americans, as distinctive and as marked as though theirs had been a nationality stamped with centuries of transmission; and, lastly, there were the English, already presented to our reader in an early chapter,—Lady Lackington and her friend Lady Grace,—having, in a caprice of a moment, descended to see "what the whole thing was like."

"No presentations, my Lord, none whatever," said Lady Lackington, as she arranged the folds of her dress, on assuming a very distinguished position in the room. "We have only come for a few minutes, and don't mean to make acquaintances."

"Who is the little pale woman with the turquoise ornaments?" asked Lady Grace.

"The Princess Labanoff," said his Lordship, blandly bowing.

"Not she who was suspected of having poisoned—"

"The same."

"I should like to know her. And the man,—who is that tall, dark man, with the high forehead?"

"Glumthal, the great Frankfort millionnaire."

"Oh, present him, by all means. Let us have him here," said Lady Lackington, eagerly. "What does that little man mean by smirking in that fashion,—who is he?" asked she, as Mr. O'Reilly passed and repassed before her, making some horrible grimaces that he intended to have represented as fascinations.

"On no account, my Lord," said Lady Lackington, as though replying to a look of entreaty from his Lordship.

"But you 'd really be amused," said he, smiling. "It is about the best bit of low comedy—"

"I detest low comedy."

"The father of your fair friends, is it not?" asked Lady Grace, languidly.

"Yes. Twining admires them vastly," said his Lordship, half maliciously. "If I might venture—"

"Oh dear, no; not to me," said Lady Grace, shuddering. "I have little tolerance for what are called characters. You may present your Hebrew friend, if you like."

"He's going to dance with the Princess; and there goes Twining, with one of my beauties, I declare," said Lord Lackington. "I say, Spicer, what is that dark lot, near the door?"

"American trotters, my Lord; just come over."

"You know them, don't you?"

"I met them yesterday at dinner, and shall be delighted to introduce your Lordship. Indeed, they asked me if you were not the Lord that was so intimate with the Prince of Wales."

"How stupid! They might have known, even without the aid of a Peerage, that I was a schoolboy when the Prince was a grown man. The tall girl is good-looking; what's her name?"

"She's the daughter of the Honorable Leonidas Shinbone, that's all I know,—rather a belle at Saratoga, I fancy."

"Very dreadful!" sighed Lady Grace, fanning herself; "they do make such a mess of what might be very pretty toilette. You could n't tell her, perhaps, that her front hair is dressed for the back of the head."

"No, sir; I never play at cards," said Lord Lackington, stiffly, as an American gentleman offered him a pack to draw from.

"Only a little bluff or a small party of poker," said the stranger, "for quarter dollars, or milder, if you like it."

A cold bow of refusal was the reply.

"I told you he was the Lord," said a friend, in a drawling accent "He looks as if he 'd 'mow us all down like grass.'"

Dr. Lanfranchi, the director of the establishment, here interposed, and, by a few words, induced the Americans to retire and leave the others unmolested.

"Thank you, doctor," said Lady Lackington, in acknowledgment; "your tact is always considerate,—always prompt."

"These things never happen in the season, my Lady," said he, with a very slight foreign accentuation of the words. "It is only at times like this that people—very excellent and amiable people, doubtless—"

"Oh, to be sure they are," interrupted she, impatiently; "but let us speak of something else. Is that your clairvoyant Princess yonder?"

"Yes, my Lady; she has just revealed to us what was doing at the Crimea. She says that two of the English advanced batteries have slackened their fire for want of ammunition, and that a deserter was telling Todleben of the reason at the moment She is *en rapport* with her sister, who is now at Sebastopol."

"And are we to be supposed to credit this?" asked my Lord.

"I can only aver that I believe it, my Lord," said Lanfranchi, whose massive head and intensely acute features denoted very little intellectual weakness.

"I wish you 'd ask her why are we lingering so long in this dreary place?" sighed Lady Lackington, peevishly.

"She answered that question yesterday, my Lady," replied he, quietly.

"How was that? Who asked her? What did she say?"

"It was the Baron von Glum that asked; and her answer was, 'Expecting a disappointment.'"

"Very gratifying intelligence, I must say. Did you hear that, my Lord?"

"Yes, I heard it, and I have placed it in my mind in the same category as her Crimean news."

"Can she inform us when we are to get away?" asked her Ladyship.

"She mentioned to-morrow evening as the time, my Lady," said the doctor, calmly.

A faint laugh of derisive meaning was Lady Lackington's only reply; and the doctor gravely remarked: "There is more in these things than we like to credit; perhaps our very sense of inferiority in presence of such prediction is a bar to our belief. We do not willingly lend ourselves to a theory which at once excludes us from the elect of prophecy."

"Could she tell us who'll win the Derby?" said Spicer, joining the colloquy. But a glance from her Ladyship at once recalled him from the indiscreet familiarity.

"Do you think she could pronounce whose is the arrival that makes such a clatter outside?" said Lord Lackington, as a tremendous chorus of whip-cracking announced the advent of something very important; and the doctor hurried off to receive the visitor. Already a large travelling-carriage, drawn by eight horses, and followed by a "fourgon" with four, had drawn up before the great entrance, and a courier, gold-banded and whiskered, and carrying a most imposingly swollen money-bag, was ringing stoutly for admittance. When Dr. Lanfranchi had exchanged a few words with the courier, he approached the window of the carriage, and, bowing courteously, proceeded to welcome the traveller.

"Your apartments have been ready since the sixteenth, sir; and we hoped each day to have seen you arrive."

"Have your visitors all gone?" asked the stranger, in a low quiet tone.

"No, sir; the fine weather has induced many to prolong their stay. We have the Princess Labanoff, Lord Lackington, the Countess Grembinski, the Duke of Terra di Monte, the Lady Grace—"

The traveller, however, paid little attention to the Catalogue, but with the aid of the courier on one side and his-valet on the other, slowly descended from the carriage. If he availed himself of their assistance, there was little in his appearance that seemed to warrant its necessity. He was a large, powerfully built man, something beyond the prime of life, but whose build announced considerable vigor. Slightly stooped in the shoulders, the defect seemed to add to the fixity of his look, for the head was thus thrown more forward, and the expression of the deep-set eyes, overshadowed by shaggy gray eyebrows, rendered more piercing and direct His features were massive and regular, their character that of solemnity and gravity; and as he removed his cap, he displayed a high, bold forehead with what phrenologists would have called an extravagant development of the organs of locality. Indeed, these overhanging masses almost imparted an air of retreating to a head that was singularly straight.

"A number of letters have arrived for you, and you will find them in your room, sir," continued Lanfranchi, as he escorted him towards the stairs. A quiet bow acknowledged this speech, and the doctor went on: "I was charged with a message from Lord Lackington, too, who desired me to say that he hoped to see you as soon as possible after your arrival. May I inform him when you could receive him?"

"Not to-night; some time to-morrow, about twelve o'clock, or half-past, if that will suit him," said the stranger, coldly. "Is Baron Glumthal here? Well, tell him to come up to me, and let them send me some tea."

"May I mention your arrival to his Lordship, for I know his great anxiety?"

"Just as you please," said the other, in the same quiet tone; while he bowed in a fashion to dismiss his visitor.

Having glanced casually at the addresses of a number of letters, he only opened one or two, and looked cursorily over their contents; and then opening a window which looked over the lake, he placed a chair on the balcony and sat down, as if to rest and reflect in the fresh and still night air. It was a calm and quiet atmosphere,—not a leaf stirred, not a ripple moved the glassy surface of the lake; so that, as he sat, he could overhear Dr. Lanfranchi's voice beneath announcing his arrival to Lord Lackington.

"If he can receive Glumthal, why can't he see *me?*" asked the Viscount, testily. "You must go back and tell him that I desire particularly to meet him this evening."

"If you wish, my Lord—"

"I do, sir," repeated he, more peremptorily. "Lady Lackington and myself have been sojourning here the last three weeks, awaiting this arrival, and I am at a loss to see why our patience is to be pushed further. Pray take him my message, therefore."

The doctor, without speaking, left the room at once.

Lanfranchi was some minutes in the apartment before he discovered where the stranger was sitting, and then approaching him softly he communicated his Lordship's request.

"I am afraid you must allow me to take my own way. I have contracted an unfortunate habit in that respect," said the stranger, with a quiet smile. "Give my compliments to his Lordship, and say that at twelve to-morrow I am at his orders; and tell Baron Glumthal that I expect him now."

Lanfranchi withdrew; and having whispered the message to the Baron, proceeded to make his communication to the Viscount.

"Very well, sir," said Lord Lackington, haughtily interrupting; "something like an apology. Men of this sort have a business-like standard even for their politeness, and there is no necessity for me to teach them something better;" and then, turning to Twining, he added, "That was Dunn's arrival we heard awhile ago."

"Oh, indeed! Very glad,—quite rejoiced on your account more than my own. Dunn—Dunn; remarkable man—very," said Twining, hurriedly.

"Thank Heaven! we may be able to get away from this place to-morrow or next day," said Lord Lackington, sighing drearily.

"Yes, of course; very slow for your Lordship—no society—nothing to do."

"And the weather beginning to break?" said Lord Lackington, peevishly.

"Just so, as your Lordship most justly observes,—the weather beginning to break."

"Look at that troop of horses," said the Viscount, as the postilions passed beneath the window in a long file with the cattle just released from the travelling-carriages. "There goes ten—no, but twelve posters. He travels right royally, doesn't he?"

"Very handsomely, indeed; quite a pleasure to see it," said Twining, gleefully.

"These fellows have little tact, with all their worldly shrewdness, or they 'd not make such ostentatious display of their wealth."

"Quite true, my Lord. It *is* indiscreet of them."

"It is so like saying, 'This is *our* day! '" said the Viscount.

"So it is, my Lord; and a very pleasant day they have of it, I must say; clever men—shrewd men—know the world thoroughly."

"I 'm not so very sure of that, Twining," said his Lordship, smiling half superciliously. "If they really had all the worldly knowledge you attribute to them, they 'd scarcely venture to shock the feelings of society by assumptions of this sort They would have more patience, Twining,—more patience."

"So they would, my Lord. Capital thing,—excellent thing, patience; always rewarded in the end; great fun." And he rubbed his hands and laughed away pleasantly.

"And they'll defeat themselves, that's what will come of it, sir," said Lord Lackington, not heeding the other's remark.

"I quite agree with your Lordship," chimed in Twining.

"And shall I tell you why they 'll defeat themselves, sir?"

"Like it of all things; take it as a great favor on your Lordship's part."

"For this reason, Twining, that they have no 'prestige,'—no, Twining, they have no prestige. Now, sir, wealth unassociated with prestige is just like—what shall I say?—it is, as it were, a sort of local rank,—a kind of thing like being brigadier in the Bombay Army, but only a lieutenant when you 're at home; so long, therefore, as these fellows are rich, they have their influence. Let them suffer a reverse of fortune, however, and where will they be, sir?"

"Can't possibly say; but quite certain your Lordship knows,—perfectly sure of it," rattled out Twining.

"I do, sir. It is a subject on which I have bestowed considerable thought. I may go further, and say, one which I have reduced to a sort of theory. These men are signs of the times,—emblems of our era; just like the cholera, the electric telegraph, or the gold-fields of Australia. We must not accept them as normal, do you perceive? They are the abnormal incidents of our age."

"Quite true, most just, very like the electric telegraph!" muttered Twining.

"And by that very condition only exercising a passing influence on our society, sir," said his Lordship, pursuing his own train of thought.

"Perfectly correct, rapid as lightning."

"And when they do pass away, sir," continued the Viscount, "they leave no trace of their existence behind them. The bubble buret, the surface of the stream remains without a ripple. I myself may live to see; you, in all probability, will live to see."

"Your Lordship far more likely,—sincerely trust as much," said Twining, bowing.

"Well, sir, it matters little which of us is to witness the extinction of this Plutocracy." And as his Lordship enunciated this last word, he walked off like one who had totally exhausted his subject.

CHAPTER VIII
MR. DUNN

MR. Davenport Dunn sat at breakfast in his spacious chamber overlooking the Lake of Como. In addition to the material appliances of that meal, the table was covered with newly arrived letters, and newspapers, maps, surveys, railroad sections, and Parliamentary blue-books littered about, along with chalk drawings, oil miniatures, some carvings in box and ivory, and a few bronzes of rare beauty and design. Occasionally skimming over the newspapers, now sipping his tea, or now examining some object of art through a magnifier, he dallied over his meal like one who felt the time thus passed a respite from the task of the day. At last he walked out, and, leaning over the balcony, gazed at the glorious landscape at his feet. It was early morning, and the great masses of misty clouds were slowly beginning to move up the Alps, disclosing as they went spots of bright green verdure, dark-sided ravines and cataracts, amid patches of pine forest, or dreary tracts of snow still lying deep in the mountain clefts. Beautiful as was the picture of the lake itself, and the wooded promontories along it, his eyes never turned from the rugged grandeur of the Alpine range, which he continued to gaze at for a long time. So absorbed was he in his contemplation, that he never noticed the approach of another, and Baron Glumthal was already leaning over the balustrade beside him ere he had perceived him.

"Well, is it more assuring now that you have looked at it?" asked the German, in English, of which there was the very slightest trace of a foreign accent.

"I see nothing to deter one from the project," said Dunn, slowly. "These questions resolve themselves purely into two conditions,—time and money. The grand army was only a corporal's guard, multiplied by hundreds of thousands."

"But the difficulties—"

"Difficulties!" broke in Dunn; "thank Heaven for them, Baron, or you and I would be no better off in this world than the herd about us. Strong heads and stout hearts are the breaching artillery of mankind,—you can find rank and file any day."

"When I said difficulties, I might have used a stronger word."

"And yet," said Dunn, smiling, "I'd rather contract to turn the Alps yonder, than to drive a new idea into the heads of a people. See here, now," said he, entering the room, and returning with a large plan in his hand, "this is Chiavenna. Well, the levels show that a line drawn from this spot comes out below Andeer, at a place called Mühlen,—the distance something less than twenty-two miles. By Brumall's contract, you will perceive that if he don't meet with water—"

"But in that lies the whole question," broke in the other.

"I know it, and I am not going to blink it. I mean to take the alternatives in turn."

"Shall I spare you a deal of trouble, Dunn?" said the German, laying his hand on his arm. "Our house has decided against the enterprise. I have no need to explain the reasons."

"And can you be swayed by such counsels?" cried Dunn, eagerly. "Is it possible that you will suffer yourselves to be made the dupes of a Russian intrigue?"

"Say, rather, the agents of a great policy," said Glumthal, "and you will be nearer the mark. My dear friend," added he, in a lower and more confidential tone, "have I to tell *you* that *your* whole late policy in England is a mistake, your Crimean war a mistake, your French alliance a mistake, and your present attempt at a reconciliation with Austria the greatest mistake of all?"

"You would find it a hard task to make the nation believe this," said Dunn, smiling.

"So I might; but not to convince your statesmen of it. They see it already. They perceive even now some of the perils of the coarse they have adopted."

"The old story. I have heard it at least a hundred times," broke in Dunn. "We have been overturning the breakwaters that the ocean may swamp us. But I tell *you*, Baron, that the more democratic we grow in England, the safer we become. We don't want these alliances we fancied ourselves once in need of. That family compact redounded but little to our advantage."

"So it might. But there is another compact now forming, which bodes even less favorably to you. The Church, by her Concordat, is replacing the old Holy Alliance. You 'll need the aid of the only power that cannot be drawn into this league,—I mean the only great power,—Russia."

"If you will wait till we are so minded, Baron," said Dunn, laughing, "you have plenty of time to help me with my tunnel here." And he pointed to his plans.

"And where will the world be,—I mean your world and mine,—before the pick of the workman reaches so far?" and he placed his finger on the Splugen Alps,—"answer me that. What will be the Government of France,—I don't ask who? Where will Naples be? What king will be convoking the Hungarian Diet? Who will be the Russian viceroy on the Danube?"

"Far more to the purpose were it if I could tell you how would the Three per Cents stand," broke in Dunn.

"I 'm coming to that," said the other, dryly. "No, no," said he, after a pause; "let us see this unhappy war finished,—let us wait till we know who are to be partners in the great game of European politics. Lanfranchi tells me that the French and Russians who meet here come together on the best of terms; that intimacies, and even friendships. spring up rapidly between them. This fact, if repeated in Downing Street, might be heard with some misgiving."

Though Dunn affected indifference to this remark, he winced, and walked to the window to hide his irritation.

Immediately beneath where he stood, a trellised vine-walk led down to the lake, where the boats were usually in waiting; and from this alley now a number of voices could be heard, although the speakers were entirely hidden by the foliage. The gay and laughing tones indicated a pleasure-party; and such it was, bent on a picnic to Bellaggio. Some were loud in praises of the morning, and the splendid promise of the day; others discussed how many boats they should want, and how the party was to be divided.

"The Americans with the Russians," said Twining, slapping his legs and laughing; "great friends—capital allies—what fun! Ourselves and the O'Reillys.—Spicer, look out, and see if they are coming."

"And do you mean to say you'll not come?" whispered a very soft voice, after the crowd had passed on.

"Charmante Molly!" said Lord Lackington, in his most dulcet of accents, "I am quite heart-broken at the disappointment; but when I tell you that this man has come some hundreds of miles to meet me here,—that the matter is one of deepest importance—"

"And who is he? Could you make him come too?"

"Impossible, *ma belle*. He is quite unsuited to this kind of thing,—a mere creature of parchments. The very sight of him would only suggest thoughts of foreclosing mortgages and renewal fines."

"How I hate him!"

"Do, dearest,—hate him to your heart's content,—and for nothing more than the happiness of which he robs me."

"Well, I 'm sure, I did think—" And she stopped, and seemed confused.

"And what, pray, was it that you did think?" said his Lordship, most winningly.

"I thought two things, then, if you must know," said she, archly: "first, that a great personage like your Lordship would make a very small one like this Mr. Dunn understand it was his duty to await your convenience; and my second thought was—But perhaps you don't care to hear it?"

"Of all things. Pray go on."

"Well, then, my second was that if I asked you to come, you'd not refuse me."

"What an inexorable charmer it is!" cried he, in stage fashion. "Do you fancy you could ever forgive yourself if, yielding to this temptation, I were really to miss this man?"

"You told me yourself, only yesterday," said she, "*ce que femme veut*—Besides, you'll have him all day tomorrow, and the next, and—"

"Well, so be it. See how I hug my chains!" said he, drawing her arm within his, and moving on towards the boat.

"Were you to be of that party, Baron?" asked Dunn, pointing to the crowd beside the lake.

"So I was. The Princess engaged me last night; they are going to the Plinniana and Bellaggio. Why not join us?"

"Oh, I have a score of letters to write, and double as many to read. In fact, I have kept all my work for a quiet day in this nice tranquil spot I wish I could take a week here."

"And why not do it? Have n't you yet learned that it is the world's duty to wait on *us?* For my own part, I have always found that one emerges from these secluded places with renewed energy and awakened vigor. I heard Stadeon once say that when anything puzzled him, he went to pass a day at Maria Zell, and he never came away without hitting on the solution. They are beckoning to me; so good-bye!"

"Anything puzzled him!" muttered Dunn, repeating the words of the other's story. "If he but knew that what puzzles *me* at this moment is myself!"

The very nature of the correspondence that then littered his table might well warrant what he felt. Who, and what was he, to whom great ministers wrote confidentially, and secretaries of state began, "My dear Dunn"? How had he risen to this eminence? What were the gifts by which he held, and was to maintain it? Most men who have attained to high station from small beginnings, have so conformed to the exigencies of each new change in life as to carry but little of what they started with to their position of eminence; gradually assimilating to the circumstances around them as they went, they flung the past behind them, only occupied with those qualities which should fit them for the future. Not so Davenport Dunn: he was ever present to his own eyes as the son of the very humblest parentage; as the poor boy educated by charity, struggling drearily through years of poverty,—the youth discouraged and slighted, the man repulsed and rejected. Certain incidents of his life never left him; there they were, as if photographed on his heart; and at will he could behold himself as he was turned away ignominiously from Kellett's house; or a morning scarce less sad, as he learned his rejection for the sizarship; or the day still more bitter that Lord Glengariff put him out of doors, with words of insult and shame. Like avenging spirits, these memories travelled with him wherever he journeyed. They sat beside him as he dined at great men's tables; they loitered with him in his lonely walks, and whispered into his ear in the dark hours of the night. No high-hearted hope, no elevating self-reliance, had sustained him through these youthful reverses; each new failure, on the contrary, seemed to have impressed him more and more strongly with the conviction that the gifts which win success in life had not been vouchsafed him; that his abilities were of that humble order which never elevate their possessor above mere mediocrity; that if he meant to strive for the great prizes of life, it must be less by addressing himself to great intellectual efforts than by a patient study of men themselves,—of their frailties, their weaknesses, and their follies. Whatever he had seen of the world had shown him how invariably the greatest minds were alloyed with some deteriorating influence, and that passions of one kind or other, ambitions more or less worthy, even the subtlety of flattery, swayed those whose intellects soared loftily among their fellows. "I cannot share in the tilt with these," said he. "Mine are no gifts of eloquence or imaginative power; I am not versed in the mysteries of science, nor deep-read in the intricacies of law. Let me, however, see if I cannot, by dexterity, accomplish what is denied to my strength. Every man, whatever his station, covets wealth. The noblest and the meanest, the man dignified by exalted aspirations, the true creature of selfish enjoyments, are all alike enlisted in the pursuit. Let me consider how this common tendency may be best turned to account. To enrich others, it is not necessary that I should be wealthy myself. The geographer may safely dictate the route by which the explorer is to journey through a desert he has never travelled himself. The great problems of finance can be worked by suggestions in a garret, though their application may demand millions." Starting thus from an humble attorney in a country town, he gradually grew to be known as a most capable adviser in all monetary matters. Rich men consulted him about profitable investments and safe employment of their capital; embarrassed men confided to him their difficulties, and sought his aid to meet them; speculators asked his advice as to this or that venture; and even those who gambled on the eventful fortunes of a ministry were fain to be guided by his wise predictions. "Dunn has got me the money on reasonable terms;" "Dunn has managed to let me have five per cent;" "Dunn assures me I may risk this;" "Dunn tells me that they 'll carry the bill next session,"—such and such things were the phrases one heard at every turn, till his opinion became a power in the land, and he grew to feel it so.

This first step led to another and higher one. Through the moneyed circumstances of men he came to learn their moral natures: against what temptations this one was proof; to what that other would yield; what were the goals for which each was striving; what the secret doubts and misgivings that beset them. What the doctor was to the world of sickness and infirmity did he become to the world of human passion and desire. Men came to him with the same unreserve; they stripped before him and laid bare the foul spots of their heart's disease, as though it were but repeating the story to themselves. Terrible and harrowing as are the tales which reach the physician's ears, the stories revealed to his were more terrible and harrowing still. They came to him with narratives of reckless waste and ruin; with histories of debt that dated a century back; with worse, far worse,—with tales of forgery and fraud. Crimes for which the law would have exacted its last expiation were whispered to him in that dreary confessional, his private office, and the evidences of guilt placed in his hands that he might read and reflect over them. And as the doctor moves through life with the sad knowledge of all the secret suffering around him,—how little that "flush" indicates of health, how faintly beats the heart that seems to swell with happiness,—so did this man walk a world that was a mere hospital ward of moral rottenness. Why should the priest and the physician be the only men to trade upon the infirmities of human nature? Why should they be the sole depositaries of those mysteries by which men's actions can be swayed and moulded? By what temptations are men so assailable as those that touch their material fortunes, and why not make this moral country an especial study? Such were his theory and his practice.

There is often a remarkable fitness—may we call it a "pre-established harmony"?—between men and the circumstances of their age, and this has led to the opinion that it is by the events themselves the agents are developed; we incline to think differently, as the appearance of both together is rather in obedience to some over-ruling edict of Providence which has alike provided the work and the workmen. It would be a shallow reading of history to imagine Cromwell the child of the Revolution, or Napoleon as the accident of the battle of the sections.

Davenport Dunn sprang into eminence when, by the action of the Encumbered Estates Court, a great change was operated in the condition of Ireland. To grasp at once the immense consequences of a tremendous social revolution—to foresee even some of the results of this sweeping confiscation—required no common knowledge of the country, and no small insight into its habits. The old feudalism that had linked the fate of a starving people with the fortunes of a ruined gentry was to be extinguished at once, and a great experiment tried. Was Ireland to be more governable in prosperity than in adversity? This was a problem which really might not seem to challenge much doubt, and yet was it by no means devoid of difficulty to those minds who had long based their ideas of ruling that land on the principles of fomenting its dissensions and separating its people. Davenport Dunn saw the hesitation of the moment, and offered himself at once to solve the difficulty. The transfer of property might be conducted in such a way as to favor the views of a particular party in the state; the new proprietary might be selected, and the aim of a government consulted in the establishment of this new squirearchy. He thought so, at least, and, what is more, he persuaded a chief secretary to believe him.

Nothing reads more simply than the sale of an encumbered estate: "In the matter of Sir Roger O'Moore, Bart, Brian O'Moore, and Margaret Halliday, owners, and Paul May-bey, petitioner, the Commissioners will, on Friday next, at the hour of noon,"—and so on; and then come the descriptive particulars of Carrickross, Dummaymagan, and Lantygoree, with Griffith's valuation and the ordnance survey, concluding with a recital of all the penalties, reservations, covenants, clauses, &c., with the modest mention of twenty-odd pounds some shillings tithe-rent charge, for a finish. To dispossess of this a man that never really owned it for the last forty years, and invest it in another, who never saw it, was the easy operation of the auctioneer's hammer; and with a chief commissioner to ratify the sale, few things seemed easier than the whole process. Still, there are certain aspects in the transaction which suggest reflection. What were the ties, what the relations, between the original owner and the tenantry who held under him? What kind of social system had bound them,—what were the mutual services they rendered each other? For the reverence and respect tendered on one side, and for the thousand little charities and kindnesses bestowed on the other, what was to be the compensation? How was that guidance and direction, more or less inherent in those who are the heads of a neighborhood, to be replaced? Was it quite certain that the incoming proprietor would care to study the habits, the tastes, and the tempers of the peasantry on his estate, learn their ways, or understand their difficulties? And, lastly, what new political complexion would the country wear? Would it become more Conservative or more Whig, more Democratic or more Saxon?

Davenport Dunn's opinion was that the case was precisely that of a new colony, where the first settlers, too busy about their material interests to care for mere speculative questions, would attach themselves heartily to any existing government, giving their adhesion to whatever afforded protection to their property and safety to their lives. "Take this new colony," said he, "into your especial care, and their sons and grandsons will be yours after-wards. A new regiment is being raised; write your own legends on their colors, and they are your own." He sketched out a system by which this new squirearchy was to be dealt with,—how courted, flattered, and rewarded. He showed how, in attaching them to the State, the government of the country might be rendered more easy, and the dreaded influence of the priest be antagonized most effectually; and, finally, demonstrated that Ireland, which had been the stereotyped difficulty of every administration, might now be turned into a stronghold against opposition.

To replace the great proprietary whose estates were now in the market by a new constituency in accordance with his views was, therefore, his general scheme, and he addressed himself to this task with all his peculiar energy. He organized the registry of all the encumbered estates of Ireland, with every detail which could illustrate the various advantages; he established an immense correspondence with English capitalists eager for new investments; he possessed himself of intimate knowledge of all the variations and fluctuations which attend the money market at certain periods, so that he knew the most favorable moments to suggest speculation; and, lastly, he had craft enough to carry his system into operation without any suspicion being attached to it; and was able to say to a Viceroy, "Look and judge for yourself, my Lord, whose influence is now paramount in Ireland."

Truly, it was not easy for a government to ignore him; his name turned up at every moment. From the stirring incident of a great county election to the small contest for a poor-law guardianship, he figured everywhere, until every question of policy became coupled with the inevitable demand, "What does Dunn think of it?"

Like all men of strong ambition, he encouraged few or no intimacies; he had actually no friendships. He wanted no counsels; nor would he have stooped to have laid a case for advice before any one. Partly in consequence of this, he was spoken of generally in terms of depreciation and discredit. Some called him lucky,—a happy phrase that adapts itself to any fancy; some said he was a commonplace, vulgar fellow, with certain business aptitudes, but quite incapable of any wide or extended views; some, again, went further, and said he was the mere tool of certain clever heads that did not care to figure in the foreground; and not a few wondered that "a man of this kind" should have ever attained to any eminence or station in the land.

"You 'll see how his Excellency will turn him to account; he knows how to deal with fellows of this stamp," said a private secretary in the Castle.

"I have no doubt, sir, Mr. Davenport Dunn would agree with you," said the Attorney-General, with a sneer; "but the opinion would be bad in law!"

"He 's not very much of a churchman, I suspect," whispered a bishop; "but we find him occasionally useful."

"He serves *our* purpose!" pompously spoke a country gentleman, who really, in the sentiment, represented a class.

Such was the man who now sat alone, communing with himself, in his room at the Villa d'Este. Let us believe that he had enough to think of.

CHAPTER IX
A DAY ON THE LAKE OF COMO

We fully sympathize with Lord Lackington, who preferred the picnic and the society of Miss Molly O'Reilly to the cares of business and an interview with Davenport Dunn. The Lake of Como, on a fine day of summer or early autumn, and with a heart moderately free from the anxieties and sorrows of life, is a very enjoyable locality, and essentially so to a man of the world like the noble Viscount, who liked to have the more romantic features of the scene blended with associations of ease and pleasure, and be able to turn from the contemplation of Alpine ruggedness to the sight of some terraced garden, glowing in the luxuriance of its vegetation. Never, perhaps, was there ever a spot so calculated to appeal successfully to the feelings of men of his stamp. There was mountain grandeur and desolation, snow-peak and precipice; but all in the back distance, not near enough to suggest even the fear of cold, or the disagreeable idea of a sledge journey. There were innumerable villas of every style and class,—some spacious and splendid enough for royal residences; others coquettish little chalets, where lovers might pass the honeymoon. There were tasteful pavilions over the very lake; snug spots where solitude might love to ponder, a student read, or an idler enjoy his cigar, in the most enviable of scenes. Trellised vine-walks zigzagged up the hills to some picturesque shrine whose modest little spire rose above the olive-trees, or some rude steps in the rock led down to a little nook, whole white sands glistened beneath the crystal waters,—such a bath as no Sybarite, in all his most glowing fancy, ever imagined. And amid all and through all there was that air of wealth—that assurance of affluence and abundance—which comes so home to the hearts of men whose sense of enjoyment can only be gratified where there is to be no sacrifice to their love of ease. In the noble Viscount's estimation, the place was perfect It was even associated with the solitary bit of romance of his whole life. It was here that he passed the first few weeks after his wedding; and though he had preserved very little of those feelings which imparted happiness to that period, though her Ladyship did not recall to his mind the attractions which once had fascinated him,—new glazed and new lacquered over and over again as was the vase, "the scent of the roses had clung to it still," The distance that lends enchantment to the material has also its influence on the moral picture. Memory softens and subdues many a harsh tint, mellows many an incongruity, and blends into a pleasant harmony many things which in their proximity were the reverse of agreeable. Not that we would be understood to say that Lord Lackington's honeymoon was not like yours, an elysium of happiness and bliss; we would simply imply that, in recalling it, he only remembered the rose-tints, and never brought up one of the shadows. He had, in his own fashion, poetized that little episode of his life, when, dressed in a fancy and becoming costume, he played gondolier to his young bride, scaled the mountain to fetch her Alp-roses, and read aloud "Childe Harold," as he interpolated Harrow recollections of its author. Not one of these did he now remember; he'd as soon have dreamed of being marker at a billiard table as of playing the barcarole; and as to mountain excursions he 'd not have bargained for any success that required the exertion of a steep staircase.

"There 's a little villa in a bay somewhere hereabouts," said he, as the boat glided smoothly along; "I should like much to show it to you." This was addressed to Molly O'Reilly, who sat beside him. "Do you happen to know La Pace?" asked he of one of the boatmen.

"To be sure I do, Eccellenza. Who doesn't? My own father was barcarole there to a great Milordo, I can't say how many years back. Ah," added he, laughing, "what stories he used to have of that same Milordo, who was always dressing himself up to be as a gondolier or a chamois-hunter."

"We have n't asked for your father's memoirs, my good fellow; we only wanted you to show us where La Pace lies," said the Viscount, testily.

"There it is, then, Eccellenza," said the man, as they rounded a little promontory of rock, and came in full view of a small cove, in the centre of which stood the villa.

Untenanted and neglected as it was, there was yet about it that glorious luxuriance of vegetation, that rare growth of vines and olive and oleander and cactus which seems to more than compensate all the care and supervision of men. The overloaded orange-trees dipped their weary branches in the lake, where the golden balls rose and fell as the water surged about them. The tangled vines sprawled over the ground, staining the deep grass with their purple blood. Olive berries lay deep around, and a thousand perfumes loaded the air as the faint breeze stirred it.

"Let me show you a true Italian villa," said the Viscount, as the boat glided up to the steps cut in the marble rock. "I once passed a few weeks here; a caprice seized me to know what kind of life it would be to loiter amidst olive groves, and have no other company than the cicala and the green lizard."

"Faith, my Lord," said O'Reilly, "if you could live upon figs and lemons, you 'd have nothing to complain of; but I 'm thinking you found it lonely."

"I scarcely remember, but my impression is, I liked it," said he, with a slight hesitation. "I used to lie under the great cedar yonder, and read Petrarch."

"Capital fun—excellent—live here for two hundred a year, or even less—plenty of fish in the lake—keep the servants on watermelons," said Twining, slapping his legs, as he made this domestic calculation to himself.

"With people one liked about one," said Miss O'Reilly, "I don't see why this should n't be a delicious spot."

"There's not a hundred yards of background. You could n't give a horse walking exercise here if your life was on it," said Spicer, contemptuously.

"Splendid grapes, wonderful oranges, finest melons I ever saw,—all going to waste too," said Twining, laughing, as if such utter neglect was a very droll thing. "Get this place a bargain,—might have it for a mere nothing."

"So you might, O'Reilly," said the Viscount; "it is one of those deserted spots that are picked up for a tenth of their value; buy it, fit it up handsomely, and we'll come and spend the autumn with you,—won't we, Twining?"

"Upon my life we will, I 'll swear it; be here 1st September to the day, and stay till—as long as you please. Great fun!"

"Delicious spot to come and repose in from the cares and worries of life," said Lord Lackington, as he stretched upon a bench and began peeling an orange.

"I 'd get the blue devils in a week; I 'd be found hanging some fine morning—"

"For shame, papa," broke in Molly. "My Lord says he 'd come on a visit to us, and you know we 'd only be here in the autumn."

"Just so—come here for the wine season—get in your olives and look after your oil—great fun," chimed in Twining, merrily.

"I declare, I 'd like it of all things, would not you?" said the elder girl to Spicer, who had now begun to reflect that there was a kind of straw-yard season for men as well as for hunters,—when the great object was to live cheap and husband your resources; and as he ruminated over the lazy quietness of an existence that would cost nothing, when even his "Bell's Life" should be inserted amongst the family extraordinaires, he vouchsafed to approve the scheme; and in his mumbling tone, in imitation of Heaven knows what celebrated sporting character, he grumbled out, "Make the governor go in for it by all means!"

Twining had entered into the project most eagerly. One of the most marked traits of his singular mind was not merely to enjoy his own preeminence in wealth over so many others, but to chuckle over all the possible mistakes which *he* had escaped and *they* had fallen into. To know that there was a speculation whose temptation he had resisted and which had engulfed all who engaged in it; to see the bank fail whose directorship he had refused, or the railroad smashed whose preference shares he had rejected,—this was an intense delight to him; and on such occasions was it that he slapped his lean legs most enthusiastically, and exclaimed, "What fun!" with the true zest of enjoyment.

To plant a man of O'Reilly's stamp in such a soil seemed, therefore, about the best practical joke he had ever heard of; and so he walked him over the villa, discoursing eloquently on all the advantages of the project,— the great social position it would confer, the place he would occupy in the country, the soundness of the investment, the certainty of securing great matches for the girls. What a view that window opened of the Splugen Alps! What a delicious spot, this little room, to sip one's claret of an autumn evening! Think of the dessert growing almost into the very dining-room, and your trout leaping within a yard of the breakfast-table! Austrians charmed to have you—make you a count—a Hof something or other, at once—give you a cross—great fun, eh?—Graf O'Reilly—sound admirably—do it, by all means!

While Twining's attack was being conducted in this fashion, Lord Lackington was not less industriously pursuing his plan of campaign elsewhere. He had sauntered with Molly into the garden and a little pavilion at the end of it, where the lake was seen in one of its most picturesque aspects. It was a well-known spot to him; he had passed many an evening on that low window-seat, half dreamingly forgetting himself in the peaceful scene, half consciously recalling pleasant nights at Brookes's and gay dinners at Carlton House. Here was it that he first grew hipped with matrimony, and so sated with its happiness that he actually began to long for any little disaster that might dash the smooth monotony of his life; and yet now, by one of those strange tricks memory plays us, he fancied that the moments he had once passed here had never been equalled in all his after-life.

"I'm certain, though you won't confess," said she, after one of his most eloquent bursts of remembered enjoyment,—"I 'm certain you were very much in love those days."

"An ideal passion, perhaps, a poetized vision of that bright creature who should, one day or other, sway this poor heart;" and he flattened the creases of his spotless white waistcoat; "but if you mean that I knew of any, had ever seen any, until now, this very moment—"

"Stop! remember your promise," said she, laughing.

"But, *charmante* Molly, I 'm only mortal," said he, with an air of such superb humility that made her at once remember it was a peer who said it.

"Mortals must keep their words," said she, pertly. "The condition on which I consented to accept your companionship was—But I need n't remind you."

"No, do not, dear Molly, for I shall be delighted to forget it. You are aware that no law ever obliged a man to do what was impossible; and that to exact any pledge from him to such an end is in itself an illegality. You little suspected, therefore, that it was you, not I, was the delinquent."

"'All I know is, that you assured me you 'd not—you 'd not talk nonsense," said she, blushing deeply, half angry, half ashamed.

"Oh! never guessed you were here," broke in Twining, as he peeped through the window. "Sweet spot—so quiet and secluded—capital fun!"

"There is *such* a view from this, papa," said Molly, in some confusion at Twining's bantering look; "come round and see it."

"I have just been telling this dear girl of yours, O'Reilly, that you ought to make this place your own," said Lord Lackington. "Don't fancy you 'd be out of the world here. Why, there 's the Villa d'Este, a European celebrity at once; it will be thronged next year to suffocation. The 'Galignani,' I see, has already mentioned myself and Lady Lackington as among the visitors. These things have their effect The press in our day is an estate."

"Indeed, I 'm sure of it. There was a cousin of my wife's drew his two hundred a year out of the 'Tyrawley Express,'—a daily little paper, that, maybe, your Lordship never seen."

"When I said an estate, sir, I rather alluded to a recognized condition of power and influence than to mere wealth. Not, I will add, that I am one of those who approve of this consummation; nor can I see how men of my order can ever so regard it."

"Well," said O'Reilly, sighing, as though the confession cost something, "there 's nothing equal to a newspaper. I 'm reading 'Saunders' this eight-and-forty years, and I own to you I never found one I liked so much. For you see, my Lord, it 's the same with a paper as with your house,—you ought to know where to lay your hand on what you want. Now, you might as well put me in Buckingham Palace, and tell me to find my bedroom, as give me the 'Times' and bid me discover the Viceregal Court. If they mention it at all, it 's among the accidents and offences."

"Castle festivities—Patrick's Hall—great fun!" said Twining, laughing pleasantly, for he cherished some merry recollections of these hospitalities.

"Have you—But of course you were too young for presentation," said his Lordship to Molly.

"We were n't out; but, in any case, I 'm sure we 'd not have been there," said Molly.

"The pleasure of that presentation may perhaps be reserved for me, who knows?" said the Viscount, graciously. "If our people come in, it is the post they 'd offer me."

"Lord-Lieutenant!" said Molly, opening her eyes to the fullest.

"Even so, *ma belle*. Shall we rehearse the ceremony of presentation? Twining, do you perform the Chamberlain. Stand aside, O'Reilly; be a gentleman at large, or an Ulster King-at-arms. Now for it!" And so saying, he drew himself proudly up to an attitude of considerable dignity, while Twining, muttering to himself, "What fun!" announced aloud, "Miss Molly O'Reilly, your Excellency;" at which, and before she was aware, his Excellency stepped one step in advance, and sainted her on either cheek with a cordiality that covered her with blushes.

"That 's not it, at all, I 'm certain," said she, half angrily.

"On my life, it's the exact ceremony, and no more," said the Viscount. Then resuming the performance, he added, "Take care, Twining, that she is put on your list for the balls. O'Reilly, your niece is charming."

"My niece—sure she 's—"

"You forget, my worthy friend, that we are enacting Viceroy, and cannot charge our memory with the ties of kindred."

Spicer now came up to say that a thunderstorm was threatening, and that the wisest course would probably be to land the luncheon and remain where they were till the hurricane should pass over. The proposition was at once approved of, and the party were soon busily occupying themselves in the cares for the entertainment; all agreeing that they felt no regret at being separated from the other boat, which had proceeded up the lake; in fact, as Mr. O'Reilly said, "they were snugger as they were, without the Roosians,"—a sentiment in various ways acknowledged by the rest.

Strange freemasonry is there in conviviality. The little preparations for this picnic dinner disseminated amidst them all the fellowship of old acquaintance, and, as they assisted and aided each other, a degree of kindliness grew up that bound them together like a family. Each vied with each in displaying his power of usefulness and agreeability; even the noble Viscount, who actually did nothing what-ever, so simulated occupation and activity that he was regarded by all as the very life and soul of the party. And yet we are unjust in saying he did nothing; for he it was who, by the happy charm of his manner, the ready tact of a consummate man of the world, imparted to the meeting its great success. Unused to the agreeable qualities of such men, O'Reilly felt all the astonishment that great conversational gifts inspire, and sat amazed and delighted at the stores of pleasant stories, witty remarks, and acute observations poured out before him.

He knew nothing of the skill by which these abilities were guided, nor how, like cunning shopkeepers dressing their wares to most advantage, such men exhibit their qualities with all the artifice of display. He never suspected the subtle flattery by which he was led to fancy himself the intimate of men whose names were freely talked of before him, till at length the atmosphere of the great world was to him like the air he had breathed from childhood.

"How the Prince would have relished O'Reilly!" said the Viscount to Twining, in a whisper easily overheard. "That racy humor, that strong native common-sense, that vigorous disregard of petty obstacles wherever he is bent on following out a path,—his royal Highness would have appreciated all these."

"Unquestionably—been charmed with them—thought him most agreeable—great fun."

"You remind me of O'Kelly,—Colonel O'Kelly,—O'Reilly; strange enough, too, each of you should be of that same old Celtic blood. But, perhaps, it is just that very element that gives you the peculiar social fascination I was alluding to. You are not old enough, Twining, to remember that small house with the bay-windows opening on the Birdcage Walk; it was like a country parsonage dropped down in the midst of London, with honeysuckles over the porch, and peacocks on the lawn in front of it. O'Kelly and Payne lived there together,—the two pleasantest bachelors that ever joined in partnership. The Prince dined with them by agreement every Friday. The charm of the thing was no state, no parade, whatever. It was just as if O'Reilly here were to take this villa, and say, 'Now, Lackington, I am rich enough to enjoy myself; I don't want the worry and fatigue of hunting out the pleasant people of the world; but you know them all, you understand them,—their ways, their wants, and their requirements; just tell me, frankly, could n't we manage to make this their rallying-spot throughout Europe? Settled down here in the midst of the most lovely scenery in the world, with a good cook and a good cellar, might not this place become a perfect Paradise?'"

"If I only knew that your Lordship, just yourself alone, and, of course, the present company," added O'Reilly, with a bow round the table, "would vouchsafe me the honor of a visit, I'd be proud to be the owner of this place to-morrow. Indeed, I don't see why we would n't be as well here as traipsing over the world in dust and heat. If, then, the girls see no objection—"

"I should like it of all things, papa," broke in Miss O'Reilly.

"I am charmed with the very thought of it," cried Molly.

"Capital thought—romantic notion—save any amount of money, and no taxes," muttered Twining.

"There's no approach by land whatever," said Spicer, who foresaw that all his horse capabilities would receive no development here.

"All the better," broke in Twining; "no interlopers—no fellows cantering down to luncheon, or driving over to dine—must come by boat, and be seen an hour beforehand."

"If I know anything of my friend here," said the Viscount, "his taste will rather lie in the fashion of a warm welcome than a polite denial to a visitor. You must talk to Lanfranchi about the place to-morrow, O'Reilly. He 's a shrewd fellow, and knows how to go about these things."

"Faith, my Lord, I see everything in sunshine so long as I sit in such company. It's the very genial kind of thing I like. A few friends—if I 'm not taking too great a liberty—"

"No, by no means, O'Reilly. The esteem I feel for you, and that Twining feels for you "—here his Lordship looked over at Spicer and slightly nodded, as though to say, "There is another there who requires no formal mention in the deed "—"are not passing sentiments, and we sincerely desire they may be accepted as true friendship."

"To be sure—unquestionably—great regard—unbounded admiration—what fun!" muttered Twining, half aloud.

The evening wore along in pleasant projects for the future. Spicer had undertaken to provide workmen and artificers of various kinds to repair and decorate the villa and its grounds. He knew of such a gardener, too; and he thought, by a little bribery and a trip down to Naples, he might seduce the Prince of Syracuse's cook,—a Sicilian, worth all the Frenchmen in the world for an ultramontane "cuisine." In fact, ere the bright moonlight on the lake reminded them of their journey homeward, they had arranged a plan of existence for the O'Reillys almost Elysian in its enjoyments.

Few things develop more imaginative powers than the description of a mode of life wherein "money is no object," and wishing and having are convertible terms. Let a number of people—the least gifted though they be with the graces of fancy—so picture forth such an existence, and see how, by the mere multiplication of various tastes, they will end by creating a most voluptuous and splendid tableau. O'Reilly's counsellors were rather adepts in their way, and certainly they did not forget one single ingredient of pleasure; till, when the boat glided into the little bay of the D'Este, such a story of a life was sketched out as nothing out of fairy-land could rival.

"I 'll have it, my Lord; the place is as good as mine this minute," said O'Reilly, as he stepped on shore; and as he spoke his heart thrilled with the concentrated delights of a whole life of happiness.

CHAPTER X
A "SMALL DINNER"

Lady Lackington and Lady Grace Twining passed the morning together. Their husbands' departure on the picnic excursion offered them a suitable subject to discuss those gentlemen, and they improved the occasion to some purpose.

The Viscountess did not, indeed, lean very heavily on her Lord's failings; they were, as she described them, the harmless follies of certain middle-aged gentlemen, who, despite time and years, would still be charming and fascinating. "He likes those little easy conquests he is so sure of amongst vulgar people," said she. "He affects only to be amused by them, but he actually likes them; and then, as he never indulges in this sort of thing except in out-of-the-way places, why, there 's no great harm in it."

Lady Grace agreed with her, and sighed. She sighed, because she thought of her own burden, and how far more heavily it pressed. Twining's were no little foibles, no small weaknesses; none of his faults had their root in any easy self-deceptions. Everything he did or said or thought was maturely weighed and considered; his gay, laughing manner, his easy, light-hearted gesticulation, his ready concurrence in the humor about him, were small coin that he scattered freely while he pondered over heavy investments.

From long experience of his crafty, double-dealing nature, coupled with something very near aversion to him, Lady Grace had grown to believe that in all he said or did some unseen motive lay, and she brought herself to believe that even his avaricious and miserly habits were practised still less for the sake of saving than for some ulterior and secret end.

Of the wretched life they led she drew a dreary picture: a mock splendor for the world, a real misery at home; all the outward semblance of costly living, all the internal consciousness of meanness and privation. He furnished houses with magnificence, that he might let them; he set up splendid equipages, that, when seen, they should be sold. "My very emeralds," said she, "were admired and bought by the Duchess of Windermere. It is very difficult to say that there is anything out of which he cannot extract a profit. If my ponies were praised in the park, I knew it was only the prelude to their being at Tattersall's in the morning; even the camellia which I wore in my hair was turned to advantage, for it sold the conservatory that raised it. And yet they tell me that if—they say that—I mean—I am told that the law would not construe these as cruelty, but simply a very ordinary exercise of marital authority, something unpleasant, perhaps, but not enough to warrant complaint, still less resistance."

"But they *are* cruelties," broke in Lady Lackington; "men in Mr. Twining's rank of life do not beat their wives—"

"No, they only break their hearts," sighed Lady Grace; "and this, I believe, is perfectly legal."

"They were doing, or going to do, something about that t' other day in the Lords. That dear old man, Lord Cloudeslie, had a bill or an amendment to somebody's bill, by which—I 'm not sure I 'm quite correct about it—but I believe it gave the wife power to take her settlement. No, that is not it; she was to be able, after five years of great cruelty—I'm afraid I have no clear recollection of its provisions, but I know the odious Chancellor said it would effectually make women independent of men."

"Of course it never will become law, then," sighed Lady Grace, again.

"Who knows, dear? They are always passing something or other they 're sorry for afterwards in either House. Shall I tell you who'd know all about it?—that Mr. Davenport Dunn. He is just the kind of person to understand these things."

"Indeed!" exclaimed Lady Grace, with more animation in her manner.

"Let as ask him to dinner," said Lady Lackington; "I know him sufficiently to do so,—that is, I have met him once. He 'll be charmed, of course; and if there is anything very good and very safe to be done on the Bourse, he 'll certainly tell us."

"I don't care for the Bourse. Indeed, I have nothing to speculate with."

"That is the best reason in the world, my dear, to make a venture; at least, so my brother-in-law, Annesley, says. You are certain to come out a winner, and in my own brief experiences, I never gave anything,—I only said, 'Yes, I 'll have the shares.' They were at fifty-eight and three-quarters, they said, and sure to be at sixty-four or five; and they actually did rise to seventy, and then we sold—that is, Dunn did—and remitted me twelve hundred and fifty-three pounds odd."

"I wish he could be equally fortunate with me. I don't mean as regards money," said Lady Grace; and her cheek became crimson as she spoke.

"I have always said there's a fate in these things; and who knows if his being here Just at this moment is not a piece of destiny."

"It might be so," said the other, sadly.

"There," said Lady Lackington, as she rapidly wrote a few lines on a piece of note-paper, "that ought to do:—

> "'Dear Mr. Dunn,—If you will accept of an early dinner, with Lady Grace Twining and myself for the company, to-day,
>
> you will much oblige
>
> "'Your truly,
>
> "'Georgina Lackington.'"

"To another kind of man I'd have said something about two *pauvres femmes délaissées*, but he 'd have been frightened, and probably not come."

"Probably," said Lady Grace, with a sigh.

"Now, let us try the success of this." And she rang a bell, and despatched the note.

Lady Lackington had scarcely time to deliver a short essay on the class and order of men to which Mr. Davenport Dunn pertained, when the servant returned with the answer. It was a very formal acceptance of the invitation, "Mr. Davenport Dunn presented his compliments,"—and so on.

"Of course, he comes," said she, throwing the note away. "Do you know, my dear, I half suspect we have been indiscreet; for now that we have caught our elephant, what shall we do with him?"

"I cannot give you one solitary suggestion."

"These people are not our people, nor are their gods our gods," said Lady Lackington.

"If we all offer up worship at the same temple,—the Bourse," said Lady Grace, something sadly,—"we can scarcely dispute about a creed."

"That is only true in a certain sense," replied the other. "Money is a necessity to all; the means of obtaining it may, therefore, be common to many. It is in the employment of wealth, in the tasteful expenditure of riches, that we distinguish ourselves from these people. You have only to see the houses they keep, their plate, their liveries, their equipages, and you perceive at once that whenever they rise above some grovelling imitation they commit the most absurd blunders against all taste and propriety. I wish we had Spicer here to see about this dinner, it is one of the very few things he understands; but I suppose we must leave it to the cook himself, and we have the comfort of knowing that the criticism on his efforts will not be of a very high order."

"We dine at four, I believe," said Lady Grace, in her habitual tone of sorrow, as she swept from the room with that gesture of profound woe that would have graced a queen in tragedy.

Let us turn for a moment to Mr. Davenport Dunn. Lady Lackington's invitation had not produced in him either those overwhelming sensations of astonishment or those excessive emotions of delight which she had so sanguinely calculated on. There was a time that a Viscountess asking him thus to dinner had been an event, the very fact being one requiring some effort on his part to believe; but these days were long past. Mr. Dunn had not only dined with great people since that, but had himself been their host and entertainer. Noble lords and baronets had sipped his claret, right honorables praised his sherry, and high dignitaries condescended to inquire where he got "that exquisite port." The tremulous, faint-hearted, doubting spirit, the suspectful, self-distrusting, humble man, had gone, and in his place there was a bold, resolute nature, confident and able, daily testing his strength against some other in the ring, and as often issuing from the contest satisfied that he had little to fear from any antagonist. He was clever enough to see that the great objects in life are accomplished less by dexterity and address than by a strong, undeviating purpose. The failure of many a gifted man, and the high success of many a commonplace one, had not been without its lesson for him; and it was in the firm resolve to rise a winner that he sat down to the game of life.

Lady Lackington's invitation was, therefore, neither a cause of pleasure nor astonishment. He remembered having met her somewhere, some time, and he approached the renewed acquaintance without any one of the sentiments her Ladyship had so confidently predicted. Indeed, so little of that flurry of anticipation did he experience, that he had to be reminded her Ladyship was waiting dinner for him, before he could remember the pleasure that was before him.

It may be a very ungallant confession for this true history to make, but we cannot blink saying that Lady Lack-ington and Lady Grace both evidenced by their toilette that they were not indifferent to the impression they were to produce upon their guest.

The Viscountess was dressed in the perfection of that French taste whose chief characteristic is freshness and elegance. She was light, gauzy, and floating,—a sweeping something of Valenciennes and white muslin,— but yet human withal, and very graceful. Her friend, in deep black, with a rich lace veil fastened on her head behind, and draped artistically over one shoulder, was a charming personification of affliction not beyond consolation. When they met, it was with an exchange of looks that said, "This ought to do."

Lady Lackington debated with herself what precise manner of reception she would award to Mr. Dunn,—whether to impose by the haughty condescension of a fine lady, or fascinate by the graceful charm of an agreeable one. She was "equal to either fortune," and could calculate on success, whichever road she adopted. While she thus hesitated, he entered.

If his approach had little or nothing of the man of fashion about it, it was still a manner wherein there was little to criticise. It was not bold nor timid, and, without anything like over-confidence, there was yet an air of self-reliance that was not without dignity.

At dinner the conversation ranged over the usual topics of foreign travel, foreign habits, collections, and galleries. Of pictures and statues he had seen much, and evidently with profit and advantage; of people and society he knew next to nothing, and her Ladyship quickly detected this deficiency, and fell back upon it as her stronghold.

"When hard-worked men like myself take a holiday," said Dunn, "they are but too glad to escape from the realities of life by taking refuge amongst works of art. The painter and the sculptor suggest as much poetry as can consist with their stern notions, and are always real enough to satisfy the demand for fact."

"But would not what you call your holiday be more pleasantly passed in making acquaintances? You could of course have easy access to the most distinguished society."

"I'm a bad Frenchman, my Lady, and speak not a word of German or Italian."

"English is very generally cultivated just now,—the persons best worth talking to can speak it."

"The restraint of a strange tongue, like the novelty of a court dress, is a sad detractor from all naturalness. At least, in my own little experience with strangers, I have failed to read anything of a man's character when he addressed me in a language not his own."

"And was it essential you should have read it?" asked Lady Grace, languidly.

"I am always more at my ease when I know the geography of the land I live in," said Dunn, smiling.

"I should say you have great gifts in that way,—I mean in deciphering character," said Lady Lackington.

"Your Ladyship flatters me. I have no pretensions of the kind. Once satisfied of the sincerity of those with whom I come into contact, I never strive to know more, nor have I the faculties to attempt more."

"But, in your wide-spread intercourse with life, do you not, insensibly as it were, become an adept in reading men's natures?"

"I don't think so, my Lady. The more one sees of life the simpler does it seem, not from any study of humanity, but by the easy fact that three or four motives sway the whole world. An unsupplied want of one kind or other— wealth, rank, distinction, affection, it may be—gives the entire impulse to a character, just as a passion imparts the expression to a face; and all the diversities of temperament, like those of countenance, are nothing but the impress of a want,—you may call it a wish. Now it may be," added he, and as he spoke he stole a glance, quick as lightning, at Lady Grace, "that such experiences are more common to men like myself,—men, I mean, who are intrusted with the charge of others' interests; but assuredly I have no clew to character save in that one feature,—a want."

"But I want fifty thousand things," said Lady Lacking-ton. "I want a deal of money; I want that beautiful villa near Palermo, the 'Serra Novena;' I want that Arab pony Kratuloff rides in the park; I want, in short, everything that pleases me every hour of the day."

"These are not wants that make impulses, no more than a passing shower makes a climate," said Dunn. "What I speak of is that unceasing, unwearied desire that is with us in joy or sadness, that journeys with us and lives with us, mingling in every action, blending with every thought, and presenting to our minds a constant picture of ourselves under some wished-for aspect different from all we have ever known, where we are surrounded with other impulses and swayed by other passions, and yet still identically ourselves. Lady Grace apprehends me."

"Perhaps,—at least partly," said she, fanning herself and concealing her face.

"There are very few exempt from a temptation of this sort, or, if they be, it is because their minds are dissipated on various objects."

"I hate things to be called temptations, and snares, and the rest of it," said Lady Lackington; "it is a very tiresome cant. You may tell me while I am waiting for my fish-sauce at dinner, it is a temptation; but if you wish me really to understand the word, tell me of some wonderful speculation, some marvellous scheme for securing millions. Oh, dear Mr. Dunn, you who really know the way, will you just show me the road to—I will be moderate—about twenty thousand pounds?"

"Nothing easier, my Lady, if you are disposed to risk forty."

"But I am not, sir. I have not the slightest intention to risk one hundred. I'm not a gambler."

"And yet what your Ladyship points at is very like gambling."

"Pray place that word along with temptation, in the forbidden category; it is quite hateful to me."

"Have *you* the same dislike to chance, Lady Grace?" said he, stealing a look at her face with some earnestness.

"No," said she, in a low voice; "it is all I have to look for."

"By the way, Mr. Dunn, what are they doing in Parliament about us? Is there not something contemplated by which we can insist upon separate maintenance, or having a suitable settlement, or—"

"Separation—divorce," said Lady Grace, solemnly.

"No, my Lady, the law is only repairing an old road, not making a new one. The want of the age is cheapness,—cheap literature, cheap postage, and cheap travelling, and why not cheap divorce? Legislation now professes as its great aim to extend to the poor all the comforts of the rich; and as this is supposed to be one of them—"

"Have you any reason to doubt it, sir?" asked Lady Grace.

"Luxuries cease to be luxuries when they become common. Cheap divorce will be as unfashionable as cheap pine-apple when a coal-heaver can have it," said Lady Lackington.

"You mistake, it seems to me, what constitutes the luxury," interposed Lady Grace. "Every day of the year sees men liberated from prison, yet no one will pretend that the sense of freedom is less dear to every creature thus delivered."

"Your figure is but too like," said Dunn. "The divorced wife will be to the world only too much a resemblance of the liberated prisoner. Dark or fair, guilty or innocent, she will carry with her the opprobrium of a public trial, a discussion, and a verdict. Now, how few of us would go through an operation in public for the cure of a malady! Would we not rather hug our sorrows and our sufferings in secrecy than accept health on such conditions?"

"Not when the disease was consuming your very vitals,—not when a perpetual fever racked your brain and boiled in your blood. You'd take little heed of what is called exposure then. The cry of your heart would be, 'Save me! save me!'" As she spoke, her voice grew louder and wilder, till it became almost a shriek, and, as she ended, she lay back, flushed and panting, in her chair.

"You have made her quite nervous, Mr. Dunn," said Lady Lackington, as she arose and fanned her.

"Oh, no. It's nothing. Just let me have a little fresh air,—on the terrace. Will you give me your arm?" said Lady Grace, faintly. And Dunn assisted her as she arose and walked out. "How very delicious this is!" said she, as she leaned over the balcony, and gazed down upon the placid water, streaked with long lines of starlight. "I conclude," said she, after a little pause, "that scenes like this—moments as peacefully tranquil—are as dear to you, hard-worked men of the world, as they are to the wearied hearts of us poor women, all whose ambitions are so humble in comparison."

"We are all of us striving for the same goal, I believe," said he,—"this same search after happiness, the source of so much misery!"

"You are not married, I believe?" said she, in an accent whose very softness had a tone of friendship.

"No; I am as much alone in the world as one well can be," rejoined he, sorrowfully.

"And have you gone through life without ever meeting one with whom you would have been content to make partnership,—taking her, as those solemn words say, 'for better, for worse'?"

"They are solemn words," said he, evading her question; "for they pledge that for which it is so hard to promise,—the changeful moods which time and years bring over us. Which of us at twenty can say what he will be at thirty,—still less at fifty? The world makes us many things we never meant to be."

"So, then, you are not happy?" said she, in the same low voice.

"I have not said so much," said he, smiling sadly; "are you?"

"Can you ask me? Is not the very confidence wherewith I treat you—strangers as we were an hour back to each other—the best evidence that it is from the very depth of my misery I appeal to you?"

"Make no rash confidences, Lady Grace," said he, seriously. "They who tell of their heart's sorrows to the world are like those who count their gold before robbers. I have seen a great deal of life, and the best philosophy I have learned from it is to 'bear.' Bear everything that can be borne. You will be surprised what a load you will carry by mere practice of endurance."

"It is so easy to say to one in pain, 'Have patience,'" said she, bitterly.

"I have practised what I teach for many a year. Be assured of one thing,—the Battle of Life is waged by all. The most favored by fortune—the luckiest, as the world calls them—have their contest and their struggle. It is not for existence, but it is often for what makes existence valuable."

She sighed deeply, and, after a pause, he went on,—

"We pity the poor, weary, heart-sick litigant, wearing out life in the dreary prosecution of a Chancery suit, dreaming at night of that fortune he is never to see, and waking every day to the same dull round of pursuit. As hope flickers in his heart, suffering grows a habit; his whole nature imbibes the conflicting character of his cause; he doubts and hesitates and hopes and fears and wishes, till his life is one long fever. But infinitely more painful is the struggle of the heart whose affections have been misplaced. These are the suits over which no hope ever throws a ray. It is a long, dreary path, without a halting-place or a goal."

As he spoke, she covered her face with her handkerchief; but he could perceive that she was weeping.

"I am speaking of what I know," said he. "I remember once coming closely into relations with a young nobleman whose station, fortune, and personal advantages combined to realize all that one could fancy of worldly blessings. He was just one of those types a novelist would take to represent the most favored class of the most favored land of Europe. He had an ancient name, illustrious in various ways, a splendid fortune, was singularly endowed with abilities, highly accomplished, and handsome, and, more than all, he was gifted with that mysterious power of fascination by which some men contrive to make themselves so appreciated by others that their influence is a sort of magic. Give him an incident to relate,— let him have a passing event to tell, wherein some emotion of pity, some sentiment of devotion played a part,—and without the slightest touch of artifice, without the veriest shade of ingenuity, he could make you listen breathlessly, and hang in rapture on his words. Well, this man—of whom, if I suffer myself to speak, I shall grow wearisome in the praise—this man was heart-broken. Before he succeeded to his title, he was very poor, a subaltern in the army, with little beyond his pay. He fell in love with a very beautiful girl—I never heard her name, but I know that she was a daughter of one of the first houses in England. She returned his affection, and there was one of those thousand cases wherein love has to combat all the odds, and devotion subdue every thought that appeals to worldly pride and vanity.

"She accepted the contest nobly; she was satisfied to brave humble fortune, obscurity, exile,—everything for him—at least she said so, and I believe she thought she could keep her word. When the engagement took place—which was a secret to their families—the London season had just begun.

"It is not for me to tell you what a period of intoxicating pleasure and excitement that is, nor how in that wondrous conflict of wealth, splendor, beauty, and talent, all the fascination of gambling is imparted to a scene where, of necessity, gain and loss are alternating. It demands no common power of head and heart to resist these temptations. Apparently she had not this self-control. The gorgeous festivities about her, the splendor of wealth, and more than even that, the esteem in which it was held, struck her forcibly. She saw that the virtues of humble station met no more recognition than the false lustre of mock gems,—that ordinary gifts, illustrated by riches, became actual graces. She could not shut out the contrast between her lover, poor, unnoticed, and unregarded, and the crowd of fashionable and distinguished youths whose princely fortunes gave them place and pre-eminence. In fact, as he himself told me,—for Allington excused her—Good Heavens! are you ill?" cried be, as with a low, faint cry she sank to the ground.

"Is she dying? Good God! is she dead?" cried Lady Lackington, as she lifted the powerless arm, and held the cold hands within her own.

Lanfranchi was speedily sent for, and saw that it was merely a fainting fit.

"She was quite well previously, was she not?" asked he of Dunn.

"Perfectly so. We were chatting of indifferent matters,—of London, and the season,—when she was seized," said he. "Is there anything in the air here that disposes to these attacks?"

Lanfranchi looked at him without reply. Possibly they understood each other, for they parted without further colloquy.

CHAPTER XI
"A CONSULTATION"

It was late in the night as Lord Lackington and his friends reached the villa, a good deal wearied, very jaded, and, if the confession may be made, a little sick of each other; they parted pretty much as the members of such day-long excursions are wont to do,—not at all sorry to have reached home again, and brought their trip of pleasure to an end. Twining, of course, was the same happy-natured, gay, volatile creature that he set out in the morning. Everything went well with him, the world had but one aspect, which was a pleasant one, and he laughed and muttered, "What fun!" as in half-dogged silence the party wended their way through the garden towards the house.

"I hope these little girls may not have caught cold," said the Viscount, as he stood with Twining on the terrace, after saying "Good-night!"

"I hope so, with all my heart. Charming girls—most fascinating—father so amiable."

"Isn't that Dunn's apartment we see the light in?" asked the other, half impatiently. "I 'll go and make him a visit."

"Overjoyed to see you, greatly flattered by the attention," chimed in Twining; and while he rubbed his hands over the enchanting prospect, Lord Lackington walked away.

Not waiting for any announcement, and turning the handle of the door immediately after he had knocked at it, the Viscount entered. Whether Dunn had heard him or not, he never stirred from the table where he was writing, but continued engrossed by his occupation till his Lordship accosted him.

"I have come to disturb you, I fear, Dunn?"

"Oh! Lord Lackington, your most obedient. Too happy to be honored by your presence at any time. Just returned, I conclude?"

"Yes, only this moment," said the Viscount, sighing wearily. "These picnics are stupid inventions; they fatigue and they exhaust. They give little pleasure at the time, and none whatever to look back upon."

"Your Lordship's picture is rather a dreary one," said Dunn, smiling.

"Perfectly correct, I assure you; I went simply to oblige some country folks of yours. The O'Reillys,—nice little girls,—very natural, very pretty creatures; but the thing is a bore. I never knew any one who enjoyed it except the gentleman who gets tipsy, and *he* has an awful retribution in the next day's headache,—the terrible headache of iced rum punch."

Dunn laughed, because he saw that his Lordship expected as much; and the Viscount resumed,—

"I am vexed, besides, at the loss of time; I wanted to have my morning with *you* here."

Dunn bowed graciously, but did not speak.

"We have so much to talk over—so many things to arrange—that I am quite provoked at having thrown away a day; and you, too, are possibly pressed for time?"

He nodded in assent.

"You can give me to-morrow, however?"

"I can give you to-night, my Lord, which will, perhaps, do as well."

"But to-morrow—"

"Oh, to-morrow, my Lord, I start with Baron Glumthal for Frankfort, to meet the Elector of Darmstadt,—an appointment that cannot be broken."

"Politically most important, I have no doubt," said the Viscount, with an undisguised sarcasm in the tone.

"No, my Lord, a mere financial affair," said Dunn, not heeding the other's manner. "His Highness wants a loan, and we are willing to accommodate him."

"I wish I could find you in the same liberal spirit. It is the very thing I stand in need of Just now. In fact, Dunn, you must do it."

The half-coaxing accent of these last words was a strong contrast to the sneer of a few seconds before, and Dunn smiled as he heard them.

"I fancy, my Lord, that if you are still of the same mind as before, you will have little occasion to arrange for a loan in any quarter."

"Pooh! pooh! the scheme is absurd. It has not one, but fifty obstacles against it. In the first place, you know nothing of this fellow, or whether he can be treated with. As for myself, I do not believe one word about his claim. Why, sir, there's not a titled house in England has not at some period or other been assailed with this sort of menace. It is the stalest piece of knavery going. If you were to poll the peers to-morrow, you 'd not meet two out of ten have not been served with notice of action, or ejectment on the title; in fact, sir, these suits are a profession, and a very lucrative one, too."

Lord Lackington spoke warmly, and ere he had finished had lashed himself up into a passion. Meanwhile Duun sat patiently, like one who awaited the storm to pass by ere he advanced upon his road.

"I conclude, from your manner, that you do not agree with me?" said the Viscount.

"Your Lordship opines truly. I take a very different view of this transaction. I have had all the documents of Conway's claim before me. Far more competent judges have seen and pronounced upon them. They constitute a most formidable mass of evidence, and, save in a very few and not very important details, present an unbroken chain of testimony."

"So, then, there is a battery preparing to open fire upon us?" said the Viscount, with a laugh of ill-affected indifference.

"There is a mine whose explosion depends entirely upon your Lordship's discretion. If I say, my Lord, that I never perused a stronger case, I will also say that I never heard of one so easy of management The individual in whose favor these proofs exist has not the slightest knowledge of them. He has not a suspicion that all his worldly prospects put together are worth a ten-pound note. It is only within the last three months that I have succeeded in even discovering where he is."

"And where is he?"

"Serving as a soldier with his regiment in the Crimea. He was in hospital at Scutari when I first heard, but since that returned to duty with his regiment."

"What signifies all this? The fellow himself is nothing to us!"

Dunn again waited till this burst of anger had passed, and then resumed,—

"My Lord, understand me well. You can deal with this case now; six months hence it may be clear and clean beyond all your power of interference. If Conway's claim derive, as I have strong ground to believe it, from the elder branch, the estate and the title are both his."

"You are a hardy fellow, a very hardy fellow, Mr. Dunn, to make such a speech as this!"

"I said, 'If,' my Lord—'If' is everything here. The assumption is that Reginald Conway was summoned by mistake to the House of Peers in

Henry the Seventh's reign,—the true Baron Lackington being then an exile. It is from him this Conway's descent claims."

"I'm not going to constitute myself a Committee of Privileges, sir, and listen to all this jargon; nor can I easily conceive that the unshaken possession of centuries is to be disturbed by the romantic pretensions of a Crimean soldier. I am also aware how men of your cloth conduct these affair to their own especial advantage. They assume to be the arbiters of the destinies of great families, and they expect to be paid for their labors,—eh, is n't it so?"

"I believe your Lordship has very accurately defined our position, though, perhaps, we might not quite agree as to the character of the remuneration."

"How so? What do you mean?"

"I, for instance, my Lord, would furnish no bill of costs to either party. My relations with your Lordship are such as naturally give me a very deep interest in what concerns you; of Mr. Conway I know nothing."

"So, then, you are simply moved in this present affair by a principle of pure benevolence; you are to be a sort of providence to the House of Lackington,—eh, is that it?"

"Your Lordship's explanation is most gracious," said Dunn, bowing.

"Come, now; let us talk seriously," said the Viscount, in a changed tone. "What is it you propose?"

"What I would *suggest*, my Lord," said Dunn, with a marked emphasis on the word, "is this. Submit the documents of this claim—we can obtain copies of the most important of them—to competent opinion, learn if they be of the value I attribute to them, see, in fact, if this claim be prosecuted, whether it is likely to succeed at law, and, if so, anticipate the issue by a compromise."

"But what compromise?"

"Your Lordship has no heir. Your brother, who stands next in succession, need not marry. This point at once decided, Conway's claim can take its course after Mr. Beecher's demise. The estates secured to your Lordship for life will amply guarantee a loan to the extent you wish."

"But they are mine, sir; they are mine this moment. I can go into the market to-morrow and raise what amount I please—"

"Take care, my Lord, take care; a single imprudent step might spoil all. If you were to negotiate a mere ten thousand to-morrow, you might be met by the announcement that your whole property was about to be litigated, and your title to it contested. Too late to talk of compromise, then."

"This sounds very like a threat, Mr. Dunn."

"Then have I expressed myself most faultily, my Lord; nor was there anything less near my thoughts."

"Would you like to see my brother? He shall call on you in Dublin; you will be there by—when?"

"Wednesday week, my Lord; and it is a visit would give me much pleasure."

"If I were to tell you my mind frankly, Dunn," said the Viscount, in a more assured tone, "I 'd say, I would not give a ten-pound note to buy up this man's whole claim. Annesley, however, has a right to be consulted; he has an interest only second to my own. See him, talk it over with him, and write, to me."

"Where shall I address you, my Lord?"

"Florence; I shall leave this at once,—to-night," said Lord Lackington, impatiently; for, somehow,—we are not going to investigate wherefore,—he was impatient to be off, and see no more of those he had been so intimate with.

CHAPTER XII
ANNESLEY BEECHER'S "PAL"

Lord Lackington was not much of a letter-writer; correspondence was not amongst the habits of his day. The society in which he moved, and of which, to some extent, he was a type, cared more for conversational than epistolary graces. They kept their good things for their dinner-parties, and hoarded their smart remarks on life for occasions where the success was a personal triumph. Twice or thrice, however, every year, he was obliged to write. His man of business required to be reminded of this or that necessity for money, and his brother Annesley should also be admonished, or reproved, or remonstrated with, in that tone of superiority and influence so well befitting one who pays an annuity to him who is the recipient. In fact, around this one circumstance were grouped all the fraternal feelings and brotherly interest of these two men. One hundred and twenty-five pounds sterling every half-year represented the ties of blood that united them; and while it offered to the donor the proud reflection of a generous self-sacrifice, it gave to him who received the almost as agreeable occasion for sarcastic allusion to the other's miserly habits and sordid nature, with a contrast of what he himself had done were their places in life reversed.

It was strange enough that the one same incident should have begotten such very opposite emotions; and yet the two phrases, "If you knew all I have done for him," and the rejoinder, "You 'd not believe the beggarly pittance he allows me," were correct exponents of their several feelings.

Not impossible is it that each might have made out a good case against the other. Indeed, it was a theme whereon, in their several spheres, they were eloquent; and few admitted to the confidence of either had not heard of the utter impossibility of doing anything for Annesley,—his reckless folly, his profligacy, and his waste; and, on the other hand, "the incredible meanness of Lackington, with at least twelve thousand a year, and no children to provide for, giving me the salary of an upper butler." Each said far too much in his own praise not to have felt, at least, strong misgivings in his conscience. Each knew far too well that the other had good reason in many things he said; but so long had their plausibilities been repeated, that each ended by satisfying himself he was a paragon of fraternal affection, and, stranger still, had obtained for this opinion a distinct credence in their several sets in society; so that every peer praised the Viscount, and every hard-up younger son pitied poor Annesley, and condemned the "infamous conduct of the old coxcomb his brother."

"That scampish fellow's conduct is killing poor Lackington," would say a noble lord.

"Annesley can't stand old Lackington's treatment much longer," was the commentary of half-pay captains of dragoons.

Had you but listened to Lord Lackington, he would have told you of at least fifty distinct schemes he had contrived for his brother's worldly success, all marred and spoiled by that confounded recklessness, "that utter disregard, sir, of the commonest rules of conduct that every man in life is bound to observe." He might have been, by this time, colonel of the Fifty-something; he might have been governor of some fortunate island in the Pacific; consul-general at Sunstroke Town, in Africa, where, after three years, you retire with a full pension. If he 'd have gone into the Church, — and there was no reason why he should n't, — there was the living of St. Cuthbert-in-the-Vale, eight hundred a year, ready for him. Every Administration for years back had been entreated in his favor; and from Ordnance clerkships to Commissions in Lunacy he had been offered places in abundance. Sinecures in India and jobs in Ireland had been found out in his behalf, and deputy-somethings created in Bermuda just to provide for him.

The concessions he had made, the proxies he had given, "just for Annesley's sake," formed a serious charge against the noble Lord's political consistency; and he quoted them as the most stunning evidences of fraternal love, and pointed out where he had gone against his conscience and his party as to a kind of martyrdom that made a man illustrious forever.

As for Annesley, his indictment had, to the full, as many counts. What he might have been, — not in a mere worldly sense, not as regards place, pension, or emolument, but what in integrity, what in fair fame, what in honorable conduct and unblemished character, if Lackington had only dealt fairly with him, — "there was really no saying." The noble motives which might have prompted, the high aspirations that might have moved him, all the generous impulses of a splendid nature were there, thwarted, baffled, and destroyed by Lackington's confounded stupidity. What the Viscount ought to have done, what precise species of culture he should have devoted to these budding virtues, how he ought to have trained and trellised these tender shoots of aspiring goodness, he never exactly detailed. It was only clear that, whatever the road, he had never taken it; and it was really heart-breaking to hear what the world had lost in public and private virtues, all for Lackington's indolence and folly.

"He never gave me a chance, sir,—not one chance," would he say. "Why, he knows Palmerston just as well as I know you; he can talk to Lord Derby as freely as I am speaking at this minute; and, would you believe it? he wouldn't say, 'There's Annesley—my brother Annesley—wants that commissionership or that secretary's place. Annesley 's a devilish clever fellow,—up to a thing or two,—ask Grog Davis if he ain't. Just try to get between him and the ropes, that's all; see if he does n't sleep with one eye open. 'Do you tell me there's one of them would refuse him? Grog said to his face, at Epsom Downs, the morning Crocus was scratched, 'My Lord,' says he, 'take all you can get upon Annesley; make your book on him; he's the best horse in your lot, and it's Grog Davis says it.'"

Very true was it that Grog Davis said so. Nay, to enjoy the pleasure of hearing him so discourse was about the greatest gratification of Annesley Beecher's present life. He was poor and discredited. The Turf Club would not have him; he durst not show at Tattersall's. Few would dine, none discount him; and yet that one man's estimate of his gifts sustained him through all. "If Grog be right—and he ought to be, seeing that a more dodgy, crafty fellow never lived—I shall come all round again. He that never backed the wrong horse could n't be far astray about men. He thinks I've running in me yet; *he* sees that I 'll come out one of these days in top condition, and show my number from the stand-house." To have had the greatest opinion in Equity favorable to your cause in Chancery, to have known that Thesiger or Kelly said your case was safe, to learn that Faraday had pronounced your analysis correct, or White, of Cowes, had approved of the lines of your new yacht,—would any of them be very reassuring sensations; and yet were they as nothing to the unbounded confidence imparted to Beecher's mind by the encouraging opinion of his friend Grog Davis. It is only justice to say that Beecher's estimate of Davis was a feeling totally free of all the base alloy of any self-interest. With all Grog's great abilities, with talents of the very highest order, he was the reverse of a successful man. Trainer, auctioneer, sporting character, pugilist, publican, and hell-keeper, he had been always unlucky. He had his share of good things,—more than his share. He had been in at some of the "very best-robberies" ever done at Newmarket. The horses he had "nobbled," the jockeys "squared," the owners "hocussed," were legion. All the matches he had "made safe," all the fights he had sold, would have filled five columns of "Bell's Life." In whatever called itself "sport" he had dabbled and cheated for years; and yet, there he was, with all his successes and all his experiences, something more than fifteen thousand pounds worse than ruined.

Worthy reader, have you stood by while some enthusiastic admirer of Turner's later works has, in all the fervor of his zeal, encomiumized one of those strange, incomprehensible creations, where cloud and sea, atmosphere, shadow and smoke, seem madly commingled with tall masts piercing the lurid vapor, and storm-clouds drifting across ruined towers? If at first you gladly welcomed any guidance through the wondrous labyrinth, and you accepted gratefully the aid of one who could reconcile seeming incongruities, and explain apparent difficulties, what was your disappointment, at last, to discover that from some defect of organization, some absent power of judgment, you could not follow the elucidation; that you saw no power in this, no poetry in that; that no light gleamed into *your* soul out of all that darkness, nor any hope into *your* heart, from the mad confusion of that chaos? Pretty much the same mystification had it been to you to have listened to Annes-ley Beecher's account of his friend Grog Davis. It was evident that *he* saw the reason for everything,—he could account for all; but, alas! the explanatory gift was denied him. The very utmost you could attain to was a glimmering perception that there were several young men of rank and station who had only half trusted the distinguished Davis, and in their sparing confidence had rescued themselves from his knavery; that very artful combinations occasionally require confederates, and confederates are not always loyal; that Grog occasionally did things with too high a hand,— in plain words, reserved for himself more than his share of the booty; and, in fact, that, with the best intentions and the most decided determination to put others "into the hole," he fell in himself, and so completely, too, that he had never been able to show his head out of it ever since.

If, therefore, as we have said, Annesley Beecher's explanation of these tangled skeins was none of the clearest, there was nothing daunting to himself in that difficulty. On the contrary, he deemed his intimacy with Grog as one of his greatest privileges. Grog had told him things that he would not tell to another man breathing; he had seen, in Grog's own hand, what would, if not hang him, give him twenty years at Norfolk Island; he knew that Grog had done things no man in England but himself had ever dreamed of; in fact, as Othello's perils had won the fair Desdemona's love, Grog Davis's rascalities had captivated Beecher's admiration; and, as the recruit might gaze upon the thickly studded crosses on the breast of some glorious soldier, so did he venerate the proofs of the thousand-and-one knaveries of one who for thirty-odd years had been a "leg" and a swindler.

Let us present Captain Davis—for by that title was he popularly known—to our reader. He was a short, red-faced—very red-faced—man, with a profusion of orange-red hair, while he wore beard and whiskers in that form so common in our Crimean experiences. He was long-armed and bandy, the legs being singularly short and muscular. He affected dress, and was remarkable for more ostentation of velvet than consisted with ordinary taste, and a far greater display of rings, charms, and watch trinkets than is common even to gentlemen of the "Jewish persuasion." The expression of the man's face was eminently determination, and his greenish-gray eyes and thin-lipped, compressed mouth plainly declared, "Bet with me or not,—if you give me the shadow of a shade of impertinence I 'll fasten a quarrel upon you of which all your rank and station won't protect you from the consequences. I can hit a sixpence at twenty paces, and I 'll make you feel that fact in every word you say to me. In my brevet rank of the turf you can't disown me, and if you try, mine the fault if you succeed." He had been out three or four times in very sanguinary affairs, so that the question as to "meeting" him was a settled point. He was one of those men to whom the epithet "dangerous" completely applies; he was dangerous alike to the young fellow entering life, unsuspectful of its wiles and ignorant of its rascalities; dangerous in the easy facility with which he would make foolish wagers, and lend even large sums on the very slightest acquaintance. He seemed so impressed with his theory that everybody ought to have all the enjoyment he liked, there was such a careless good-nature about him, such an uncalculating generosity, an air of such general kindliness, that very young men felt at once at ease in his company; and if there were sundry things in his manner that indicated coarseness or bad breeding, if his address was vulgar and his style "snobbish," there were sufficient traits of originality about him to form a set-off for these defects, and "Old Grog" was pronounced an "out-and-out good fellow," and always ready "to help one at a pinch."

Such was he to the very young men just passing the threshold of life; to the older hands—fellows versed in all its acts and ways—he showed no false colors; such, then, he was, the character which no disguise conceals,—"the leg;" one whose solvency may be counted on more safely than his honesty, and whose dealings, however based on roguery, are still guided by that amount of honor which is requisite for transactions amongst thieves. There was an impression, too,—we have no warranty for saying how far it was well founded,—that Grog was behind the scenes in transactions where many high and titled characters figured; that he was confederate in affairs of more than doubtful integrity; and that, if he liked, he could make revelations such as all the dark days at Tattersall's never equalled. "They 'll never push *me* to the wall," he would say, "take my word for it; they 'll not make Grog Davis turn Queen's evidence," was the boastful exclamation of his after-dinner hours: and he was right. He could have told of strange doings with arsenic in the stable, and, stranger still, with hocussed negus in the back parlor; he had seen the certain favorite for the Oaks carted out stiff and cold on the morning that was to have witnessed her triumph; and he had opened the door for the ruined heir as he left his last thousand on the green baize of the hell table. He was so accustomed to all the vicissitudes of fortune—that is, he was so habituated to aid the goddess in the work of destiny—that nothing surprised him; and his red, carbuncled face and jaundiced eye never betrayed the slightest evidence of anything like emotion or astonishment

How could Beecher have felt any other than veneration for one so gifted? He approached him as might some youthful artist the threshold of Michael Angelo; he felt, when with him, that he was in the presence of one whose maxims were silver and whose precepts were gold, and that to the man who could carry away those experiences the secrets of life were no longer mysteries.

All the delight an old campaigner might have felt had the Great Duke vouchsafed to tell him of his achievements in the Peninsula—how he had planned the masterly defences of Torres Vedras, or conceived the bold advance upon Spain—would have been but a weak representation of the eager enjoyment Beecher experienced when Grog narrated some of his personal recollections: how he had squared Sir Toby at Manchester; the way he had won the York Handicap with a dead horse; and the still prouder day when, by altering the flags at Bolton, he gained twenty-two thousand pounds on the Great National Steeplechase. Nor was it without a certain vaingloriousness that Grog would speak of these, as, cigar in mouth and his hands deep in his breeches pockets, he grunted out, in broken sentences, the great triumphs of his life.

We began this chapter by saying that Lord Lackington was not an impassioned letter-writer; and here we are discoursing about Mr. Davis and his habits, as if these topics could possibly have any relation to the noble Viscount's ways; and yet they are connected, for it was precisely to read one of his Lordship's letters to his friend that Beecher was now Grog's guest, seated opposite to him at the fire, in a very humble room of a very humble cottage on the strand of Irish-town. Grog had sought this retirement after the last settling at Newmarket, and had been, in popular phrase, "missing" since that event.

"Well, it's a long one, at all events," said Mr. Davis, as he glanced through his double eyeglass at the letter Beecher handed him,—"so long that I 'll be sworn it had no enclosure. When a man sends the flimsy, he spares you the flourish!"

"Right there, Grog. It's all preach and no pay; but read it" And he lighted his cigar, and puffed away.

"'Lake of Como, Oct 15

"What 's the old cove about up at Como so late in the season?"

"Read it, and you 'll know all," said the other, sententiously.

"'Dear Annesley,—I have been plotting a letter to you these half-dozen weeks; but what with engagements, the heat, and that insurmountable desire to defer whatever can by possibility be put off, all my good intentions have turned out tolerably like some of your own,—pleasant memories, and nothing more. Georgina, too, said—'

"Who's Georgina?"

"My sister-in-law."

"What's she like,—you never spoke of her?"

"Oh, nothing particular. She was a Ludworth; they 're a proud set, but have n't a brass farthing among them."

"Why did he marry her?"

"Who knows? He liked her, I believe," said he, after a pause, as though, failing a good and valid reason, he gave the next best that offered.

"'Georgina, too, said she 'd write, but the chances are her own commissions would have been the burden of her letter. She has never forgotten that bargain of Mechlin lace you once procured her, and always speculates on some future exercise of your skill.'"

Annesley burst into a hearty laugh, and said,—

"It was amongst the trumpery they gave me at Antwerp for a bill of three hundred and fifty pounds; I got a Rubens,—a real Rubens, of course,—an ebony cabinet, and twenty yards of coffee-colored 'point de Bruxelles,' horrid trash; but no matter, I never paid the bill, and Georgina thought the lace a dead bargain at forty louis."

"So that it squared you both?" said Grog.

"Just so, Master Davis. Read on."

"'You must see the utter impossibility of my making any increase to your present allowance—'"

"Hang me if I do, then!"

"'—present allowance. The pressure of so many bad years, the charges of aiding the people to emigrate, and the cost of this confounded war, have borne very heavily upon us all, and condemned us to economies that we never dreamed of. For myself, I have withdrawn my subscription from several charities, and will neither give a cup at the Broome Regatta, nor my accustomed ten pounds towards the race ball. I wish I could impress you with the necessity of similar sacrifices: these are times when every man must take his share of the national burdens, and reduce his habits of indulgence in conformity with national exigency.'"

"It 's all very fine to talk of cutting your coat, but when you have n't got any cloth at all, Master Davis—"

"Well, I suppose you must take a little of your neighbor's—if it don't suit you to go naked. This here noble Lord writes 'like a book;' but when he says, 'I 'm not a-goin' to stump it,' there 's no more to be said. You don't want to see the horse take his gallops that you know is to be scratched on the day of the race,—that's a mere piece of idle curiosity, ain't it?"

"Quite true, Grog."

"Well, it's clear he won't He says he won't, and that's enough.—'We have come abroad for no other reason than economy, and are only looking for a place inexpensive enough for our reduced means.' What's his income?"

"Better than twelve thousand a year."

"Has he debts?"

"Well, I suppose he may; everybody has."

"Ay," said Grog, dryly, and read on.—"'The Continent, however, is not the cheap place it once was,—rent, servants, markets, all are dearer,—and I 'm quite satisfied you find Ireland much less expensive than any other part of Europe,'—which means, 'Stay there,'—eh?"

"No, I don't take it that way," said Beecher, reddening.

"But I do, and I 'll maintain it," reiterated Grog. "He's a knowing one, that same noble Viscount; he's not the flat you always thought he was. He can square his own book, he can.—As to any prospect of places, I tell you, frankly, there is none. These competitive humbugs they call examinations do certainly stop a number of importunate people, but the vigilance of Parliament exercises a most overbearing tyranny on the ministers; and then the press! Now, we might tide over the House, Annesley, but the press would surely ruin all. If you were gazetted to-day Consul to the least-known South American republic,—commissioner for the sale of estates in the planet Saturn,—those fellows would have a leader on you to-morrow, showing what you did fifteen years ago at Ascot,—all your outlawries, all your actions in bankruptcy. They 'd begin saying, 'Is this the notorious Hon.

Annesley Beecher? or are we mistaken in supposing that the gentleman here referred to is the same lately mentioned in our columns as the friend and associate of the still more famous Grog Davis?'"

"He's cool, he is, the noble Lord," said Davis, laying down the letter, while Beecher laughed till his eyes ran over with tears. "Now, I 'd trouble his Lordship to tell *me*," continued Grog, "which had the worst of that same acquaintance, and which was more profitable to the other. If the famous Grog were to split upon the notorious Annes-ley, who 'd come last out of the bag?"

"You need n't take it so seriously as all that, Grog," said Beecher, in a placable tone.

"Why, when I'm told that one of the hardest things to be laid to *your* charge is the knowing *me*, it's high time to be serious, I think; not but I might just throw a shell into the enemy's own camp. The noble Lord ain't so safe as he fancies. I was head-waiter at Smykes's,—the old Cherry-tree, at Richmond—the night Mat Fortescue was ruined. I could tell the names of the partners even yet, though it's a matter of I won't say how many years ago; and when poor Fortescue blew his brains out, I know the man who drove his phaeton into town and said, 'Fortescue never had a hand light enough for these chestnuts. I always knew what I could do with them if they were my own.'"

"Lackington never said that. I 'll take my oath of it he never did!" cried Beecher, passionately.

"Take your oath of it!" said Davis, with an insulting sneer. "Do you mind the day old Justice Blanchard—it was at the York assizes—said, 'Have a care, Mr. Beecher, what you are about to swear; if you persist in affirming that document, the consequences may be more serious than you apprehend?' And do you remember you did n't swear?"

"I 'll tell you what, Master Grog," said Beecher, over whose face a sudden paleness now spread, "you may speak of *me* just as you like. You and I have been companions and pals for many a day; but Lackington is the head of my family, he has his seat in the Peers, he can hold up his head with the best in England, and I 'll not sit here to listen to anything against him."

"You won't, won't you?" said Grog, placing a hand on either knee, and fixing his fiery gray eyes on the other's face. "Well, then, I 'll tell you that you *shall!* Sit down, sir,—sit down, I say, and don't budge from that chair till I tell you! Do you see that hand? and that arm,—grasp it, squeeze it,— does n't feel very like the sinews of a fellow that feared hard labor. I was the best ten stone seven man in England the year I fought Black Joe, and I 'm as tough this minute, so that Norfolk Island needn't frighten me; but the Hon. Annesley Beecher would n't like it, I 'll promise him. He 'd have precious pains in the shoulder-blades, and very sore feelings about the small of the back, after the first day's stone-breaking. Now, don't provoke me, that's all. When the world has gone so bad with a man as it has with *me* the last year or two, it's not safe to provoke him,—it is not."

"I never meant to anger you, old fellow," began Annesley.

"Don't do it, then,—don't, I say," repeated the other, doggedly; and he resumed the letter, saying: "When you 're a-writing the answer to this here letter, just ask Grog Davis to give you a paragraph. Just say, 'Grog, old fellow, I 'm writing to my noble brother; mayhap you have a message of some kind or other for him,' and you 'll see whether he has or not."

"You 're a rum one, Master Davis," said Beecher, with a laugh that revealed very little of a heart at ease.

"I'm one that won't stand a fellow that doesn't run straight with me,— that's what I am. And now for the noble Viscount." And he ran his eyes over the letter without reading aloud. "All this here is only saying what sums he has paid for you, what terrible embarrassment your debts have caused him. Lord love him! it's no new thing to hear of in this life that paying money is no pleasure. And then it finishes, as all the stories usually do, by his swearing he won't do it any more. 'I think,' he says, 'you might come round by a fortunate hit in marriage; but somehow you blundered in every case that I pointed out to you—'"

"That's too bad!" cried Beecher, angrily. "The only thing he ever 'put me on' was an iron-master's widow at Barnstable, and I found that the whole concern was under a contract to furnish rails for a Peruvian line at two pounds ten a ton under the market price of iron."

"It was *I* discovered that!" broke in Grog, proudly.

"So it was, old fellow; and you got me off the match without paying forfeit."

"Well, this here looks better," continued Grog, reading.

"Young and handsome, one of two daughters of an old Irish provision merchant come abroad for the first time in their life, and consequently new to everything. The name's O'Reilly, of Mary's Abbey, so that you can have no difficulty in accurately learning all about him in Dublin. Knowing that these things are snapped up immediately in the cities, I have induced O'R. to take a villa on the lake here for the present, so that if your inquiries turn out satisfactorily, you can come out at once, and we 'll find the birds where I have landed them.'"

"That's business-like,—that's well and sensibly put," said Davis, in a voice of no counterfeited admiration.

He read on: "'O'R. talks of forty thousand to each, but, with the prospect of connecting himself with people of station, might possibly come down more handsomely in one case, particularly when brought to see that the other girl's prospects will be proportionately bettered by this alliance; at all events, no time is to be lost in the matter, and you can draw on me, at two months, for fifty pounds, which will carry you out here, and where, if you should not find me, you will have letters of presentation to the O'R.'s. It is not a case requiring either time or money,—though it may call for more energy and determination than you are in the habit of exercising. At the proper moment I shall be ready to contribute all in my power.'

"What does that mean?" said Davis.

"I can't even guess; but no matter, the thing sounds well. You can surely learn all about this O'Reilly?"

"That's easy enough."

"I say, I say, old fellow," cried Beecher, as he flung his cigar away and walked up and down the room briskly, "this would put us all on our legs again. Wouldn't I 'go a heavy pot' on Rolfs stable! I 'd take Coulton's three-year-old for the Canterbury to-morrow, I would! and give them twelve to twenty in hundreds on the double event. We'd serve them out, Master Grog—we'd give them such a shower-bath, old boy! They say I'm a flat, but what will they say when A. B.'s number hangs out at the Stand-house?"

"There's not much to do on the turf just now," said Grog, dryly. "They 've spoiled the turf," said he, as he lighted his cigar,—"clean spoiled it. Once upon a time the gents was gents, and the legs legs, but nowadays every one 'legs' it, as he can; so I 'd like to see who's to make a livin' out of it!"

"There's truth in that!" chimed in Beecher.

"So that," resumed Grog, "if you go in for this girl, don't you be making a book; there's plenty better things to be had now than the ring. There's companies, and banks, and speculations on every hand. You buy in at, say thirty, and sell out at eighty, ninety, or a hundred. I 've been a meditating over a new one I 'll tell you about another time,—let us first think about this here marriage,—it ain't impossible."

"Impossible! I should think not, Master Grog. But you will please to remember that Lackington has no child. I must succeed to the whole thing,—title and all."

"Good news for the Jews, would n't it be?" cried Davis. "Why, your outlying paper would n't leave much of a margin to live on. You owe upwards of a hundred thousand,—that you do."

"I could buy the whole concern to-morrow for five-and twenty thousand pounds. They can't touch the entail, old fellow!"

"My word on't, they 'd have it out of you, one way or other; but never mind, there's time enough to think of these things,—just stir yourself about this marriage."

"I 'll start on Monday. I have one or two trifling matters to look after here, and then I 'm free."

"What's this in the turn-down of Lackington's letter marked 'Strictly confidential'?

> "'I meant to have despatched this yesterday, but fortunately deferred doing so—fortunately, I say—as Davenport Dunn has just arrived here, with a very important communication, in which your interest is only inferior to my own. The explanation would be too long for a letter, and is not necessary besides, as D. will be in Dublin a day or two after this reaches you. See him at once; his address is Merrion Square North, and he will be fully prepared for your visit. Be on your guard. In truth, D., who is my own solicitor and man of business in Ireland, is somewhat of a crafty nature, and may have other interests in his head paramount to those of, yours,
>
> "'Lackington.'"

"Can you guess what this means, Grog? Has it any reference to the marriage scheme?"

"No; this is another match altogether," said Grog, sententiously; "and this here Dunn—I know about him, though I never seen him—is the swellest cove going. *You* ain't fit to deal with *him*—you ain't!" added he, contemptuously. "If you go and talk to that fellow alone, I know how 't will be."

"Come, come, I'm no flat"

Grog's look—one of intense derision—stopped him, and after stammering and blushing deeply, he was silent.

"You think, because you have a turn of speed among cripples, that you 're fast," said Grog, with one of his least amiable grins, "but I tell you that except among things of your own breeding, you'd never save a distance. Lord love ye! it never makes a fellow sharp to be 'done;' that's one of the greatest mistakes people ever make. It makes him suspicious,—it keeps him on the look-out, as the sailors say; but what's the use of being on the look-out if you haven't got good eyes? It's the go-ahead makes a man nowadays, and the cautious chaps have none of that. No, no; don't you go rashly and trust yourself alone with Dunn. You 'll have to consider well over this,— you 'll have to turn it over carefully in your mind. I 'd not wonder," said he, after a pause, "but you 'll have to take *me* with you!"

CHAPTER XIII
A MESSAGE FROM JACK

"He's come at last, Bella," said Kellett, as, tired and weary, he entered the little cottage one night after dark. "I waited till I saw him come out of the station at West-land Row, and drive off to his house."

"Did he see you, papa?—did he speak to you?" asked she, eagerly.

"See *me*—speak to *me!* It's little he was thinking of me, darling! with Lord Glengariff shaking one of his hands, and Sir Samuel Downie squeezing the other, and a dozen more crying out, 'Welcome home, Mr. Bunn! it is happy we are to see you looking so well; we were afraid you were forgetting poor Ireland and not coming back to us!' And by that time the carmen took up the chorus, and began cheering and hurrahing, 'Long life and more power to Davenport Dunn!' I give you my word, you'd have thought it was Daniel O'Connell, or at least a new Lord-Lieutenant, if you saw the uproar and excitement there was about him."

"And he—how did he take it?" asked she.

"Just as cool as if he had a born right to it all. 'Thank you very much,—most kind of you,' he muttered, with a little smile and a wave of his hand, as much as to say, 'There now, that'll do. Don't you see that I'm travelling *incog.*, and don't want any more homage?'"

"Oh, no, papa,—not that,—it was rather like humility—"

"Humility!" said he, bursting into a bitter laugh,—"you know the man well! Humility! there are not ten noblemen in Ireland this minute has the pride and impudence of that man. If you saw the way he walked down the steps to his carriage, giving a little nod here, and a little smile there,—maybe offering two fingers to some one of rank in the crowd—you'd say, 'There's a Prince coming home to his own country,—see how, in all their joy, he won't let them be too familiar with him!'"

"Are you quite just—quite fair in all this, dearest papa?"

"Well, I suppose I'm not," said he, testily. "It's more likely the fault lies in myself,—a poor, broken-down country gentleman, looking at everything on the dark side, thinking of the time when his own family were something in the land, and Mr. Davenport Dunn very lucky if he got leave to sit down in the servants'-hall. Nothing more likely than that!" added he, bitterly, as he walked up and down the little room in moody displeasure.

"No, no, papa, you mistake me," said she, looking affectionately at him. "What I meant was this, that to a man so burdened with weighty cares—one whose brain carries so many great schemes and enterprises—a sense of humility, proud enough in its way, might naturally mingle with all the pleasures of the moment, whispering as it were to his heart, 'Be not carried away by this flattery, be not carried away by your own esteem; it is less you than the work you are destined for that men are honoring. While they seem to cheer the pilot, it is rather the glorious ocean to which he is guiding them that they address their salutations.' Might not some such consciousness as this have moved him at such a time?"

"Indeed, I don't know, and I don't much care," said Kellett, sulkily. "I suppose people don't feel, nowadays, the way they used when I was young. There's new inventions in everything."

"Human nature is the same in all ages!" said she, faintly.

"Faith, and so much the worse for it, Bella. There's more bad than good in life,—more cruelty and avarice and falsehood than there's kindness, benevolence, and honesty. For one good-natured act I 've met with, have n't I met twenty, thirty, no, but fifty, specimens of roguery and double-dealing. If you want to praise the world, don't call Paul Kellett into court, that's all!"

"So far from agreeing with you," cried she, springing up and drawing her arm within his, "you are exactly the very testimony I'd adduce. From your own lips have I heard more stories of generosity—more instances of self-devotion, trustfulness, and true kindness—than I have ever listened to in life."

"Ay, amongst the poor, Bella,—amongst the poor!" said Kellett, half ashamed of his recantation.

"Be assured, then, that these traits are not peculiar to any class. The virtues of the poor, like their sufferings, are more in evidence than in any other condition,—their lives are laid bare by poverty; but I feel assured people are better than we think them,—better than they know themselves."

"I 'm waiting to hear you tell me that I 'm richer too," said Kellett, with a half-melancholy laugh,—"that I have an elegant credit in a bank somewhere, if I only knew where to draw upon it!"

"There is this wealth in the heart of man, if he but knew how to profit by it: it is to teach us this lesson that great men have arisen from time to time. The poets, the warriors, the explorers, the great in science, set us all the same task, to see the world fair as it really is, to recognize the good around us, to subdue the erroneous thoughts that, like poisonous weeds, stifle the wholesome vegetation of our hearts, and to feel that the cause of humanity is our cause, its triumphs our triumphs, its losses our losses!"

"It may be all as you say, Bella darling, but it's not the kind of world ever *I* saw. I never knew men do anything but cheat each other and tell lies; and the hardest of it all," added he, with a bitter sigh, "that, maybe, it is your own flesh and blood treats you worst!"

This reflection announced the approach of gloomy thoughts. This was about the extent of any allusion he would ever make to his son, and Bella was careful not to confirm him in the feeling by discussing or opposing it. She understood his nature well. She saw that some fortunate incident or other, even time, might dissipate what had never been more than a mere prejudice, while, if reasoned with, he was certain to argue himself into the conviction that of all the rubs he had met in life his son Jack's conduct was the hardest and the worst.

The long and painful silence that now ensued was at length broken by a loud knocking at the door of the cottage, a sound so unusual as to startle them both.

"That's at *our* door, Bella," said he. "I wonder who it can be? Beecher couldn't come out this time of the night."

"There it is again," said Bella, taking a light. "I 'll go and see who's there."

"No, let me go," cried Kellett, taking the candle from her hand, and leaving the room with the firm step of a man about to confront a danger.

"Captain Kellett lives here, does n't he?" said a tall young fellow, in the dress of a soldier in the Rifles.

Kellett's heart sank heavily within him as he muttered a faint "Yes."

"I'm the bearer of a letter for him," said the soldier, "from his son."

"From Jack!" burst out Kellett, unable to restrain himself. "How is he? Is he well?"

"He's all right now; he was invalided after that explosion in the trenches, but he's all right again. We all suffered more or less on that night;" and his eyes turned half inadvertently towards one side, where Kellett now saw that an empty coat-sleeve was hanging.

"It was there you left your arm, then, poor fellow," said Kellett, taking him kindly by the hand. "Come in and sit down; I'm Captain Kellett. A fellow-soldier of Jack's, Bella," said Kellett, as he introduced him to his daughter; and the young man bowed with all the ease of perfect good-breeding.

"You left my brother well, I hope?" said Bella, whose womanly tact saw at once that she was addressing her equal.

"So well that he must be back to his duty ere this. This letter is from him; but as he had not many minutes to write, he made me promise to come and tell you myself all about him. Not that I needed his telling me, for I owe my life to your son, Captain Kellett; he carried me in on his back under the sweeping fire of a Russian battery; two rifle bullets pierced his chako as he was doing it; he must have been riddled with shot if the Russians had not stopped their fire."

"Stopped their fire!"

"That they did, and cheered him heartily. How could they help it! he was the only man on that rude glacis, torn and gullied with shot and shell."

"Oh, the noble fellow!" burst out the girl, as her eyes ran over.

"Is n't he a noble fellow?" said the soldier. "We don't want for brave fellows in that army; but show me one will do what he did. It was a shot carried off this," said he, touching the empty sleeve of his jacket; "and I said something—I must have been wandering in my mind—about a ring my mother had given me, and it was on the finger of that poor hand. Well, what does Jack Kellett do, while the surgeon was dressing my wound, but set off to the place where I was shot down, and, under all that hailstorm of Minié-balls, brought in the limb. That's the ring,—he rescued it at the risk of his life. There's more than courage in that; there's a goodness and kindness of heart worth more than all the bravery that ever stormed a battery."

"And yet he left me,—deserted his poor father!" cried old Kellett, sobbing.

"If he did so, it was to make a name for you that the first man in England might be proud of."

"To go off and list as a common soldier!" said Kellett; and then, suddenly shocked at his own rudeness, and shamed by the deep blush on Sybella's face, he stammered out, "Not but I've known many a man with good blood in his veins,—many a born gentleman,—serving in the ranks."

"Well, I hope so," said the other, laughing with a hearty good-nature. "It's not exactly so common a thing with us as with our worthy allies the French; but every now and then you'll find a firelock in the hands that once held a double-barrelled Manton, and maybe knocked over the pheasants in his own father's preserves."

"Indeed, I have heard of such things," said Kellett, with a sigh; but he was evidently lending his assent on small security, because he cared little for the venture.

"How poor Jack loves you!" cried Bella, who, deep in her brother's letter, had paid no attention to what was passing; "he calls you Charley,—nothing but Charley."

"My name is Charles Conway," said the young man, smiling pleasantly.

"'Charley,'" read she, aloud, "'my banker when I have n't a shilling, my nurse in hospital, my friend always,—he 'll hand you this, and tell you all about me. How the dear old dad will love to hear his stories of campaigning life, so like his own Peninsular tales! He'll see that the long peace has not tamed the native pluck of the race, but that the fellows are just as daring, just as steady, just as invincible as ever they were; and he'll say, too, that to have won the friendship of such a comrade I must have good stuff in me also.'"

"Oh, if he hadn't gone away and left his old father!" broke in Kellett, lamentingly; "sure it was n't the time to leave me."

"Wasn't it, though?" broke in the soldier; "I differ with you there. It was the very moment that every fellow with a dash of spirit about him should have offered his services. We can't all have commissions,—we can't all of us draw handsome allowances from our friends; but we can surely take our turn in the trenches, and man a battery; and it's not a bad lesson to teach the common fellow, that for pluck, energy, and even holding out, the gentleman is at least his equal."

"I think it's the first of the name ever served in the ranks," said the old man, who, with a perverse obstinacy, would never wander from this one idea.

"How joyously he writes!" continued Bella, as she bent over the letter: "'I see by the papers, dearest Bella, that we are all disgusted and dispirited out here,—that we have nothing but grievances about green coffee and raw pork, and the rest of it; don't believe a word of it. We do curse the Commissariat now and then. It smacks like epicurism to abuse the rations; but ask Charley if these things are ever thought of after we rise from dinner and take a peep at those grim old earthworks, that somehow seem growing every day, or if we grumble about fresh vegetables as we are told off for a covering party. There's plenty of fighting; and if any man has n't enough in the regular way, he can steal out of a clear night and have a pop at the Russians from a rifle-pit. I 'm twice as quick a shot as I was when I left home, and I confess the sport has double the excitement of my rambles after grouse over Mahers Mountain. It puts us on our mettle, too, to see our old enemies the French taking the work with us; not but they have given us the lion's share of it, and left our small army to do the same duties as their large one. One of the regiments in our brigade, rather than flinch from their share, returned themselves twelve hundred strong, while they had close upon three hundred sick,—ay, and did the work too. Ask dad if his Peninsulars beat that? Plenty of hardships, plenty of roughing, and plenty of hard knocks there are, but it's the jolliest life ever a fellow led, for all that. Every day has its own story of some dashing bit of bravery, that sets us all wild with excitement, while we wonder to ourselves what do you all think of us in England. Here comes an order to summon all to close their letters, and so I shut up, with my fondest affection to the dear old dad and yourself.

"'Ever yours,

"'Jack Kellett.

"'As I don't suppose you'll see it in the "Gazette," I may as well say that I 'm to be made a corporal on my return to duty. It's a long way yet to major-general, but at least I 'm on the road, Bella.'"

"A corporal! a corporal!" exclaimed Kellett; "may I never, if I know whether it's not a dream. Paul Kellett's eldest son—Kellett of Kellett's Court—a corporal!"

"My father's prejudices all attach to the habits of his own day," said Bella, in a low voice, to the soldier,—"to a time totally unlike the present in everything."

"Not in everything, Miss Kellett," said the youth, with a quiet smile. "Jack has just told you that all the old ardor, all the old spirit, is amongst the troops. They are the sons and grandsons of the gallant fellows that beat the French out of Spain."

"And are *you* going back?" asked Kellett, half moodily, and scarcely knowing what he said.

"They won't have me," said the soldier, blushing as he looked at his empty sleeve; "they want fellows who can handle a Minié rifle."

"Oh, to be sure—I ought to have known—I was forgetting," stammered he out, confusedly; "but you have your pension, anyhow."

"I've a kind old mother, which is better," said the youth, blushing deeper again. "She only gave me a short leave to run over and see Jack Kellett's family; for she knows Jack, by name at least, as if he were her own."

To Bella's questions he replied that his mother had a small cottage near Bettws, at the foot of Snowdon; it was one of the most picturesque spots of all Wales, and in one of those sunny nooks where the climate almost counterfeits the South of Europe.

"And now you'll go back, and live tranquilly there," said the girl, half dreamily, for her thoughts were wandering away Heaven knows where.

The youth saw the preoccupation, and arose to take his leave. "I shall be writing to Jack to-morrow, Captain Kellett," said he. "I may say I have seen you well and hearty, and I may tell the poor fellow—I 'm sure you 'll let me tell him—that you have heartily forgiven him?" Old Kellett shook his head mournfully; and the other went on: "It's a hard thing of a dark night in the trenches, or while you lie on the wet ground in front of them, thinking of home and far away, to have any one thought but love and affection in your heart It does n't do to be mourning over faults and follies, and grieving over things one is sorry for. One likes to think, too, that they who are at home, happy at their firesides, are thinking kindly of us. A man's heart is never so stout before the enemy as when he knows how dear he is to some one far away."

As the youth spoke these words half falteringly, for he was naturally bashful and timid, Bella turned her eyes fully upon his, with an interest she had not felt before, and he reddened as he returned her gaze.

"I 'm sure you forgive me, sir," said he, addressing Kellett. "It was a great liberty I took to speak to you in this fashion; but I was Jack's comrade,—he told me every secret he had in the world, and I know how the poor fellow would march up to a Russian battery to-morrow with an easier heart than he'd hear one hard word from you."

"Ask Bella there if I ever said a word, ever as much as mentioned his name," said Kellett, with all the self-satisfaction of egotism.

Bella's eyes quickly turned towards the soldier, with an expression so full of significance that he only gave a very faint sigh, and muttered,—

"Well, I can do no more; when I next hear from Jack, sir, you shall know it." And with this he moved towards the door.

Bella hastily whispered a few words in her father's ear, to which, as he seemed to demur, she repeated still more eagerly.

"How could we, since it's Sunday, and there will be Beecher coming out?" muttered he.

"But this is a gentleman, papa; his soldier jacket is surely no disgrace—"

"I couldn't, I couldn't," muttered he, doggedly.

Again she whispered, and at last he said,—

"Maybe you 'd take your bit of dinner with us tomorrow, Conway,— quite alone, you know."

The young fellow drew himself up, and there was, for an instant, a look of haughty, almost insolent, meaning in his face. There was that, however, in Bella's which as speedily overcame whatever irritation had crossed his mind, and he politely said,—

"If you will admit me in this dress,—I have no other with me."

"To be sure,—of course," broke in Kellett. "When my son is wearing the same, what could I say against it?"

The youth smiled good-naturedly at this not very gracious speech; mayhap the hand he was then holding in his own compensated for its rudeness, and his "Good-bye!" was uttered in all frankness and cordiality.

CHAPTER XIV
A DINNER AT PAUL KELLETT'S

To all you gentlemen who live at home at ease there are few things less troublesome than the arrangement of what is called a dinner-party. Some difficulty may possibly exist as to the guests. Lady Mary may be indisposed. It might not be quite right to ask Sir Harry to meet the Headleys. A stray embarrassment or two will arise to require a little thought or a little management The material details, however, give no care. There is a stereotyped mode of feeding one's friends, out of which it is not necessary, were it even possible, to issue. Your mock-turtle may have a little more or less the flavor of Madeira; your salmon be somewhat thicker in the shoulder; your sirloin be a shade more or less underdone; your side dishes a little more or less uneatable than your neighbor's; but, after all, from the caviare to the cheese, the whole thing follows an easy routine, and the dinner of No. 12 is the fac-simile of the dinner at No. 13; and the same silky voice that whispers "Sherry, sir?" has its echo along the whole street The same toned-down uniformity pervades the intellectual elements of the feast; all is quiet, jogtrot, and habitual; a gentle atmosphere of murmuring dulness is diffused around, very favorable to digestion, and rather disposing to sleep.

How different are all these things in the case of the poor man, especially when he happens to be a reduced gentleman, whose memories of the past are struggling and warring with exigencies of the present and the very commonest necessities are matters of gravè difficulty.

Kellett was very anxious to impress his son's friend with a sense of his social standing and importance, and he told Bella "not to mind spending the whole week's allowance, just to show the soldier what Jack's family was." A leg of mutton and a little of Kinnahan's port constituted, in his mind, a very high order of entertainment; and these were at once voted. Bella hoped that after the first outburst of this ostentatious fit he would fall back in perfect indifference about the whole matter; but far from it,—his waking thought in the morning was the dinner; and when she remarked to him at breakfast on the threatening aspect of the clouds, his reply was, "No matter, dear, if we have plenty of capers." Even the unhappy possibility of Beecher's "dropping in" was subordinate to his wish to cut a figure on the occasion;

and he pottered about from the dining-room to the kitchen, peeped into saucepans, and scrutinized covered dishes with a most persistent activity. Nor was Bella herself quite averse to all this. She saw in the distance—remotely it might be—the glimmering of a renewed interest about poor Jack. "The pleasure this little incident imparts," thought she, "will spread its influence wider. He 'll talk of him too; he 'll be led on to let him mingle with our daily themes. Jack will be one of us once more after this;" and so she encouraged him to make of the occasion a little festival.

What skill did she not practise, what devices of taste not display, to cover over the hard features of their stern poverty! The few little articles of plate which remained after the wreck of their fortune were placed on the sideboard, conspicuous amongst which was a cup "presented by his brother officers to Captain Paul Kellett, on his retirement from the regiment, with which he had served thirty-eight years,"—a testimonial only exhibited on the very most solemn occasions. His sword and sash—the same he wore at Waterloo—were arrayed over the fireplace, and his Talavera chako—grievously damaged by a French sabre—hung above them. "If he begins about 'that expedition,'"—it was thus he always designated the war in the Crimea,—"Bella, I 'll just give him a touch of the real thing, as we had it in the Peninsula! Faith, it wasn't digging holes in the ground we were then;" and he laughed to himself at the absurdity of the conceit.

The few flowers which the garden owned at this late season, humble and common as they were, figured on the chimney-piece, and not a resource of ingenuity was neglected to make that little dinner-room look pleasant and cheery. Fully a dozen times had Kellett gone in and out of the room, never weary of admiring it, and as constantly muttering to himself some praise of Bella, to whose taste it was all owing. "I 'd put the cup in the middle of the table, Bella. The wallflowers would do well enough at the sideboard. Well, maybe you 're right, darling; it is less pretentious, to be sure. And be careful, dear, that old Betty has a clean apron. May I never, but she's wearing the same one since Candlemas! And don't leave her any corks to draw; she's the devil for breaking them into the bottle. I 'll sit here, where I can have the screw at my hand. There 's a great convenience in a small room, after all. By the good day, here 's Beecher!" exclaimed he, as that worthy individual approached the door.

"What's all this for, Kellett, old boy? Are you expecting the Viceroy, or celebrating a family festival, eh? What does it mean?"

"'T is a mutton chop I was going to give a friend of Jack's,—a young fellow that brought me a letter from him yesterday."

"Oh! your son Jack. By the way, what's his regiment,—Light Dragoons, is n't it?"

"No; the Rifles," said Kellett, with a short cough.

"He's pretty high up for his lieutenancy by this, ain't he?" said Beecher, rattling on. "He Joined before Alma, didn't he?"

"Yes; he was at the battle," said Kellett, dryly; for though he had once or twice told his honorable friend that Jack was in the service, he had not mentioned that he was in the ranks. Not that Annesley Beecher would have, in the least, minded the information. The fact could not by possibility have touched himself; it never could have compelled *him* to mount guard, do duty in the trenches, eat Commissariat biscuit, or submit to any of the hardships soldiery inflicts; and he 'd have heard of Jack's fate with all that sublime philosophy which teaches us to bear tranquilly the calamities of others.

"Why don't you stir yourself to get him a step? There's nothing to be had without asking! ay, worse than asking,—begging, worrying, importuning. Get some fellow in one of the offices to tell you when there's a vacancy, and then up and at them. If they say, 'We are only waiting for an opportunity, Captain Kellett,' you reply, 'Now's your time then, Groves of the Forty-sixth is gone "toes up;" Simpson, of the Bays, has cut his lucky this morning.' That's the way to go to work."

"You are wonderful!" exclaimed Kellett, who really did all but worship the worldly wisdom of his friend.

"I 'd ask Lackington, but he 's no use to any one. Just look at my own case." And now he launched forth into the theme he really loved and never found wearisome. His capacity for anything—everything, his exact fitness for fifty opposite duties, his readiness to be a sinecurist, and his actual necessity for a salary, were subjects he could be eloquent on; devoting occasional passing remarks to Lackington's intense stupidity, who never exerted himself for him, and actually "thought him a flat." "I know you won't believe—but he does, I assure you—he thinks me a flat!"

Before Kellett could fully rally from the astounding force of such an unjustifiable opinion, his guest, Conway, knocked at the door.

"I say, Kellett, there comes an apology from your friend."

"How so?" asked Kellett, eagerly.

"I just saw a soldier come up to the door, and the chances are it 's an officer's servant with a note of excuse."

The door opened as he spoke, and Conway entered the room. Kellett met him with an honest cordiality, and then, turning to Beecher, said,—

"My son's friend and comrade,—Mr. Annesley Beecher;" and the two men bowed to each other, and exchanged glances that scarcely indicated much pleasure at the acquaintance.

"Why, he 's in the ranks, Kellett," whispered Beecher, as he drew him into the window.

"So is my son," said Kellett, with a gulp that half choked him.

"The deuce he is; you never told me that. And is this our dinner company?"

"I was just going to explain—Oh, here's Bella!" and Miss Kellett entered, giving such a cordial greeting to the soldier that made Beecher actually astounded.

"What's his name, Kellett?" said Beecher, half languidly.

"A good name, for the matter of that; he's called Conway."

"Conway—Conway?" repeated Beecher, aloud; "we have fortieth cousins, Conways. There was a fellow called Conway in the Twelfth Lancers that went a tremendous pace; they nicknamed him the 'Smasher,' I don't know why. Do you?" said he, addressing the soldier.

"I 've heard it was from an awkward habit he had of putting his heel on snobs."

"Oh! you know him, perhaps?" said Beecher, affectedly.

"Why, as I was the man myself, I ought, according to the old adage, to say I knew but little of him."

"You Conway of the Twelfth! the same that owned Brushwood and Lady Killer, that won the Riddlesworth?"

"You're calling up old memories to me," said the youth, smiling, "which, after all, I 'd just as soon forget."

"And you were an officer in the Lancers!" exclaimed Kellett, eagerly.

"Yes; I should have had my troop by this if I hadn't owned those fortunate three-year-olds Mr. Beecher has just reminded me of. Like many others, whom success on the turf has misled, I went on madly, quite convinced I had fortune with me."

"Ah!" said Beecher, moralizing, "there's no doing a good stroke of work without the legs. Cranley tried it, Hawchcome tried it, Ludborough tried it, but it won't do. As Grog Davis says, 'you must not ignore existing interests.'"

"There's another name I have n't heard for many a year. What a scoundrel that fellow was! I 've good ground for believing that this Davis it was poisoned Sir Aubrey, the best horse I ever owned. Three men of his stamp would make racing a sport unfit for gentlemen."

"Miss Kellett, will you allow me?" said Beecher, offering his arm, and right well pleased that the announcement of dinner cut short the conversation.

"A nice fellow that friend of your brother's," muttered he, as he led her along; "but what a stupid thing to go and serve in the ranks! It's about the last step I 'd ever have thought of taking."

"I'm certain of it," said Bella, with an assent so ready as to sound like flattery.

As the dinner proceeded, old Kellett's astonishment continued to increase at the deference paid by Beecher to every remark that fell from Conway. The man who had twice won "the Bexley," and all but won "the Elms;" he who owned Sir Aubrey, and actually took the odds against all "Holt's stable," was no common celebrity. In vain was it Conway tried to lead the conversation to his friend Jack,—what they had seen, and where they had been together,—Beecher would bring them back to the Turf and the "Racing Calendar." There were so many dark things he wanted to know, so much of secret history he hoped to be enlightened in; and whenever, as was often the case, Conway did not and could not give him the desired information, Beecher slyly intimated by a look towards Kellett that he was a deep fellow; while he muttered to himself, "Grog Davis would have it out of him, notwithstanding all his cunning."

Bella alone wished to hear about the war. It was not alone that her interest was excited for her brother, but in the great events of that great struggle her enthusiastic spirit found ample material for admiration. Conway related many heroic achievements, not alone of British soldiers, but of French and even Russians. Gallantry, as he said, was of no nation in particular,—there were brave fellows everywhere; and he told, with all the warmth of honest admiration, how daringly the enemy dashed into the lines at night and confronted certain death, just for the sake of causing an interruption to the siege, and delaying, even for a brief space, the advance of the works. Told, as these stories were, with all the freshness which actual observation confers, and in a spirit of unexaggerated simplicity, still old Kellett heard them with the peevish jealousy of one who felt that they were destined to eclipse in their interest the old scenes of Spain and Portugal. That any soldiers lived nowadays like the old Light Division, that there were such fellows as the fighting Fifth, or Crawfurd's Brigade, no man should persuade him; and when he triumphantly asked if they had n't as good a general as Sir Arthur Welles-ley, he fell back, laughing contemptuously at the idea of such being deemed war at all, or the expedition, as he would term it, being styled a campaign.

"Remember, Captain Kellett, we had a fair share of your old Peninsular friends amongst us,—gallant veterans, who had seen everything from the Douro to Bayonne."

"Well, and did n't they laugh at all this? did n't they tell you fairly it was not fighting?"

"I 'm not so sure they did," said Conway, laughing good-naturedly. "Gordon told an officer in my hearing, that the charge up the heights at the Alma reminded him strongly of Harding's ascent of the hills at Albuera."

"No, no, don't say that; I can't stand it!" cried Kellett, peevishly; "sure if it was only that one thinks they were Frenchmen—Frenchmen, with old Soult at their head—at Albuera—"

"There's nothing braver than a Russian, sir, depend on 't," said the youth, with a slight warmth in his tone.

"Brave if you like; but, you see, he isn't a soldier by nature, like the Frenchman; and yet we beat the French, thrashed him from the sea to the Pyrenees, and over the Pyrenees into France."

"What's the odds? You'd not do it again; or, if you did, not get Nap to abdicate. I 'd like to have two thousand to fifty on the double event," said Beecher, chuckling over an imaginary betting-book.

"And why not do it again?" broke in Bella. "Is it after listening to what we have heard this evening that we have cause for any faint-heartedness about the spirit of our soldiery? Were Cressy or Agincourt won by braver fellows than now stand entrenched around Sebastopol?"

"I don't like it; as Grog says, 'never make a heavy book on a waiting race!'"

"I conclude, then," said Conway, "you are one of those who augur ill of our success in the present war?"

"I 'd not stake an even fifty, on either side," said Beecher, who had shrewd suspicions that it was what he 'd have called a "cross," and that Todleben and Lord Raglan could make "things comfortable" at any moment.

"I see Miss Bella's of my mind," added he, as he perceived a very peculiar smile just parting her lips.

"I suspect not, Mr. Beecher," said she, slyly.

"Why did you laugh, then?"

"Shall I tell you? It was just this, then, passing in my mind. I was wondering within myself whether the habit of reducing all men's motives to the standard of morality observable in the 'ring' more often lead to mistakes, or the contrary."

"I sincerely trust that it rarely comes right," broke in Conway. "I was close upon four years on the turf, as they call it; and if I had n't been ruined in time, I 'd have ended by believing that an honest man was as great a myth as anything we read of amongst the heathen gods."

"That all depends upon what you call honest," said Beecher.

"To be sure it does; you 're right there," chimed in Kellett; and Beecher, thus seconded, went on, —

"Now, I call a fellow honest when he won't put his pal into a hole; when he 'll tell him whenever he has got a good thing, and let him have his share; when he'll warn him against a dark lot, and not let him 'in' to oblige any one, — that's honesty."

"Well, perhaps it is," said Conway, laughing. "The Russians said it was mercy t' other day, when they went about shooting the wounded. There's no accounting for the way men are pleased to see things."

"I 'd like to have *your* definition of honesty," said Beecher, slightly piqued by the last remark.

"How can you expect me to give you one? Have I not just told you I was for more than three years on the turf, had a racing stable, and dealt with trainers and jocks?" He paused for a second or two, and then, in a stronger voice, went on: "I cannot believe that the society of common soldiers is a very high standard by which to measure either manners or motives; and yet I pledge my word to it, that my comrades, in comparison with my old companions of the turf, were unexceptionable gentlemen. I mean that, in all that regards truthfulness, fair dealing, and honorable intercourse, it would be insult to compare them."

"Ah, you see," said Beecher, "you got it 'all hot,' as they say. You 're not an unprejudiced juryman. They gave you a bucketing, — I heard all about it. If Corporal Trim had n't been doctored, you 'd have won twelve thousand at Lancaster."

Conway smiled good-humoredly at the explanation thus suggested, but said nothing.

"Bother it for racing," said Kellett "I never knew any real taste for horses or riding where there was races. Instead of caring for a fine, showy beast, a little thick in the shoulder, square in the joints, and strong in the haunch, they run upon things like greyhounds, all drawn up behind and low before; it's a downright misery to mount one of them."

"But it's a real pleasure to see him come in first, when your book tells you seven to one in your favor. Talk of sensations," said he, enthusiastically; "where is there the equal of that you feel when the orange and blue you have backed with a heavy pot comes pelting round the corner, followed by two,—then three,—all punishing, your own fellow holding on beautifully, with one eye a little thrown backward to see what's coming, and that quiet, calm look about the mouth that says, 'I have it.' Every note of the wild cheer that greets the winner is applause to your own heart; that deafening yell is your own song of triumph."

"Listen to him!—that's his hobby," cried Kellett, whose eyes glistened with excitement at the description, and who really felt an honest admiration for the describer. "Ah, Beecher, my boy!—you're at home there."

"If they'd only give me a chance, Paul,—one chance!"

Whether it was that the expression was new and strange to him, or that the energy of the speaker astonished him, but Conway certainly turned his eyes towards him in some surprise; a sentiment which Beecher at once interpreting as interest, went on,—

"*You*," said he,—"*you* had many a chance; *I* never had one. You might have let them all in, you might have landed them all—so they tell me, at least—if you'd have withdrawn Eyetooth. He was own brother to Aurelius, and sure to win. Well, if you'd have withdrawn him for the Bexley, you'd have netted fifty thousand. Grog—I mean a fellow 'well up' among the legs—told me so."

"Your informant never added what every gentleman in England would have said of me next day," said Conway. "It would have been neither more nor less than a swindle. The horse was in perfect health and top condition,—why should I not have run him?"

"For no other reason that I know, except that you'd have been richer by fifty thousand for not doing it."

"Well," said Conway, quietly, "it's not a very pleasant thing to be crippled in this fashion; but I'd rather lose the other arm than do what you speak of. And if I did n't know that many gentlemen get a loose way of talking of fifty things they 'd never seriously think of doing, I 'd rather feel disposed to be offended at what you have just said."

"Offended! of course not,—I never dreamed of anything offensive. I only meant to say that they call *me* a flat; but hang me if I'd have let them off as cheaply as you did."

"Then they're at perfect liberty to call me a flat also," said Conway, laughing. "Indeed, I suspect I have given them ample reason to think me one."

The look of compassionate pity Beecher bestowed on him as he uttered these words was as honest as anything in his nature could be.

It was in vain Bella tried to get back the conversation to the events of the campaign, to the scenes wherein poor Jack was an actor. Beecher's perverse activity held them chained to incidents which, to him, embraced all that was worth living for. "You must have had some capital things in your time, though. You had some race-horses, and were well in with Tom Nolan's set," said he to Conway.

"Shall I tell you the best match I ever had,—at least, the one gave me most pleasure?"

"Do, by all means," said Beecher, eagerly, "though I guess it already. It was against Vickersley, even for ten thousand, at York."

"No," said the other, smiling.

"Well, then, it was the Cotswold,—four miles in two heats. You won it with a sister to Ladybird."

"Nor that, either; though by these reminiscences you show me how accurately you have followed my humble fortunes."

"There 's not a man has done anything on the turf for fifty years I can't give you his history; not a horse I won't tell you all his performances, just as if you were reading it out of the 'Racing Calendar.' As 'Bell's Life' said t' other day, 'If Annesley Beecher can't answer that question,'—and it was about Running Rein,—'no man in England can.' I'm 'The Fellow round the corner' that you always see alluded to in 'Bell.'"

"Indeed!" exclaimed Conway, with assumed deference.

"That I am,—Kellett knows it. Ask old Paul there,—ask Grog,—ask any one you like, whether A. B. is up to a thing or two. But we 're forgetting this match,—the best thing you said you ever had."

"I 'm not so sure you 'll be of my mind when you hear it," said Conway, smiling. "It was a race we had t' other day in the Crimea,—a steeplechase, over rather a stiff course, with Spanish ponies; and I rode against Lord Broodale, Sir Harry Curtis, and Captain Marsden, and won five pounds and a dozen of champagne. My comrades betted something like fifty shillings on the match, and there would have been a general bankruptcy in the company if I had lost. Poor Jack mortgaged his watch and a pilot coat that he was excessively proud of,—it was the only bit of mufti in the battalion, I think; but he came off all right, and treated us all to a supper with his winnings, which, if I don't mistake, did n't pay more than half the bill."

"Good luck to him, and here's his health," cried Kellett, whose heart, though proof against all ordinary appeals to affection, could not withstand this assault of utter recklessness and improvidence. "He's my own flesh and blood, there's no denying it."

If Conway was astounded at this singular burst of paternal affection, he did not the less try to profit by it, and at once began to recount the achievements of his comrade, Jack Kellett. The old man listened half doggedly at first, but gradually, as the affection of others for his son was spoken of, he relaxed, and heard, with an emotion he could not easily repress, how Jack was beloved by the whole regiment,—that to be his companion in outpost duty, to be stationed with him in a battery, was a matter of envy. "I won't say," said Conway, "that every corps and every company has not fellows brave as he; but show me one who 'll carry a lighter spirit into danger, and as soft a heart amid scenes of cruelty and bloodshed. So that if you asked who in our battalion is the pluckiest, who the most tenderhearted, who the most generous, and who the least given to envy, you'd have the one answer, 'Jack Kellett,' without a doubt."

"And what will it all do for him?" broke in the old man, resorting once more to his discontent.

"What will it do for him? What has it done for him? Is it nothing that in a struggle history will make famous a man's name is a household word; that in a war where deeds of daring are so rife, his outnumbers those of any other? It's but a few weeks back a Sardinian staff-officer, coming to our head-quarters on business, asked if the celebrated 'Bersagliere' was there,— so they call riflemen,—and desired to see him; and, better than that, though he didn't know Jack's name, none doubted who was meant, but Jack Kellett was sent for on the instant. Now, that I call fame."

"Will it get him his commission?" said Beecher, knowingly, as though by one shrewd stroke of intelligence he had embraced the entire question.

"A commission can be had for four hundred and fifty pounds, and some man in Parliament to ask for it. But what Jack has done cannot be bought by mere money. Do you go out there, Mr. Beecher, just go and see for yourself—it's well worth the while—what stuff fellows are made of that face danger every day and night, without one thought above duty, never expecting, never dreaming that anything they do is to have its personal benefit, and would far rather have their health drunk by their comrades than be quoted in the 'Times.' You'll find your old regiment there,—you were in the Fusilier Guards, weren't you?"

"Yes, I tried soldiering, but I did n't like it," said Beecher; "and it was better in my day than *now*, they tell me."

A movement of impatience on Conway's part was suddenly interrupted by Kellett, saying, "He means that the service is n't what it was; and indeed he's right there. I remember the time there wasn't a man in the Eighty-fifth could n't carry away three bottles of Bennett's strong port, and play as good a rubber, afterwards, as Hoyle himself."

"It's the snobbery I was thinking of," said Beecher; "fellows go into the army now who ought to be counter-jumping."

"I don't know what they ought to be doing," broke in Conway, angrily, "but I could tell you something of what they are doing; and where you are to find men to do it better, I 'm not so clear. I said a few moments back, you ought to go out to the Crimea; but I beg to correct myself,—it is exactly what you ought not to do."

"Never fear, old fellow; I never dreamed of it. Give you any odds you like, you 'll never see my arrival quoted at Balaklava."

"A thousand pardons, Miss Kellett," whispered Conway, as he arose, "but you see how little habit I have of good company; I'm quite ashamed of my warmth. May I venture to come and pay you a morning visit before I go back?"

"Oh, by all means; but why not an evening one? You are more certain to find us."

"Then an evening one, if you'll allow me;" and shaking Kellett's hand warmly, and with a cold bow to Beecher, he withdrew.

"Wasn't he a flat!" cried Beecher, as the door closed after him. "The Smasher—that was the name he went by—went through an estate of six thousand a year, clean and clear, in less than four years, and there he is now, a private soldier with one arm!"

"Faith, I like him; he's a fine fellow," said Kellett, heartily.

"Ask Grog Davis if he'd call him a fine fellow," broke in Beecher, sneeringly; "there's not such a spoon from this to Newmarket. Oh, Paul, my hearty, if I had but one, just one of the dozen chances he has thrown away! But, as Grog says, 'a crowbar won't make a cracksman;' nor will a good stable of horses, and safe jocks 'bring a fellow round,' if he hasn't it here." And he touched his forehead with his forefinger most significantly.

Meanwhile Charles Conway sauntered slowly back to town, on the whole somewhat a sadder man than he had left it in the morning. His friend Jack had spoken much to him of his father and sister, and why or to what extent he knew not, but somehow they did not respond to his own self-drawn picture of them. Was it that he expected old Kellett would have been a racier version of his son,—the same dashing, energetic spirit,—seeing all for the best in life, and accepting even its reverses in a half-jocular humor? Had he hoped to find in him Jack's careless, easy temper,—a nature so brimful of content as to make all around sharers in its own blessings; or had he fancied a "fine old Irish gentleman" of that thoroughbred school he had so often heard of?

Nor was he less disappointed with Bella; he thought she had been handsomer, or, at least, quite a different kind of beauty. Jack was blue-eyed and Saxon-looking, and he fancied that she must be a "blonde," with the same frank, cheery expression of her brother; and he found her dark-haired and dark-skinned, almost Spanish in her look,—the cast of her features grave almost to sadness. She spoke, too, but little, and never once reminded him, by a tone, a gesture, or a word, of his old comrade.

Ah! how these self-created portraits do puzzle and disconcert us through life! How they will obtrude themselves into the foreground, making the real and the actual but mere shadows in the distance! What seeming contradiction, too, do they create as often as we come into contact with the true, and find it all so widely the reverse of what we dreamed of! How often has the weary emigrant sighed over his own created promised land in the midst of the silent forest or the desolate prairie! How has the poor health-seeker sunk heavy-hearted amid scenes which, had he not misconstrued them to himself, he had deemed a paradise!

These "phrenographs" are very dangerous paintings, and the more so that we sketch them in unconsciously.

"Jack is the best of them; that's clear," said Conway, as he walked along; and yet, with all his affection for him, the thought did not bring the pleasure it ought to have done.

CHAPTER XV
A HOME SCENE

When Paul Kellett described Mr. Davenport Dunn's almost triumphal entry into Dublin, he doubtless fancied in his mind the splendors that awaited him at home; the troops of servants in smart liveries, the homage of his household, and the costly entertainment which most certainly should celebrate his arrival. Public rumor had given to the hospitalities of that house a wide extended fame. The fashionable fishmonger of the capital, his Excellency's "purveyor" of game, the celebrated Italian warehouse, all proclaimed him their best customer. "Can't let you have that turbot, sir, till I hear from Mr. Dunn." "Only two pheasants to be had, sir, and ordered for Mr. Dunn." "The white truffles only taken by one gentleman in town. None but Mr. Dunn would pay the price." The culinary traditions of his establishment threw the Castle into the background, and Kellett revelled in the notion of the great festivity that now welcomed his return. "Lords and earls—the biggest salmon in the market—the first men of the land—and lobster sauce—ancient names and good families—with grouse, and 'Sneyd's Twenty-one'—that 's what you may call life! It is wonderful, wonderful!" Now, when Paul enunciated the word "wonderful" in this sense, he meant it to imply that it was shameful, distressing, and very melancholy for the prospects of humanity generally. And then he amused himself by speculating whether Dunn liked it all,—whether the unaccustomed elegance of these great dinners did not distress and pain him rather than give pleasure, and whether the very consciousness of his own low origin wasn't a poison that mingled in every cup he tasted.

"It's no use talking," muttered he to himself; "a man must be bred to it, like everything else. The very servants behind his chair frighten him; he's, maybe, eating with his knife, or he's putting salt where he ought to put sugar, or he does n't take the right kind of wine with his meat. Beecher says he 'd know any fellow just by that, and then it's 'all up' with him. Wonderful, wonderful!"

How would it have affected these speculations had Kellett known that, while he was indulging them, Dunn had quietly issued by a back door from his house, and, having engaged a car, set out towards Clontarf? A drearier drive of a dreary evening none need wish for. Occasional showers were borne on the gusty wind, swooping past as though hurrying to some elemental congress far away, while along the shore the waves beat with that irregular plash that betokens wild weather at sea. The fitful moonlight rather heightened than diminished the dismal aspect of the scenery. For miles the bleak strand stretched away, no headland nor even a hillock marking the coast; the spectral gable of a ruined church being the only object visible against the leaden sky. Little garlands of paper, the poor tributes of the very poor, decorated the graves and the head-stones, and, as they rustled in the night wind, sounded like ghostly whisperings. The driver piously crossed himself as they passed the "un-cannie" spot, but Dunn took no heed of it. To wrap his cloak tighter about him, to shelter more closely beneath his umbrella, were all that the dreary scene exacted from him; and except when a vivid flash of lightning made the horse swerve from the road and dash down into the rough shingle of the strand, he never adverted to the way or the weather.

"What's this,—where are we going?" cried he, impatiently.

"'T is the flash that frightened the beast, yer honner," said the man; "and if it was plazin' to you, I 'd rather tarn back again."

"Turn back—where to?"

"To town, yer honner."

"Nothing of the kind; drive on, and quickly too. We have five miles yet before us, and it will be midnight ere we get over them at this rate."

Sulkily and unwillingly did he obey; and, turning from the shore, they entered upon a low, sandy road that traversed a wide and dreary tract, barely elevated a few feet above the sea. By degrees the little patches of grass and fern disappeared, and nothing stretched on either side but low sand hummocks, scantily covered with rushes. Sea-shells crackled beneath the wheels as they went, and after a while the deep booming of the sea thundering heavily along a sandy shore, apprised them that they had crossed the narrow neck of land which divided two bays.

"Are you quite certain you I 've taken the right road, my man?" cried Dunn, as he observed something like hesitation in the other's manner.

"It ought to be somewhere hereabout we turn off," said the man, getting down to examine more accurately from beneath. "There was a little cross put up to show the way, but I don't see it."

"But you have been here before. Ton told me you knew the place."

"I was here onst, and, by the same token, I swore I'd never come again. I lamed the best mare I ever put a collar on, dragging through this deep sand. Wirra, wirra! why the blazes would n't he live where other Christians do! There it is now; I see a light. Ah! bother them, it's out again."

Pushing forward as well as he might in the direction he had seen the light, he floundered heavily on, the wheels sinking nearly to the axles, and the horse stumbling at every step.

"Your horse is worth nothing, my good fellow; he has n't strength to keep his legs," said Dunn, angrily.

"Good or bad, I'll give you lave to broil me on a gridiron if ever ye catch me coming the same road again. Ould Duun won't have much company if he waits for me to bring them."

"I'll take good care not to tempt you!" said Dunn, angrily.

And now they plodded on in moody silence till they issued forth upon a little flat space, bounded on three sides by the sea, in the midst of which a small two-storied house stood, defended from the sea by a rough stone breakwater that rose above the lower windows.

"There it is now, bad luck to it!" said the carman, savagely, for his horse was so completely exhausted that he was obliged to walk at his head and lift him at every step.

"You may remain here till I want you," said Dunn, getting down and plodding his way through the heavy sand. Flakes of frothy seadrift swept past him as he went, and the wild wind carried the spray far inland in heavy showers, beating against the walls and windows of the lonely house, and making the slates rattle. A low wall of large stones across the door showed that all entrance by that means was denied; and Dunn turned towards the back of the house, where, sheltered by the low wall, a small door was detectable. He knocked several times at this before any answer was returned; when, at last, a harsh voice from within called out, —

"Don't ye hear who it is? confound ye! Open the door at once!" and Dunn was admitted into a large kitchen, where in a great straw chair beside the fire was seated the remains of a once powerful man, and who, although nearly ninety years of age, still preserved a keen eye, a searching look, and a quick impatience of manner rarely observable at his age.

"Well, father, how are you?" said Dunn, taking him affectionately by both hands, and looking kindly in his face.

"Hearty, — stout and hearty," said the old man. "When did you arrive?"

"A couple of hours ago. I did not wait for anything but a biscuit and a glass of wine, when I set out here to see you. And you are well?"

"Just as you see: an odd pain or so across the back, and a swimming of the head,—a kind of giddiness now and then, that's all. Put the light over there till I have a look at you. You 're thinner, Davy,—a deal thinner, than when you went away."

"I have nothing the matter with me; a little tired or so, that's all," said Dunn, hastily. "And how are things doing here, father, since I left?"

"There's little to speak of," said the old man. "There never is much doing at this season of the year. You heard, of course, that Gogarty has lost his suit; they 're moving for a new trial, but they won't get it. Lanty Moore can't pay up the rest of the purchase for Slanestown, and I told Hankes to buy it in. Kelly's murderer was taken on Friday last, near Kilbride, and offers to tell, God knows what, if they won't hang him; and Sir Gilbert North is to be the new Secretary, if, as the 'Evening Mail' says, Mr. Davenport Dunn concurs in the appointment"—and here the old man laughed till his eyes ran over. "That's all the news, Davy, of the last week; and now tell me yours. The papers say you were dining with kings and queens, and driving about in royal coaches all over the Continent,—was it true, Davy?"

"You got my letters, of course, father?"

"Yes; and I could n't make out the names, they were all new and strange to me. I want to have from yourself what like the people are,—are they as hard-working, are they as 'cute as our own? There's just two things now in the world,—coal and industry,—sorra more than that And so you dined with the King of France?"

"With the Emperor, father. I dined twice; he took me over to Fontainebleau and made me stay the day."

"You could tell him many a thing he'd never hear from another, Davy; you could explain to him what's doing here, and how he might imitate it over there,—rooting out the old vermin and getting new stock in the land,— eh, Davy?"

"He needs no counsels, at least from such as me," said Dunn.

"Faith, he might have worse, far worse. An Encumbered Estate Court would do all his work for him well, and the dirty word 'Confiscation' need never be uttered!"

"He knows the road he wants to go," said Dunn, curtly.

"So he may; but that does n't prove it 's the best way."

"Whichever path he takes he'll tread it firmly, father, and that's more than half the battle. If you only saw what a city he has made Paris—"

"That's just what I don't like. What's the good of beautifying and gilding or ornamenting what you 're going to riddle with grape and smash with round shot? It's like dressing a sweep in a field-marshal's uniform, And we all know where it will be to-morrow or next day."

"That we don't, sir. You 're not aware that these spacious thoroughfares, these wide squares, these extended terraces, are so contrived that columns may march and manoeuvre in them, squadrons charge, and great artillery act through them. The proudest temples of that splendid city serve as bastions; the great Louvre itself is less a palace than a fortress."

"Ay, ay, ay," cackled the old man, to whom these revelations opened a new vista of thought. "But what's the use of it, after all, Davy? He must trust somebody; and when it comes to that with anybody in life, where 's his security, tell me that? But let us talk about home. Is it true the Ministry is going out?"

"They're safer than ever; take my word for it, father, that these fellows know the trick of it better than all that went before them. They 'll just do whatever the nation and the 'Times' dictate to them; a little slower, mayhap, than they are ordered, but they 'll do it They have no embarrassments of a policy of any kind; and the only pretence of a principle they possess is to sit on the Treasury benches."

"And they 're right, Davy,—they 're right," said the old man, energetically.

"I don't doubt but they are, sir; the duty of the pilot is to take charge of the ship, but not to decide the port she sails for."

"I wish you were one of them, Davy; they'd suit you, and you 'd suit *them*."

"So we should, sir; and who knows what may turn up? I'm not impatient"

"That's right, Davy; that's the lesson I always taught you; wait,—wait!"

"When did you see Driscoll, father?" asked Dunn, after a pause.

"He was here last week; he's up to his ears about that claim to the Beecher estate, Lord—Lord—What's his—"

"Lackington."

"Yes, Lord Lackington. He says if you were once come home, you 'd get him leave to search the papers in the Record Tower at the Castle, and that it would be the making of himself if anything came out of it."

"He's always mare's-nesting, sir," said Dunn, carelessly.

"Faith, he has contrived to feather his own nest, anyhow," said the old man, laughing. "He lent Lord Glengariff five thousand pounds t' other day at six per cent, and on as good security as the Bank."

"Does he pretend to have discovered anything new with respect to that claim?"

"He says there's just enough to frighten them, and that *your* help—the two of ye together—could work it well."

"He has not, then, found out the claimant?"

"He has his name, and the regiment he's in, but that's all. He was talking of writing to him."

"If he's wise, he'll let it alone. What chance would a poor soldier in the ranks have against a great lord, if he had all the right in the world on his side?"

"So I told him; but he said we could make a fine thing out of it, for all that; and, somehow, Davy, he's mighty seldom mistaken."

"If he be, sir, it is because he has hitherto only meddled with what lay within his power. He can scheme and plot and track out a clew in the little world he has lived in; but let him be careful how he venture upon that wider ocean of life where his craft would be only a cock-boat."

"He hasn't *your* stuff in him, Davy," cried the old man, in ecstasy; and a very slight flush rose to the other's cheek at the words, but whether of pride, or shame, or pleasure, it were hard to say. "I 've nothing to offer you, Davy, except a cut of cold pork; could you eat it?" said the old man.

"I'm not hungry, father; I'm tired somewhat, but not hungry."

"I'm tired, too," said the old man, sighing; "but, to be sure, it's time for me,—I 'll be eighty-nine if I live till the fourth of next month. That's a long life, Davy."

"And it has been an active one, sir."

"I 've seen great changes in my time, Davy," continued he, following out his own thoughts. "I was in the Volunteers when we bullied the English, and they 've paid us off for it since, that they have! I was one of the jury when Jackson died in the dock, and if he was alive now, maybe it's a lord of the Treasury he 'd be. Everything is changed, and everybody too. Do you remember Kellett, of Kellett's Court, that used to drive on the Circular Road with six horses?"

Dunn nodded an assent.

"His liveries were light-blue and silver, and Lord Castletown's was the same; and Kellett said to him one day, 'My Lord,' says he, 'we're always mistaken for each other; could n't we hit on a way to prevent it?' 'I'm willing,' says my Lord, 'if I only knew how.' 'Then I 'll tell you,' says Kellett; 'make your people follow your own example and turn their coats,—that'll do it,' says he." And the old man laughed till his eyes swam. "What's become of them Kelletts?" added he, sharply.

"Ruined,—sold out"

"To be sure, I remember all about it; and the young fellow,—Paul was his name,—where's he?"

"He's not so very young now," said Dunn, smiling; "he has a clerkship in the Customs,—a poor place it is."

"I'm glad of it," said he, fiercely; "there was an old score between us,— that's his father and me,—and I knew I would n't die till it was settled."

"These are not kindly feelings, father," said Dunn, mildly.

"No; but they 're natural ones, and that's as good," said the old man, with an energy that seemed to defy his age. "Where would I be now, where would you, if it was only kindness we thought of? There wasn't a man in all Ireland I wanted to be quite with so much as old Kellett of Kellett's Court; and you'd not wonder if you knew why; but I won't tell."

Davenport Dunn's cheek grew crimson and then deadly pale, but he never uttered a word.

"And what's more," continued the old man, energetically, "I'd pay the debt off to his children and his children's children with interest, if I could."

Still was the other silent; and the old man looked angry that he had not succeeded in stimulating the curiosity he had declared he would not gratify.

"Fate has done the work already, sir," said Dunn, gravely. "Look where *we* are, and where *they!*"

"That 's true,—that's true; we have a receipt in full for it all; but I 'd like to show it to him. I 'd like to say to him, 'Mr. Kellett, once upon a time, when my son there was a child—'"

"Father, father, these memories can neither make us wiser nor happier," broke in Dunn, in a voice of deep emotion. "Had I taken upon me to carry through life the burden of resentments, my back had been broken long ago; and from your own prudent counsels I learned that this could never lead to success. The men whom destiny has crushed are like bankrupt debtors, and to pursue them is but to squander your own resources."

The old man sat moodily, muttering indistinctly to himself, and evidently little moved by the words he had listened to.

"Are you going away already?" cried he, suddenly, as Dunn rose from his chair.

"Yes, sir; I have a busy day before me to-morrow, and need some sleep to prepare for it."

"What will you be doing to-morrow, Davy?" asked the old man, while a bright gleam of pride lighted up his eyes and illuminated his whole face.

"I have deputations to receive,—half a dozen, at least. The Drainage Commission, too, will want me, and I must contrive to have half an hour for the Inland Navigation people; then the Attorney-General will call about these prosecutions, and I have not made up my mind about them; and the Castle folk will need some clew to my intentions about the new Secretary; there are some twenty provincial editors, besides, waiting for directions, not to speak of private and personal requests, some of which I must not refuse to hear. As to letters, three days won't get through them; so that you see, father, I do need a little rest beforehand."

"God bless you, my boy,—God bless you, Davy," cried the old man, tenderly, grasping his hand in both his own. "Keep the head clear, and trust nobody; that's the secret,—trust nobody; the only mistakes I ever made in life was when I forgot that rule." And affectionately kissing him, the father dismissed his son, muttering blessings on him as he went.

CHAPTER XVI
DAVIS VERSUS DUNN

Davenport Dunn had not exaggerated when he spoke of a busy day for the morrow. As early as eight o'clock was he at breakfast, and before nine the long back parlor, with its deep bay-window, was crowded like the waiting-room of a fashionable physician. Indeed, in the faces of anxiety, eagerness, and impatience of those assembled there, there was a resemblance. With a tact which natural shrewdness and long habit could alone confer, Mr. Clowes, the butler, knew exactly where each arrival should be introduced; and while railway directors, bank governors, and great contractors indiscriminately crowded the large dining-room, peers and right honorables filled the front drawing-room, the back one being reserved for law officers of the Crown, and such secret emissaries as came on special mission from the Castle. From the hall, crammed with frieze-coated countryfolk, to the little conservatory on the stairs, where a few ladies were grouped, every space was occupied. Either from previous acquaintance, or guided by the name of the visitor, Mr. Clowes had little difficulty in assigning him his fitting place, dropping, as he accompanied him, some few words, as the rank and station of the individual might warrant his addressing to him. "I 'll let Mr. Dunn know your Lordship is here this instant; he is now just engaged with the Chief Baron." — "He 'll see you, Sir Samuel, next." — "Mr. Wilcox, you have no chance for two hours; the Foyle deputation is just gone in." — "You need scarcely wait to-day, Mr. Tobin; there are eighteen before you." — "Colonel Craddock, you are to come on Saturday, and bring the plans with you." — "Too late, Mr. Dean; his Grace the Archbishop waited till a quarter to eleven, the appointment is now for to-morrow at one." — "No use in staying, my honest fellow, your own landlord could n't see Mr. Dunn to-day." In the midst of such brief phrases as these, while he scattered hopes and disappointments about him, he suddenly paused to read a card, stealing a quick glance at the individual who presented it "'Mr. Annesley Beecher.' By appointment, sir?"

"Well, I suppose I might say yes," muttered the visitor, while he turned to a short and very overdressed person at his side for counsel in the difficulty.

"To be sure—by appointment," said the other, confidently, while he bestowed on the butler a look of unmistakable defiance.

"And this—gentleman—is with you, sir?" asked the butler, pausing ere he pronounced the designation. "Might I request to have his name?"

"Captain Davis," said the short man, interposing. "Write it under your own, Beecher."

While Mr. Annesley Beecher was thus occupied,—and, sooth to say, it was an office he did not discharge with much despatch,—Clowes had ample time to scan the appearance and style of the strangers.

"If you 'll step this way, sir," said Clowes, addressing Beecher only, "I'll send in your card at once." And he ushered them as he spoke into the thronged dinner-room, whose crowded company sat silent and moody, each man regarding his neighbor with a kind of reproachful expression, as though the especial cause of the long delay he was undergoing.

"You ought to 'tip' that flunkey, Beecher," said Davis, as soon as they were alone in a window.

"Haven't the tin, Master Grog!" said the other, laughing; while he added, in a lower voice, "Do you know, Grog, I don't feel quite comfortable here. Rather mixed company, ain't it, for a fellow who only goes out of a Sunday?"

"All safe," muttered Davis. "These all are bank directors or railway swells. I wish we had the robbing of them!"

"Good deal of humbug about all this, ain't there?" whispered Beecher, as he threw his eyes over the crowded room.

"Of course there is," replied the other. "While he's keeping us all kicking our shins here, he's reading the 'Times,' or gossiping with a friend, or weighing a double letter for the post. It was the dentists took up the dodge first, and the nobs followed them."

"I 'm not going to stand it much longer, Grog. I tell you I don't feel comfortable."

"Stuff and nonsense! You don't fancy any of these chaps has a writ in his pocket, do you? Why, I can tell you every man in the room. That little fellow, with the punch-colored shorts, is chairman of the Royal Canal Company. I know *him*, and he knows *me*. He had me 'up' about a roulette-table on board of one of the boats, and if it had n't been for a trifling incident that occurred to his wife at Boulogne, where she went for the bathing, and which I broke to him in confidence—But stay, he's coming over to speak to me."

"How d'ye do, Captain Davis?" said the stranger, with the air of a man resolved to brave a difficulty, while he threw into the manner a tone of haughty patronage.

"Pretty bobbish, Mr. Hailes; and *you*, the same I hope."

"Well, thank you. You never paid me that little visit you promised at Leixlip."

"I 've been so busy of late; up to my ears, as they say. Going to start a new company, and thinking of asking your assistance too."

"What's the nature of it?"

"Well, it's a kind of a mutual self-securing sort of thing against family accidents. You understand,—a species of universal guarantee to insure domestic peace and felicity,—a thing that will come home to us all; and I only want a few good names in the direction, to give the shares a push."

Beecher looked imploringly, to try and restrain him; but he went on,—

"May I take the liberty to put you down on the committee of management?"

Before any answer could come to this speech, Mr. Clowes called out in a deep voice,—

"Mr. Annesley Beecher and Captain Davis;" and flung wide the door for them to pass out.

"Why did you say that to him, Grog?" whispered Beecher, as they moved along.

"Just because I was watching the way he looked at me. He had a hardy, bold expression on his face that showed he needed a reminder, and so I gave him one. Always have the first blow when you see a fellow means to strike you."

Mr. Davenport Dunn rose as the visitors entered the' room, and having motioned to them to be seated, took his place with his back to the fire,—a significant intimation that he did not anticipate a lengthy review. Whether it was that he had not previously settled in his own mind how to open the object of his visit, or that something in Dunn's manner and appearance unlike what he anticipated had changed his intention; but certain is it that Beecher felt confused and embarrassed, and when reminded by Dunn's saying, "I am at your service, sir," he turned a most imploring look towards Davis to come to his rescue. The captain, however, with more tact, paid no attention to the appeal; and Beecher, with an immense effort, stammered out, "I have taken the liberty to call on you. I have come here today in consequence of a letter—that is, my brother, Lord Lackington—You know my brother?"

"I have that honor, sir."

"Well, in writing to me a few days back, he added a hurried postscript, saying he had just seen you; that you were then starting for Ireland, where, on your arrival, it would be well I should wait upon you at once."

"Did his Lordship mention with what object, sir?"

"I can't exactly say that he did. He said something about your being his man of business, thoroughly acquainted with all his affairs, and so, of course, I expected—I believed, at least—that you might be able to lead the way,—to show me the line of country, as one might call it," added he, with a desperate attempt to regain his ease by recurring to his favorite phraseology.

"Really, sir, my engagements are so numerous that I have to throw myself on the kindness of those who favor me with a call to explain the object of their visit."

"I haven't got Lackington's letter about me; but if I remember aright, all he said was, 'See Dunn as soon as you can, and he 'll put you up to a thing or two,' or words to that effect."

"I regret deeply, sir, that the expressions give me no clew to the matter in hand."

"If this ain't fencing, my name isn't Davis," said Grog, breaking in. "You know well, without any going about the bush, what he comes about; and all this skirmishing is only to see if he's as well 'up' as yourself in his own business. Now then, no more chaff, but go in at once."

"May I ask who is this gentleman?"

"A friend,—a very particular friend of mine," said Beecher, quickly,— "Captain Davis."

"Captain Davis," repeated Dunn, in a half voice to himself, as if to assist his memory to some effort,—"Captain Davis."

"Just so," said Grog, defiantly,—"Captain Davis."

"Does his Lordship's letter mention I should have the honor of a call from Captain Davis, sir?"

"No; but as he's my own intimate friend,—a gentleman who possesses all my confidence,—I thought, indeed, I felt, the importance of having his advice upon any questions that might arise in this interview."

"I 'm afraid, sir, you have subjected your friend to a most unprofitable inconvenience."

"The match postponed till further notice," whispered Grog.

"I beg pardon, sir," said Dunn, not overhearing the remark.

"I was a saying that no race would come off to-day, in consequence of the inclemency of the weather," said Grog, as he adjusted his shirt collar.

"Am I to conclude, then," said Beecher, "that you have not any communication to make to me?"

"No, you ain't," broke in Grog, quickly. "He don't like me, that's all, and he has n't the manliness to say it."

"On the contrary, sir, I feel all the advantage of your presence on this occasion, all the benefit of that straightforward manner of putting the question which saves us so much valuable time."

Grog bowed an acknowledgment of the compliment, but with a grin on his face that showed in what spirit he accepted it.

"Lord Lackington did not speak to you about my allowance?" asked Beecher, losing all patience.

"No, sir, not a word."

"He did not allude to a notion—he did not mention a plan—he did not discuss people called O'Reilly, did he?" asked he, growing more and more confused and embarrassed.

"Not a syllable with reference to such a name escaped him, sir."

"Don't you see," said Grog, rising, "that you 'll have to look for the explanation to the second column of the 'Times,' where 'A. B. will hear something to his advantage if he calls without C.D.'?"

Davenport Dunn paid no attention to this remark, but stood calmly impassive before them.

"It comes to this, then, that Lackington has been hoaxing me," said Beecher, rising, with an expression of ill-temper on his face.

"I should rather suggest another possibility," said Dunn, politely; "that, knowing how far his Lordship has graciously reposed his own confidence in me, he has generously extended to me the chance of obtaining the same position of trust on the part of his brother,—an honor I am most ambitious to attain. If you are disengaged on Sunday next," added he, in a low voice, "and would favor me with your company at dinner, alone,—quite alone—"

Beecher bowed an assent in silence, casting a cautious glance towards Davis, who was scanning the contents of the morning paper.

"Till then," muttered Dunn, while he added aloud, "A good-morning," and bowed them both to the door.

"Well, you are a soft un, there's no denying it," said Davis, as they gained the street.

"What d'ye mean?" cried Beecher, angrily.

"Why, don't you see how you spoiled all? I'd have had the whole story out of him, but you would n't give me time to 'work the oracle.' He only wanted to show us how cunning he was,—that he was deep and all that; and when he saw that we were all wonder and amazement about his shrewdness, then he 'd have gone to business."

"Not a bit of it, Master Grog; that fellow's wide awake, I tell you."

"So much the worse for you, then, that's all."

"Why so?"

"Because you're a going to dine with him on Sunday next, all alone. I heard it, though you did n't think I was listening, and I saw the look that passed, too, as much as to say, 'We 'll not have that fellow;' and that's the reason I say, 'So much the worse for you.'"

"Why, what can he do, with all his craft? He can't make me put my name to paper; and if he did, much good would it do him."

"*You* can't make running against the like of him," said Grog, contemptuously. "He has an eye in his head like a dog-fox. *You* 've no chance with him. He could n't double on me,—he 'd not try it; but he 'll play *you* like a trout in a fish-pond."

"What if I send him an excuse, then,—shall I do that?"

"No. You must go, if it was only to show that you suspect nothing; but keep your eyes open, watch the ropes, and come over to me when the 'heat is run.'"

And with this counsel they parted.

CHAPTER XVII
THE "PENSIONNAT GODARDE"

Let us ask our reader to turn for a brief space from these scenes and these actors, and accompany us to that rich plain which stretches to the northwest of Brussels, and where, on the slope of the gentle hill, beneath the royal palace of Lacken, stands a most picturesque old house, known as the Château of the Three Fountains. The very type of a château of the Low Countries, from its gabled fronts, all covered with festooned rhododendron, to its trim gardens, peopled with leaden deities and ornamented by the three fountains to which it owes its name, nothing was wanting. From the plump little figure who blew his trumpet on the weather-vane, to the gaudily gilded pleasure-boat that peeped from amidst the tall water-lilies of the fish-pond, all proclaimed the peculiar taste of a people who loved to make nature artificial, and see the instincts of their own quaint natures reproduced in every copse and hedgerow around them.

All the little queer contrivances of Dutch ingenuity were there,—mock shrubs, which blossomed as you touched a spring; jets, that spurted out as you trod on a certain spot; wooden figures, worked by mechanisms, lowered the drawbridge to let you pass; nor was the toll-keeper forgotten, who touched his cap in salutation. Who were they who had designed all these pleasant conceits, and what fate had fallen on their descendants, we know not. At the time we speak of, the château was a select Pensionnat for ten young ladies, presided over by Madame Godarde, "of whom all particulars might be learned at Cadel's Library, Old Bond Street, or by personal application to the Rev. Pierre Faucher, Evangelical Minister, Adam Street, Strand, London." It was, as we have said, select,—the most select of Pensionnats. The ten young ladies were chosen after investigations the most scrutinizing; the conditions of the admission verged on the impossible. The mistress realized in her person all the rare attributes of an elevated rank and a rigid Protestantism, while the educational programme was little short of a fellowship course. Just as being a guardsman is supposed to confer a certain credit over a man's outset in life, it was meant that being an *élève* of Madame Godarde should enter the world with a due and becoming *prestige*; for while the range of acquirements included something at least from every branch of human science, the real superiority and strength of the establishment lay in the moral culture observed there; and as the female teachers were selected from amongst the models of the sex, the male instructors were warranted as having triumphed over temptations not inferior to St. Anthony's. The ritual of the establishment well responded to all the difficulties of admission. It was almost conventual in strictness; and even to the uniform dress worn by the pupils there was much that recalled the nunnery. The quiet uniformity of an unbroken existence, the changeless fashion of each day's life, impressed even young and buoyant hearts, and toned down to seriousness spirits that nature had formed to be light and joyous. One by one, they who had entered there underwent this change; a little longer might be the struggle with some, the end was alike to all; nay, not to all! there was one whose temperament resisted to the last, and who, after three years of the durance, was just as unbroken in spirit, just as high in heart, just as gay, as when she first crossed the threshold. Gifted with one of those elastic natures which rise against every pressure, she accepted every hardship as the occasion for fresh resource, and met each new infliction, whether it were a severe task, or even punishment, with a high-hearted resolve not to be vanquished. There was nothing in her appearance that indicated this hardihood: she was a fair, slight girl, whose features were feminine almost to childishness. The gray-blue eyes, shaded with deep lashes; the beautifully formed mouth, on which a half-saucy smile so often played; a half-timid expression conveyed in the ever-changing color of her cheek, — suggested the expression of a highly impressionable and undecided nature; yet this frail, delicate girl, whose birdlike voice reminded one of childhood, swayed and ruled all her companions. She added to these personal graces abilities of a high order. Skilled in every accomplishment, she danced and sang and drew and played better than her fellows; she spoke several modern languages fluently, and even caught up their local dialects with a quickness quite marvellous. She could warble the Venetian barcarole with all the soft accents of an Adriatic tongue, or sing the Bauerlied of the Tyrol with every cadence of the peasant's fancy. With a memory so retentive that she could generally repeat what she had once read over attentively, she had powers of mimicry that enabled her to produce at will everything noticeable that crossed her. A vivid fancy, too, threw its glittering light over all these faculties, so that even the commonplace incidents of daily life grouped themselves dramatically in her mind, and events the least striking were made the origin of situation and sentiment, brilliant with wit and poetry.

Great as all these advantages were, they were aided, and not inconsiderably, by other and adventitious ones. She was reputed to be a great heiress. How and when and why this credit attached to her, it were hard to say; assuredly she had never given it any impulse. She spoke, indeed, constantly of her father—her only living relation—as of one who never grudged her any indulgence, and she showed her schoolfellows the handsome presents which from time to time he sent her; these in their costliness—so unlike the gifts common to her age—may possibly have assisted the belief in her great wealth. But however founded, the impression prevailed that she was to be the possessor of millions, and in the course of destiny, to be what her companions called her in jest—a Princess.

Nor did the designation seem ill applied. Of all the traits her nature exhibited, none seemed so conspicuous as that of "birth." The admixture of timidity and haughtiness, that blended gentleness with an air of command, a certain instinctive acceptance of whatever deference was shown her as a matter of right and due, all spoke of "blood;" and her walk, her voice, her slightest gesture, were in keeping with this impression. Even they who liked her least, and were most jealous of her fascination, never called her Princess in any mockery. No, strange enough, the title was employed with all the significance of respect, and as such did she receive it.

If it were not that, in her capricious moods, Nature has moulded stranger counterfeits than this, we might incur some risk of incredulity from our reader when we say that the Princess was no other than Grog Davis's daughter!

Davis had been a man of stratagems from his very beginning in life. All his gains had been acquired by dexterity and trick. Whatever he had accomplished was won as at a game where some other paid the loss. His mind, consequently, fashioned itself to the condition in which he lived, and sharpness and shrewdness and over-reaching seemed to him not alone the only elements of success, but the only qualities worth honoring. He had seen honesty and imbecility so often in company that he thought them convertible terms; and yet this man—"leg," outcast, knave that he was—rose above all the realities of a life of roguery in one aspiration,—to educate his child in purity, to screen her from the contamination of his own set, to bring her up amongst all the refining influences of care and culture, and make her, as he said to himself, "the equal of the best lady in the land!" To place her amongst the well-born and wealthy, to have her where her origin could not be traced, where no clew would connect her with himself, had cost him a greater exercise of ingenuity than the deepest scheme he had ever plotted on the turf. That exchange of references on which Madame Godarde's exclusiveness so peremptorily insisted was only to be met at heavy cost. The distinguished baronet who stood sponsor to Grog Davis's respectability received cash for the least promising of promissory notes in return, and the lady who waited on Madame Godarde in her brougham "to make acquaintance with the person who was to have charge of her young relative," was the distracted mother of a foolish young man who had given bills to Davis for several thousands, and who by this special mission obtained possession of the documents. In addition to these direct, there were many other indirect sacrifices. Grog was obliged for a season to forego all the habits and profits of his daily life, to live in a sort of respectable seclusion, his servants in mourning, and himself in the deepest sable for the loss of a wife who had died twelve years before. In fact, he had to take out a species of moral naturalization, the details of which seemed interminable, and served to convince him that respectability was not the easy, indolent thing he had hitherto imagined it.

If Davis had been called on to furnish a debtor and creditor account of the transaction, the sum spent in the accomplishment of this feat would have astonished his assignee. As he said himself, "Fifteen hundred would n't see him through it." It is but fair to say that the amount so represented comprised the very worst of bad debts, but Grog cared little for that; his theory was that there was n't the difference between a guinea and a pound in the best bill from Baring's and the worst paper in Holywell Street. "You can always get either your money or your money's worth," said he, "and very frequently the last is the better of the two."

If it was a proud day for the father as he consigned his daughter to Madame Godarde's care, it was no less a happy one for Lizzy Davis, as she found herself in the midst of companions of her own age, and surrounded with all the occupations and appliances of a life of elegance. Brought up from infancy in a small school in a retired part of Cornwall, she had only known her father during the two or three off months of that probationary course of respectability we have alluded to. With all his affection for his child, and every desire to give it utterance, Davis was so conscious of his own defects in education, and the blemishes which his tone of mind and thought would inevitably exhibit, that he had to preserve a sort of estrangement towards her, and guard himself against whatever might prejudice him in her esteem. If, then, by a thousand acts of kindness and liberality he gained on her affection, there was that in his cold and distant manner that as totally repelled all confidence. To escape from the dull uniformity of that dreary home, where a visitor never entered, nor any intercourse with the world was maintained, to a scene redolent of life, with gay light-hearted associates, all pursuing the same sunny paths, to engage her brilliant faculties in a variety of congenial pursuits, wherein there was only so much of difficulty as inspired zeal, to enter on an existence wherein each day imparted the sense of new acquirement, was a happiness that verged on ecstasy. It needed not all the flatteries that surrounded her to make this seem a paradise; but she had these, too, and in so many ways. Some loved her light-heartedness, and that gay spirit that floated like an atmosphere about her; others praised her gracefulness and her beauty; some preferred to these, those versatile gifts of mind that gave her the mastery over whatever she desired to learn; and there were those who dwelt on the great fortune she was to have, and the great destiny that awaited her.

How often in the sportive levity of happy girlhood had they asked her what life she should choose for herself, — what station, and what land to live in! They questioned her in all sincerity, believing she had but to wish, to have the existence that pleased her. Then what tender caresses followed, — what flattering entreaties that the dear Princess would not forget Josephine or Gertrude or Julia, in the days of her greatness, but would recognize those who had been her loved schoolfellows years before!

"What a touchstone of your tact will it be, Lizzy, when you 're a duchess," said one, "to meet one of us in a watering-place or on a steamboat, and to explain, delicately enough, not to hurt us, to his Grace the Duke that you knew us as girls, and how provoking if you should call me Jane or Clara!"

"And then the charming condescension of your inquiry if we were married, though a half-bashful and an awkward-looking man should be standing by at our interview, waiting to be presented, and afraid to be spoken to. Or worse than that, the long, terrible pauses in conversation, which show how afraid you are lest we should tumble into reminiscences."

"Oh, Lizzy darling," cried another, "do be a duchess for a moment, and show how you would treat us all. It would be charming."

"You seem to be forgetting, mesdames," said she, haughtily, "what an upstart you are making of me. This wondrous elevation, which is at once to make me forget my friends and myself, does not present to my eyes the same dazzling effect. In fact, I can imagine myself a duchess to-morrow without losing either my self-respect or my memory."

"Daisy dearest, do not be angry with us," cried one, addressing her by the pet name which they best loved to call her.

"I am rather angry with myself that I should leave no better impression behind me. Yes," added she, in a tone of sadness, "I am going away."

"Oh, darling Lizzy, — oh, Daisy, don't say so," broke out so many voices together.

"Too true! dearest friends," said she, throwing her arms around those nearest to her. "I only learned it this morning. Madame Godarde came to my room to say papa had written for me, and would come over to fetch me in about a fortnight I ought doubtless to be so happy at the prospect of going home; but I have no mother,—I have not either brother or sister; and here, amidst you, I have every tie that can attach the heart. When shall I ever live again amidst such loving hearts?—when shall life be the happy dream I have felt it here?"

"But think of us, Daisy, forlorn and deserted," cried one, sobbing.

"Yes, Lizzy," broke in another, "imagine the day-by-day disappointments that will break on us as we discover that this pleasure or that spot owed its charm to you,—that it was your voice made the air melody, your accents gave the words their feeling! Fancy us as we find out—as find out we must—that the affection we bore you bound us into one sisterhood—"

"Oh," burst Lizzy in, "do let me carry away some of my heart to him who should have it all, and make not my last moments with you too painful to bear. Remember, too, that it is but a passing separation; we can and we will write to each other. I 'll never weary of hearing all about you and this dear spot. There's not a rosebud opening to the morning air but will bring some fragrance to my heart; and that dear old window! how often shall I sit at it in fancy, and look over the fair plain before us. Bethink you, too, that I am only the first launched into that wide ocean of life where we are all to meet hereafter."

"And be the dear, dear friends we now are," cried another. And so they hung upon her neck and kissed her, bathing her soft tresses with their tears, and indulging in all the rapture of that sorrow no ecstasy of joy can equal.

CHAPTER XVIII
SOME DOINGS OF MR. DRISCOLL

"There it is, Bella," said Kellett, as he entered the cottage at nightfall, and threw a sealed letter on the table. "I hadn't the courage to open it. A fellow came into the office and said, 'Is one Kellett here? This is a letter from Mr. Davenport Dunn.' *He* was Mister, and I was *one* Kellett. Wasn't I low enough when I couldn't say a word to it?—wasn't I down-in the world when I had to bear it in silence?"

"Shall I read it for you?" said she, gently.

"Do, darling; but before you begin, give me a glass of whiskey-and-water. I want courage for it, and something tells me, Bella, I'll need courage too."

"Come, come, papa, this is not like yourself; this is not the old Albuera spirit you are so justly proud of."

"Five-and-thirty years' hard struggling with the world never improved a man's pluck. There was n't a fellow in the Buffs had more life in him than Paul Kellett. It was in general orders never to sell my traps or camp furniture when I was reported missing; for, as General Pack said, 'Kellett is sure to turn up to-morrow or the day after.' And look at me now!" cried he, bitterly; "and as to selling me out, they don't show me much mercy, Bella, do they?"

She made no reply, but slowly proceeded to break the seal of the letter.

"What a hurry ye're in to read bad news!" cried he, peevishly; "can't you wait till I finish this?" And he pointed to the glass, which he sipped slowly, like one wishing to linger over it.

A half-melancholy smile was all her answer, and he went on,—

"I'm as sure of what's in that letter there as if I read it. Now, mark my words, and I'll just tell you the contents of it: Kellett's Court is sold, the first sale confirmed, and the Master's report on your poor mother's charge is unfavorable. There's not a perch of the old estate left us, and we're neither more nor less than beggars. There it is for you in plain English."

"Let us learn the worst at once, then," said she, resolutely, as she opened the letter.

"Who told you that was the worst?" broke he in, angrily. "The worst isn't over for the felon in the dock when the judge has finished the sentence; there's the 'drop' to come, after that."

"Father, father!" cried she, pitifully, "be yourself again. Remember what you said the other night, that if we had poor Jack back again you'd not be afraid to face life in some new world beyond the seas, and care little for hardships or humble fortune if we could only be together."

"I was dreaming, I suppose," muttered he, doggedly.

"No; you were speaking out of the fulness of your love and affection; you were showing me how little the accidents of fortune touch the happiness of those resolved to walk humbly, and that, once divested of that repining spirit which was ever recalling the past, we should confront the life before us more light of heart than we have felt for many a year."

"I wonder what put it in my head," muttered he, in the same despondent tone.

"Your own stout heart put it there. You were recalling what young Conway was telling us about poor Jack's plans and projects; and how, when the war was over, he 'd get the Sultan to grant him a patch of land close to the Bosphorus, where he'd build a little kiosk for us all, and we 'd grow our own corn and have our own vines and fig-trees, seeking for nothing but what our own industry should give us."

"Dreams, dreams!" said he, sighing drearily. "You may read the letter now." And she began,—

> "Sir,—By direction of Mr. Davenport Dunn, I have to
> acquaint you that the Commissioners, having overruled the
> objections submitted by him, will on Tuesday next proceed
> to the sale of the lands of Kellett's Court, Gorestown, and
> Kilinaganny, free of all charges and encumbrances thereon,
> whether by marriage settlement — "

"I told you,—that's just what I was saying," burst in Kellett; "there's not sixpence left us!"

She ran hurriedly over to herself the tiresome intricacies that followed, till she came to the end, where a brief postscript ran,—

"As your name is amongst those to be reduced in consequence of the late Treasury order regarding the Customs, Mr. Dunn hopes you will lose no time in providing yourself with another employment, to which end he will willingly contribute any aid in his power."

A wild, hysterical burst of laughter broke from Kellett as she ceased.

"Isn't there any more good news, Bella? Look over it carefully, darling, and you 'll surely discover something else."

The terrible expression of his face shocked her, and she could make no reply.

"I 'll wager a crown, if you search well, you 'll see something about sending me to jail, or, maybe, transporting me. — Who's that knocking at the door there?" cried he, angrily, as a very loud noise resounded through the little cottage.

"'T is a gentleman without wants to speak to the master," said the old woman, entering.

"I 'm engaged, and can't see anybody," rejoined Kellett, sternly.

"He says it's the same if he could see Miss Bella," reiterated the old woman.

"He can't, then; she 's engaged too."

The woman still lingered at the door, as if she expected some change of purpose.

"Don't you hear me? — don't you understand what I said?" cried he, passionately.

"Tell him that your master cannot see him," said Bella.

"If I don't make too bould, — if it's not too free of me, — maybe you 'd excuse the liberty I 'm taking," said a man, holding the door slightly open, and projecting a round bullet head and a very red face into the room.

"Oh, Mr. Driscoll," cried Bella. "Mrs. Hawkshaw's brother, papa," whispered she, quietly, to her father, who, notwithstanding the announcement, made no sign.

"If Captain Kellett would pardon my intrusion," said Driscoll, entering with a most submissive air, "he'd soon see that it was at laste with good intentions I came out all the way here on foot, and a bad night besides, — a nasty little drizzling rain and mud, — such mud!" And he held up in evidence a foot about the size of an elephant's.

"Pray sit down, Mr. Driscoll," said Bella, placing a chair for him. "Papa was engaged with matters of business when you knocked,—some letters of consequence."

"Yes, miss, to be sure, and did n't want to be disturbed," said Driscoll, as he sat down, and wiped his heated forehead. "I 'm often the same way myself; but when I 'm at home, and want nobody to disturb me, I put on a little brown-paper cap I have, and that's the sign no one's to talk to me."

Kellett burst into a laugh at the conceit, and Driscoll so artfully joined in the emotion that when it ceased they were already on terms of intimacy.

"You see what a strange crayture I am. God help me!" said Driscoll, sighing. "I have to try as many dodges with myself as others does be using with the world, for my poor head goes wanderin' away about this, that, and the other, and I 'm never sure it will think of what I want."

"That's a sad case," said Kellett, compassionately.

"I was like everybody else tell I had the fever," continued Driscoll, confidentially. "It was the spotted fever, not the scarlet fever, d' ye mind; and when I came out of it on the twenty-ninth day, I was the same as a child, simple and innocent You 'd laugh now if I told you what I did with the first half-crown I got. I bought a bag of marbles!"

And Kellett did laugh heartily; less, perhaps, at the circumstance than at the manner and look of him who told it.

"Ay, faith, marbles!" muttered Driscoll to himself; "'tis a game I'm mighty fond of."

"Will you take a little whiskey-and-water? Hot or cold?" asked Kellett, courteously.

"Just a taste, to take off the deadness of the water," said Driscoll. "I 'm obleeged to be as cautious as if I was walkin' on eggs. Dr. Dodd says to me, 'Terry,' says he, 'you had never much brains in your best days, but now you 're only a sheet of thin paper removed from an idiot, and if you touch spirits it's all up with you.'"

"That was plain speaking, anyhow," said Kellett, smiling.

"Yes," said Driscoll, while he seemed struggling to call up some reminiscence: and then, having succeeded, said, "Ay, 'There's five-and-twenty in Swift's this minute,' said he, 'with their heads shaved, and in blue cotton dressing-gowns, more sensible than yourself.' But, you see, there was one thing in my favor,—I was always harmless."

The compassionate expression with which Kellett listened to this declaration guaranteed how completely the speaker had engaged his sympathy.

"Well, well," continued Driscoll, "maybe I'm just as happy, ay, happier than ever I was! Every one is kind and good-natured to me now. Nobody takes offence at what I say or do; they know well in their hearts that I don't mean any harm."

"That you don't," broke in Bella, whose gratitude for many a passing word of kindness, as he met her of a morning, willingly seized upon the opportunity for acknowledgment.

"My daughter has often told me of the kind way you always spoke to her."

"Think of that, now," muttered Terry to himself; "and I saying all the while to my own heart, ''T is a proud man you ought to be to-day, Terry Driscoll, to be giving good-morning to Miss Kellett of Kellett's Court, the best ould blood in your own county.'"

"Your health, Driscoll,—your health," cried Kellett, warmly. "Let your head be where it will, your heart's in the right place, anyhow."

"Do you say so, now?" asked he, with all the eagerness of one putting a most anxious question.

"I do, and I'd swear it," cried Kellett, resolutely. "'Tis too clever and too 'cute the world's grown; they were better times when there was more good feeling and less learning."

"Indeed—indeed, it was the remark I made to my sister Mary the night before last," broke in Driscoll. "'What is there,' says I, 'that Miss Kellett can't teach them? They know the rule of three and What 's-his-name's Questions as well as I know my prayers. You don't want them to learn mensuration and the use of the globes?' 'I'll send them to a school in France,' says she; 'it's the only way to be genteel.'"

"To a school in France?" cried Bella; "and is that really determined on?"

"Yes, miss; they 're to go immediately, and ye see that was the reason I walked out here in the rain to-night I said to myself, 'Terry,' says I, 'they 'll never say a word about this to Miss Kellett till the quarter is up; be off, now, and break it to her at once.'"

"It was so like your own kind heart," burst out Bella.

"Yes," muttered Driscoll, as if in a revery, "that's the only good o' me now,—I can think of what will be of use to others."

"Did n't I tell you we were in a vein of good luck, Bella?" said Kellett, between his teeth; "didn't I say awhile ago there was more coming?"

"'But,' says I to Mary," continued Driscoll, "'you must take care to recommend Miss Kellett among your friends—'"

Kellett dashed his glass down with such force on the table as to frighten Driscoll, whose speech was thus abruptly cut short, and the two men sat staring fixedly at each other. The expression of poor Terry's vacant face, in which a struggling effort to deprecate anger was the solitary emotion readable, so overcame Kellett's passion that, stooping over, he grasped the other's hand warmly, and said,—

"You 're a kind-hearted creature, and you 'd never hurt a living soul. I 'm not angry with you."

"Thank you, Captain Kellett,—thank you," cried the other, hurriedly, and wiped his brow, like one vainly endeavoring to follow out a chain of thought collectedly. "Who is this told me that you had another daughter?"

"No," said Kellett; "I have a son."

"Ay, to be sure! so it was a son, they said, and a fine strapping young fellow too. Where is he?"

"He 's with his regiment, the Rifles, in the Crimea."

"Dear me, now, to think of that,—fighting the French, just the way his father did."

"No," said Kellett, smiling, "it 's the Russians he 's fighting, and the French are helping him to do it."

"That's better any day," said Driscoll; "two to one is a pleasanter match. And so he's in the Rifles?" And here he laid his head on his hand and seemed lost in thought. "Is he a captain?" asked he, after a long pause.

"No, not yet," said Kellett, while his cheek flushed at the evasion he was practising.

"Well, maybe he will soon," resumed the other, relapsing once more into deep thought. "There was a young fellow joined them in Cork just before they sailed, and I lent him thirty shillings, and he never paid me. I wonder what became of him? Maybe he's killed."

"Just as likely," said Kellett, carelessly.

"Now, would your son be able to make him out for me?—not for the sake of the money, for I would n't speak of it, but out of regard for him, for I took a liking to him; he was a fine, handsome fellow, and bold as a lion."

"He mightn't be in Jack's battalion, or he might, and Jack not know him. What was his name?" said Kellett, in some confusion.

"I 'll tell you if you 'll pledge your word you 'll never say a syllable about the money, for I can't think but he forgot it."

"I 'll never breathe a word about it."

"And will you ask your son all about him,—if he likes the sarvice, or if he 'd rather be at home, and how it agrees with him?" "And the name?"

"The name?—I wrote it down on a bit of paper just for my own memory's sake, for I forget everything; the name is Conway,—Charles Conway."

"Why, that's the very—" When he got so far, a warning look from Bella arrested Kellett's voice, and he ceased speaking, looking eagerly at his daughter for some explanation. Had he not been so anxious for some clew to her meaning, he could scarcely have failed to be struck by the intense keenness of the glance Driscoll turned from the countenance of the father to that of the daughter. She, however, marked it, and with such significance that a deathlike sickness crept suddenly over her, and she sank slowly down into a seat.

"You ware saying, 'That's the very—'" said Driscoll, repeating the words, and waiting for the conclusion.

"The very name we read in a newspaper," said Bella, who, with a sort of vague instinct of some necessity for concealment, at once gave this evasive reply. "He volunteered for somewhere, or was first inside a battery, or did something or other very courageous."

"It was n't killed he was?" said Driscoll, in his habitual tone.

"No, no," cried Kellett, "he was all safe."

"Isn't it a queer thing? but I'd like to hear of him! There was some Conway s connections of my mother's, and I can't get it out of my head but he might be one of them. It's not a common name, like Driscoll."

"Well, Jack will, maybe, be able to tell you about him," said Kellett, still under the spell of Bella's caution.

"If you would tell me on what points you want to be informed," said Bella, "I shall be writing to my brother in a day or two. Are there any distinct questions you wish to be answered?"

The calm but searching glance that accompanied these few words gradually gave way to an expression of pity as Bella gazed at the hopeless imbecility of poor Driscoll's face, wherein not a gleam of intelligence now lingered. It was as if the little struggle of intellect had so exhausted him that he was incapable of any further effort of reason. And there he sat, waiting till the returning tide of thought should flow back upon his stranded intelligence.

"Would you like him to be questioned about the family?" said she, looking good-naturedly at him.

"Yes, miss,—yes," said he, half dreamily; "that is, I would n't like my own name, poor crayture as I am, to be mentioned; but if you could anyways find out if he was one of the Conway s of Abergedley,—they were my mother's people,—if you could find out that for me, it would be a great comfort."

"I'll charge myself with the commission," said Bella, writing down the words "Conway of Abergedley."

"Now there was something else, if my poor head could only remember it," said Driscoll, whose countenance displayed the most complete picture of a puzzled intelligence.

"Mix yourself another tumbler, and you'll think of it by and by," said Kellett, courteously.

"Yes," muttered Driscoll, accepting the suggestion at once. "It was something about mustard-seed, I think," added he, after a pause; "they say it will keep fresh for two years if you put it in a blue-paper bag,—deep blue is best" A look of sincere compassion passed between Kellett and his daughter, and Driscoll went on, "I don't think it was that, though, I wanted to remember." And he fell into deep reflection for several minutes, at the end of which he started abruptly up, finished off his glass, and began to button up his coat in preparation for the road.

"Don't go till I see what the night looks like," cried Kellett, as he left the room to examine the state of the weather.

"If I should be fortunate enough to obtain any information, how shall I communicate with you?" asked Bella, addressing him hastily, as if to profit by the moment of their being alone.

Driscoll looked fixedly at her for a second or two, and gradually the expression of his face settled down into its habitual cast of unmeaning imbecility, while he merely muttered to himself, "No evidence; throw out the bills."

She repeated her question, and in a voice to show that she believed herself well understood.

"Yes!" said he, with a vacant grin, — "yes! but they don't agree with everybody."

"There's a bit of a moon out now, and the rain has stopped," said Kellett, entering, "so that it would n't be friendly to detain you."

"Good-night, good-night," said Driscoll, hurriedly; "that spirit is got up to my head. I feel it. A pleasant journey to you both, and be sure to remember me to Mrs. Miller." And with these incoherent words he hastened away, and his voice was soon heard singing cheerily as he plodded his way towards Dublin. "That's the greatest affliction of all," said Kellett, as he sat down and sipped his glass. "There 's nothing like having one's faculties, one's reason, clear and unclouded. I would n't be like that poor fellow there to be as rich as the Duke of Leinster."

"It is a strange condition," said Bella, thoughtfully. "There were moments when his eyes lighted up with a peculiar significance, as if, at intervals, his mind had regained all its wonted vigor. Did you remark that?"

"Indeed, I did not. I saw nothing of the kind," said Kellett, peevishly. "By the way, why were you so cautious about Conway?"

"Just because he begged that his name might not be mentioned. He said that some trifling debts were still hanging over him, from his former extravagance; and though all in course of liquidation, he dreaded the importunate appeals of creditors so certain to pour in if they heard of his being in Dublin."

"Every one has his troubles!" muttered Kellett, as he sank into a moody reflection over his own, and sipped his liquor in silence.

Let us now follow Driscoll, who, having turned the corner of the lane, out of earshot of the cottage, suddenly ceased his song, and walked briskly along towards town. Rapidly as he walked, his lips moved more rapidly still, as he maintained a kind of conversation with himself, bursting out from time to time with a laugh, as some peculiar conceit amused him. "To be sure, a connection by the mother's side," said he. "One has a right to ask after his own relations! And, for all I know, my grandmother was a Conway. The ould fool was so near pokin' his foot in it, and letting out that he knew him well. She's a deep one, that daughter; and it was a bould stroke the way she spoke to me when we were alone. It was just as much as to say, 'Terry, put your cards down, for I know your hand.' 'No, miss,' says I, 'I've a thrump in the heel of my fist that ye never set eyes on. Ha, ha, ha!' but she's deep for all that, — mighty deep; and if it was safe, I wish we had her in the plot! Ay! but is it safe, Mr. Driscoll? By the virtue of your oath, Terry Driscoll, do you belave she wouldn't turn on you? She's a fine-looking girl, too," added he, after an interval. "I wish I knew her sweetheart, for she surely has one. Terry, Terry, ye must bestir yourself; ye must be up early and go to bed late, my boy. You 're not the man ye were before ye had that 'faver,'—that spotted faver!"—here he laughed till his eyes ran over. "What a poor crayture it has left ye; no memory, no head for anything!" And he actually shook with laughter at the thought. "Poor Terry Driscoll, ye are to be pitied!" said he, as he wiped the tears from his face. "Is n't it a sin and a shame there's no one to look after ye?"

CHAPTER XIX
DRISCOLL IN CONFERENCE

"Not come in yet, sir; but he is sure to be back soon," said Mr. Clowes, the butler, to Terry Driscoll, as he stood in the hall of Mr. Davenport Dunn's house, about eleven o'clock of the same night we have spoken of in our last chapter.

"You're expecting him, then?" asked Driscoll, in his own humble manner.

"Yes, sir," said Clowes, looking at his watch; "he ought to be here now. We have a deal of business to get through to-night, and several appointments to keep; but he'll see you, Mr. Driscoll. He always gives directions to admit *you* at once."

"Does he really?" asked Driscoll, with an air of perfect innocence.

"Yes," said Clowes, in a tone at once easy and patronizing, "he likes *you*. You are one of the very few who can amuse him. Indeed, I don't think I ever heard him laugh, what I 'd call a hearty laugh, except when you 're with him."

"Isn't that quare, now!" exclaimed Driscoll. "Lord knows it's little fun is in me now!"

"Come in and take a chair; charge you nothing for the sitting," said Clowes, laughing at his own smartness as he led the way into a most comfortably furnished little room which formed his own sanctum.

The walls were decorated with colored prints and drawings of great projected enterprises,—peat fuel manufactories of splendid pretensions, American packet stations on the west coast, of almost regal architecture, vied with ground-plans of public parks and ornamental model farms; fish-curing institutions, and smelting-houses, and beetroot-sugar buildings, graced scenes of the very wildest desolation, and, by an active representation of life and movement, seemed to typify the wealth and prosperity which enterprise was sure to carry into regions the very dreariest and least promising.

"A fine thing, that, Mr. Driscoll!" said Clowes, as Terry stood admiring a large and highly colored plate, wherein several steam-engines were employed in supplying mill-streams with water from a vast lake, while thousands of people seemed busily engaged in spade labor on its borders. "That is the 'Lough Corrib Drainage and Fresh Strawberry Company,' capital eight hundred thousand pounds! Chemical analysis has discovered that the soil of drained lands, treated with a suitable admixture of the alkaline carbonates, is peculiarly favorable to the growth of the strawberry,—a fruit whose properties are only now receiving their proper estimate. The strawberry, you are perhaps not aware, is a great anti-scorbutic. Six strawberries, taken in a glass of diluted malic acid of a morning, fasting, would restore the health of those fine fellows we are now daily losing in such numbers in the Crimea. I mean, of course, a regular treatment of three months of this regimen, with due attention to diet, cleanliness, and habit of exercise,—all predisposing elements removed, all causes of mental anxiety withdrawn. To this humane discovery this great industrial speculation owes its origin. There you see the engines at full work; the lake is in process of being drained, the water being all utilized by the mills you see yonder, some of which are compressing the strawberry pulp into a paste for exportation. Here are the people planting the shoots; those men in blue, with the watering-pots, are the alkaline feeders, who supply the plant with the chemical preparation I mentioned, the strength being duly marked by letters, as you see. B. C. P. means bi-carbonate of potash; S. C. S., sub-carbonate of soda; and so on. Already, sir," said he, raising his voice, "we have contracts for the supply of twenty-eight tons a week, and we hope," added he, with a tremulous fervor in his voice, "to live to see the time when the table of the poorest peasant in the land will be graced by the health-conducing condiment."

"With all my heart and soul I wish you success," said Driscoll; while he muttered under his breath what sounded like a fervid prayer for the realization of this blessed hope.

"Of that we are pretty certain, sir," said Clowes, pompously; "the shares are now one hundred and twelve,—paid up in two calls, thirty-six pounds ten shillings, *He*," said Clowes, with a jerk of his thumb towards Mr. Dunn's room, meant to indicate its owner,—"*he* don't like it; calls it a bubble, and all that, but I have, known him mistaken, sir,—ay, and more than once. You may remember that vein of yellow marble—giallo antico, they call it—found on Martin's property—That's his knock; here he comes now," cried he, hurrying away to meet his master, and leaving the story of his blunder unrelated. "All right," said Clowes, re-entering, hastily; "you can go in now. He seems in a precious humor to-night," added he, in a low whisper; "something or other has gone wrong with him."

Driscoll had scarcely closed the inner door of cloth that formed the last security of Davenport Dunn's privacy, when he perceived the correctness of Mr. Clowes's information. Dunn's brow was dark and clouded, his face slightly flushed, and his eye restless and excited.

"What is it so very pressing, Driscoll, that could n't wait till to-morrow?" said he, peevishly, and not paying the slightest attention to the other's courteous salutation.

"I thought this was the time you liked best," said Driscoll, quietly; "you always said, 'Come to me when I've done for the day—'"

"But who told you I had done for the day? That pile of letters has yet to be answered; many of them I have not even read. The Attorney-General will be here in a few minutes about these prosecutions too."

"That's a piece of good luck, anyhow," said Driscoll, quickly.

"How so? What d' ye mean?"

"Why, we could just get a kind of travelling opinion out of him about this case."

"What nonsense you talk!" said Dunn, angrily; "as if a lawyer of standing and ability would commit himself by pronouncing on a most complicated question, the details of which he was to gather from *you*!" The look and emphasis that accompanied the last word were to the last degree insulting, but they seemed to give no offence whatever to him to whom they were addressed; on the contrary, he met them with a twinkle of the eye, and a droll twist of the mouth, as he muttered half to himself,—

"Yes, God help me, I 'll never set the Liffey on fire!"

"You might, though, if you had it heavily insured," said Dunn, with a savage irony in his manner that might well have provoked rejoinder; but Driscoll was proof against whatever he didn't want to resent, and laughed pleasantly at the sarcasm.

"You were dining at the Lodge, I suppose, to-day?" asked he, eager to get the conversation afloat at any cost.

"No, at Luscombe's,—the Chief Secretary's," said Dunn, curtly.

"They say he's a clever fellow," said Driscoll.

"They are heartily welcome to this opinion who think so," broke in Dunn, peevishly. "Let them call him a fortunate one if they like, and they 'll be nearer the mark.—What of this affair?" said he, at last "Have you found out Conway?"

"No; but I learned that he dined and passed the evening with ould Paul Kellett He came over to Ireland to bring him some news of his son, who served in the same regiment, and so I went out to Kellett to pump them; but for some reason or other they're as close as wax. The daughter beats all ever you saw! She tried a great stroke of cunning with me, but it wouldn't do."

"It was your poor head and the spotted fever,—eh?" said Dunn, laughing.

"Yes," said Driscoll; "I never was rightly myself since that" And he laughed heartily.

"This is too slow for me, Driscoll; you must find out the young fellow at once, and let me see him. I have read over the statement again, and it is wonderfully complete. Hatch-ard has it now before him, and will give me his opinion by Sunday next On that same day Mr. Beecher is to dine with me; now if you could manage to have Conway here on Monday morning, I 'd probably be in a condition to treat openly with him."

"You're going too fast,—too fast, entirely," said Driscoll; "sure, if Conway sees the road before him, he may Just thravel it without us at all."

"I 'll take care he shall not know which path to take, Driscoll; trust me for that. Remember that the documents we have are all-essential to him. Before he sees one of them our terms must be agreed on."

"I'll have ten thousand paid down on the nail. 'Tis eight years I am collectin' them papers. I bought that shooting-lodge at Banthry, that belonged to the Beechers, just to search the old cupboard in the dinner-room. It was plastered over for fifty years, and Denis Magrath was the only man living knew where it was."

"I am aware of all that. The discovery—if such it prove—was all your own, Driscoll; and as to the money remuneration, I 'll not defraud you of a sixpence."

"There was twelve hundred pounds," continued Driscoll, too full of his own train of thought to think of anything else, "for a wretched ould place with the roof fallin' in, and every stack of it rotten! Eight years last Michaelmas,—that's money, let me tell you! and I never got more than thirty pounds any year out of it since."

"You shall be paid, and handsomely paid."

"Yes," said Terry, nodding.

"You can have good terms on either side."

"Yes, or a little from both," added Driscoll, dryly.

CHAPTER XX
AN EVENING WITH GROG DAVIS

It was late at night, and Grog Davis sat alone by a solitary candle in his dreary room. The fire had long burned out, and great pools of wet, driven by the beating rain through the rickety sashes, soaked the ragged carpet that covered the floor, while frequent gusts of storm scattered the slates, and shook the foundations of the frail building.

To all seeming, he paid little attention to the poor and comfortless features of the spot. A short square bottle of Hollands, and a paper of coarse cigars beside him, seemed to offer sufficient defence against such cares, while he gave up his mind to some intricate problem which he was working out with a pack of cards. He dealt, and shuffled, and dealt again, with marvellous rapidity. There was that in each motion of the wrist, in every movement of the finger, that bespoke practised manipulation, and a glance quick as lightning on the board was enough to show him how the game fared.

"Passed twelve times," muttered he to himself; then added aloud, "Make your game, gentlemen, make your game. The game is made. Red, thirty-two. Now for it, Grog,—man or a mouse, my boy. Mouse it is! by — — ," cried he, with an infamous oath. "Red wins! Confound the cards!" cried he, dashing them on the floor. "Two minutes ago I had enough to live on the rest of my days. I appeal to any man in the room," said he, with a look of peculiar defiance around him, "if he ever saw such ill luck! There's not another fellow breathing ever got it like me!" And as he spoke, he arose and walked up and down the chamber, frowning savagely, and turning glances of insolent meaning on every side of him. At last, approaching the table, he filled out a glass of gin and drank it off; and then, stooping down, he gathered up the cards and reseated himself. "Take you fifty on the first ace," cried he, addressing an imaginary bettor, while he began to deal out the cards in two separate heaps. "Won!" exclaimed he, delightedly. "Go you double or quits, sir?—Any gentleman with another fifty?—A pony if you like, sir?—Done! Won again, by jingo! This is the only game, after all; decided in a second. I make the bank, gentlemen, two hundred in the bank.

Why, where are the bettors this evening? This is only punting, gentlemen. Any one say five hundred—four—three—one hundred—for the first knave?" And the cards fell from his hands with wondrous rapidity. "Now, if no one is inclined to play, let 's have a broiled bone," said he, rising, and bowing courteously around him.

"Second the motion!" cried a cheery voice, as the door opened and Annesley Beecher entered. "Why, Grog, my hearty, I thought you had a regular flock of pigeons here. I heard you talking as I came up the stairs, and fancied you were doing a smart stroke of work."

"What robbery have *you* been at with that white choker and that gimcrack waistcoat?" said Davis, sulkily.

"Dining with Dunn, and a capital dinner he gave me. I 'm puzzled to say whether I like his wine or his cookery best."

"Were there many there?"

"None but ourselves."

"Lord! how he must have worked you!" cried Davis, with an insolent grin.

"Ain't such a flat as you think me, Master Grog. Solomon was a wise man, and Samson a strong one, and A. B. can hold his own with most 'in the ruck.'"

A most contemptuous look was the only answer Davis condescended to this speech. At last, after he had lighted a fresh cigar, and puffed it into full work, he said, "Well, what was it he had to say to you?"

"Oh, we talked away of everything; and, by Jupiter! he knows a little of everything. Such a memory, too; remembers every fellow that was in power the last fifty years, and can tell you how he was 'squared,' for it 's all on the 'cross' with *them*, Grog, just as in the ring. Every fellow rides to order, and half the running one sees is no race! Any hot water to be had?"

"No, there's cold in that jug yonder. Well, go on with Dunn."

"He is very agreeable, I must say; for, besides having met everybody, he knows all their secret history,—how this one got out of his scrape, and why that went into the hole. You see in a moment how much he must be trusted, and that he can make his book on life as safe as the Bank of England. Fearfully strong that gin is!"

"No, it ain't," said Grog, rudely; "it's not the velvety tipple Dunn gave you, but it's good British gin, that's what it is."

"You would n't believe, too, how much he knows about women! He's up to everything that's going on in town. Very strange that, for a fellow like him! Don't you think so?"

Davis made no answer, but puffed away slowly. "And after women, what came next?"

"He talked next—let me see—about books. How he likes Becky Sharp,—how he enjoys her! He says that character will do the same service as the published discovery of some popular fraud; and that the whole race of Beckys now are detected swindlers,—nothing less."

"And what if they are? Is that going to prevent their cheating? Hasn't the world always its crop of flats coming out in succession like green peas? What did he turn to after that?"

"Then we had a little about the turf."

"He don't know anything about the turf!" said Grog, with intense contempt.

"I 'm not so sure of that," said Beecher, cautiously.

"Did he speak of *me* at all?" said Grog, with a peculiar grin.

"No; only to ask if you were the same Captain Davis that was mentioned in that affair at Brighton."

"And what did you say?"

"Said! Not knowing, could n't tell, Master Grog. Knew you were a great friend of my brother Lackington's, and always hand and glove with Blanchard and the swells."

"And how did he take that?"

"Said something about two of the same name, and changed the subject."

Davis drew near the table, and taking up the cards began to shuffle them slowly, like one seeking some excuse for a moment of uninterrupted reflection. "I've found out the way that Yankee fellow does the king," said he, at last. "It's not the common bridge that everybody knows. It's a Mississippi touch, and a very neat one. Cut them now wherever you like."

Beecher cut the cards with all due care, and leaned eagerly over the table.

"King of diamonds!" cried Grog, slapping the card on the board.

"Do it again," said Beecher, admiringly; and once more Davis performed the dexterous feat.

"It's a nick!" cried Beecher, examining the edge of the card minutely.

"It ain't no such thing!" said Davis, angrily. "I'd give you ten years to find it out, and twenty to do it, and-you 'd fail in both."

"Let's see the dodge, Grog," said Beecher, half-coaxingly.

"You don't see *my* hand till you put *yours* on the table," said Davis, fiercely. Then crossing his arms before him, and fixing his red fiery eyes on Beecher's face, he went on, "What do you mean by this fencing — just tell me what you mean by it?"

"I don't understand you," said Beecher, whose features were now of ashy paleness.

"Then you shall understand me!" cried Davis, with an oath. "Do you want me to believe that Dunn had you to dine with him all alone, just to talk about politics, of which you know nothing, or books, of which you know less; that he 'd give you four precious hours of a Sunday evening to bear your opinions about men or women or things in general? Do you ask me to swallow that, sir?"

"I ask you to swallow nothing," stammered out Beecher, in whose heart pride and fear were struggling for the mastery. "I have told you what we spoke of. If anything else passed between us, perhaps it was of a private and personal nature; perhaps it referred to family topics; perhaps I might have given a solemn assurance not to reveal the subject of it to any one."

"You did, — did you?" said Davis, with a sneer.

"I said, perhaps I might have done so. I did n't say I had."

"And so you think — you fancy — that you 're a going to double on me," said Davis, rising, and advancing towards him with a sort of insulting menace. "Now, look here, my name ain't Davis but if ever you try it — try it, I say, because, as to doing it, I dare you to your face — but if you just try it, twelve hours won't pass over till the dock of a police court is graced by the Honorable Annesley Beecher on a charge of forgery."

"Oh, Davis!" cried Beecher, as he placed his hands over the other's lips, and glanced in terror through the room. "There never was anything I did n't tell you, — you 're the only man breathing that knows me."

"And I do know you, by Heaven, I do!" cried the other, savagely; "and I know you'd sneak out of my hands to-morrow, if you dared; but this I tell you, when you leave *mine* it will be to exchange into the turnkey's. You fancy that because I see you are a fool that I don't suspect you to be a crafty one. Ah! what a mistake you make there!"

"But listen to me, Grog,—just hear me."

"My name 's Davis, sir,—Captain Davis,—let me hear you call me anything else!"

"Well, Davis, old fellow,—the best and truest friend ever fellow had in the world,—now what's all this about? I 'll tell you every syllable that passed between Dunn and myself. I'll give you my oath, as solemnly as you can dictate it to me, not to conceal one word. He made me swear never to mention it. It was *he* that imposed the condition on me. What he said was this: 'It's a case where you need no counsel, and where any counsel would be dangerous. He who once knows your secret will be in a position to dictate to you. Lord Lackington must be your only adviser, since his peril is the same as your own.'"

"Go on," said Davis, sternly, as the other seemed to pause too long.

Beecher drew a long breath, and, in a voice faint and broken, continued: "It's a claimant to the title,—a fellow who pretends he derives from the elder branch,—the Conway Beechers. All stuff and nonsense,—they were extinct two hundred years ago,—but no matter, the claim is there, and so circumstantially got up, and so backed by documents and the rest of it, that Lackington is frightened,—frightened out of his wits. The mere exposure, the very rumor of the thing, would distract *him*. He's proud as Lucifer,— and then he's hard up; besides, he wants a loan, and Dunn tells him there's no getting it till this affair is disposed of, and that he has hit on the way to do it."

"As how?" said Davis, dryly.

"Well," resumed Beecher, whose utterance grew weaker and less audible at every word, "Lackington, you know, has no children. It 's very unlikely he ever will now; and Dunn's advice is that for a life interest in the title and estates I should bind myself not to marry. That fellow then, if he can make good his claim, comes in as next of kin after *me*; and as to who or what comes after *me*," cried he, with more energy, "it matters devilish little. Once 'toes up' and Annesley Beecher won't fret over the next match that comes off,—eh, Grog, old fellow?" And he endeavored by a forced jocularity to encourage his own sinking heart.

"Here's a shindy!" said Grog, as he mixed himself a fresh tumbler and laid his arms crosswise on the table; "and so it's no less than the whole stakes is on this match?"

"Title and all," chimed in Beecher.

"I was n't thinking of the title," said Grog, gruffly, as he relapsed into a moody silence. "Now, what does my Lord say to it all?" asked he, after a long pause.

"Lackington?—Lackington says nothing, or next to nothing. You read the passage in his letter where he says, 'Call on Dunn,' or 'Speak to Dunn,' or something like that,—he did n't even explain about what; and then you may remember the foolish figure we cut on that morning we waited on Dunn ourselves, not being able to say why or how we were there."

"I remember nothing about cutting a foolish figure anywhere or any time. It's not very much *my* habit. It ain't *my* way of business."

"Well, I can't say as much," said Beecher, laughing; "and I own frankly I never felt less at ease in my life."

"That's *your* way of business," said Grog, nodding gravely at him.

"Every fellow is n't born as sharp as you, Davis. Samson was a wise man—no, Solomon was a wise man—"

"Leave Samson and Solomon where they are," said Grog, puffing his cigar. "What we have to look to here is whether there be a claim at all, and then what it's worth. The whole affair may be just a cross between this fellow Dunn and one of his own pals. Now, it's my Lord's business to see to that. *You* are only the *second* horse all this while. If my Lord knows that he can be disqualified, he's wide awake enough to square the match, he is. But it maybe that Dunn hasn't put the thing fairly before him. Well, then, you must compare your book with my Lord's. You'll have to go over to him, Beecher." And the last words were uttered with a solemnity that showed they were the result of a deep deliberation.

"It's all very well, Master Davis, to talk of going over to Italy; but where's the tin to come from?"

"It must be had somehow," said Davis, sententiously. "Ain't there any fellows about would give you a name to a bit of stiff, at thirty-one days' date?"

"Pumped them all dry long ago!" said Beecher, laughing. "There's not a man in the garrison would join me to spoil a stamp; and, as to the civilians, I scarcely know one who isn't a creditor already."

"You are always talking to me of a fellow called Kellett,—why not have a shy at *him*?"

"Poor Paul!" cried Beecher, with a hearty laugh. "Why, Paul Kellett's ruined—cleaned out—sold in the Encumbered what d'ye-call-'ems, and has n't a cross in the world!"

"I ought to have guessed as much," growled out Grog, "or he'd not have been on such friendly terms with *you*."

"A polite speech that, Grog," said Beecher, smiling.

"It's true, and that's better," said Davis. "The only fellows that stick close to a man in his poverty are those a little poorer than himself."

"Not but, if he had it," said Beecher, following up his own thoughts, — "not but, if he had it, he's just the fellow to do a right good-natured thing."

"Well, I suppose he's got his name, — they have n't sold *that*, have they?"

"No, but it's very much like the estate," said Beecher. "It's far too heavily charged ever to pay off the encumbrances."

"Who minds that, nowadays? A bad bill is a very useful thing sometimes. It's like a gun warranted to burst, and you can always manage to have it in the right man's hands when it comes the time for the explosion."

"You *are* a rum un, Davis, — you *are*, indeed," said Beecher, admiringly; for it was in the delivery of such wise maxims that Davis appeared to him truly great.

"Get him down for fifty, — that ain't much, — fifty at three months. My Lord says he 'll stand fifty himself, in that letter I read. It was to help you to a match, to be sure; but that don't matter. There can be no question of marrying now. Let me see how this affair is going to turn. Well, I'll see if I can't do something myself. I've a precious lot of stamped paper there," — and he pointed to an old secretary, — "if I could hit upon a sharp fellow to work it."

"You are a trump, Grog!" cried Beecher, delightedly.

"If we had a clear two hundred, we could start to-morrow," said Grog, laying down his cigar, and staring steadfastly at him.

"Why, would *you* come, too?" muttered Beecher, who had never so much as imagined the possibility of this companionship on the Continent.

"I expect I would," said Davis, with a very peculiar grin. "It ain't likely you'd manage an affair like this without advice."

"Very true, — very true," said Beecher, hurriedly. "But remember, Lackington is my brother, — we 're both in the same boat."

"But not with the same skulls," said Grog. And he grinned a savage grin at the success of his pun.

Beecher, however, so far from appreciating the wit, only understood the remark as a sneer at his intelligence, and half sulkily said, —

"Oh! I'm quite accustomed to that, now,—I don't mind it."

"That's right,—keep your temper," said Grog, calmly; "that's the best thing in *your* book. You 're what they call good-tempered. And," added he, in the moralizing tone, "though the world does take liberties with the good-tempered fellows, it shies them many a stray favor,—many a sly five-pun'-note into the bargain. I've known fellows go through life—and make a rare good thing of it, too—with no other stock-in-trade than this same good temper."

Beecher did not pay his habitual attention to Grog's words, but sat pondering over all the possible and impossible objections to a tour in such company. There were times and places where men might be seen talking to such a man as Davis. The betting-ring and the weighing-stand have their privileges, just like the green-room or the "flats," but in neither case are the intimacies of such localities exactly of a kind for parade before the world. Of all the perils of such a course none knew better than Beecher. What society would think,—what clubs would say of it,—he could picture to his mind at once.

Now, there were very few of life's casualties of which the Honorable Annesley Beecher had not tasted. He knew what it was to have his bills protested, his chattels seized, his person arrested; he had been browbeaten by Bankruptcy Commissioners, and bullied by sheriffs' officers; tradesmen had refused him credit; tailors abjured his custom; he had "burned his fingers" in one or two not very creditable transactions; but still, with all this, there was yet one depth to which he had not descended,—he was never seen in public with a "wrong man." He had a jerk of the head, a wink, or a glance for the leg who met him in Piccadilly, as every one else had. If he saw him in the garden of the Star and Garter, or the park at Greenwich, he might even condescend to banter him on "looking jolly," and ask what new "robbery" he was in for; but as to descending to intimacy or companionship openly before the gaze of the world, he 'd as soon have thought of playing cad to a 'bus, or sweep at a crossing.

It was true the Continent was not Hyde Park,—the most strait-laced and well-conducted did fifty things there they had never ventured on at home. Foreign travel had its license, and a passport was a sort of plenary indulgence for many a social transgression; but, with all this, there were a few names—about half a dozen in all Europe—that no man could afford to link his own along with.

As for Grog, he was known everywhere. From Ostend to Odessa his fame extended, and there was scarcely a police prefect in the travelled districts of the Continent that had not a description of his person, and some secret instructions respecting him. From many of the smaller states, whose vigilance is in the ratio of their littleness, he was rigidly excluded; so that in his journeying through Europe, he was often reduced to a zigzag and erratic procedure, not unlike the game known to schoolboys as scotch-hop. In the ten minutes—it was not more—that Beecher passed in recalling these and like facts to his memory, his mind grew more and more perplexed; nor was the embarrassment unperceived by him who caused it. As Davis sipped and smoked, he stole frequent glances at his companion's face, and strove to read what was passing in his mind. "It may be," thought Grog, "he does n't see his way to raising the money. It may be that his credit is lower in the market than I fancied; or"—and now his fiery eyes grew fiercer and his lip more tense—"or it may be that he doesn't fancy *my* company. If I was only sure it was *that*," muttered he between his teeth; and had Annesley Beecher only chanced to look at him as he said it, the expression of that face would have left a legacy of fear behind it for many a day.

"Help yourself," said Grog, passing the bottle across the table,—"help yourself, and the gin will help you, for I see you are 'pounded.'"

"Pounded? No, not a bit; nothing of the kind," said Beecher, blushing. "I was thinking how Lackington would take all this; what my Lady would say to it; whether they 'd regard it seriously, or whether they 'd laugh at my coming out so far about nothing."

"They'll not laugh, depend on't; take my word for it, they won't laugh," said Davis, dryly.

"Well, but if it all comes to nothing,—if it be only a plant to extort money?"

"Even that ain't anything to laugh at," said Davis. "I 've done a little that way myself, and yet I never saw the fellow who was amused by it."

"So that you really think I ought to go out and see my brother?"

"I'm sure and certain that we must go," said Davis, just giving the very faintest emphasis to the "we."

"But it will cost a pot of money, Grog, even though I should travel in the cheapest way,—I mean, the cheapest way possible for a fellow as well known as I am."

This was a bold stroke; it was meant to imply far more than the mere words announced. It was intended to express a very complicated argument in a mere innuendo.

"That's all gammon," said Grog, rudely. "We don't live in an age of couriers and extra-post; every man travels by rail nowadays, and nobody cares whether you take a coupé or a horse-box; and as to being known, so am I, and almost as well known as most fellows going."

This was pretty plain speaking; and Beecher well knew that Davis's frankness was always on the verge of the only one thing that was worse than frankness.

"After all," said Beecher, after a pause, "let the journey be ever so necessary, I have n't got the money."

"I know you haven't, neither have I; but we shall get it somehow. You 'll have to try Kellett; you 'll have to try Dunn himself, perhaps. I don't see why you should n't start with him. *He* knows that you ought to confer with my Lord; and he could scarce refuse your note at three months, if you made it—say fifty."

"But, Grog," said Beecher, laying down his cigar, and nerving himself for a great effort of cool courage, "what would suffice fairly enough for one, would be a very sorry allowance for two; and as the whole of my business will be with my own brother,—where of necessity I must be alone with him,—don't you agree with me that a third person would only embarrass matters rather than advance them?"

"No!" said Grog, sternly, while he puffed his cigar in measured time.

"I 'm speaking," said Beecher, in a tone of apology,—"I'm speaking, remember, from my knowledge of Lackington. He's very high and very proud,—one of those fellows who 'take on,' even with their equals; and with myself, he never forgets to let me feel I'm a younger brother."

"He would n't take any airs with *me*," said Grog, insolently. And Beecher grew actually sick at the bare thought of such a meeting.

"I tell you frankly, Davis," said he, with the daring of despair, "it wouldn't do. It would spoil all. First and foremost, Lackington would never forgive me for having confided this secret to any one. He'd say, and not unfairly either, 'What has Davis to do with this? It's not the kind of case he is accustomed to deal with; his counsel could n't possibly be essential here.' *He* does n't know," added he, rapidly, "your consummate knowledge of the world; *he* hasn't seen, as I have, how keenly you read every fellow that comes before you."

"We start on Monday," said Grog, abruptly, as he threw the end of his cigar into the fire; "so stir yourself, and see about the bills."

Beecher arose and walked the room with hurried strides, his brow growing darker and his face more menacing at every moment.

"Look here, Davis," cried he, turning suddenly round and facing the other, "you assume to treat me as if I was a—schoolboy;" and it was evident that he had intended a stronger word, but had not courage to utter it, for Davis's wicked eyes were upon him, and a bitter grin of irony was already on Grog's mouth as he said,—

"Did you ever try a round with *me* without getting the worst of it? Do you remember any time where you came well out of it? You 've been mauled once or twice somewhat roughly, but with the gloves on,—always with the gloves on. Now, take my advice, and don't drive me to take them off,—don't! You never felt my knuckles yet,—and, by the Lord Harry, if you had, you'd not call out 'Encore.'"

"You just want to bully me," said Beecher, in a whimpering tone.

"Bully you,—bully *you!*" said Davis, and his features put on a look of the most intense scorn as he spoke. "Egad!" cried he, with an insolent laugh, "you know very little about either of us."

"I'd rather you'd do your worst at once than keep threatening me in this fashion."

"No, you would n't; no—no—nothing of the kind," said Davis, with a mockery of gentleness in his voice and manner.

"May I be hanged if I would not!" cried Beecher, passionately.

"It ain't hanging now,—they 've made it transportation," said Davis, with a grin; "and them as has tried it says the old way was easiest." And in the slang style of the last words there was a terrible significance,—it was as though a voice from the felons' dock was uttering a word of warning. Such was the effect on Beecher that he sank slowly down into a seat, silent and powerless.

"If you had n't been in this uncommon high style tonight," said Grog, quietly, "I'd have told you some excellent reasons for what I was advising. I got a letter from Spicer this morning. He, and a foreign fellow he calls Count Lienstahl,—it sounds devilish like 'lie and steal,' don't it?—have got a very pretty plant together, and if they could only chance upon a good second-rate horse, they reckon about eight or ten hundred in stakes alone this coming spring. They offer me a share if I could come out to them, and mean to open the campaign at Brussels. Now, there's a thing to suit us all,—'picking for every one,' as they say in the oakum-sheds."

"Cochin China might be had for five hundred; or there's Spotted Snake, they want to sell him for anything he'll bring," said Beecher, with animation.

"They could manage five hundred at least, Spicer says. We 're good for about twelve thousand francs, which ought to get us what we're looking for."

"There's Anchovy Paste—"

"Broke down before and behind."

"Hop the Twig, own sister to Levanter; ran second for the Colchester Cup—"

"Mares don't answer abroad."

"Well, what do you say to Mumps?"

"There's the horse for the Continent. A great heavy-headed, thick-jawed beast, with lazy action, and capped hocks. He's the animal to walk into a foreign jockey club. Oh, if we had him!"

"I know where he is!" exclaimed Beecher, in ecstasy. "There 's a Brummagem fellow driving him through Wales,—a bagman,—and he takes him a turn now and then for the county stakes that offer. I 'll lay my head on't we get him for fifty pounds."

"Come, old fellow," said Grog, encouragingly, "you *have* your wits about you, after all. Breakfast here to-morrow, about twelve o'clock, and we 'll see if we can't arrange the whole affair. It's a sure five hundred apiece, as if we had it here;" and he slapped his pockets as he spoke.

Beecher shook his friend's hand with a warmth that showed all his wonted cordiality, and with a hearty "Good-night!" they separated.

Grog had managed cleverly. He had done something by terror, and the rest he had accomplished by temptation. They were the two only impulses to sway that strange temperament.

CHAPTER XXI
A DARK DAY

It was the day appointed for the sale of Kellett's Court, and a considerable crowd was assembled to witness the proceeding. Property was rapidly changing hands; new names were springing up in every county, and old ones were growing obsolete. Had the tide of conquest and confiscation flowed over the land, a greater social revolution could not have resulted; and while many were full of hope and confidence that a new prosperity was about to dawn upon Ireland, there were some who continued to deplore the extinction of the old names, and the exile of the old families, whose traditions were part of the history of the country.

Kellett's Court was one of those great mansions which the Irish gentlemen of a past age were so given to building, totally forgetting how great the disproportion was between their house and their rent-roll. Irregular, incongruous, and inelegant, it yet, by its very size and extent, possessed a certain air of grandeur. Eighty guests had sat down to table in that oak wainscoted dinner-room; above a hundred had been accommodated with beds beneath that roof; the stables had stalls for every hunting-man that came; and the servants' hall was a great galleried chamber, like the refectory of a convent, in everything save the moderation of the fare.

Many were curious to know who would purchase an estate burdened by so costly a residence, the very maintenance of which in repair constituted a heavy annual outlay. The gardens, long neglected and forgotten, occupied three acres, and were themselves a source of immense expense; a considerable portion of the demesne was so purely ornamental that it yielded little or no profit; and, as an evidence of the tastes and habits of its former owners, the ruins of a stand-house marked out where races once were held in the park, while hurdle fences and deep drains even yet disfigured the swelling lawn.

Who was to buy such a property was the question none could answer. The house, indeed, might be converted into a "Union," if its locality suited; it was strong enough for a jail, it was roomy enough for a nunnery. Some averred the Government had decided on purchasing it for a barrack; others pretended that the sisterhood of the Sacred Heart had already made their bargain for it; yet to these and many other assertions not less confidently uttered there were as many demurrers.

While rumors and contradictions were still buzzed about, the Commissioner took his place on the bench, and the clerk of the Court began that tedious recital of the circumstances of the estate with whose details all the interested were already familiar, and the mere curious cared not to listen to. An informality on a former day had interfered with the sale, a fact which the Commissioner alluded to with satisfaction, as property had risen largely in value in the interval, and he now hoped that the estate would not alone clear off all the charges against it, but realize something for its former owner. A confused murmur of conversation followed this announcement. Men talked in knots and groups, consulted maps and rent-rolls, made hasty calculations in pencil, whispered secretly together, muttering frequently the words "Griffith," "plantation measure," "drainage," and "copyhold," and then, in a half-hurried, half-wearied way, the Court asked, "Is there no bidding after twenty-seven thousand five hundred?"

"Twenty-eight!" said a deep voice near the door.

A long, dreary pause followed, and the sale was over.

"Twenty-eight thousand!" cried Lord Glengariff; "the house alone cost fifty."

"It's only the demesne, my Lord," said some one near; "it's not the estate is sold."

"I know it, sir; but the demesne contains eight hundred acres, fully wooded, and enclosed by a wall.—Who is it for, Dunn?" asked he, turning to that gentleman.

"In trust, my Lord," was the reply.

"Of that I am aware, sir; you have said as much to the Court."

Dunn bent over, and whispered some words in his ear.

"Indeed!" exclaimed the other, with evident astonishment; "and intending to reside?" added he.

"Eventually, I expect so," said Dunn, cautiously, as others were now attending to the conversation.

Again Lord Glengariff spoke; but, ere he had finished, a strange movement of confusion in the body of the Court interrupted him, while a voice hoarse with passionate meaning cried out, "Is the robbery over?—is it done?" and a large, powerful man, his face flushed, and his eyes glaring wildly, advanced through the crowd to the railing beneath the bench. His waistcoat was open, and he held his cravat in one hand, having torn it off in the violence of his excitement.

"Who is this man?" asked the Commissioner, sternly.

"I'll tell you who I am,—Paul Kellett, of Kellett's Court, the owner of that house and estate you and your rascally miscreants have just stolen from me,—ay, stolen is the word; law or justice have nothing to do with it. Your Parliament made it law, to be sure, to pamper your Manchester upstarts who want to turn gentlemen—"

"Does any one know him?—has he no friends who will look after him?" said the Commissioner, leaning over and addressing those beneath in a subdued voice.

"Devil a friend in the world! It's few friends stick to the man whose property comes here. But don't make me out mad. I 'm in my full senses, though I had enough to turn fifty men to madness."

"I know him, my Lord; with the permission of the Court, I 'll take charge of him," said Dunn, in a tone so low as to be audible only to a few. Kellett, however, was one of them, and he immediately cried out,—

"Take charge of me! Ay, that he will. He took charge of my estate, too, and he 'll do by *me* what he did with the property,—give a bargain of me!"

A hearty burst of laughter filled the hall at this sally; for Dunn was one of those men whose prosperity always warrants the indulgence of a sarcasm. The Court, however, could no longer brook the indecorous interruption, and sternly ordered that Kellett might be removed.

"My dear Mr. Kellett, pray remember yourself; only recollect where you are; such conduct will only expose you—"

"Expose me! do you think I've any shame left in me? Do you think, when a man is turned out to starve on the roads, that he cares much what people say of him?"

"This interruption is intolerable," said the Commissioner. "If he be not speedily removed, I 'll order him into the custody of the police."

"Do, in God's name," cried Kellett, calmly. "Anything that will keep me from laying hands on myself, or somebody else, will be a charity."

"Come with me, Kellett,—do come along with *me!*" said Dunn, entreatingly.

"Not a step,—not an inch. It was going with *you* brought me here. This man, my Lord," cried he, addressing the Court with a wild earnestness,— "this man said to me that this was the time to sell a property,—that land was rising every day; that if we came into the Court now, it's not twenty, nor twenty-five, but thirty years' purchase—"

"I am sorry, sir," said the Commissioner, sternly, "that you will give me no alternative but that of committing you; such continued disrespect of Court cannot longer be borne."

"I 'm as well in jail as anywhere else. You 've robbed me of my property, I care little for my person. I'll never believe it's law,—never! You may sit up with your wig and your ushers and your criers, but you are just a set of thieves and swindlers, neither more nor less. Talk of shame, indeed! I think some of yourselves might blush at what you 're doing. There, there, I 'm not going to resist you," said he to the policeman; "there's no need of roughness. Newgate is the best place for me now. Mind," added he, turning to where the reporters for the daily press were sitting,—"mind and say that I just offered a calm protest against the injustice done me; that I was civilly remonstrating with the Court upon what every man—"

Ere he could finish, he was quietly removed from the spot, and before the excitement of the scene had subsided, he was driving away rapidly towards Newgate.

"Drunk or mad,—which was it?" said Lord Glengariff to Davenport Dunn, whose manner was scarcely as composed as usual.

"He has been drinking, but not to drunkenness," said Dunn, cautiously. "He is certainly to be pitied." And now he drew nigh the bench and whispered a few words to the Commissioner.

Whatever it was that he urged—and there was an air of entreaty in his manner—did not seem to meet the concurrence of the judge. Dunn pleaded earnestly, however; and at last the Commissioner said, "Let him be brought up tomorrow, then, and having made a suitable apology to the Court, we will discharge him." Thus ended the incident, and once more the clerk resumed his monotonous readings. Townlands and baronies were described, valuations quoted, rights of turbary defined, and an ancient squirearchy sold out of their possessions with as little commotion or excitement as a mock Claude is knocked down at Christie's. Indeed, of so little moment was the scene we have mentioned deemed, that scarcely half a dozen lines of the morning papers were given to its recital. The Court and its doings were evidently popular with the country at large, and one of the paragraphs which readers read with most pleasure was that wherein it was recorded that estates of immense value had just changed owners, and that the Commissioner had disposed of so many thousands' worth of landed property within the week.

Sweeping measures, of whatever nature they be, have always been in favor with the masses; never was any legislation so popular as the guillotine!

Evening was closing in, the gloomy ending of a gloomy day in winter, and Sybella Kellett sat at the window anxiously watching for her father's return. The last two days had been passed by her in a state of feverish uneasiness. Since her father's attendance at the custom-house ceased,—. for he had been formally dismissed at the beginning of the week,—his manner had exhibited strange alternations of wild excitement and deep depression. At times he would move hurriedly about, talking rapidly, sometimes singing to himself; at others he would sit in a state of torpor for hours. He drank, too, affecting some passing pain or some uneasiness as an excuse for the whiskey-bottle; and when gently remonstrated with on the evil consequences, became fearfully passionate and excited. "I suppose I 'll be called a drunkard next; there 's nothing more likely than I 'll be told it was my own sottish habits brought all this ruin upon me. 'He 's a sot.'—'He 's never sober.'—'Ask his own daughter about him.'" And then stimulating himself, he would become furious with rage. As constantly, too, did he inveigh against Dunn, saying that it was he that ruined him, and that had he not listened to his treacherous counsels he might have arranged matters with his creditors. From these bursts of passion he would fall into moods of deepest melancholy, accusing his own folly and recklessness as the cause of all his misfortunes, and even pushing self-condemnation so far as to assert that it was his misconduct and waste had driven poor Jack from home and made him enlist as a soldier.

Bella could not but see that his intellect was affected and his judgment impaired, and she made innumerable pretexts to be ever near him. Now she pretended that she required air and exercise, that her spirits were low, and needed companionship. Then she affected to have little purchases to make in town, and asked him to bear her company. At length he showed a restlessness under this restraint that obliged her to relax it; he even dropped chance words as if he suspected that he was the object of some unusual care and supervision. "There's no need of watching me," said he, rudely, to her on the morning that preceded the sale; "I 'm in no want of a keeper. They 'll see Paul Kellett 's not the man to quail under any calamity; the same to-day, to-morrow, and the next day. Sell him out or buy him in, and you 'll never know by his face that he felt it."

He spoke very little on that morning, and scarcely tasted his breakfast. His dress was more careful than usual; and Bella, half by way of saying something, asked if he were going into Dublin.

"Into Dublin! I suppose I am, indeed," said he, curtly, as though giving a very obvious reply. "Maybe," added he, after a few minutes,—"maybe you forget this is the seventeenth, and that this is the day for the sale."

"I did remember it," said she, with a faint sigh, but not daring to ask how his presence there was needed.

"And you were going to say," added he, with a bitter smile, "what did that matter to me, and that wasn't wanted. Neither I am,—I 'm neither seller nor buyer; but still I 'm the last of the name that lived there,—I was Kellett of Kellett's Court, and there 'll never be another to say the same, and I owe it to myself to be there to-day,—just as I 'd attend a funeral,—just as I 'd follow the hearse."

"It will only give you needless pain, dearest father," said she, soothingly; "pray do not go."

"Faith, I'll go if it gave me a fit," said he, fiercely. "They may say when they go home, 'Paul Kellett was there the whole time, as cool as I am now; you 'd never believe it was the old family place—the house his ancestors lived in for centuries—was up for sale; there he was, calm and quiet If that is n't courage, tell me what is.'"

"And yet I 'd rather you did not go, father. The world has trials enough to tax our energies, that we should not go in search of them."

"That's a woman's way of looking at it," said he, contemptuously.

"A man with a man's heart likes to meet danger, just to see how he 'll treat it."

"But remember, father—"

"There, now," said he, rising from the table, "if you talked till you were tired, I 'd go still. My mind is made up on it."

Bella turned away her head, and stole her handkerchief to her eyes.

"I know very well," burst he in, bitterly, "that the blackguard newspapers to-morrow will just be as ready to abuse me for it. It would have been more dignified, or more decent, or something or other, if Mr. Kellett had not appeared at the sale; but I 'll go, nevertheless, if it was only to see the man that's to take our place there! Wait dinner for me till six,—that is, if there 's any dinner at all." And, with a laugh of bitterest meaning, he left the room, and was soon seen issuing from the little garden into the road.

What a sad day, full of gloomy forebodings, was that for her! She knew well how all the easy and careless humor of her father had been changed by calamity into a spirit fierce and resentful; that, suspectful of insult on every hand, he held himself ever prepared to meet the most harmless remark with words of defiance. An imaginary impression that the world had agreed to scorn him, made him adopt a bearing at once aggressive and offensive; and he who was once a proverb for good temper became irritable and savage to a degree.

What might not come of such a temperament, tried in its tenderest spot? What might occur to expose him to the heartless sneers of those who neither knew his qualities nor his trials? These were her thoughts as she walked to and fro in her little room, unable to read, unable to write, though she made several attempts to begin a letter to her brother. The dark future also lowered before, without one flicker of light to pierce its gloom. How were they to live? In a few days more they would be at the end of their frail resources,—something less than two pounds was all that they had in the world. How she envied those in some foreign land who could stoop to the most menial labor, unseen and unremembered by their own. How easily, she thought, poverty might be borne, if divested of the terrible contrast with a former condition. Could they by any effort raise the means to emigrate,—and where to? Might not Mr. Dunn be the person to give counsel in such a case? From all she had heard of him, he was conversant with every career, every walk, and every condition. Doubtless he could name the very colony, and the very spot to suit them,—nor impossible that he might aid them to reach it. If they prospered, they could repay him. They might pledge themselves to such a condition on this head as he would dictate. How, then, to approach him? A letter? And yet a letter was always so wanting in the great requisite of answering doubts as they arose, and meeting difficulties by ready re-Joinder. A personal interview would do this. Then why not ask for an audience of him? "I'll call upon him at once," said she; "he may receive me without other solicitation,—my name will surely secure me that much of attention." Would her father approve of such a step?—would it not appear to his eyes an act of meanness and dependence?—might not the whole scheme be one to which he would offer opposition? From conflicts like these she came back to the dreary present and wondered what could still delay his coming. It was a road but little travelled; and as she sat watching at the window, her eyes grew wearied piercing the hazy atmosphere, darkening deeper and deeper as night drew near. She endeavored to occupy herself in various ways: she made little preparations for his coming; she settled his room neatly, over and over; she swept the hearth, and made a cheerful fire to greet him; and then, passing into the kitchen, she looked after the humble dinner that awaited him. Six o'clock passed, and another weary hour followed. Seven,—and still he came not. She endeavored to divert her thoughts into thinking of the future she had pictured to herself. She tried to fancy the scenery, the climate, the occupation of that dream-land over the seas; but at every bough that beat against the window by the wind, at every sound of the storm without, she would start up, and hasten to the door to listen.

It was now near eight o'clock; and so acute had her hearing become by intense anxiety that she could detect the sounds of a footfall coming along the plashy road. She did not venture to move, lest she should lose the sound, and she dreaded, too, lest it should pass on. She bent down her head to hear; and now, oh, ecstasy of relief! she heard the latch of the little wicket raised, and the step upon the gravel-walk within. She rushed at once to the door, and, dashing out into the darkness, threw herself wildly upon his breast, saying, "Thank God you are come! Oh, how I have longed for you, dearest, dearest father!" And then as suddenly, with a shriek, cried out, "Who is it? Who is this?"

"Conway,—Charles Conway. A friend,—at least, one who would wish to be thought so."

With a wild and rapid utterance she told him of her long and weary watch, and that her fears—mere causeless fears, she said she knew they were—had made her nervous and miserable. Her father's habits, always so regular and homely, made even an hour's delay a source of anxiety. "And then he had not been well for some days back,—circumstances had occurred to agitate him; things preyed upon him more heavily than they had used. Perhaps it was the dreary season—perhaps their solitary kind of life—had rendered them both more easily depressed. But, somehow—" She could not go on; but hastening towards the window, pressed her hands to her face.

"If you could tell me where I would be likely to hear of him,—what are his haunts in town—"

"He has none,—none whatever. He has entirely ceased to visit any of his former friends; even Mr. Beecher he has not called on for months long."

"Has he business engagements in any quarter that you know of?"

"None now. He did hold an office in the Customs, but he does so no longer. It is possible—just possible—he might have called at Mr. Dunn's, but he could not have been detained there so late as this. And if he were—" She stopped, confused and embarrassed.

"As to that," said he, catching at her difficulty with ready tact, "I could easily pretend it was my own anxiety that caused the visit. I could tell him it was likely I should soon see Jack again, and ask of him to let me be the bearer of some kind message to him."

"Yes, yes," muttered Bella, half vacantly; for he had only given to his words the meaning of a mere pretext.

"I think you may trust to me that I will manage the matter delicately. He shall never suspect that he has given any uneasiness by his absence."

"But even this," said she, eagerly, "condemns me to some hours longer of feverish misery. You cannot possibly go back to town and return here in less than two—perhaps three hours."

"I 'll try and do it in half the time," said Conway, rising, and taking his cap. "Where does Mr. Dunn live?"

"In Menion Square. I forget the number, but it does not matter; every one knows his house. It is on the north side."

"You shall see me before—What o'clock is it now?"

"Half-past eight," said she, shuddering, as she saw how late it was.

"Before eleven, I promise you confidently,—and earlier if I can."

"You know my father so very little—so very recently," said Sybella, with some confusion, "that it may be necessary to guard you,—that is, you ought to be made aware that on this day the estate our family has held for centuries was sold. It is true we are no poorer than we were yesterday; the property we called our own, and from habit believed to be such, had been mortgaged this many a year. Why or how we ever fancied that one day or other we should be in a position to pay off the encumbrances, I cannot tell you; but it is true that we did so fancy, and used to talk of that happy event as of one we felt to be in store for us. Well, the blow has fallen at last, and demolished all our castle-building! Like storm-tossed vessels, we saw ships sinking on every side, and yet caught at hope for ourselves. This hope has now left us. The work of this morning has obliterated every trace of it. It is of this, then, I would ask you to be mindful when you see my poor father. He has seen ruin coming this many a year; it never came face to face with him till to-day. I cannot tell how he may brave it, though there was a time I could have answered for his courage."

"Jack Kellett's father could scarcely be deficient in that quality," said Conway, whose flashing eyes showed that it was Jack's sister was uppermost in his mind as he spoke.

"Oh," said she, sorrowfully, "great as the heroism is that meets death on the field of battle, it is nothing to the patient and enduring bravery that confronts the daily ills of life,—confronts them nobly, but in humility, neither buoyed up by inordinate hope, nor cast down by despondency, but manfully resolved to do one's best, and, come what may, to do it without sacrifice of self-respect. Thus meeting fate, and with a temper that all the crosses of life have not made irritable nor suspectful, makes a man to my eyes a greater hero than any of those who charge in forlorn hopes, or single-handed rush up the breach torn by grape-shot." Her cheek, at first pale, grew deeper and deeper red, and her dark eyes flashed till their expression became almost wild in brilliancy, when, suddenly checking her passionate mood, she said, "It were better I should go along with you,—better, at least, I were at hand. He will bear much from me that he would not endure from another, and I will go." So saying, she hastened from the room, and in a moment came back shawled and ready for the road.

"What a night for you to venture out," said Conway; "and I have got no carriage of any kind."

"I am well accustomed to brave bad weather, and care nothing for it."

"It is raining fearfully, and the waves are washing clear over the low sea-wall," said he, trying to dissuade her.

"I have come out here on many such nights, and never the worse for it. Can't you fancy Jack Kellett's sister equal to more than this?" said she, smiling through all her sadness, as she led the way to the door.

And now they were upon the road, the wild rain and the gusty wind beating against them, and almost driving them back. So loud the storm that they did not try to speak, but with her arm close locked within his own, Conway breasted the hurricane with a strange sensation of delight he had never known before.

Scarcely a word passed between them as they went; as the rain beat heavily against her he would try as well as he could to shelter her; when the cutting wind blew more severely, he would draw her arm closer within his own; and yet, thus in silence, they grew to each other like friends of many a year. A sense of trustfulness, a feeling of a common object too, sufficed to establish between them a sentiment to be moulded by the events of after-life into anything. Ay, so is it! Out of these chance affinities grow sometimes the passion of a life, and sometimes the disappointments that embitter existence!

"What a good fortune it was that brought you to my aid to-night," said she; "I had not dared to have come this long road alone."

"What a good fortune mine to have even so humble a service to render you! Jack used to talk to me of you for hours long. Nights just like this have we passed together; he telling me about your habits and your ways, so that this very incident seems to fit into the story of your life as an every-day occurrence. I know," continued he, as she seemed to listen attentively, "how you used to ride over the mountains at home, visiting wild and out-of-the-way spots; how you joined him in his long fishing excursions, exploring the deep mountain gorges while he lingered by the riverside. The very names you gave these desolate places—taken from old books of travel—showed me how a spirit of enterprise was in your heart."

"Were they not happy days!" murmured she, half to herself.

"They must have been," said he, ardently; "to hear of them has charmed the weariest watches of the night, and made me long to know you."

"Yes; but I am not what I was," said she, hastily. "Out of that dreamy, strange existence I have awakened to a world full of its own stern realities. That pleasant indolence has ill prepared me for the road I must travel; and it was selfish too! The vulgarest cares of every-day life are higher aims than all the mere soarings of imagination, and of this truth I am only now becoming aware."

"But it was for never neglecting those very duties Jack used to praise you; he said that none save himself knew you as other than the careful mistress of a household."

"Poor fellow! ours was an humble retinue, and needed little guidance."

"I see," said Conway, "you are too proud to accept of such esteem as mine; but yet you can't prevent me offering it."

"Have I not told you how I prize your kindness?" said she, gently.

"Will you let me think so?" cried Conway, pressing her arm closely; and again they were silent Who knows with what thoughts?

How dreary did the streets seem as they entered Dublin! The hazy lamps, dulled by the fast-falling rain, threw a misty light through the loaded atmosphere; the streets, deserted by all but the very poorest were silent and noiseless, save for the incessant plash of the rain; few lights were seen on any side, and all was darkness and gloom. Wearily they plodded onward, Sybella deeply sunk in her own thoughts as to the future, and Conway, too respectful of her feelings to interrupt her, never uttered a word as they went. At last they reached Merrion Square, and after some little search stood at the door of Mr. Davenport Dunn. Sybella drew a heavy sigh as Conway knocked loudly, and muttered to herself, "Heaven grant me good tidings of my father!"

CHAPTER XXII
AFTER A DINNER-PARTY

Mr. Davenport Dunn had a dinner-party,—he entertained the notables of the capital; and a chief secretary, a couple of judges, a poor-law commissioner, and some minor deities, soldier and civilian, formed his company. They were all social, pleasant, and conversational. The country was growing governable, calendars were light, military duty a mere pastime, and they chatted agreeably over reminiscences of a time—not very remote neither—when Rockites were rife, jails crammed, and the fatigues and perils of a soldier not inferior to those of actual warfare.

"To our worthy host here!" said the Chief Baron, eying his claret before the light,—and it was a comet vintage,—"to our worthy host here are we indebted for most of this happy change."

"Under Providence," whispered the oily Dean of the Chapel Royal.

"Of course, so I mean," said the judge, with that kind of impatience he would have met a needless suggestion in court. "Great public works, stupendous enterprises, and immense expenditure of capital have encountered rebellion by the best of all methods,—prosperity!"

"Is it really extinct,—has Lazarus died, or is he only sleeping?" interposed a small dark-eyed man, with a certain air of determination and a look of defiance that seemed to invite discussion.

"I should, at all events, call it a trance that must lead to perfect recovery," said the Chief Secretary. "Ireland is no longer a difficulty."

"She may soon become something more," said the dark man; "instead of embarrassing your counsels, she may go far towards swaying and controlling them. The energies that were once wasted in factious struggles at home here, may combine to carry on a greater combat in England; and it might even happen that your statesmen might look back with envy to days of orange-and-green memory."

"She would gladly welcome the change you speak of." said the Secretary.

"I'm not so sure of that, sir; you have not already shown yourselves so very tolerant when tried. It is but a few years ago, and your bar rebelled at the thought of an Irishman being made Master of the Rolls in England, and that Irishman, Plunkett."

"I must say," burst in the Attorney-General, fresh from his first session in Parliament, and, more still, his first season in town, "this is but a prejudice,—an unjust prejudice. I can assert for myself that I never rose in the House without experiencing a degree of attention,—a deference, in short—"

"Eminently the right of one whose opinions were so valuable," said the Secretary, bowing blandly, and smiling.

"You did not lash them too often nor too much, Hutchard," said the dark man. "If I remember aright, you rose once in the session, and that was to move an adjournment."

"Ah, Lindley," said the other, good-humoredly, "you are an unforgiving enemy." Then, turning to the Chief Secretary, he said: "He cannot pardon my efforts, successful as they have been, to enable the Fellows of the University to marry. He obtained his fellowship as a safe retirement, and now discovers that his immunity is worth nothing."

"I beg pardon," said Lindley; "I have forgiven you long ago. It was from your arguments in its favor the measure was so long resisted. You are really blameless in the matter!"

The sharp give and take of these sallies—the fruit of those intimacies which small localities produce—rather astonished the English officials, and the Secretary and the Commissioner exchanged glances of significant import; nor was this lost on the Chief Baron, who, to change the topic, suddenly asked,—

"Who bought that estate—Kellett's Court, I think they call it—was sold this morning?"

"I purchased it in trust," said Dunn, "for an English peer."

"Does he intend ever to reside there?"

"He talks of it, my Lord," said Dunn, "the way men talk of something very meritorious that they mean to do—one day or other."

"It went, I hear, for half its value," remarked some one.

"A great deal above that, I assure you," said Dunn. "Indeed, as property is selling now, I should not call the price a bad one."

"Evidently Mr. Kellett was not of your mind," said the former speaker, laughing.

"I 'm told he burst into court to-day and abused every one, from the Bench to the crier, called the sale a robbery, and the judge a knave."

"Not exactly that. He did, it is true, interrupt the order of the Court, but the sale was already concluded. He used very violent language, and so far forgot his respect for the Bench as to incur the penalty of a committal."

"And was he committed?" asked the Secretary.

"He was; but rather as a measure of precaution than punishment. The Court suspected him to be insane." Here Dunn leaned over and whispered a few words in the Secretary's ear. "Nor was it without difficulty," muttered he, in a low tone. "He continued to inveigh in the most violent tone against us all; declared he 'd never leave the Jail without a public apology from the Bench; and, in fact, conducted himself so extravagantly that I half suspected the judge to be right, and that there was some derangement in the case."

"I remember Paul Kellett at the head of the grand jury of his county," said one.

"He was high sheriff the first year I went that circuit," said the judge.

"And how has it ended?—where is he now?" whispered the Secretary.

"I persuaded him to come home here with me, and after a little calming down he became reasonable and has gone to his own house, but only within the last hour. It was that my servant whispered me, when he last brought in the wine."

"And I suppose, after all," said the Poor-Law Commissioner, "there was nothing peculiar in this instance; his case was one of thousands."

"Quite true, sir," said Lindley. "Statistical tables can take no note of such-like applicants for out-door relief; all are classified as paupers."

"It must be acknowledged," said the Secretary, in a tone of half rebuke, "that the law has worked admirably; there is but one opinion on that subject in England."

"I should be greatly surprised were it otherwise," said Lindley; "I never heard that the Cornish fishermen disparaged shipwrecks!"

"Who is that gentleman?" whispered the Secretary to Dunn.

"A gentleman very desirous to be Crown Prosecutor at Melbourne," said Dunn, with a smile.

"He expresses himself somewhat freely," whispered the other.

"Only here, sir,—only here, I assure you. He is our stanchest supporter in the College."

"Of course we shall take Sebastopol, sir," said a colonel from the end of the table. "The Russians are already on half rations, and their ammunition is nigh exhausted." And now ensued a lively discussion of military events, wherein the speakers displayed as much confidence as skill.

"It strikes me," said Lindley, "we are at war with the Emperor Nicholas for practising pretty much the same policy we approve of so strenuously for ourselves. He wanted to treat Turkey like an encumbered estate. There was the impoverished proprietor, the beggared tenantry, the incapacity for improvement,—all the hackneyed arguments, in fact, for selling out the Sultan that we employ so triumphantly against the Irish gentleman."

"Excuse me," said the Attorney-General, "he wanted to take forcible possession."

"Nothing of the kind. He was as ready to offer compensation as we ourselves are when we superannuate a clerk or suppress an office. His sole mistake was that he proposed a robbery at the unlucky moment that the nation had taken its periodical attack of virtue,—we were in the height of our honest paroxysm when he asked us to be knaves; and hence all that has followed."

"You estimate our national morality somewhat cheaply, sir," said the Commissioner.

"As to morals, I think we are good political economists. We buy cheaply, and endeavor, at least, to sell in the dearest markets."

"No more wine, thank you," said the Secretary, rising. "A cup of coffee, with pleasure."

It was a part of Davenport Dunn's policy to sprinkle his dinner company with men like Lindley. They were what physicians call a sort of mild irritants, and occasionally very useful in their way; but, in the present instance, he rather suspected that the application had been pushed too far, and he approached the Secretary in the drawing-room with a kind of half apology for his guest.

"Ireland," said he, "has always possessed two species of place-hunters: the one, patiently supporting Government for years, look calmly for the recognition of their services as a debt to be paid; the other, by an irritating course of action, seem to indicate how vexatious and annoying they may prove if not satisfactorily dealt with. Lindley is one of these, and he ought to be provided for."

"I declare to you, Dunn," said the Secretary, as he drew his arm within the other's, and walked with him into the back drawing-room, "these kind of men make government very difficult in Ireland. There is no reserve—no caution about them. They compromise one at every step. You are the only Irishman I ever met who would seem to understand the necessity of reserve."

Dunn bowed twice. It was like the acknowledgment of what he felt to be a right.

"I go further," said the other, warming; "you are the only man here who has given us real and effective support, and yet never asked for anything."

"What could I wish for better than to see the country governed as it is?" said Dunn, courteously.

"All are not inspired so patriotically, Dunn. Personal advantages have their influence on most men."

"Of course,—naturally enough. But I stand in no need of aid in this respect I don't want for means. I could n't, if you offered it, take office; my hands are too full already, and of work which another might not be able to carry out. Rank, of course—distinction—" and he stopped, and seemed confused.

"Well, come, we might meet you there, Dunn," said the other, coaxingly. "Be frank with me. What do you wish for?"

"My family is of humble origin, it is true," said Dunn; "but, without invidious reflection, I might point to some others—" Again he hesitated.

"*That* need not be an obstacle," said the Secretary.

"Well, then, on the score of fortune, there are some poorer than myself in—in—" He stopped again.

"Very few as wealthy, I should say, Dunn,—very few, indeed. Let me only know your wishes. I feel certain how they will be treated."

"I am aware," said Dunn, with some energy, "that you incur the risk of some attack in anything you would do for me. I am necessarily in scant favor with a large party here. They would *assail you*, they would *vilify me*; but that would pass over. A few weeks—a few months at furthest—"

"To be sure,—perfectly correct It would be mere momentary clamor. Sir Davenport Dunn, Baronet, would survive—"

"I beg pardon," said Dunn, in a voice tremulous with emotion. "I don't think I heard you aright; I trust, at least, I did not."

The Secretary looked quickly in his face, and saw it pale, the lips slightly quivering, and the brow contracted.

"I was saying," said he, in a voice broken and uncertain, "that I'm sure the Premier would not refuse to recommend you to her Majesty for a baronetcy."

"May I make so bold as to ask if you have already held any conversation with the Minister on this subject?"

"None, whatever. I assure you, most solemnly, that I have no instructions on the subject, nor have I ever had any conversation with him on the matter."

"Then let me beg you to forget what has just passed between us. It is, after all, mere chit-chat. That's a Susterman's, that portrait you are looking at," said he, eager to change the topic. "It is said to be a likeness of Bianca Capello."

"A very charming picture, indeed; purchased, I suppose, in your last visit abroad."

"Yes; I bought it at Verona. Its companion, yonder, was a present from the Archduke Stephen, in recognition, as he was gracious enough to call it, of some counsels I had given the Government engineers about drainage in Hungary. Despotic governments, as we like to term them, have this merit, at least,—they confer acts of munificent generosity."

The Secretary muttered an assent, and looked confused.

"I reaped a perfect harvest of crosses and decorations," continued Dunn, "during my tour. I have got cordons from countries I should be puzzled to point out on the map, and am a noble in almost every land of Europe but my own."

"Ours is the solitary one where the distinction is not a mere title," said the other, "and, consequently, there are graver considerations about conferring it than if it were a mere act of courtesy."

"Where power is already acquired there is often good policy in legitimatizing it," said Dunn, gravely. "They say that even the Church of Rome knows how to affiliate a heresy.—Well, Clowes, what is it?" asked he of the butler, who stood awaiting a favorable moment to address him. He now drew nigh, and whispered some words in his ear.

"But you said I was engaged—that I had company with me?" said Dunn, in reply.

"Yes, sir, but she persisted in saying that if I brought up her name you would certainly see her, were it but for a moment This is her card."

"Miss Kellett," said Dunn to himself. "Very well. Show her into the study, I will come down.—It is the daughter of that unfortunate gentleman we were speaking of awhile ago," said he, showing the card. "I suppose some new disaster has befallen him. Will you excuse me for a moment?"

As Dunn slowly descended the stairs, a very strange conflict was at work within him. From his very boyhood there had possessed him a stern sentiment of vengeance against the Kellett family. It was the daily lesson his father repeated to him. It grew with his years, and vague and unmeaning as it appeared, it had the force of an instinct. His own memory failed him as to all the circumstances of an early insult, but enough remained to make him know that he had been ignominiously treated and expelled from the house. In the great career of his life, with absorbing cares and high interests around him, he had little time for such memories, but in moments of solitude or of depression the thought would come up, and a sense of vindictive pleasure fill him, as he remembered, in the stern words of his father, where was *he*, and where were *they?* In the protection he had that very day assumed to throw over Kellett in the Court, there was the sentiment of an insolent triumph; and here was again the daughter of the once proud man supplicating an interview with him.

These were his thoughts as he entered the room where Sybella Kellett was standing near the fire. She had taken off her bonnet, and as her long hair fell down, and her dripping clothes clung to her, the picture of poverty and destitution her appearance conveyed revolted against the sentiment which had so lately filled him, and it was in a voice of gentle meaning he asked her to be seated.

"Can you tell me of my father, sir?" said she, eagerly, and not heeding his words; "he left home early this morning, and has never returned."

"I can tell you everything, Miss Kellett," said he, in a kind voice. "It will reassure you at once when I say he is well. Before this he is at home again."

The young girl clasped her hands closely, and her pale lips murmured some faint words.

"In a moment of excitement this morning he said something to offend the Court. It was an emergency to try a calmer temper, perhaps, than his; indeed, he ought not to have been there; at all events, he was betrayed into expressions which could not be passed over in mere silence, and he was committed—"

"To prison?" said she, faintly.

"Yes, he was taken into custody, but only for a few hours. I obtained his release soon after the Court rose. The difficulty was to make him accept of his liberation. Far from having calmed down, his passion had only increased, and it was only after much entreaty that he consented to leave the jail and come here with me. In fact, it was under the pretence of drawing up a formal protest against his arrest that he did come, and he has been employed in this manner till about an hour ago, when one of my clerks took charge of him to convey him home. A little quietness and a little rest will restore him perfectly, however, and I have no doubt to-morrow or next day will leave no trace of this excitement."

"You have been most kind," said she, rising, "and I am very grateful for it. We owe much to you already, and this last but increases the debt."

Dunn stood silently contemplating her, as she replaced her bonnet and prepared for the road. At last he said, "Have you come all this way on foot and alone?"

"On foot, but not alone; a comrade of my brother's—a fellow-soldier of his—kindly gave me his escort. He is waiting for me now without."

"Oh, then, the adventure has had its compensation to a certain degree," said Dunn, with a smile of raillery.

"Either I do not understand you, or you mistake me,—which is it?" said she, boldly.

"My dear young lady," said Dunn, hastily, "do not let me offend you. There is everything in what you have done this night to secure you respect and esteem. We live in a time when there is wonderfully little of personal devotion; and commonplace men like myself may well misjudge its sacrifices."

"And yet it is precisely from you I should have expected the reverse. If great minds are tainted with littleness, where are we to look for high and noble sentiments?" She moved towards the door as she spoke; and Dunn, anticipating her, said,—

"Do not go for a moment; let me offer you some refreshment, even a glass of wine. Well, then, your friend? It is scarcely courteous to leave him outside in such weather."

"Pray forgive me not accepting your offer; but I am impatient to be at home again. My father, too, will be distressed at my absence."

"But I will send my carriage with you; you shall not walk," said he, ringing the bell.

"Do not think me ungrateful, but I had rather return as I came. You have no idea, sir, how painfully kindness comes to hearts like ours. A sense of pride sustains us through many a trial; break down this, and we are helpless."

"Is it that you will accept nothing at my hands,—even the most commonplace of attentions? Well, I'll try if I cannot be more fortunate elsewhere;" and so saying, he hurried at once from the room. Before Sybella could well reflect on his words, he was back again, followed by Charles Conway.

"Miss Kellett was disposed to test your Crimean habits again, my good fellow," said Dunn, "by keeping you out there under this terrible rain, and I perceive you have got some rough treatment already;" and he looked at the armless sleeve of his jacket.

"Yes," said Conway, laughing, "a piece of Russian politeness!"

Few as were the words, the tone and manner of the speaker struck Dunn with astonishment, and he said,—

"Have you been long in the service?"

"Some years," was the short reply.

"It's very strange," said Dunn, regarding him fixedly, "but your features are quite familiar to me. You are very like a young officer who cut such a dash here formerly,—a spendthrift fellow, in a Lancer regiment."

"Pray don't involve yourself in any difficulty," said Conway, "for, perhaps—indeed, I 'm convinced—you are describing myself."

"Conway, of the Twelfth?"

"The same, at your service,—at least, in so far as being ruined and one-armed means the same with the fellow who had a good fortune, and two hands to scatter it."

"I must go. I 'm impatient to be away," said Sybella, eagerly.

"Then there is the carriage at the door," said Dunn. "This time I have resolved to have my way;" and he gave her his arm courteously to conduct her.

"Could you call upon me to-morrow—could you breakfast with me, Mr. Conway?" said Dunn, as he gave him his hand at parting; "my request is connected with a subject of great importance to yourself."

"I 'm your man," said Conway, as he followed Sybella into the carriage. And away they drove.

CHAPTER XXIII
A BREAKFAST-TABLE

When, punctual to the appointed time, Charles Conway presented himself at Mr. Dunn's door, he learned to his astonishment that that gentleman had gone out an hour before to breakfast with the Chief Secretary in the Park.

"But I came by invitation to breakfast with your master," said he.

"Possibly so," said Clowes, scanning the simply clad soldier before him. "He never mentioned it to me; that's all I know."

Conway stood for a moment, half uncertain what to say; then, with a quiet smile, he said, "Pray tell him that I was here,—my name is Conway."

"As to the breakfast part of the matter," said Clowes, who felt "rather struck" by something in the soldier's manner, as he afterwards expressed it, "I 'm just about to take mine; you might as well join me."

Conway looked him full in the face,—such a stare was it as a man gives when he questions the accuracy of his own senses; a slight flush then rose to his cheek, and his lip curled, and then, with a saucy laugh that seemed to combat the passing irritation he was suffering, he said, "It's not a bad notion, after all; I'm your man."

Now, though Mr. Clowes had anticipated a very different reception to his politeness, he said nothing, but led the way into his sanctum, trusting to the locality and its arrangement to have their due effect upon his guest. Indeed, in this respect, he did but fair justice to the comforts around him.

The breakfast-table, placed close to a cheerful fire, was spread with every luxury of that meal. A small spirit lamp burned under a dish of most appetizing cutlets, in the midst of various kinds of bread, and different sorts of preserves. The grateful odor of mocha mingled with the purer perfume of fresh flowers, which, although in midwinter, were never wanting at Mr. Clowes's breakfast-table, while in the centre rose a splendid pineapple, the first of the season, duly offered by the gardener to the grand vizier of Davenport Dunn.

"I can promise you a better breakfast than *he* would have given you," said Clowes, as he motioned his guest to a seat, while he significantly jerked his thumb towards Dunn's study. "*He* takes tea and dry toast, and he quite forgets to order anything else. He has some crank or other about beginning the day with a light meal; quite a mistake,—don't you think so?"

"This is not the most favorable moment to make me a convert to that opinion," said Conway, laughing. "I must confess I incline to *your* side of the controversy."

"There are herrings there," said Clowes, "and a spatchcock coming. You see," continued he, returning to the discussion, "he overworks—he does too much—taxes his powers beyond their strength—beyond any man's strength;" and here Mr. Clowes threw himself back in his chair, and looked pompously before him, as though to say, Even Clowes would n't have constitution for what *he* does.—"A man must have his natural rest, sir, and his natural support;" and in evidence of the last, he re-helped himself to the Strasburg pâté.

"Your words are wisdom, and washed down with such Bordeaux I 'd like to see who 'd gainsay them," said Conway, with a droll twinkle of the eye.

"Better coffee, that, I fancy, than you got in the Crimea," said Clowes, pointing to the coffee-pot.

"I suspect Lord Raglan himself never saw such a breakfast as this. May I ask if it be your every-day meal?"

"We change slightly with the seasons. Oysters and Sauterne suit spring; and then, when summer sets in, we lean towards the subacid fruits and claret-cup. Dash your pineapple with a little rum,—it's very old, and quite a liqueur."

"This must be a very jolly life of yours," said Conway, as he lighted his cigarette and placed his feet on the fender.

"You 'd prefer it to the trenches or the rifle-pits, I suspect," said Clowes, laughing, "and small blame to you. It was out there you lost your arm, I suppose?"

Conway nodded, and puffed on in silence.

"A bad business,—a bad business we 're making of it all! The Crimea was a mistake; we should have marched direct to Moscow,—Moscow or St Petersburg,—I don't care which."

"Nor should I, if we could get there," said Conway, quietly.

"Get there,—and why not? Fifty thousand British bayonets are a match for the world in arms. It is a head we want, sir,—capacity to deal with the great questions of strategy. Even you yourself must have remarked that we have no generalship,—no guidance—"

"I won't say that," said Conway, quietly. "We're knocking hard at Sebastopol, and all we can say is we have n't found the weak spot yet."

"The weak spot! Why, it 's all weak,—earthworks, nothing but earthworks! Now, don't tell me that Wellington would have minded earthworks! Ah, we have fallen upon sad times!" sighed he, piteously. "Our land commanders say earthworks are impregnable; our admirals say stone walls can't be attacked."

Conway laughed again, and lighted a fresh cigarette.

"And what pension have you for that?" asked Clowes, glancing at the empty sleeve.

"A mere trifle; I can't exactly tell you, for I have not applied for it"

"I would, though; I 'd have it out of them, and I 'd have whatever I could, besides. They 'd not give *you* the Bath; that they keep for gentlemen—"

Conway took his cigar from his lips, and while his cheek burned, he seemed about to reply; then, resuming his smoking, he lay back and said nothing.

"After all," said Clowes, "there must be distinctions of rank. One regrets, one deplores, but can't help it Look at all the attempts at equality, and see their failures. No, sir, you have *your* place in the social scale, and I have *mine*."

Now, when Mr. Clowes had enunciated this sentiment, he seemed suddenly to be struck by its severity; for he added, "Not but that every man is respectable in his own rank; don't imagine that I look down upon you."

Conway's eyes opened widely as he stared at him, and he puffed his cigar a little more energetically, but never spoke.

"You 've done with the service, I suppose?" said Clowes, after a while.

"I'm afraid so," said Conway, sighing.

"Well, *he*"—and he jerked his thumb towards Dunn's room—"he is the man to help you to something snug. He can give away places every hour of the day. Ay, sir," said he, warming, "he can make anything, from an archbishop to a barony constable."

"I rather fear that my capacity for employment might not be found very remarkable. I have idle habits and ways," said Conway, smiling.

"Bad things, my friend,—bad things for any man, but especially for a poor one. I myself began life in an humble way,—true, I assure you; but with industry, zeal, and attention, I am what you see me."

"That *is* encouraging, certainly," said Conway, gravely.

"It is so, and I mention it for your advantage."

Charles Conway now arose, and threw the half-smoked cigar into the fire. The movement betokened impatience, and, sooth to say, he was half angry with himself; for, while disposed to laugh at the vanity and conceit of the worthy butler, he still felt that he was his guest, and that such ridicule was ill applied to one whose salt he had eaten.

"You're not going without seeing him?" said Clowes. "He 's sure to be in before noon. We are to receive the Harbor Commissioners exactly at twelve."

"I have a call to make, and at some distance off in the country, this morning."

"Well, if I can be of any use to you, just tell me," said Clowes, good-naturedly. "My position here—one of trust and confidence, you may imagine—gives me many an opportunity to serve a friend; and I like you. I was taken with your manner as you came into the hall this morning, and I said to myself, 'There 's good stuff in that young fellow, whoever he is.' And I ain't wrong. You have some blood in you, I'll be bound."

"We used to be rather bumptious about family," said Conway, laughing; "but I suspect the world has taught us to get rid of some of our conceit."

"Never mind the world. Pride of birth is a generous prejudice. I have never forgotten that my grandfather, on the mother's side, was a drysalter. But can I be of any use to you? that's the question."

"I 'm inclined to think not; though I 'm just as grateful to you. Mr. Dunn asked me here this morning, I suspect, to talk over the war with me. Men naturally incline to hear what an eyewitness has to say, and he may have fancied I could have mentioned some new fact, or suggested some new expedient, which in these days seems such a fashionable habit, when everybody has his advice to proffer."

"No, no," said Clowes, shaking his head; "it could n't be that. *We* have been opposed to this war from the beginning. It was all a mistake, a dead mistake. Aberdeen agreed with us, but we were outvoted. They would have a fight. They said we wanted something to get cotton-spinning out of our blood; and, egad! I suspect they've got it.

"Our views," continued Clowes, pompously, "were either a peace or a march to St. Petersburg. This French alliance is a rotten thing, sir. That Corsican will double on us. The very first moment any turn of fortune gives France an advantage, *he 'll* make peace, and leave us all the obloquy of a reluctant assent. That's *his* view,—that's mine, too; and we are seldom mistaken."

"For all that, I wish I were back there again," said Conway. "With every one of its hardships—and they were no trifles—it was a better life than this lounging one I lead now. Tell Mr. Dunn that I was here. Say that I enjoyed your excellent hospitality and pleasant company; and accept my hearty thanks for both." And with a cordial shake of the hand, Conway wished him "Good-bye," and departed.

"That's just the class of men we want in our army," said Clowes, as he followed him with his eyes. "A stamp somewhat above the common,—a very fine young fellow too."

In less than a quarter of an hour after Conway's departure, Davenport Dunn's carriage drew up at his door, and Mr. Clowes hastened to receive his master.

"Are they out, sir,—are they out?" said he, eagerly, as he followed him into the study.

"Yes," said Dunn; "but everything is still at sixes and sevens. Lord Derby has been sent for, and Lord John sent for, and Lord Palmerston sent for, but nothing decided on,—nothing done."

"And how will it end?" asked Clowes, like one waiting for the solution of a difficulty.

"Who has called this morning?" said Dunn, curtly. "Has Lord Glengariff been here?"

"No, sir. Sir Jacob Harris and the Drumsna Directors are all in waiting, and a rather promiscuous lot are in the back parlor. A young soldier, too, was here. He fancied you had asked him to breakfast, and so I made him join mine."

"Indeed!" exclaimed Dunn. "I forgot all about that engagement. How provoking! Can you find out where he is stopping?"

"No. But he's sure to drop in again: I half promised him a sort of protection; and he looks a shrewd sort of fellow, and not likely to neglect his hits."

A strange twinkle shone in Dunn's eyes as he heard this speech, and a queer motion at the angle of his mouth accompanied it, but he never spoke a word.

As for Conway, meanwhile, he was briskly stepping out towards Clontarf, to inquire after poor Kellett, whose state was one to call for much anxiety. To the intense excitement of the morning there had succeeded a dull and apathetic condition, in which he seemed scarcely to notice anything or anybody. A look half weary, half vacant, was in his eye; his head was drooped; and a low muttering to himself was the only sign he gave of any consciousness whatever. Such was his state when Conway left the cottage late on the night before, with a promise to be back there again early the next morning.

Conway saw that the shutters of the little drawing-room were half closed as he entered the garden, and his quiet, cautious knock at the door denoted the fear at his heart. From the window, partly open, came a low, moaning sound, which, as he listened, he discovered to be the sick man's voice.

"He was just asking if you had come," said Bella. "He has been talking of poor Jack, and fancies that you have some tidings of him." And so saying, she led him into the house.

Seated before the fire, in a low chair, his hands resting on his knees, and his gaze fixed on the embers, Kellett never turned his head round as they entered, nor did he notice Bella, as, in a soft, low voice, she mentioned Conway's name.

"He has come out to see you, dear papa; to sit with you and keep you company, and talk about dear Jack."

"Ay!" said the sick man, in a vague, purposeless tone; and Conway now took a seat at his side, and laid one of his hands over his.

"You are better to-day, Captain Kellett, ain't you?" said he, kindly.

"Yes," said he, in the same tone as before.

"And will be still better to-morrow, I trust, and able to come out and take this long walk with me we have so often promised ourselves."

Kellett turned and looked him full in the face. The expression of his features was that of one vainly struggling with some confusion of ideas, and earnestly endeavoring to find his way through difficulties, and a faint, painful sigh at last showed that the attempt was a failure.

"What does this state mean? Is it mere depression, or is it serious illness?" whispered Bella.

"I am not skilful enough to say," replied Conway, cautiously; "but I hope and trust it is only the effect of a shock, and will pass off as it came."

"Ay," said Kellett, in a tone that startled them, and for a moment they fancied he must have overheard them; but one glance at his meaningless features showed that they had no ground for their fears.

"The evil is deeper than that," whispered Bella, again. "This cold dew on his forehead, those shiverings that pass over him from time to time, and that look in his eye, such as I have never seen before, all betoken a serious malady. Could you fetch a doctor,—some one in whom you place confidence?"

"I do know of one, in whom I have the fullest reliance," said Conway, rising hastily. "I'll go for him at once."

"Lose not a moment, then," said Bella, as she took the place he had just vacated, and placed her hand on her father's, as Conway had done.

Kellett's glance slowly followed Conway to the door, and then turned fully in Bella's face, while, with a voice of a thrilling distinctness, he said, "Too late, darling,—too late!"

The tears gushed from Bella's eyes, and her lips trembled; but she never uttered a word, but sat silent and motionless as before.

Kellett's eyes were now bent upon her fixedly, with an expression of deep and affectionate interest; and he slowly drew his hand from beneath hers, and placed his arm around her.

"I wish he was come, darling," said he, at last.

"Who, papa?—the doctor?" asked Bella.

"The doctor!—no, not the doctor," said he, sighing heavily.

"It is poor Jack you are thinking of," said she, affectionately.

"Poor, sure enough," muttered he; "we're all poor now." And an inexpressible misery was in his face as he spoke.

Bella wished to speak words of comfort and encouragement; she longed to tell him that she was ready and willing to devote herself to him; that in a little time, and by a little effort on their part, their changed fortunes would cease to fret them; that they would learn to see how much of real happiness can consist with narrow means, but she knew not in what spirit her words might be accepted; a chance phrase, an accidental expression, might jar upon some excited feeling, and only irritate where it was meant to soothe, and so she only pressed her lips to his hand and was silent.

The sick man's head gradually declined lower and lower, his breathing grew heavier, and he slept. The long dreary day dragged on its weary hours, and still Sybella sat by her father's side watching and waiting. It was already dusk, when a carriage stopped at the little gate and Conway got out, and was quickly followed by another. "The doctor, at last," muttered Sybella, gently moving from her place; and Kellett awoke and looked at him.

Conway had barely time to whisper the name of the physician in Bella's ear, when Sir Maurice Dashwood entered. There was none of the solemn gravity of the learned doctor, none of the catlike stealthiness of the fashionable practitioner, in his approach. Sir Maurice advanced like a man entering a drawing-room before a dinner-party, easy, confident, and affable. He addressed a few words to Miss Kellett, and then placing his chair next her father's, said, —

"I hope my old brother officer does n't forget me. Don't you remember Dashwood of the 43d?"

"The wildest chap in the regiment," muttered Kellett, "though he was the surgeon. Did you know him, sir?"

"I should think I did," said the doctor, smiling; "he was a great chum of yours, was n't he? You messed together in the Pyrenees for a whole winter."

"A wild chap, — could never come to any good," went on Kellett to himself. "I wonder what became of him."

"I can tell you, I think. Meanwhile, let me feel your pulse. No fixed pain here," said he, touching the region of the heart. "Look fully at me. Ah, it is there you feel it," said he, as he touched the other's forehead; "a sense of weight rather than pain, isn't it?"

"It's like lead I feel it," said Kellett; "and when I lay it down, I don't think I 'll ever be able to lift it up again."

"That you will, and hold it high too, Kellett," said the doctor, warmly. "You must just follow my counsels for a day or two, and we shall see a great change in you."

"I 'll do whatever you bid me, but it's no use, doctor; but I 'll do it for her sake there." And the last words were in a whisper.

"That's spoken like yourself, Kellett," said the other, cheerily. "Now let me have pen and ink."

As the doctor sat down to a table, he beckoned Bella to his side, and writing a few words rapidly on the paper before him, motioned to her to read them.

She grasped the chair as she read the lines, and it shook beneath her hand, while an ashy pallor spread over her features.

"Ask him if I might have a little brandy-and-water, Bella," said the sick man.

"To be sure you may," said Sir Maurice; "or, better still, a glass of claret; and it so happens I have just the wine to suit him. Conway, come back with me, and I 'll give you a half-dozen of it."

"And is there nothing—is there no—" Bella could utter no more, when a warning of the doctor's hand showed that her father's eyes were on her.

"Come here, Bella," said he, in a low tone,—"come here to me. There's a pound in my waistcoat-pocket, in my room; put a shilling inside of it, for it's a guinea he ought to have, and gold, by rights, if we had it. And tell him we 'll send for him if we want to see him again. Do it delicately, darling, so as not to let him know. Say I 'm used to these attacks; say they're in the family; say—But there, they are driving away,—they're off! and he never waited for his fee! That's the strangest thing of all." And so he fell a-thinking over this curious fact, muttering from time to time to himself, "I never heard of the like before."

CHAPTER XXIV
THE COTTAGE

Davenport Dunn had but little leisure to think about Conway or poor Kellett. A change of Ministry had just occurred in England, and men's minds were all eagerly speculating who was "to come in." Crowds of country gentlemen flocked up to Dublin, and "rising men" of all shades of opinion anxiously paraded their own claims to notice. Dunn's house was besieged from morning to night by visitors, all firmly persuaded that he must know more of the coming event than any one. Whether such was really the case, or that he deemed it good policy to maintain the delusion, Dunn affected a slight indisposition, and refused to admit any visitor. Mr. Clowes, indeed, informed the inquirers that it was a mere passing ailment,—"a slight derangement in the bronchi," he said; but be rigidly maintained the blockade, and suffered none to infringe it.

Of course, a hundred rumors gave their own version of this illness. It was spleen; it was indignation; the Government had thrown him over: he had been refused the secretaryship which he had formerly applied for. Others averred that his attack was most serious,—an ossification or a scirrhus of some cartilage, a thing always fatal and dreadfully painful. Some went further. It was his prosperity was in peril. Over-speculation had jeopardized him, and he was deep in the "Crédit Mobilier." Now, all this while, the disappointed politician, the hopeless invalid, and the ruined speculator ate and drank well, received and wrote replies to innumerable confidential notes from those in power, and carefully drew up a list of such as he desired to recommend to the Government for place and employment.

Every morning Sir Maurice Dashwood's well-appointed cab drew up at his door, and the lively baronet would dash up the stairs to Dunn's room with all the elasticity of youth, and more real energy than is the fortune of one young fellow in a thousand. With a consummate knowledge of men and the world, he was second to none in his profession. He felt he could afford to indulge the gay and buoyant spirits with which Nature had blessed him, and even, doctor that he was, take his share in all the sports of the field and all the pleasures of society.

"Well, Dunn," cried he, gayly, one morning, as he entered the carefully darkened room where the other sat, surrounded with papers and deep in affairs, "I think you may accept your bill of health, and come out of dock tomorrow. They are gazetted now, and the world as wise as yourself."

"So I mean to do," said Dunn. "I intend to dine with the Chancellor. What is said about the new Government?"

"Very little. There is really little to say. They are nearly the same pieces, only placed differently on the board. This trumpery cry about 'right men in right places' will lead to all kinds of confusion, since it will eternally suggest choice, which, in plain words, means newspaper dictation."

"As good as any other dictation: better in one respect, for it so often recants its judgments," said Dunn, sarcastically.

"Well, they are unanimous about *you* this morning. They are all eagerly inquiring in what way the Government propose to recognize the services of one of the ablest men and most disinterested patriots of our day."

"I don't want anything from them," said Dunn, testily, and walking to the window to avoid the keen, sharp glance the other bent upon him.

"The best way to get it when you *do* want," said Dash-wood. "By the way, what's our new Viceroy like?"

"A very good appointment, indeed," said Dunn, gravely.

"Oh, I don't mean that. I want to know what he is personally: is he stiff, haughty, grave, gay, stand-off, or affable?"

"I should say, from what I have seen of Lord Allington, that he is one of those men who are grave without sadness—"

"Come, come, never mind the antithesis; does he care for society, does he like sport, is he free-handed, or has he only come here with the traditional policy to 'drain Ireland'?"

"You 'll like him much," said Dunn, in his natural voice, "and he 'll like *you*."

Sir Maurice smiled, as though to say, "I could answer as much for myself;" and then asked, "Have you known him long?"

"No; that is, not very long," said Dunn, hesitating, "nor very intimately. Why do you ask?"

"Just because I want to get something,—at once too. There's a poor fellow, a patient of mine now,—we were brother officers once,—in a very sad way. Your friends of the Encumbered Court have Just been selling him out, and by the shock they have so stunned him that his brain has been attacked; at present it does not seem so formidable, but it will end in softening, and all the rest of it. Now, if they 'd make him something at once,—quickly it must be,—he could drop out on some small retired allowance,—anything, in short, that would support him."

"But what is it to be?" asked Dunn.

"Whatever you like to make him. It can scarcely be a bishop, for he's not in orders; nor a judge, for he was not called to the bar; but why not a commissioner of something? You have them for all purposes and of all degrees."

"You take a low estimate of commissionerships, I perceive," said Dunn, smiling.

"They are row-boats, where two or three pull, and the rest only dip their oars. But come, promise me you 'll look to this; take a note of the name,—Paul Kellett a man of excellent family, and once with a large landed property."

"I know him," said Dunn, with a peculiar significance.

"And know nothing to his disadvantage, I'm certain. He was a good officer and a kind-hearted fellow, whom we all liked. And there he is now," added he, after a pause, "with a charming girl—his daughter—and I really don't believe they have a five-pound note in the world. You must do this for me, Dunn. I 'm bent upon it!"

"I'll see what can be done about it. Anything like a job is always a difficulty."

"And everything is a job here, Dunn, and no man knows better how to deal with one." And so saying, and with a pleasant laugh, the gay-hearted doctor hurried away, to carry hope, and some portion at least of his own cheery nature, into many a darkened sick-room.

Though several names were announced with pressing entreaties for an audience, Dunn would see no one. He continued to walk up and down the room deep in thought, and seemed resolved that none should interrupt him. There were events enough to occupy, cases enough to engage him,—high questions of policy, deep matters of interest, all that can stimulate ambition, all that can awaken energy,—and yet, amidst all, where were his thoughts straying? They were away to the years of his early boyhood, when he had been Paul Kellett's playfellow, and when he was admitted—a rare honor—to the little dinner of the nursery! What a strange thing it was that it was "there and then" his first studies of life and character should have been made; that it was there and then he first moulded himself to the temper and ways of another, conforming to caprices and tending to inclinations not his own. Stern tyrants were these child masters! How they *did* presume upon their high station, how severely did they make him feel the distance between them, and what arts did they teach him,—what subtle devices to outwit their own imperiousness and give him the mastery over them! To these memories succeeded others more painful still; and Dunn's brow contracted and his lips became tight-drawn as he recollected them.

"I suppose even my father would allow that the debt is acquitted now," muttered he to himself. "I 'll go and see them!" said he, after a moment; "such a sight will teach me how far I have travelled in life."

He gently descended a private stair that led to the garden, and, passing out by the stables, soon gained the street Walking rapidly on to the first stand, he engaged a car, and started for Clontarf.

If Davenport Dunn never gave way to a passion for revenge in life, it was in some sort because he deemed it a luxury above his means. He often fancied to himself that the time might come when he could indulge in this pleasure, just as now he revelled in a thousand others, which once had seemed as remote. His theory was that he had not yet attained that eminence whence he could dispense with all aid, and he knew not what man's services at any moment might be useful to him. Still, with all this, he never ceased to enjoy whatever of evil fortune befell those who even in times past had injured him. To measure their destiny with his now, was like striking a balance with Fate,—a balance so strong in his favor; and when he had not actually contributed to their downfall, he deemed himself high-minded, generous, and pure-hearted.

It was reflecting in this wise he drove along, and at last drew up at Kellett's door; his knock was answered by Sybella herself, whose careworn features and jaded look scarcely reminded him of her appearance when first he saw her, flushed and excited by exercise.

"I thought I'd come myself and ask after him," said Dunn, as he explained the object of his visit.

"He has scarce consciousness enough to thank you," said she, mournfully, "but *I* am very grateful to you;" and she preceded him into the room, where her father sat in the selfsame attitude as before.

"He doesn't know me," whispered Dunn, as the sick man's gaze was turned to him without the slightest sign of recognition,—"he does n't know me!"

"I do. I know you well, Davenport Dunn, and I know why you come here," said Kellett, with a distinctness that startled them both. "Leave us alone together, Bella darling; we want to talk privately."

Sybella was so astounded at this sudden show of intelligence that she scarcely knew how to take it, or what to do; but at a gesture from Dunn, she stepped noiselessly from the room, and left them together.

"You must not excite yourself, Kellett, nor prejudice your prospect of recovery by any exertion; there will be time enough for matters of business hereafter—"

"No, there won't; that's the reason I want to talk to you now," said Kellett, sharply. "I know well enough my life is short here."

Dunn began some phrase of cheering meaning; but the other stopped him abruptly, and said,—

"There, there, don't be losing time that way. Is that the touch of a man long for this world?" and he laid on the other's hand his own hot and burning fingers. "I said I knew why you came here, Dunn," continued he, more strongly; "it was to look at your work. Ay, just so. It was *you* brought me to this, and you wanted to see it. Turn your eyes round the room, and you 'll see it's poor enough. Look in at that bedroom there, and you 'll say it could n't be much more humble! I pawned my watch yesterday; there's all that's out of it;" and he showed some pieces of silver and copper mixed together in the palm of his hand; "there's not a silver spoon left, so that you see you 've done it well!"

"My dear Kellett, these words of yours have no meaning in them—"

"Maybe not; but maybe you understand them, for all that! Look here, now, Dunn," said he, clutching his hand in his own feverish grasp; "what the Child begins the Man finishes! I know you well, and I 've watched you for many a year. All your plans and schemes never deceived *me*; but it's a house of cards you 're building, after all! What I knew about you as a boy others may know as a man; and I would n't believe St. Peter if he told me you only did it *once!*"

"If this be not raving, it is a deliberate insult!" muttered Dunn, sternly, while he rudely pushed away the other's hand, and drew back his chair.

"Well, it's not raving, whatever it is," said Kellett, calmly. "The cold air of the earth that's opening for me clears my brain, and I know well the words I 'm saying, and the warning I 'm giving you. Tell the people fairly that it's only scheming you were; that the companies are a bubble and the banks a sham; that you 're only juggling this man's credit against that, making the people think that you have the confidence of the Government, and the Government believe that you can do what you like with the people. Go at once and publish it, that you are only cheating them all, or you 'll have a gloomier ending even than this!"

"I came out of compassion for you."

"No, you did n't, not a bit of it. You came to tell old Mat Dunn that the score was wiped off; *he* came to the window here this morning and looked in at me."

"My father? Impossible! He's nearly ninety, and barely able to move about a room."

"I don't care for that: there he was, where you see that bush, and he leaned on the window-sill and looked at me; and he wiped the glass, where his breath dulled it, twice. Then I gave a shout at him that sent him off. They had to carry him to the car outside."

"Is this true?" cried Dunn, eagerly.

"If I had had but the strength to bring me to the window, it's little I 'd have minded his white hair."

"If you had dared!" said Dunn, rising, and no longer able to control his anger.

"Don't go yet; I have more to say to you," cried he, stretching out his hands towards him. "You think, because your roguery is succeeding, that you are great and respected. Not a bit; the gentlemen won't have you, and your own sort won't have you. There's not an honest man would eat your salt,—there's not an honest girl would bear your name. There you stand, as much alone in the world as if you came out of another country, and you 're the only man in Ireland does n't see it."

Dunn darted from the room as the last words were uttered, and gained the road. So overwhelmed was he by rage and astonishment that it was some minutes ere he could remember where he was or whither he would go.

"To Beldoyle," said he to the carman, pointing in the direction of the low shore, where his father lived; "drive your best pace." Then suddenly changing his mind, he said, "No, to town."

"Is he gone, Bella?" said Kellett, as his daughter entered.

"Yes; and before I could thank him for his coming."

"I think I said enough," said he, with a fierce laugh, which made her suddenly turn and look at him.

It was all she could do to repress a sudden cry of horror; for one side of his face was distorted by palsy, and the mouth drawn all awry.

"What's this here, Bella?" said he, trying to touch his cheek with his hand; "a kind of stiffness—a sort of—Eh, are you crying, darling?"

"No; it was something in my eye pained me," said she, turning away to hide her face.

"Give me a looking-glass, quickly," cried he.

"No, no," said she, forcing a laugh; "you have not shaved these two days, and you are quite neglected-look-ing. You sha'n't see yourself in such a state."

"Bring it this minute, I say," said he, passionately, and in a voice that grew less and less articulate every moment.

"Now pray be patient, dearest papa."

"Then I'll go for it myself;" and with these words he grasped the arm of the chair and tried to rise.

"There, there," said she, softly forcing him back into his seat, "I 'll fetch it at once. I wish you would be persuaded, dear papa—" began she, still holding the glass in her hands. But he snatched it rudely from her, and placed it before him.

"That's what it is," said he, at last; "handsome Paul Kellett they used to call me at Corfu. I wonder what they'd say now?"

"It is a mere passing thing, a spasm of some kind."

"Ay," said he, with a mocking laugh, to which the distortion imparted a shocking expression. "Both sides will be the same—to-morrow or next day—I know that."

She could hear no more, but, covering her face with her hands, sobbed bitterly.

Kellett still continued to look at himself in the glass; and whether the contortion was produced by the malady or a passing emotion, a half-sardonic laugh was on his features as he said, "I was wrong when I said I'd never be chapfallen."

CHAPTER XXV
A CHURCHYARD

There come every now and then, in our strange climate, winter days which imitate the spring, with softened sunlight, glistening leaves, and warbling birds; even the streams unite in the delusion, and run clearly along with eddying circles, making soft music among the stones. These delicious intervals are full of pleasant influences, and the garden breath that floats into the open drawing-room brings hope as well as health on its wings. It was on such a morning a little funeral procession entered the gateway of the ruined church at Kellester, and wound its way towards an obscure corner where an open grave was seen. With the exception of one solitary individual, it was easy to perceive that they who followed the coffin were either the hired mourners, or some stray passers-by indulging a sad curiosity in listlessness. It was poor Kellett's corpse was borne along, with Conway walking after it.

The mournful task over, and the attendants gone, Conway lingered about among the graves, now reading the sad records of surviving affection, now stopping to listen to the high-soaring lark whose shrill notes vibrated in the thin air. "Poor Jack!" thought he, aloud; "he little knows the sad office I have had this morning. He always was talking of home and coming back again, and telling his dear father of all his campaigning adventures; and so much for anticipation—beneath that little mound of earth lies all that made the Home he dreamed of! He's almost the last of the Albueras," said he, as he stood over the grave; and at the same time a stranger drew near the spot, and, removing his hat, addressed him by name. "Ah! Mr. Dunn, I think?" said Conway.

"Yes,"-said the other; "I regret to see that I am too late. I wished to pay the last tribute of respect to our poor friend, but unfortunately all was over when I arrived."

"You knew him intimately, I believe?" said Conway.

"From boyhood," said Dunn, coughing, to conceal some embarrassment. "Our families were intimate; but of him, personally, I saw little: he went abroad with his regiment, and when he returned, it was to live in a remote part of the country, so that we seldom met."

"Poor fellow!" muttered Conway, "he does seem to have been well-nigh forgotten by every one. I was alone here this morning."

"Such is life!" said Dunn.

"But such ought not death to be," rejoined Conway. "A gallant old soldier might well have been followed to his last billet by a few friends or comrades; but he was poor, and that explains all!"

"That is a harsh judgment for one so young as you are."

"No: if poor Kellett had fallen in battle, he had gone to his grave with every honor to his memory; but he lived on in a world where other qualities than a soldier's are valued, and he was forgotten,—that's the whole of it!"

"We must think of the daughter now; something must be done for her," said Dunn.

"I have a plan about that, if you will kindly aid me with it," said Conway, blushing as he spoke. "You are aware, perhaps, that Jack Kellett and I were comrades. He saved my life, and risked his own to do it, and I owe him more than life in the cheery, hearty spirit he inspired me with, at a time when I was rather disposed to sulk with the whole world; so that I owe him a heavy debt." Here he faltered, and at last stopped, and it was only as Dunn made a gesture to him to continue, that he went on: "Well, I have a dear, kind old mother, living all alone in Wales,—not over well off, to be sure, but quite able to do a kind thing, and fully as willing. If Miss Kellett could be induced to come and stay with her,—it might be called a visit at first,—time would gradually show them how useful they were to each other, and they 'd find they need n't—they could n't separate. That's my plan; will you support it?"

"I ought to tell you, frankly, that I have no presumption to counsel Miss Kellett. I never saw her till the night you accompanied her to my house; we are utter strangers to each other therefore. There is, however, sufficient in your project to recommend itself, and if anything I can add will aid it, you may reckon upon me; but you will yourself see whether my counsels be admissible. There is only one question I would ask,—you 'll excuse the frankness of it for the sincerity it guarantees,—Miss Kellett, although in poverty, was the daughter of a gentleman of fortune,—all the habits of her life were formed in that station; now, is it likely—I mean—are your mother's circumstances—"

"My mother has something like a hundred a year in the world," broke in Conway, hastily. "It's a poor pittance, I know, and you would be puzzled to say how one could eke out subsistence on it, but she manages it very cleverly."

"I had really no intention to obtrude my curiosity so far," said Dunn, apologizing. "My object was to show you, generally, that Miss Kellett, having hitherto lived in a condition of comfort—"

"Well, we 'll do our best—I mean my mother will," said Conway. "Only say you will recommend the plan, and I 'm satisfied."

"And for yourself—have you no project, no scheme of life struck out? A man so full of youth and energy should not sink into the listless inactivity of a retired soldier."

"You forget this," said Conway, pointing to his armless sleeve.

"Many a one-armed officer leads his squadron into fire; and your services—if properly represented, properly supported—would perhaps meet recognition at the Horse Guards. What say you, would you serve again if they offered you a cornetcy?"

"Would I?—would I bless the day that brought me the tidings? But the question is not of *me*," said he, proudly; and he turned away to leave the spot. Dunn followed him, and they walked out into the road together. A handsome chariot, splendid in all its appointments, and drawn by two powerful thoroughbreds, awaited the rich man's coming, and the footman banged down the steps with ostentatious noise as he saw him approach.

"Let the carriage follow," said Dunn to the servant, and walked on at Conway's side. "If it was not that I am in a position to be of service to you, my observation would be a liberty," said Dunn; "but I have some influence with persons in power—"

"I must stop you at once," said Conway, good-humoredly. "I belong to a class which does not accept of favors except from personal friends; and though I fully recognize your kind intentions towards me, remember we are strangers to each other."

"I should wish to forget that," said Dunn, courteously.

"I should still be ungracious enough to bear it in mind. Come, come, Mr. Dunn," said he, "this is not the topic I want you to be interested in. If you can bring some hope and comfort into that little cottage yonder, you will do a far greater kindness than by any service you can render one like me."

"It would scarcely be advisable to do anything for a day or two?" said Dunn, rather asking the question.

"Of course not. Meanwhile I 'll write to my mother, and she shall herself address Miss Kellett, or, if you think it better, she 'd come over here."

"We 'll think over that. Come back with me to town and eat your dinner with me, if you have no engagement."

"Not to-day,—excuse me to-day. I am low and out of sorts, and I feel as if I 'd rather be alone."

"Will you let me see you to-morrow, or the day after?"

"The day after to-morrow be it. By that time I shall have heard from my mother," said Conway. And they parted.

Long after Mr. Dunn's handsome equipage had driven away, Charles Conway continued to linger about the neighborhood of the little cottage. The shutters were closed, and no smoke issued from the chimney, and it looked dreary and desolate. Again and again would he draw near the little wicket and look into the garden. He would have given all he possessed to have been able to ask after her,—to have seen any one who could have told him of her,—how she bore up in her dread hour of trial; but none was to be seen. More than once he adventured to approach the door, and timidly stood, uncertain what to do, and then, cautiously retracing his steps, he regained the road, again to resume his lonely watch. And so the noon passed, and the day waned, and evening drew nigh, and there he still lingered. He thought that when night closed in, some flickering light might give sign of life within,—some faint indication of her his heart was full of; but all remained dark, silent, and cheerless. Even yet could he not bear to leave the spot, and it was already far into the night ere he turned his steps towards Dublin.

Let us go back for a moment to Mr. Davenport Dunn, who was not the only occupant of the handsome chariot that rolled smoothly back to town. Mr. Driscoll sat in one corner; the blind carefully down, so as to screen him from view.

"And that was Conway!" said he, as soon as Dunn had taken his seat. "Wasn't I right when I said you were sure to catch him here?"

"I knew as much myself," said Dunn, curtly.

"Well, and what is he like?—is he a chap easy to deal with?—is he any way deep?"

"He's as proud as Lucifer,—that 's all I can make out of him; and there are few things harder to manage than real pride."

"Ay, if you can't get round it," said Driscoll, with a sly twinkle of the eye.

"I have no time for such management," said Dunn, stiffly.

"Well, how did he take what you said to him? Did he seem as if he 'd enter into the business kindly?"

"You don't suppose that I spoke to him about his family or his fortune, do you? Is it in a chance meeting like this that I could approach a subject full of difficulty and complication? You have rare notions of delicacy and address, Driscoll!"

"God help me! I'm a poor crayture, but somehow I get along for all that, and I 'm generally as far on my road at the end of the day as them that travels with four posters."

"You'd make a pretty mess of whatever required a light hand and a fine touch, that I can tell you. The question here lies between a peer of the realm with twelve thousand a year, and a retired soldier with eightpence a day pension. It does not demand much thought to see where the balance inclines."

"You're forgetting one trifling matter. Who has the right to be the peer with the twelve thousand a year?"

"I am not forgetting it; I was going to it when you stopped me. Until we have failed in obtaining our terms from Lord Lackington—"

"Ay, but what are the terms?" broke in Driscoll, eagerly.

"If you interrupt me thus at every moment, I shall never be able to explain my meaning. The terms are for yourself to name; you may write the figures how you please. As for me, I have views that in no way clash with yours. And to resume: until we fail with the Viscount, we have no need of the soldier. All that we have to think of as regards Conway is, that he falls into no hands but our own, that he should never learn anything of his claim, nor be within reach of such information till the hour when we ourselves think fit to make it known to him—"

"He oughtn't to keep company with that daughter of Paul Kellett, then," broke in Driscoll. "There's not a family history in the kingdom she hasn't by heart."

"I have thought of that already, and there is some danger of such an occurrence."

"As how?"

"Young Conway is at this very moment plotting how she may be domesticated with his mother, somewhere in Wales, I believe."

"If he's in love with her, it will be a bad business," said Driscoll. "She does be reading and writing, too, from morning till night. There's no labor nor fatigue she's not equal to, and all the searches and inquiries that weary others she'd go into out of pure amusement. Now, if she was ever to be with his mother, and heard the old woman talk about family history, she 'd be at it hard and fast next morning."

"There is no need she should go there."

"No. But she must n't go,—must never see her."

"I think I can provide for that. It will be somewhat more difficult to take him out of the way for the present. I wish he were back in the Crimea."

"He might get killed—"

"Ay, but his claim would not die. Look here, Driscoll," said he, slowly; "I ventured to tell him this morning that I would assist him with my influence if he wishes to re-enter the service as an officer, and he resented the offer at once as a liberty. Now, it might be managed in another way. Leave me to think it over, and perhaps I can hit upon the expedient. The Attorney-General is to report upon the claims to me to-morrow, next day I'm to see Conway himself, and then you shall learn all."

"I don't like all these delays," began Driscoll; but at a look from Dunn he stopped, and held down his head, half angry, half abashed.

"You advance small loans of money on approved security, Driscoll," said Dunn, with a dry expression of the mouth. "Perhaps some of these mornings you may be applied to for a few hundreds by a young fellow wishing to purchase his commission,—you understand me?"

"I believe I do," said Driscoll, with a significant smile.

"You 'll not be too hard on him for the terms, especially if he has any old family papers to deposit as security,—eh?"

"Just so—just so. A mere nominal guarantee," said Driscoll, still laughing. "Oh, dear! but it's a queer world, and one has to work his wits hard to live in it." And with this philosophic explanation of life's trials, Mr. Driscoll took his leave of Dunn, and walked homeward.

CHAPTER XXVI
THE OSTEND PACKET

It was a wild, stormy night, with fast-flying clouds above, and a heavy rolling sea below, as the "Osprey" steamed away for Ostend, her closed hatchways and tarpaulined sailors, as well as her sea-washed deck and dripping cordage, telling there was "dirty weather outside." Though the waves broke over the vessel as she lay at anchor, and the short distance between the shore and her gangway had to be effected at peril of life, the captain had his mail, and was decided on sailing. There were but three passengers: two went aboard with the captain; the third was already on deck when they arrived, and leisurely paraded up and down with his cigar, stopping occasionally to look at the lights on shore, or cast a glance towards the wild chaos of waves that raged without.

"Safe now, I suppose, Grog?" muttered Beecher, as the vessel, loosed from her last mooring, turned head to sea out of the harbor.

"I rather suspect you are," said Davis, as he struck a light for his cigar. "Few fellows would like to swim out here with a judge's warrant in his mouth such a night as this."

"I don't like it overmuch myself," said Beecher; "there's a tremendous sea out there, and she's only a cockleshell after all."

"A very tidy one, sir, in a sea, I promise you," said the Captain, overhearing, while with his trumpet he bellowed forth some directions to the sailors.

"You've no other passengers than ourselves, have you?" asked Beecher.

"Only that gentleman yonder," whispered the Captain, pointing towards the stranger.

"Few, I take it, fancy coming out in such weather," said Beecher.

"Very few, sir, if they have n't uncommonly strong reasons for crossing the water," replied the Captain.

"I think he had you there!" growled Grog in his ear. "Don't you go poking nonsense at fellows like that. Shut up, I tell you! shut up!"

"I begin to feel it deuced cold here," said Beecher, shuddering.

"Come down below, then, and have something hot. I 'll make a brew and turn in," said Davis, as he moved towards the ladder. "Come along."

"No, I must keep the deck, no matter how cold it is. I suffer dreadfully when I go below. Send me up a tumbler of rum-and-water, Davis, as hot as may be."

"You 'd better take your friend's advice, sir," said the Captain. "It will be dirty weather out there, and you 'll be snugger under cover." Beecher, however, declined; and the Captain, crossing the deck, repeated the same counsel to the other passenger.

"No, I thank you," said he, gayly; "but if one of your men could spare me a cloak or a cape, I 'd be much obliged, for I am somewhat ill-provided against wet weather."

"I can let you have a rug, with pleasure," said Beecher, overhearing the request; while he drew from a recess beneath the binnacle one of those serviceable aids to modern travel in the shape of a strong woollen blanket.

"I accept your offer most willingly, and the more so as I suspect I have had the honor of being presented to you," said the stranger. "Do I address Mr. Annesley Beecher?"

"Eh?—I'm not aware—I'm not quite sure, by this light," began Beecher, in considerable embarrassment, which the other as quickly perceived, and remedied by saying,—

"I met you at poor Kellett's. My name is Conway."

"Oh, Conway,—all right," said Beecher, laughing. "I was afraid you might be a 'dark horse,' as we say. Now that I know your colors, I'm easy again."

Conway laughed too at the frankness of the confession, and they turned to walk the deck together.

"You mentioned Kellett. He 's gone 'toes up,' is n't he?" said Beecher.

"He is dead, poor fellow," said Conway, gravely. "I expected to have met you at his funeral."

"So I should have been had it come off on a Sunday," said Beecher, pleasantly; "but as in seeing old Paul 'tucked in' they might have nabbed me, I preferred being reported absent without leave."

"These were strong reasons, doubtless," said Conway, dryly.

"I liked the old fellow, too," said Beecher. "He was a bit of a bore, to be sure, about Arayo Molinos, and Albuera, and Soult, and Beresford, and the rest of 'em; but he was a rare good one to help a fellow at a pinch, and hospitable as a prince."

"That I 'm sure of!" chimed in Conway.

"I know it, I can swear to it; I used to dine with him every Sunday, regularly as the day came. I'll never forget those little tough legs of mutton,—wherever he found them there's no saying,—and those hard pellets of capers, like big swan-shot, washed down with table beer and whiskey-grog, and poor Kellett thinking all the while he was giving you haunch of venison and red hermitage."

"He 'd have given them just as freely if he had them," broke in Conway, half gruffly.

"That he would! He did so when he had it to give,—at least, so they tell me, for I never saw the old place at Kellett's Town, or Castle Kellett—"

"Kellett's Court was the name."

"Ay, to be sure, Kellett's Court. I wonder how I could forget it, for I'm sure I heard it often enough."

"One forgets many a thing they ought to remember," said Conway, significantly.

"Hit him again, he hasn't got no friends!" broke in Beecher, laughing jovially at this rebuke of himself. "You mean, that I ought to have a fresher memory about all old Paul's kindnesses, and you 're right there; but if you knew how hard the world has hit *me*, how hot they 've been giving it to me these years back, you 'd perhaps not lean so heavily on me. Since the Epsom of '42," said he, solemnly, "I never had one chance, not one, I pledge you my sacred word of honor. I 've had my little 'innings,' you know, like every one else,—punted for five-pun-notes with the small ones, but never a real chance. Now, I call that hard, deuced hard."

"I suppose it *is* hard," said Conway; but, really, it would have been very difficult to say in what sense his words should be taken.

"And when a fellow finds himself always on the wrong side of the road," said Beecher, who now fancied that he was taking a moralist's view of life, and spoke with a philosophic solemnity,—"I say, when a fellow sees that, do what he will, he's never on the right horse, he begins to be soured with the world, and to think that it's all a regular 'cross.' Not that I ever gave in. No! ask any of the fellows up at Newmarket—ask the whole ring—ask—" he was going to say Grog Davis, when he suddenly remembered the heavy judgment Conway had already fulminated on that revered authority, and then, quickly correcting himself, he said, "Ask any of the legs you like what stuff A. B. 's made of,—if he ain't hammered iron, and no mistake!"

"But what do you mean when you say you never gave in?" asked Conway, half sternly.

"What do I mean?" said Beecher, repeating the words, half stunned by the boldness of the question,—"what do I mean? Why, I mean that they never saw me 'down,'—that no man can say Annesley Beecher ever said 'die.' Have n't I had my soup piping hot,—spiced and peppered too! Was n't I in for a pot on Blue Nose, when Mope ran a dead heat with Belshazzar for the Cloudeslie,—fifteen to three in fifties twice over, and my horse running in bandages, and an ounce of corrosive sublimate in his stomach! Well, you 'd not believe it,—I don't ask any one to believe it that did n't see it,—but I was as cool as I am here, and I walked up to Lady Tinkerton's drag and ate a sandwich; and when she said, 'Oh! Mr. Beecher, do come and tell me what to bet on,' I said to her, 'Quicksilver's the fastest of metals, but don't back it just now.' They had it all over the course in half an hour: 'Quicksilver's the fastest of metals—'"

"I'm afraid I don't quite catch your meaning."

"It was alluding to the bucketing, you know. They 'd just given Blue Nose corrosive sublimate, which is a kind of quicksilver."

"Oh, I perceive," said Conway.

"Good,—wasn't it?" said Beecher, chuckling. "Let A. B. alone to 'sarve them out,'—that's what all the legs said!" And then he heaved a little sigh, as though to say that, after all, even wit and smartness were only a vanity and a vexation of spirit, and that a "good book" was better than them all.

"I detest the whole concern," said Conway. "So long as gentlemen bred and trained to run their horses in honorable rivalry, it was a noble sport, and well became the first squirearchy of the world; but when it degenerated into a field for every crafty knave and trickster,—when the low cunning of the gambler succeeded to the bold daring of the true lover of racing,—then the turf became no better than the *rouge et noir* table, without even the poor consolation of thinking that chance was any element in the result."

"Why, what would you have? It's a game where the best player wins, that's all," broke in Beecher.

"If you mean it is always a contest where the best horse carries away the prize, I enter my denial to the assertion. If it were so, the legs would have no existence, and all that classic vocabulary of 'nobbling,' 'squaring,' and so on, have no dictionary."

"It's all the same the whole world over," broke in Beecher. "The wide-awake ones will have the best seat on the coach."

Conway made no reply; but the increased energy with which he puffed his cigar bespoke the impatience he was suffering under.

"What became of the daughter?" asked Beecher, abruptly; and then, not awaiting the answer, went on: "A deuced good-looking girl, if properly togged out, but she had n't the slightest notion of dressing herself."

"Their narrow fortune may have had something to say to that," said Conway, gravely.

"Where there's a will, there's a way,—that 's my idea. I was never so hard up in life but I could make my tailor torn me out like a gentleman. I take it," added he, returning to the former theme, "she was a proud one. Old Kellett was awfully afraid of doing many a thing from the dread of her knowing it. He told me so himself."

"Indeed!" exclaimed Conway, with evident pleasure in the tone.

"I could have helped him fifty ways. I knew fellows who would have 'done' his bills,—small sums, of course,—and have shoved him along pleasantly enough, but *she* would n't have it at any price."

"I was not aware of that," remarked Conway, inviting, by his manner, further revelations.

Beecher, however, mistaking the source of the interest he had thus excited, and believing that his own craft and shrewdness were the qualities that awakened respect, went on to show how conversant he was with all financial operations amongst Jews and money-lenders, proudly declaring that there was not a "man on town" knew the cent per centers as he did.

"I've had my little dealings with them," said he, with some vanity in the manner. "I 've had my paper done when there was n't a fellow on the 'turf' could raise a guinea. You see," added he, lowering his voice to a whisper that implied secrecy, "I could do them a service no money could repay. I was up to all that went on in life and at the clubs. When Etheridge got it so heavy at the 'Rag,' I warned Fordyce not to advance him beyond a hundred or two. I was the only gentleman knew Brookdale's horse could win 'the Ripsley.' The legs, of course, knew it well before the race came off. Jemmy could have had ten thousand down for his 'book.' Ah! if you and I had only known each other six years ago, what a stroke of work we might have done together! Even now," said he, with increased warmth of voice, "there's a deuced deal to be done abroad. Brussels and Florence are far from worked out; not among the foreigners, of course, but our own fellows,—the young Oxford and Cambridge 'saps,'—the green ones waiting for their gazette in the Guards! Where are you bound for?—what are you doing?" asked he, as if a sudden thought had crossed his mind.

"I am endeavoring to get back to the Crimea," said Conway, smiling at the prospect which the other had with such frankness opened to him.

"The Crimea!" exclaimed Beecher, "why, that is downright madness; they 're fighting away there just as fresh as ever. The very last paper I saw is filled with an account of a Russian sortie against our lines, and a lot of our fellows killed and wounded."

"Of course there are hard knocks—"

"It's all very well to talk of it that way, but I think you might have been satisfied with what you saw, I 'd just as soon take a cab down to Guy's, or the Middlesex Hospital, and ask one of the house-surgeons to cut me up at his own discretion, as go amongst those Russian savages. I tell you it don't pay,—not a bit of it!"

"I suppose, as to the paying part, you 're quite right; but, remember, there are different modes of estimating the same thing. Now, I like soldiering—"

"No accounting for tastes," broke in Beecher. "I knew a fellow who was so fond of the Queen's Bench Prison he would n't let his friends clear him out; but, seriously speaking, the Crimea 's a bad book."

"I should be a very happy fellow to-night if I knew how I could get back there. I 've been trying in various ways for employment in any branch of the service. I 'd rather be a driver in the Wagon Train than whip the neatest four-in-hand over Epsom Downs."

"There 's only one name for that," said Beecher; "at least, out of Hanwell."

"I 'd be content to be thought mad on such terms," said Conway, good-humoredly, "and not even quarrel with those who said so!"

"I 've got a better scheme than the Crimea in my head," said Beecher, in a low, cautious voice, like one afraid of being overheard. "I 've half a mind to tell you, though there 's one on board here would come down pretty heavily on me for peaching."

"Don't draw any indignation on yourself on *my* account," said Conway, smiling. "I'm quite unworthy of the confidence, and utterly unable to profit by it."

"I 'm not so sure of that," responded Beecher. "A fellow who has got it so hot as you have, has always his eyes open ever after. Come a little to this side," whispered he, cautiously. "Did you remark my going forward two or three times when I came on board?"

"Yes, I perceived that you did so."

"You never guessed why?"

"No; really I paid no particular attention to it."

"I 'll tell you, then," whispered he, still lower, "it was to look after a horse I 've got there. 'Mumps,' that ran such a capital second for the Yarmouth, and ran a dead heat afterwards with Stanley's 'Cross-Bones,' he's there!" and his voice trembled between pride and agitation.

"Indeed!" exclaimed Conway, amused at the eagerness of his manner.

"There he is, disguised as a prize bull for the King of Belgium. Nobody suspects him,—nobody could suspect him, he 's so well got up, horns and all. Got him on board in the dark in a large roomy box, clap posters to it on the other side, and 'tool' him along to Brussels. That's what I call business! Now, if you wait a week or two, you can lay on him as deep as you like. We'll let the Belgians 'in,' before we 've done with them. We run him under the name of 'Klepper;' don't forget it,—Klepper!"

"I 've already told you I 'm unworthy of such a confidence; you only risk yourself when you impart a secret to indiscretion like mine."

"You'd not blow us?" cried Annesley, in terror.

"The best security against my doing so accidentally is that I may be hundreds of miles away before your races come off."

For a minute or two Beecher's misery was extreme. He saw how his rashness had carried him away to a foolish act of good-nature, and had not even reaped thanks for his generosity. What would he not have given to recall his words?—what would he not have done to obliterate their impression? At last a sudden thought seemed to strike him, and he said,—

"There are two of us in 'the lay,' and my 'pal' is the readiest pistol in Europe."

"I 'll not provoke any display of his skill, depend on 't," said Conway, controlling, as well as he could, the inclination to laugh out.

"He'd tumble you over like winking if you sold him. He 'd make it as short work with myself if he suspected me."

"I'd rather have a quieter sort of colleague," said Conway, dryly.

"Oh! but he's a rare one to 'work the oracle.' Solomon was a wise man—"

"What infernal balderdash are you at with Solomon and Samson, there?" shouted out Grog Davis, who had just been looking after the horse-box in the bow. "Come down below, and have a glass of brandy-and-water."

"I 'll stay where I am," said Beecher, sulkily, and walked away in dudgeon from the spot.

"I think I recognize your friend's voice," said Conway, when Beecher next joined him. "If I 'm right, it's a fellow I 've an old grudge against."

"Don't have it out, then,—that's all," broke in Beecher, hastily. "I 'd just as soon go into a cage and dispute a bone with one of Van Amburgh's tigers, as I 'd 'bring *him* to book.'"

"Make your mind easy about that," said Conway. "I never go in search of old scores. I would only say, don't leave yourself more in his power than you can easily escape from. As for myself, it's very unlikely I shall ever see him again."

"I wish you'd given up the Crimea," said Beecher, who, by one of the strange caprices of his strange nature, began to feel a sort of liking for Conway.

"Why should I give it up? It's the only career I 'm fit for,—if I even be fit for that, which, indeed, the Horse Guards don't seem to think. But I 've got an old friend in the Piedmontese service who is going out in command of the cavalry, and I 'm on my way now to Turin to see whether he cannot make me something,—anything, in short, from an aide-de-camp to an orderly. Once before the enemy, it matters wonderfully little what rank a man holds."

"The chances of his being knocked over are pretty much alike," said Beecher, "if that's what you mean."

"Not exactly," said Conway, laughing, "not exactly, though even in *that* respect the calculation is equal."

They now walked the deck step for step together in silence. The conversation had arrived at that point whence, if not actually confidential, it could proceed no further without becoming so, and so each appeared to feel it, and yet neither was disposed to lead the way. Beecher was one of those men who regard the chance persons they meet with in life just as they would accidental spots where they halt when on a journey,—little localities to be enjoyed at the time, and never, in all likelihood, revisited. In this way they obtained far more of his confidence than if he was sure to be in constant habits of intercourse with them. He felt they were safe depositaries, just as he would have felt a lonely spot in a wood a secure hiding-place for whatever he wanted to conceal. Now he was already—we are unable to say why—disposed to like Conway, and he would gladly have revealed to him much that lay heavily at his heart,—many a weighty care, many a sore misgiving. There was yet remaining in his nature that reverence and respect for honesty of character which survives very often a long course of personal debasement, and he felt that Conway was a man of honor. Such men he very well knew were usually duped and done,—they were the victims of the sharp set he himself fraternized with; but, with all that, there was something about them that he still clung to, just as he might have clung to a reminiscence of his boy-days.

"I take it," said he, at last, "that each of us have caught it as heavily as most fellows going. *You*, to be sure, worse than myself,—for I was only a younger son."

"*My* misfortunes," said Conway, "were all of my own making. I squandered a very good fortune in a few years, without ever so much as suspecting I was in any difficulty; and, after all, the worst recollection of the past is, how few kindnesses, how very few good-natured things a fellow does when he leads a life of mere extravagance. I have enriched many a money-lender, I have started half a dozen rascally servants into smart hotel-keepers, but I can scarcely recall five cases of assistance given to personal friends. The truth is, the most selfish fellow in the world is the spendthrift."

"That 's something new to me, I must own," said Beecher, thoughtfully; but Conway paid no attention to the remark. "My notion is this," said Beecher, after a pause,—"do what you will, say what you will, the world won't play fair with you!"

Conway shook his head dissentingly, but made no reply, and another and a longer silence ensued.

"You don't know my brother Lackington?" said Beecher, at length.

"No. I have met him in the world and at clubs, but don't know him."

"I 'll engage, however, you 've always heard him called a clever fellow, a regular sharp fellow, and all that, just because he's the Viscount; but he is, without exception, the greatest flat going,—never saw his way to a good thing yet, and if you told him of one, was sure to spoil it. I 'm going over to see him now," added he, after a pause.

"He 's at Rome, I think, the newspapers say?"

"Yes, he's stopping there for the winter." Another pause followed, and Beecher threw away the end of his cigar, and, sticking an unlighted one in his mouth, walked the deck in deep deliberation. "I 'd like to put a case to you for your opinion," said he, as though screwing himself to a great effort. "If you stood next to a good fortune,—next in reversion, I mean,—and that there was a threat—just a threat, and no more—of a suit to contest your right, would you accept of a life interest in the property to avoid all litigation, and secure a handsome income for your own time?"

"You put the case too vaguely. First of all, a mere threat would not drive me to a compromise."

"Well, call it more than a threat; say that actual proceedings had been taken,—not that I believe they have; but just say so."

"The matter is too complicated for my mere Yes or No to meet it; but on the simple question of whether I should compromise a case of that nature, I'd say No. I'd not surrender my right if I had one, and I 'd not retain possession of that which did n't belong to me."

"Which means, that you 'd reject the offer of a life interest?"

"Yes, on the terms you mention."

"I believe you 're right. Put the bold face on, and stand the battle. Now the real case is this. My brother Lack-ington has just been served with notice—"

Just as Beecher had uttered the last word, his arm, which rested on the binnacle against which he was standing, was grasped with such force that he almost cried out with the pain, and at the same instant a muttered curse fell upon his ear.

"Go on," said Conway, as he waited to hear more.

Beecher muttered some unintelligible words about feeling suddenly chilled, and "wanting a little brandy," and disappeared down the stairs to the cabin.

"I heard you," cried Davis, as soon as the other entered,—"I heard you! and if I hadn't heard you with my own ears, I 'd not have believed it! Have n't I warned you, not once but fifty times, against that confounded peaching tongue of yours? Have n't I told you that if every act of your life was as pure and honest as you know it is not, your own stupid talk would make an indictment against you? You meet a fellow on the deck of a steamer—"

"Stop there!" cried Beecher, whose temper was sorely tried by this attack. "The gentleman I talked with is an old acquaintance; he knows me,— ay, and what's more, he knows *you!*"

"Many a man knows *me*, and does not feel himself much the better for his knowledge!" said Davis, boldly.

"Well, I believe our friend here would n't say he was the exception to that rule," said Beecher, with an ironical laugh.

"Who is he?—what's his name?"

"His name is Conway; he was a lieutenant in the 12th Lancers, but you will remember him better as the owner of Sir Aubrey."

"I remember him perfectly," replied Davis, with all his own composure,—"I remember him perfectly,—a tall, good-looking fellow, with short moustaches. He was—except yourself—the greatest flat I ever met in the betting-ring; and that's a strong word, Mr. Annesley Beecher,—ain't it?"

"I suspect you 'd scarcely like to call him a flat to-day, at least, to his face," said Beecher, angrily.

A look of mingled insolence and contempt was all the answer Davis gave this speech; and then half filling a tumbler with brandy, he drank it off, and said slowly,—

"What *I* would dare to do, *you* certainly would never suspect,—that much I 'm well aware of. What *you* would dare is easily guessed at."

"I don't clearly understand you," said Beecher, timidly.

"*You* 'd dare to draw me into a quarrel on the chance of seeing me 'bowled over,'" said Davis, with a bitter laugh. "*You* 'd dare to see me stand opposite another man's pistol, and pray heartily at the same time that his hand might n't shake, nor his wrist falter; but I've got good business habits about me, Master Beecher. If you open that writing-desk, you 'll own few men's papers are in better order, or more neatly kept; and there is no satisfaction I could have to offer any one would n't give me ample time to deposit in the hands of justice seven forged acceptances by the Honorable Annesley Beecher, and the power of attorney counterfeited by the same accomplished gentleman's hand."

Beecher put out his hand to catch the decanter of brandy; but Davis gently removed the bottle, and said, "No, no; that's only Dutch courage, man; nerve yourself up, and learn to stand straight and manfully, and when you say, 'Not guilty,' do it with a bold look at the jury box.'"

Beecher dropped into his seat, and buried his head between his hands.

"I often think," said Davis, as he took out his cigar-case and proceeded to choose a cigar,—"I often think it would be a fine sight when the swells—the fashionable world, as the newspapers call them—would be pressing on to the Old Bailey to see one of their own set in the dock. What nobs there would be on the Bench! All Brookes's and the Wyndham scattered amongst the bar. The 'Illustrated News' would have a photographic picture of you, and the descriptive fellows would come out strong about the way you recognized your former acquaintances in court. Egad! old Grog Davis would be quite proud to give his evidence in such company!' How long have you been acquainted with the prisoner in the dock, Mr. Davis?' cried he, aloud, imitating the full and imperious accents of an examining counsel. 'I have known him upwards of fifteen years, my Lord. We went down together to Leeds in the summer of 1840 on a little speculation with cogged dice—'"

Beecher looked up and tried to speak, but his strength failed him, and his head fell heavily down again on the table.

"There, 'liquor up,' as the Yankees say," cried Davis, passing the decanter towards him. "You 're a poor chicken-hearted creature, and don't do much honor to your 'order.'"

"You 'll drive me to despair yet," muttered Beecher, in a voice scarcely above a whisper.

"Not a bit of it, man; there's pluck in despair! You 'll never go that far!"

Beecher grasped his glass convulsively; and as his eyes flashed wildly, he seemed for a moment as if about to hurl it in the other's face. Davis's look, however, appeared to abash him, and with a low, faint sigh he relinquished his hold, while his head fell forward on his bosom.

Davis now drew near the fire, and with a leg on either side of it, smoked away at his ease.

CHAPTER XXVII
A VISIT OF CONDOLENCE

"I think she will *see* me," said Davenport Dunn, to the old woman servant who opened the door to him at the Kelletts' cottage, "if you will tell her my name: Mr. Dunn,—Mr. Davenport Dunn."

"She told me she 'd not see anybody, sir," was the obdurate reply.

"Yes; but I think when you say who it is—"

"She would not see that young man that was in the regiment with her brother, and he was here every day, wet or dry, to ask after her."

"Well, take in my card now, and I 'll answer for it she'll not refuse me."

The old woman took the card half sulkily from his hand, and returned in a few minutes to say that Miss Kellett would receive him.

Dressed in mourning of the very humblest and cheapest kind, and with all the signs of recent suffering and sorrow about her, Sybella Kellett yet received Mr. Dunn with a calm and quiet composure for which he was scarcely prepared.

"If I have been importunate, Miss Kellett," said he, "it is because I desire to proffer my services to you. I feel assured that you will not take ill this assistance on my part I would wish to be thought a friend—"

"You were so to my father, sir," said she, interrupting, while she held her handkerchief to her eyes.

Dunn's face grew scarlet at these words, but, fortunately for him, she could not see it.

"I had intended to have written to you, sir," said she, with recovered composure. "I tried to do so this morning, but my head was aching so that I gave it up. I wanted your counsel, and indeed your assistance. I have no need to tell you that I 'm left without means of support. I do not want to burden relatives, with whom, besides, I have had no intercourse for years; and my object was to ask if you could assist me to a situation as governess, or, if not, to something more humble still. I will not be difficult to please," said she, smiling sadly, "for my pretensions are of the very humblest."

"I 'm aware how much you underrate them. I 'm no stranger to Miss Kellett's abilities," said Dunn, bowing.

She scarcely moved her head in acknowledgment of this speech, and went on: "If you could insure me immediate occupation, it would serve to extricate me from a little difficulty at this moment, and relieve me from the embarrassment of declining ungraciously what I cannot accept of. This letter here is an invitation from a lady in Wales to accept the hospitality of her house for the present; and however deeply the kindness touches me, I must not avail myself of it. You may read the letter," said she, handing it to him.

Dunn perused it slowly, and, folding it up, laid it on the table again.

"It is most kindly worded, and speaks well for the writer," said he, calmly.

"I feel all its kindness," said she, with a slight quivering of the lip. "It comes when such is doubly precious, but I have my reasons against accepting it."

"Without daring to ask, I can assume them, Miss Kellett. I am one of those who believe that all efforts in life to be either good or great should strike root in independence; that he who leans upon another parts with the best features of identity, and loses himself in suiting his tastes to another's."

She made no reply, but a slight flush on her cheek, and an increased brightness in her eye, showed that she gave her full concurrence to the words.

"It is fortunate, Miss Kellett," said he, resuming, "that I am the bearer of a proposition which, if you approve of, meets the case at once. I have been applied to by Lord Glengariff to find a lady who would accept the situation of companion to his daughter. He has so far explained the requirements he seeks for, that I can answer for Miss Kellett being exactly everything to fulfil them."

"Oh, sir!" broke she in, "this is in no wise what I desired. I am utterly unfitted for such a sphere and such associations. Remember how and where my life has been passed. I have no knowledge of life, and no experience of society."

"Let me interrupt you. Lord Glengariff lives completely estranged from the world in a remote part of the country. Lady Augusta, his only unmarried daughter, is no longer young; they see no company; indeed, their fortune is very limited, and all their habits of the very simplest and least expensive.

It was remembering this very seclusion, I was glad to offer you a retreat so likely to meet your wishes."

"But even my education is not what such persons would look for. I have not one of the graceful accomplishments that adorn society. My skill as a musician is very humble; I cannot sing at all; and though I can read some modern languages, I scarcely speak them."

"Do not ask me to say how much I am aware of your capacity and acquirements, Miss Kellett. It is about two months back a little volume came into my hands which had once been yours; how it ceased to be so I don't choose to confess; but it was a work on the industrial resources of Ireland, annotated and commented on by *you*. I have it still. Shall I own to you that your notes have been already used by me in my reports, and that I have adopted some of the suggestions in my recommendations to Government? Nay, if you doubt me, I will give you the proof."

"I left such a volume as you speak of at Mr. Hawkhaw's, and believed it had been mislaid."

"It was deliberately stolen, Miss Kellett, that's the truth of it. Mr. Driscoll chanced to see the book, and happened to show it to me. I could not fail to be struck with it, the more as I discovered in your remarks hints and suggestions, coupled with explanations, that none had ever offered me."

"How leniently you speak of my presumption, sir!"

"Say, rather, how sincerely I applaud your zeal and intelligence,—the book bespeaks both. Now, when I read it, I wished at once to make your acquaintance. There were points wherein you were mistaken; there were others in which you evidently see further than any of us. I felt that if time, and leisure, and opportunity of knowledge were supplied, these were the studies in which you might become really proficient. Lord Glengariff s proposal came at the very moment. It was all I could desire for you,—a quiet home, the society of those whose very breeding is acted kindliness."

"Oh, sir! do not flatter me into the belief that I am worthy of such advantages."

"The station will gain most by your association with it, take my word for that."

How was it that these words sent a color to her cheek and a courage to her heart that made her for a moment forget she was poor and fatherless and friendless? What was it, too, that made them seem less flattery than sound, just, and due acknowledgment? He that spoke them was neither young, nor handsome, nor fascinating in manner; and yet she felt his praise vibrate within her heart strangely and thrillingly.

He spoke much to her about her early life,—what she had read, and how she was led to reflect upon themes so unlikely to attract a young girl's thoughts. By degrees, as her reserve wore off, she ventured to confess what a charm the great men of former days possessed for her imagination,—how their devotion, their courage, their single-heartedness animated her with higher hopes for the time when Ireland should have the aid of those able to guide her destinies and make of her all that her great resources promised.

"The world of contemporaries is seldom just to these," said Dunn, gravely; "they excite envy rather than attract friendship, and then they have often few of the gifts which conciliate the prejudices around them."

"What matter if they can live down these prejudices?" cried she, warmly; then blushing at her own eagerness, she said, falteringly, "How have I dared to speak of these things, and to *you?*"

Dunn arose and walked to the window, and now a long pause occurred in which neither uttered a word.

"Is this cottage yours, Miss Kellett?" said he, at last.

"No; we had rented it, and the time expires in a week or two."

"And the furniture?"

"It was hired also, except a very few articles of little or no value."

Dunn again turned away, and seemed lost in deep thought; then, in a voice of some uncertainty and hesitation, said: "Your father's affairs were complicated and confused,—there were questions of law, too, to be determined about them,—so that, for the present, there is no saying exactly how they stand; still, there will be a sum,—a small one, unfortunately, but still a sum available to you, which, for present convenience, you must allow me to advance to you."

"You forget, sir, that I have a brother. To him, of right, belongs anything that remains to us."

"I had, indeed, forgotten that," said Dunn, in some confusion, "and it was just of him I wanted now to speak. He is serving as a soldier with a Rifle regiment in the Crimea. Can nothing be done to bring him favorably before the notice of his superiors? His gallantry has already attracted notice; but as his real station is still unknown, his advancement has been merely that accorded to the humblest merits. I will attend to it. I 'll write about him this very day."

"How I thank you!" cried she, fervently; and she bent down and pressed her lips to his hand.

A cold shivering passed over Dunn as he felt the hot tears that fell upon his hand, and a strange sense of weakness oppressed him.

"It will make your task the lighter," cried she, eagerly, "to know that Jack is a soldier in heart and soul,—brave, daring, and high-hearted, but with a nature gentle as a child's. There was a comrade of his here the other day, one whose life he saved—"

"I have seen Conway," said Dunn, dryly, while he scanned her features closely.

No change of color nor voice showed that she felt the scrutiny, and in a calm tone she went on: "I know so little of these things that I do not know, if my dear brother were made an officer to-morrow, whether his want of private fortune would prevent his acceptance of the rank, but there surely must be steps of advancement open to men poor as he is."

"You may trust all to me," interrupted Dunn. "Once that you consider me as your guardian, I will neglect nothing that concerns you."

"Oh, how have I deserved such kindness!" cried she, trying to smother her emotion.

"You must call me your guardian, too, and write to me as such. The world is of such a temper that it will serve you to be thought my ward. Even Lady Augusta Arden herself will feel the force of it." There was a kind of rude energy in the way these last words were uttered that gave them a character almost defiant.

"You are, then, decided that I ought to take the situation?" said she. And already her manner had assumed the deference of one seeking direction.

"Yes, for the present it is all that could be desired. There will be no necessity of your continuing there if it should ever be irksome to you. Upon this, as upon all else, I trust you will communicate freely with me."

"I should approach an actual duty—a task—with far more confidence than I feel in offering to accommodate myself to the ways and tempers of utter strangers."

"Very true," said he; "but when I have told you about them they will be strangers no longer. People are easily comprehended who have certain strong ruling passions. They have only one, and that the very simplest of all motives,—pride. Let me tell you of them." And so he drew his chair to her side, and began to describe the Ardens.

We do not ask the reader to follow Davenport Dunn in his sketch; enough that we say his picture was more truthful than flattering, for he portrayed traits that had often given him offence and suffering. He tried to speak with a sort of disinterested coldness,—a kind of half-pitying indifference about "ways and notions" that people estranged from "much intercourse with the world *will* fall into;" but his tone was, in spite of himself, severe and resentful, and scarcely compensated by his concluding words, "though, of course, to *you* they will be amiable and obliging."

"How I wish I could see them, though only for a minute!" said she, as he finished.

"Have you such confidence, then, in your power of detecting character at sight?" asked he, with a keen and furtive glance.

"My gift is generally enough for my own guidance," said she, frankly; "but, to be sure, it has only been exercised amongst the country people, and they have fewer disguises than those we call their betters."

"I may write word, then, that within a week you will be ready," said Dunn, rising. "You will find in that pocket-book enough for any immediate outlay,—nay, Miss Kellett, it is your own,—I repeat it, all your own. I am your guardian, and no more." And with a stiffness of manner that almost repelled gratitude, he took his leave and withdrew. As he gained the door, however, he stopped, and after a moment came back into the room. "I should like to see you again before you leave; there are topics I would like to speak with you on. May I come in a day or two?"

"Whenever and as often as you please."

Dunn took her hand and pressed it tenderly. A deep crimson overspread her face as she said "Good-bye!" and the carriage had rolled away ere she knew that he was gone.

CHAPTER XXVIII
THE HERMITAGE AT GLENGARIFF

Beside a little arm of the sea, and surrounded by lofty mountains, stood the cottage of Lord Glengariff. It was originally built as a mere fishing-lodge, a resting-place in the bathing-season, or a spot to visit when it was the pleasure of its owners to affect retirement and seclusion. Then would the Earl and his Countess and the Ladies Julia and Jemima come down to the Hermitage with a sort of self-approving humility that seemed to say, "Even *we* know how to chastise pride, and vanity, and the sinful lusts of the flesh." Whether it was that these seasons of mortification became more frequent, or that they required more space, we cannot say; but, in course of time, the hermitage extended its limbs, first in one direction, and then in another, till at length it grew to be a very commodious house, with ample rooms and every imaginable comfort, Owing to the character of the architecture, too, it gained in picturesque effect by these successive additions; and in its jutting projections, its deep-shadowed courts, and its irregular line of roof, it presented a very pleasing specimen of that half-Elizabethan cottage so rarely hit upon in any regular plan. As the fortunes of the noble house declined,—the Earl's ancestors had been amongst the most extravagant of Irish gentry,—the ancient castle of Holt-Glengariff, where they had long resided, was sold, and the family settled down to live at the Hermitage. At first the change was supposed to be merely temporary,—"they were going to live in London or in Brighton; they were about to establish themselves in Paris; her Ladyship was ordered to Italy,"—a variety of rumors, in fact, were afloat to explain that the sunshine of their presence in that lonely glen would be but brief and short-lived. All the alterations that might be made in the cottage or its grounds, all the facilities of approach by land and water, all the beneficial changes in the village itself, were alluded to as projects for the day when they would come back there; for my Lord said he "really liked the place,"—a species of avowal that was accepted by the neighborhood as the proudest encomium man could pronounce upon their "happy valley."

With all these plans and intentions, it was now eighteen years, and the Earl had never quitted the Hermitage for any longer journey than an occasional trip to Dublin. The Countess had taken a longer road than that over the Alps, and lay at rest in the village churchyard. The Ladies Georgina,

Arabella, and Julia had married off, and none remained but Lady Augusta Arden, of whom we have already made brief mention to our readers in a former chapter.

We did but scant justice to Lady Augusta when we said that she had once been handsome: she was so still. She had fine eyes and fine teeth; a profusion of brown hair of the very silkiest; her figure was singularly graceful; and, baring a degree of haughtiness,—a family trait,—her manner was unexceptionably good and pleasing. Both the Earl and his daughter had lived too long amongst those greatly inferior to them in rank and fortune not to conceive a very exaggerated estimate of themselves.

No Pasha was ever more absolute than my Lord in the little village beside him; his will was a sort of firman that none dreamed of disputing; and, indeed, the place men occupied in the esteem of their fellows there, was little else than a reflex of how they were regarded at the Hermitage. We never scruple to bestow a sort of derisive pity upon the savage who, having carved his deity out of a piece of wood, sits down to worship him; and yet, what an unconscious imitation of the red man is all our adulation of great folks! We follow him to the very letter, not only in investing the object of our worship with a hundred qualities that he has not, but we make him the butt of our evil passions, and in the day of our anger and disappointment we turn round and rend him! Not that the villagers ever treated my Lord in this wise,—they were still in the stage "of worship;" they had been at "their offices," fathers and grandfathers, for many a year, and though some were beginning to complain that their knees were getting sore, none dreamed of getting on their legs! The fact was, that even they who liked the religion least thought it was not worth while abjuring the faith of their fathers, especially when they could not guess what was to replace it; and so my Lord dictated and decided and pronounced for the whole neighborhood; and Lady Augusta doctored and model-schooled and loan-funded them to her heart's content. Nay, we are wrong! It was all in the disappointed dreariness of an unsatisfied heart that she took to benevolence! Oh, dear! what a sorry search is that after motives, if one only knew how much philanthropy and active charity have come of a breach of promise to marry! Not that Lady Augusta had ever stood in this position, but either that she had looked too high, or was too hard to please, or from some other cause, but she never married.

The man who has no taste for horsemanship consoles himself for the unenjoyed pleasure by reading of the fractured ribs and smashed collarbones of the hunting-field. Was it in something of this spirit that Lady

Augusta took an especial delight in dwelling in her mind and in her letters on all the disagreeables of her sisters' wedded life? The extravagance of men, their selfishness, their uncomplying habits, the odious tyranny of their tempers, were favorite themes with her, dashed with allusions to every connubial contingency, from alimony to the measles in the nursery! At last, possibly because, by such frequent recurrence to the same subjects, she had no longer anything new to say on them, or perhaps—it is just possible—that the themes themselves had less interest for others than for herself, her sisters seemed to reply less regularly than of old. Their answers were shorter and drier; and they appeared neither to care so much for sympathy and condolence as formerly; and, in fact, as Lady Augusta said to herself, "They were growing inured to ill-treatment!" And if half of us in this world only knew of the miseries we are daily suffering, and which sympathetic friends are crying over, what a deal of delightful affliction might we enjoy that we now are dead to! What oppressive governments do we live under, what cruel taskmasters, what ungrateful publics, not to speak of the more touching sorrows of domestic life,—the undervaluing parents and unsympathizing wives! Well, one thing is a comfort: there are dear kind hearts in mourning over all these for us, anxiously looking for the day we may awaken to a sense of our own misery!

It was of a cheery spring morning, sunlit and breezy, when, in the chirping songs of birds, the rustling leaves, and fast-flowing rivulets, Nature seems to enjoy a more intense vitality, that the Earl sat at breakfast with his daughter. A fairer prospect could hardly be seen than that which lay before the open windows in front of them. The green lawn, dotted with clumps of ancient trees, inclined with many a waving slope to the sea, which in a long narrow arm pierced its way between two jutting headlands,—the one bold, rocky, and precipitous; the other grass-covered and flowery, reflecting its rich tints in the glassy water beneath. The sea was, indeed, calm and still as any lake, and, save when a low, surging sound arose within some rocky cavern, as silent and noiseless. The cattle browsed down to the very water's edge, and the nets of the fishermen hung to dry over the red-berried foliage of the arbutus. They who looked—when they did, perchance, look on this scene—gazed with almost apathy on it. Their eyes never brightened as the changing sunlight cast new effects upon the scene. Nor was this indifference the result of any unconsciousness of its beauty. A few months back it was the theme of all their praises. Landscape-painters and photographers were invited specially to catch its first morning tints, its last mellow glow at sunset. The old Lord said it was finer than Sorrento, equal to anything in Greece.

If the Mediterranean were bluer, where was there such emerald verdure,—where such blended coloring of heaths, purple and blue and violet,—in what land did the fragrance of the white thorn so load the warm atmosphere? Such, and such like, were the encomiums they were wont to utter; and wherefore was it that they uttered them no more? The explanation is a brief one. A commission, or a deputation, or a something as important, had come down to examine Bantry Bay, and investigate its fitness to become a packet station for America. In the course of this examination, a scientific member of the body had strayed down to Glengariff, where, being of a speculative as well as of a scientific turn, he was struck by its immense capabilities. What a gem it was, and what might it not be made! It was Ireland in the tropics,—"the Green Isle" in the Indian Ocean! Only imagine such a spot converted into a watering-place! With a lodge for the Queen on that slope sheltered by the ilex-copse, crescents, and casinos, and yacht stations, and ornamental villas rose on every side by his descriptive powers, and the old Earl—for he was dining with him—saw at one glance how he had suddenly become a benefactor of mankind and a millionnaire. "That little angle of the shore yonder, my Lord,—the space between the pointed rock and the stone-pine trees,—is worth fifty thousand pounds; the crescent that would stand there would leave many an untenanted house at Kemp Town. I 'll engage myself to get you a thousand guineas for that small bit of tableland to the right; the Duke of Uxmore is only waiting to hit upon such a spot. Here, too, where we sit, must be the hydropathic establishment. You can't help it, my Lord, you must comply. This park will bring you in a princely revenue. It is gold,—actual gold,—every foot of it! There 's not a Swiss cottage in these woods won't pay cent per cent!"

Mr. Galbraith—such was his name—was of that pictorially gifted order of which the celebrated George Robins was once chief. He knew how to dress his descriptions with the double attraction of the picturesque and the profitable, so that trees seemed to bend under golden fruit, and the sea-washed rocks looked like "nuggets."

If there be something very seductive in the prospect of growing immensely rich all at once, there is a terrible compensation in the utter indifference inflicted on us as to all our accustomed pleasures in life. The fate of Midas seems at once our own; there is nothing left to us but that one heavy and shining metal of all created blessedness! Lord Glengariff was wont to enjoy the lonely spot he lived in with an intense appreciation of its beauty. He never wearied of watching the changing effects of season on a scene so full of charm; but now he surveyed it with a sense of fidgety impatience, eager for the time when the sounds of bustle and business should replace the stillness that now reigned around him.

"This is from Dunn," said he, breaking open a large, heavy-sealed letter which had just arrived. His eyes ran hastily along it, and he exclaimed peevishly, "No prospectus yet; no plan issued; nothing whatever announced. 'I have seen Galbraith, and had some conversation with him about your harbor.' My harbor!"

"Go on," said Lady Augusta, mildly.

"Why, the insolent upstart has not even listened to what was said to him. My harbor! He takes it for granted that we were wanting to make this a packet station for America, and he goes on to say that the place has none of the requisite qualifications,—no depth of water! I wish the fellow were at the bottom of it! Really, this is intolerable. Here is a long lecture to me not to be misled by those 'speculation-mongers who are amongst the rife products of our age.' I ask you, if you ever heard of impertinence like that? This fellow—the arch-charlatan of his day, the quack *par excellence* of his nation—dares to warn *me* against the perils of his class and kindred! Only listen to this, Gusty," cried he, bursting into a fit of half-angry laughter: "'I am disposed to think that, by drawing closer to the present party in power, you could serve your interests much more effectively than by embarking in any schemes of mere material benefit. Allington'—he actually calls him Allington!—'dropped hints to this effect in a confidential conversation we held last evening together, and I am in hopes that, when we meet, you will enter into our views.' Are the coronets of the nobility to be put up to sale like the acres of the squirearchy? or what is it this fellow is driving at?" cried he, flinging down the letter in a rage, and walking up and down the room. "The rule of O'Connell and his followers was mild and gentle and forbearing, compared with the sway of these fellows. In the one case we had a fair stand-up fight,—opinion met opinion, and the struggle was an open one; but here we have an organized association to investigate the state of our resources, to pry into our private affairs, learning what pressure bears upon us here, what weak spot gives way there. They hold our creditors in leash, to slip them on us at any moment; and the threat of a confiscation—for it is just that, and nothing less—is unceasingly hanging over us!"

He stopped short in his torrent of passion, for the white sail of a small fishing-craft that just showed in the offing suddenly diverted his thoughts to that vision of prosperity he so lately revelled in,—that pleasant dream of a thriving watering-place, bright, sunny, and prosperous, the shore dotted with gayly caparisoned donkeys, and the sea speckled with pleasure-boats. All the elements of that gay Elysium came up before him,—the full tide of fortune setting strongly in, and coming to his feet. Galbraith, who revelled in millions, whose rapid calculations rarely descended to ignoble thousands, had constantly impressed upon him that if Dunn only took it up, the project was already accomplished. "He'll start you a company, my Lord, in a week; a splendid prospectus and an admirable set of names on the direction, with a paid-up capital, to begin with, of—say £30,000. He knows to a nicety how many Stock Exchange fellows, how many M.P.'s, how many county gentlemen to have. He 'll stick all the plums in the right place too; and he'll have the shares quoted at a premium before the scrip is well out in the market. Clever fellow, my Lord,—vastly clever fellow, Dunn!" And so the Earl thought, too, till the letter now before him dashed that impression with disappointment.

"I 'll tell you what it is, Gusty," said he, after a pause,—"we must ask him down here. It is only by an actual inspection of the bay that he can form any just conception of the place. You must write to him for me. This gouty knuckle of mine makes penwork impossible. You can say—Just find a sheet of paper, and I 'll tell you what to say." Now, the noble Earl was not as ready at dictation as he had fancied; for when Lady Augusta had opened her writing-desk, arranged her writing-materials, and sat, pen in hand, awaiting his suggestions, he was still pacing up and down the room, muttering to himself in broken and unconnected phrases, quite unsuited to the easy flow of composition. "I suppose, Gusty,—I take it for granted,—you must begin, 'My dear sir,'—eh?—or, perhaps, better still, 'Dear Mr. Dunn.'"

"'Dear Mr. Dunn,'" said she, not looking up from the paper, but quietly retouching the last letters with her pen.

"But I don't see why, after all, we should follow this foolish lead," said he, proudly. "The acceptance he meets from others need not dictate to us, Gusty. I 'd say, 'The Earl of Glengariff'—or, 'I am requested by Lord Glen-gariff—'"

"'My father, Lord Glengariff,'" interposed she, quietly.

"It sounds more civilly, perhaps. Be it so;" and again he walked up and down, in the same hard conflict of composition. At length he burst forth: "There 's nothing on earth more difficult than addressing a man of this sort. You want his intimacy without familiarity. You wish to be able to obtain the benefit of his advice, and yet not incur the infliction of his dictation. In fact, you are perfectly prepared to treat him as a valued guest, provided he never lapses into the delusion that he is your friend. Now, it would take old Metternich to write the sort of note I mean."

"If I apprehend you, your wish is to ask him down here on a visit of a few days, with the intimation that you have a matter of business to communicate—"

"Yes, yes," said he, impatiently, "that's very true. The business part of the matter should come in incidentally, and yet the tone of the invitation be such as to let him distinctly understand that he does not come without an express object Now you have my meaning, Gusty," said he, with the triumphant air of one who had just surmounted a difficulty.

"If I have, then, I am as far as ever from knowing how to convey it," said she, half peevishly. "I'd simply say, 'Dear Sir,' or, 'Dear Mr. Dunn,—There is a question of great moment to myself, on which your advice and counsel would be most valuable to me. If you could spare me the few days a visit would cost you, and while giving us the great pleasure of your society—'"

"Too flattering, by half. No, no," broke he in again. "I 'll tell you what would be the effect of all that, Gusty,"—and his voice swelled out full and forcibly,—"the fellow would come here, and, before a week was over, he 'd call me Glengariff!"

She grew crimson over face and forehead and neck, and then almost as quickly pale again; and, rising hastily from the table, said, "Really, you expect too much from my subtlety as a note-writer. I think I 'd better request Mr. Dunn to look out for one of those invaluable creatures they call companions, who pay your bills, correct your French notes, comb the lapdog, and scold your maid for you. *She* might be, perhaps, equal to all this nice diplomacy."

"Not a bad notion, by any means, Gusty," said he, quickly. "A clever woman would be inestimable for all the correspondence we are like to have soon; far better than a man,—less obtrusive, more confidential, not so open to jobbery; a great point,—a very great point. Dunn's the very man, too, to find out the sort of person we want."

"Something more than governess, and less than lady," said she, half superciliously.

"The very thing, Gusty,—the very thing. Why, there are women with breeding enough to be maids of honor, and learning sufficient for a professor, whose expectations never rise beyond a paltry hundred a year— what am I saying?—sixty or seventy are nearer the mark. Now for it, Gusty.

Make this object the substance of your letter. You can have no difficulty in describing what will suit us. We live in times, unfortunately, when people of birth and station are reduced to straitened circumstances on every hand. It reminds me of what poor Hammersley used to say,—'Do you observe,' said he, 'that whenever there's a great smash on the turf, you 'll always see the coaches horsed with thoroughbreds for the next year or two!'"

"A very unfeeling remark, if it mean anything at all." "Never mind. Write this letter, and say at the foot of it, 'We should be much pleased if, in your journeys 's out'—he's always coming down to Cork and the neighborhood—you could give us a few days at Glengariff Hermitage. My father has certain communications to make to you, which he is confident would exempt your visit from the reproach of mere idleness.' He'll take that; the fellow is always flattered when you seem impressed by the immensity of his avocations!" And with a hearty chuckle at the weakness he was triumphing over, the old Lord left the room, while his daughter proceeded to compose her letter.

CHAPTER XXIX
A MORNING AT OSTEND

It would never have occurred to the mind of any one who saw Annesley Beecher and Davis, as they sat at breakfast together in Ostend, that such a scene as we have described could have occurred between them. Not only was their tone frank and friendly with each other, but a gay and lively spirit pervaded the conversation, and two seemingly more light-hearted fellows it were hard to find.

As the chemist is able by the minutest drop, an almost imperceptible atom of some subtle ingredient, to change the properties of some vast mass, altering color and odor and taste at once, so did the great artist Grog Davis know how to deal with the complicated nature of Beecher, that he could at any moment hurl him down into the blackest depths of despair, or elevate him to the highest pinnacle of hope and enjoyment. The glorious picture of a race-course, with all its attendant rogueries, betting-stands crammed with "fats," a ring crowded with "green-horns," was a tableau of which he never wearied. Now, this was a sort of landscape Grog touched off neatly. All the figures he introduced were life-studies, every tint and shade and effect taken carefully from nature. With a masterly hand he sketched out a sort of future campaign, artfully throwing Beecher himself into the foreground, and making him fancy that he was in some sort necessary to the great events before them.

"Mumps did not touch his hock, I hope, when he kicked there?" asked Beecher.

"Call him Klepper,—never forget that," remonstrated Grog; "he's remarkably like Mumps, that's all; but Mumps is in Staffordshire,—one of the Pottery fellows has him."

"So he is," laughed Beecher, pleasantly. "I know the man that owns him."

"No, you don't," broke in Davis; "you've only heard his name,—it is Coulson or Cotton, or something like that. One thing, however, is certain: he values him at twelve hundred pounds, and we 'd sell our horse for eight."

"So we would, Grog, and be on the right side of the hedge too."

"He'd be dog cheap for it," said Davis; "he's one of those lazy beggars that never wear out. I 'd lay an even thousand on it that he runs this day two years as he does to-day, and even when he has n't speed for a flat race he 'll be a rare steeple-chase horse."

Beecher's eyes glistened, and he rubbed his hands with delight as he heard him.

"I do like an ugly horse," resumed Davis; "a heavy-shouldered beast, with lob-ears, lazy eyes, and capped hocks, and if they know how to come out a stable with a 'knuckle over' of the pastern, or a little bit lame, they 're worth their weight in gold."

What a merry laugh was Beecher's as he listened!

"Blow me!" cried Grog, in a sort of enthusiasm, "if some horses don't seem born cheats,—regular legs! They drag their feet along, all weary and tired; if you push them a bit, they shut up, or they answer the whip with a kind of shrug, as if to say, 'It ain't any use punishing me at all,' the while they go plodding in, at the tail of the others, till within five, or maybe four lengths of the winning-post, and then you see them stretching—it ain't a stride, it's a stretch—you can't say how it's done, but they draw on—on—on, till you see half a head in front, and there they stay—just doing it—no more."

"Mumps is exactly—"

"Klepper,—remember, he's Klepper," said Grog, mildly.

"Klepper, to be sure,—how can I forget it?"

"I hope that fellow Conway is off," said Grog.

"Yes, he started by the train for Liege,—third class too,—must be pretty hard up, I take it, to travel that way."

"Good enough for a fellow that has been roughing it in the ranks these two years."

"He's a gentleman, though, for all that," broke in Beecher.

"And Strawberry ran at Doncaster, and I saw him t' other day in a 'bus. Now, I 'd like to know how much better he is for having once been a racer?"

"Blood always tells—"

"In a horse, Beecher, in a horse, not in a man. Have n't I got a deal of noble blood in my veins?—ain't I able to show a thoroughbred pedigree?" said he, mockingly. "Well, let me see the fellow will stand at eight paces from the muzzle of a rifle-pistol more cool, or who'll sight his man more calm than I will." There was a tinge of defiance in the way these words were said that by no means contributed to the ease of him who heard them.

"When do we go for Brussels, Grog?" asked he, anxious to change the subject.

"Here's the map of the country," said Davis, producing a card scrawled over with lines and figures. "Brussels, the 12th and 14th; Spa, the 20th; Aix, the 25th. Then *you* might take a shy at Dusseldorf, *I* can't; I winged a Prussian major there five years ago, and they won't let me in. I 'll meet you at Wiesbaden, and we 'll have a week at the tables. You 'll have to remember that I 'm Captain Christopher so long as we're on the Rhine; once at Baden, 'Richard's himself again!'"

"Is this for either of you, gentlemen?" said the waiter, presenting an envelope from the telegraph-office.

"Yes; I'm Captain Davis," said Grog, as he broke the seal.

"'Is the Dean able to preach?—may we have a collection?—Telegraph back.—Tom,'" read? Davis, slowly, aloud; and then added, "Ain't he a flat to be always telegraphing these things? As if every fellow in the office couldn't see his game!"

"Spicer, is it?" asked Beecher.

"Yes; he wants to hear how the horse is,—if there's good running in him, and what he's to lay on; but that's no way to ask it. I mind the day, at Wolverton, when Lord Berrydale got one of these: 'Your mother is better,—they are giving her tonics.' And I whispered to George Rigby, 'It 's about Butterfly his mare, that's in for the York, and that's to say, "She's all safe, lay heavy on it." And so I hedged round, and backed her up to eight thousand,—ay, and I won my money; and when Berrydale said to me after the race was over, 'Grog,' says he, 'you seem to have had a glimpse of the line of country this time,' says I to him; 'Yes, my Lord,' says I; 'and I 'm glad to find the tonics agree with your Lordship's mother.' Did n't he redden up to the roots of his hair! and when he turned away he said, 'There's no coming up to that fellow Davis!'"

"But I wonder you let him see that you were in his secret," said Beecher.

"That was the way to treat *him*. If it was Baynton or Berries, I'd not have said a word; but I knew Berrydale was sure to let me have a share in the first good thing going just out of fear of me, and so he did; that was the way I came to back Old Bailey."

It was now Beecher's turn to gaze with admiring wonder at this great intelligence, and certainly his look was veneration itself.

"Here's another despatch," cried Davis, as the waiter presented another packet like the former one. "We 're like Secretaries of State to-day," added he, laughing, as he tore open the envelope. This time, however, he did not read the contents aloud, but sat slowly pondering over the lines to himself.

"It's not Spicer again?" asked Beecher.

"No," was the brief reply.

"Nor that other fellow,—that German with the odd name?"

"No."

"Nothing about Mumps,—Klepper, I mean,—nothing about him?"

"Nothing; it don't concern him at all. It's not about anything you ever heard of before," said Davis, as he threw a log of wood on the fire, and kicked it with his foot. "I 'll have to go to Brussels to-night. I 'll have to leave this by the four o'clock train," said he, looking at his watch. "The horse is n't fit to move for twenty-four hours, so you 'll remain here; he must n't be left without one of us, you know."

"Of course not. But is there anything so very urgent—"

"I suppose a man is best judge of his own affairs," said Davis, rudely.

Beecher made no reply, and a long and awkward silence ensued.

"Let him have one of the powders in a linseed mash," said Davis, at last, "and see that the bandages are left on—only a little loose—at night. Tom must remain with him in the box on the train, and I 'll look out for you at the station. If we shouldn't meet, come straight to the Hôtel Tirlemont, where all will be ready for you."

"Remember, Grog, I've got no money; you haven't trusted me with a single napoleon."

"I know that; here's a hundred francs. Look out sharp, for you 'll have to account for every centime of it when we meet. Dine upstairs here, for if you go down to the ordinary you 'll be talking to every man Jack you meet,—ay, you know you will."

"Egad! it's rather late in the day to school me on the score of manners."

"I 'm not a-talking of manners, I 'm speaking of discretion,—of common prudence,—things you 're not much troubled with; you 're just as fit to go alone in life as I am to play the organ at an oratorio."

"Many thanks for the flattery," said Beecher, laughing.

"What would be the good of flattering you?" broke out Grog. "You ain't rich, that one could borrow from you; you haven't a great house, where one could get dinners out of you; you 're not even the head of your family, that one might draw something out of your rank,—you ain't anything."

"Except *your* friend, Grog Davis; pray don't rob me of that distinction," said Beecher, with a polished courtesy the other felt more cutting than any common sarcasm.

"It's the best leaf in your book, whatever you may think of it," said Davis, sternly; "and it will be a gloomy morning for you whenever you cease to be it."

"I don't intend it, old fellow; I 'll never tear up the deed of partnership, you may rely upon that. The old-established firm of Beecher and Davis, or Davis and Beecher—for I don't care which—shall last *my* time, at least;" and he held out his hand with a cordiality that even Grog felt irresistible, for he grasped and shook it heartily.

"If I could only get you to run straight, I 'd make a man of you," said Grog, eying him fixedly. "There's not a fellow in England could do as much for you as I could. There's nobody knows what's in you as I do, and there's nobody knows where you break down like *me*."

"True, O Grog, every word of it."

"I 'd put you in the first place in the sporting world,—I 'd have your name at the top of the list at 'the turf.' In six months from this day—this very day—I 'd bind myself to make Annesley Beecher the foremost man at Newmarket. But just on one condition."

"And that?"

"You should take a solemn oath—I 'd make it a solemn one, I promise you—never to question anything I decided in your behalf, but obey me to the letter in whatever I ordered. Three months of that servitude, and you 'd come out what I 've promised you."

"I 'll swear it this moment," cried Beecher.

"Will you?" asked Davis, eagerly.

"In the most solemn and formal manner you can dictate on oath to me. I 'll take it now, only premising you 'll not ask me anything against the laws."

"Nothing like hanging, nor even transportation," said Grog, laughing, while Beecher's face grew crimson, and then pale. "No,—no; all I 'll ask is easily done, and not within a thousand miles of a misdemeanor. But you shall Just think it over quietly. I don't want a 'catch match.' You shall have time to reconsider what I have said, and when we meet at Brussels you can tell me your mind."

"Agreed; only I hold *you* to your bargain, remember, if *I* don't change."

"I'll stand to what I've said," said Davis. "Now, remember, the Hotel Tirlemont; and so, good-bye, for I must pack up."

When the door closed after him, Annesley Beecher walked the room, discussing with himself the meaning of Davis's late words. Well did he know that to restore himself to rank and credit and fair fame was a labor of no common difficulty. How was he ever to get back to that station, forfeited by so many derelictions! Davis might, it is true, get his bills discounted,—might hit upon fifty clever expedients for raising the wind,—might satisfy this one, compromise with that; he might even manage so cleverly that racecourses and betting-rooms would be once more open to him. But what did—what could Grog know of that higher world where once he had moved, and to which, by his misdeeds, he had forfeited all claim to return? Why, Davis did n't even know the names of those men whose slightest words are verdicts upon character. All England was not Ascot, and Grog only recognized a world peopled with gentlemen riders and jocks, and a landscape dotted with flagstaffs, and closed in with a stand-house.

"No, no," said he to himself; "that's a flight above you, Master Davis. It 's not to be thought of."

CHAPTER XXX
THE OPERA

A dingy old den enough is the Hôtel Tirlemont, with its low-arched *porte-cochere*, and its narrow windows, small-paned and iron-barred. It rather resembles one of those antiquated hostels you see in the background of an Ostade or a Teniers than the smart edifice which we nowadays look for in an hotel. Such was certainly the opinion of Annesley Beecher as he arrived there on the evening after that parting with Davis we have just spoken of. Twice did he ask the guide who accompanied him if this was really the Tirlemont, and if there were not some other hotel of the same name; and while he half hesitated whether he should enter, a waiter respectfully stepped forward to ask if he were the gentleman whose apartment had been ordered by Captain Davis,—a demand to which, with a sullen assent, he yielded, and slowly mounted the stairs.

"Is the Captain at home?" asked he.

"No, sir; he went off to the railway station to meet you. Mademoiselle, however, is upstairs."

"Mademoiselle!" cried Beecher, stopping, and opening wide his eyes in astonishment. "This *is* something new," muttered he. "When did she come?"

"Last night, sir, after dinner."

"Where from?"

"From a Pensionnat outside the Porte de Scharbeck, I think, sir; at least, her maid described it as in that direction."

"And what is she called,—Mademoiselle Violette, or Virginie, or Ida, or what is it, eh?" asked he, jocularly.

"Mademoiselle, sir,—only Mademoiselle,—the Captain's daughter!"

"His daughter!" repeated he, in increased wonderment, to himself. "Can this be possible?"

"There is no doubt of it, sir. The lady of the Pensionnat brought her here last night in her own carriage, and I heard her, as she entered the salon, say,

'Now, Mademoiselle, that I have placed you in the hands of your father—' and then the door closed."

"I never knew he had a daughter," muttered Beecher to himself. "Which is my room?"

"We have prepared this one for you, but to-morrow you shall have a more comfortable one, with a look-out over the lower town."

"Put me somewhere where I sha'n't hear that confounded piano, I beg of you. Who is it rattles away that fashion?"

"Mademoiselle, sir."

"To be sure,—I ought to have guessed it; and sings too, I'll be bound?"

"Like Grisi, sir," responded the waiter, enthusiastically; for the Tirlemont, being frequented by the artistic class, had given him great opportunity for forming his taste.

Just at this moment a rich, full voice swelled forth in one of the popular airs of Verdi, but with a degree of ease and freedom that showed the singer soared very far indeed above the pretensions of mere amateurship.

"Wasn't I right, sir?" asked the waiter, triumphantly. "You'll not hear anything better at the Grand Opera."

"Send me up some hot water, and open that portmanteau," said Beecher, while he walked on towards the door of the salon. He hesitated for a second or two about then presenting himself; but as he thought of Grog Davis, and what Grog Davis's daughter must be like, he turned the handle and entered.

A lady rose from the piano as the door opened, and even in the half-darkened room Beecher could perceive that she was graceful, and with an elegance in her gesture for which he was in no wise prepared.

"Have I the honor to address Miss Davis?"

"You are Mr. Annesley Beecher, the gentleman my papa has been expecting," said she, with an easy smile. "He has just gone off to meet you."

Nothing could be more commonplace than these words, but they were uttered in a way that at once declared the breeding of the speaker. She spoke to a friend of her father, and there was a tone of one who felt that even in a first meeting a certain amount of intimacy might subsist between them.

"It's very strange," said Beecher, "but your father and I have been friends this many a year—close friends too—and I never as much as suspected he had a daughter. What a shame of him not to have given me the pleasure of knowing you before!"

"It was a pleasure he was chary enough of to himself," said she, laughing. "I have been at school nearly four years, and have only seen him once, and then for a few hours."

"Yes—but really," stammered out Beecher, "fascinations—charms such as—"

"Pray, sir, don't distress yourself about turning a compliment. I'm quite sure I'm very attractive, but I don't in the least want to be told so. You see," she added, after a pause, "I 'm presuming upon what papa has told me of your old friendship to be very frank with you."

"I am enchanted at it," cried Beecher. "Egad! if you. 'cut out all the work,' though, I 'll scarcely be able to follow you."

"Ah! so here you are before me," cried Davis, entering and shaking his hand cordially. "You had just driven off when I reached the station. All right, I hope?"

"All right, thank you."

"You 've made Lizzy's acquaintance, I see, so I need n't introduce you. *She* knows you this many a day."

"But why have I not had the happiness of knowing *her?*" asked Beecher.

"How 's Klepper?" asked Grog, abruptly. "The swelling gone out of the hocks yet?"

"Yes; he's clean as a whistle."

"The wind-gall, too,—has that gone?"

"Going rapidly; a few days' walking exercise will make him perfect."

"No news of Spicer and his German friend,—though I expected to have had a telegraph all day yesterday. But come, these are not interesting matters for Lizzy,—we 'll have up dinner, and see about a box for the opera."

"A very gallant thought, papa, which I accept with pleasure."

"I must dress, I suppose," said Beecher, half asking; for even yet he could not satisfy his mind what amount of observance was due to the daughter of Grog Davis.

"I conclude you must," said she, smiling; "and I too must make a suitable toilette;" and, with a slight bow and a little smile, she swept past them out of the room.

"How close you have been, old fellow,—close as wax,—about this," said Beecher; "and hang me, if she mightn't be daughter to the proudest Duke in England!"

"So she might," said Grog; "and it was to make her so, I have consented to this life of separation. What respect and deference would the fellows show *my* daughter when I wasn't by? How much delicacy would she meet with when the fear of an ounce ball wasn't over them? And was I going to bring her up in such a set as you and I live with? Was a young creature like that to begin the world without seeing one man that wasn't a leg, or one woman that wasn't worse? Was it by lessons of robbery and cheating her mind was to be stored? And was she to start in life by thinking that a hell was high society? Look at her *now*," said he, sternly, "and say if I was in Norfolk Island to-morrow, where 's the fellow that would have the pluck to insult her? It is true *she* doesn't know me as you and the others know me; but the man that would let her into *that* secret would never tell her another." There was a terrible fierceness in his eye as he spoke, and the words came from him with a hissing sound like the venomous threatenings of a serpent. "*She* knows nothing of *my* life nor *my* ways. Except your own name, she never heard me mention one of the fellows we live with. She knows *you* to be the brother of Lord Viscount Lack-ington, and that you are the Honorable Annesley Beecher, that's all she knows of *you*; ain't that little enough?"

Beecher tried to laugh easily at this speech; but it was only a very poor and faint attempt, after all.

"She thinks *me* a man of fortune, and *you* an unblemished gentleman; and if that be not innocence, I 'd like to know what is! Of where, how, and with whom we pick up our living, she knows as much as *we* do about the Bench of Bishops."

"I must confess I don't think the knowledge would improve her!" said Beecher, with a laugh.

A fierce and savage glance from Davis, however, very quickly arrested his jocularity; and Beecher, in a graver tone, resumed: "It was a deuced fine thing of you, Grog, to do this. There 's not another fellow living would have had the head to think of it But now that she has come home to you, how do you mean to carry on the campaign? A girl like that can't live secluded from the world, — she must go out into society? Have you thought of that?"

"I have thought of it," rejoined Davis, bluntly, but in a tone that by no means invited further inquiry.

"Her style and her manner fit her for the best set anywhere—"

"That's where I intend her to be," broke in Davis.

"I need scarcely tell as clever a fellow as you," said Beecher, mildly, "that there's nothing so difficult as to find footing among these people.

Great wealth may obtain it, or great patronage. There are women in London who can do that sort of thing; there are just two or three such, and you may imagine how difficult it is to secure their favor."

"They 're all cracked teacups, those women you speak of; one has only to know where the flaw is, and see how easily managed they are!"

Beecher smiled at this remark; he chuckled to himself, too, to see that for once the wily Grog Davis had gone out of his depth, and adventured to discuss people and habits of which he knew nothing; but, unwilling to prolong a controversy so delicate, he hurried away to his room to dress. Davis, too, retired on a similar errand, and a student of life might have been amused to have taken a peep into the two dressing-rooms. As for Beecher, it was but the work of a few minutes to array himself in dinner costume. It was a routine task that he performed without a thought on its details. All was ready at his hand; and even to the immaculate tie, which seemed the work of patience and skill, he despatched the whole performance in less than a quarter of an hour. Not so Davis: he ransacked drawers and portmanteaus; covered the bed, the chairs, and the table with garments; tried on and took off again; endeavored to make colors harmonize, or hit upon happy contrasts. He was bent on appearing a "swell;" and, unquestionably, when he did issue forth, with a canary-colored vest, and a green coat with gilt buttons, his breast a galaxy of studs and festooned chains, it would have been unfair to say he had not succeeded.

Beecher had but time to compliment him on his "get up," when Miss Davis entered. Though her dress was simply the quiet costume of a young unmarried girl, there was in her carriage and bearing, as she came in, all the graceful ease of the best society; and lighted up by the lamps of the apartment, Beecher saw, to his astonishment, the most beautiful girl he had ever beheld. It was not alone the faultless delicacy of her face, but there was that mingled gentleness and pride, that strange blending of softness and seriousness, which sit so well on the high-born, giving a significance to every gesture or word of those whose every movement is so measured, and every syllable so carefully uttered. "Why was n't she a countess in her own right?" thought he; "that girl might have all London at her feet."

The dinner went on very pleasantly. Davis, too much occupied in listening to his daughter or watching the astonishment of Beecher, scarcely ever spoke; but the others chatted away about whatever' came uppermost in a light and careless tone that delighted him.

Beecher was not sorry at the opportunity of a little dis-play. He was glad to show Davis that in the great world of society he could play no insignificant part; and so he put forth all his little talents as a talker, with choice anecdotes of "smart people," and the sayings and doings of a set which, to Grog, were as much myths as the inscriptions on an Assyrian monument. Lizzy Davis evidently took interest in his account of London and its life. She liked, too, to hear about the families of her schoolfellows, some of whom bore "cognate" names, and she listened with actual eagerness to descriptions of the gorgeous splendor and display of a town "season."

"And I am to see all these fine things, and know all these fine people, papa?" asked she.

"Yes, I suppose so,—one of these days, at least," muttered Grog, not caring to meet Beecher's eye.

"I don't think you care for this kind of life so much as Mr. Beecher, pa. Is their frivolity too great for your philosophy?"

"It ain't that!" muttered Grog, growing confused.

"Then do tell me, now, something of the sort of people you are fond of; the chances are that I shall like them just as well as the others."

Beecher and Davis exchanged glances of most intense significance; and were it not from downright fear, Beecher would have burst out laughing.

"Then I will ask Mr. Beecher," said she, gayly. "*You 'll* not be so churlish as papa, I 'm certain. *You 'll* tell me what his world is like?"

"Well, it's a very smart world too," said Beecher, slyly enjoying the malicious moment of worrying Grog with impunity. "Not so many pretty women in it, perhaps, but plenty of movement, plenty of fun,—eh, Davis? Are you fond of horses, Miss Davis?"

"Passionately; and I flatter myself I can ride too. By the way, is it true, papa, you have brought a horse from England for me?"

"Who could have told you that?" said Davis, almost sternly.

"My maid heard it from a groom that has just arrived, but with such secrecy that I suppose I have destroyed all the pleasure of the surprise you intended me; never mind, dearest pa, I am just as grateful—"

"Grateful for nothing," broke in Davis. "The groom is a prating rascal, and your maid ought to mind her own affairs." Then reddening to his temples with shame at his ill-temper, he added, "There is a horse, to be sure, but he ain't much of a lady's palfrey."

"What would you say to her riding Klepper in the Allée Verte,—it might be a rare stroke?" asked Beecher, in a whisper to Davis.

"Do you think that *she* is to be brought into *our* knaveries? Is *that* all you have learned from what I 've been saying to you?" whispered Davis, with a look of such savage ferocity that Beecher grew sick at heart with terror.

"I 'm sorry to break in upon such confidential converse," said she, laughingly, "but pray remember we are losing the first scene of the opera."

"I 'm at your orders," said Beecher, as, with his accustomed easy gallantry, he stepped forward to offer her his arm.

The opera was a favorite one, and the house was crowded in every part. As in all cities of a certain rank, the occupants of the boxes, with a few rare exceptions, were the same well-known people who, night after night, follow along the worn track of pleasure. To them the stage is but a secondary object, to which attention only wanders at intervals. The house itself, the brilliant blaze of beauty, the splendor of diamonds, the display of dress, and, more than all these, the subtle by-play of intrigue, detectable only by eyes deep-skilled and trained,—these form the main attractions of a scene wherein our modern civilization is more strikingly exhibited than in any other situation.

Scarcely had Lizzy Davis taken her seat than a low murmur of wondering admiration ran through the whole house, and, in the freedom which our present-day habits license, every opera-glass was turned towards her. Totally unconscious of the admiration she was exciting, her glances ranged freely over the theatre in every part, and her eyes were directed from object to object in amazement at the gorgeousness of the scene around her. Seated far back in the box, entirely screened from view, her father, too, perceived nothing of that strange manifestation wherein a sort of homage is blended with a degree of impertinence, but watched the stage with intense eagerness. Very different from the feelings of either father or daughter were the feelings of Annesley Beecher. He knew well the opera and its habits, and as thoroughly saw that it is to the world of fashion what Tattersall's or the turf is to the world of sport,—the great ring where every match is booked, every engagement registered, and every new aspirant for success canvassed and discussed. There was not a glance turned towards the unconscious girl at his side but he could read its secret import. How often had it been his own lot to stare up from his stall at some fair face, unknown to that little world which arrogates to itself all knowledge, and mingle his criticism with all the impertinences fashion loves to indulge in! The steady stare of some, the unwilling admiration of others, the ironical gaze of more, were all easy of interpretation by him, and for the very first time in his life he became aware of the fact that it was possible to be unjust with regard to the unknown.

As the piece proceeded, and her interest in the play increased, a slightly heightened color and an expression of half eagerness gave her beauty all that it had wanted before of animation, and there was now an expression of such captivation on her face that, carried away by that mysterious sentiment which sways masses, sending its secret spell from heart to heart, the whole audience turned from the scene to watch its varying effects upon that beautiful countenance. The opera was "Rigoletto," and she continued to translate to her father the touching story of that sad old man, who, lost to every sentiment of honor, still cherished in his heart of hearts his daughter's love. The terrible contrast between his mockery of the world and his affection for his home, the bitter consciousness of how he treated others, conjuring up the terrors of what yet might be his own fate, came to him in her words, as the stage revealed their action, and gradually he leaned over in his eagerness till his head projected outside the box.

"There—was n't I right about her?" said a voice from one of the stalls beneath. "That's Grog Davis. I know the fellow well."

"I 've won my wager," said another. "There 's old Grog leaning over her shoulder, and there can't be much doubt about her now."

"Annesley Beecher at one side, and Grog Davis at the other," said a third, make the case very easy reading. "I 'll go round and get presented to her."

"Let us leave this, Davis," whispered Beecher, while he trembled from head to foot,—"let us leave this at once. Come down to the crush-room, and I 'll find a carriage."

"Why so—what do you mean?" said Davis; and as suddenly he followed Beecher's glance towards the pit, whence every eye was turned towards them.

That glance was not to be mistaken. It was the steady and insolent stare the world bestows upon those who have neither champions nor defenders; and Davis returned the gaze with a defiance as insulting.

"For any sake, Davis, let us get away," whispered Beecher again. "Only think of *her*, if there should be any exposure!"

"Exposure!—how should there? Who 'd dare—"

Before he could finish, the curtain at the back of the box was rudely drawn aside, and a tall, handsome man, with a certain swaggering ease of manner that seemed to assert his right to be there if he pleased, came forward, saying,—

"How goes it, Davis? I just caught a glimpse of that charming—"

"A word with you, Captain Hamilton," said Davis, between his teeth, as he pushed the other towards the door.

"As many as you like, old fellow, by and by. For the present, I mean to establish myself here."

"That you sha'n't, by Heaven!" cried Davis, as he placed himself in front of him. "Leave this, sir, at once."

"Why, the fellow is deranged," said Hamilton, laughing; "or is it jealousy, old boy?"

With a violent push Davis drove him backwards, and ere he could recover, following up the impulse, he thrust him outside the box, hurriedly passing outside, and shutting the door after him.

So rapidly and so secretly had all this occurred, that Lizzy saw nothing of it, all her attention being eagerly fixed on the stage. Not so Beecher. He had marked it all, and now sat listening in terror to the words of high altercation in the lobby. From sounds that boded like insult and outrage, the noise gradually decreased to more measured tones; then came a few words in whisper, and Davis, softly drawing the curtain, stepped gently to his chair at his daughter's back. A hasty sign to Beecher gave him to understand that all was settled quietly, and the incident was over.

"You 'll not think me very churlish if I rob you of one act of the opera, Lizzy?" said Davis, as the curtain fell; "but I have a racking headache, which all this light and heat are only increasing."

"Let us go at once, dearest papa," said she, rising. "You should have told me of this before. There, Mr. Beecher, you needn't leave this—"

"She's quite right," said Davis; "you must remain."

And the words were uttered with a certain significance that Beecher well understood as a command.

It was past midnight when Annesley Beecher returned to the hotel, and both Davis and his daughter had already gone to their rooms.

"Did your master leave any message for me?" said he to the groom, who acted as Davis's valet.

"No, sir, not a word."

"Do you know, would he see me? Could you ask him?" said he.

The man disappeared for a few minutes, and then coming back, said, "Mr. Davis is fast asleep, sir, and I dare not disturb him."

"Of course not," said Beecher, and turned away.

"How that fellow can go to bed and sleep, after such a business as that!" muttered Beecher, as he drew his chair towards the fire, and sat ruminating over the late incident. It was in a spirit of triumphant satisfaction that he called to mind the one solitary point in which he was the superior of Davis,—class and condition,—and he revelled in the thought that men like Grog make nothing but blunders when they attempt the habits of those above them. "With all his shrewdness," said he to himself, half aloud, "he could not perceive that he has been trying an impossibility. She is beyond them all in beauty, her manners are perfect, her breeding unexceptionable; and yet, there she is, Grog Davis's daughter! Ay, Grog, my boy, you 'll see it one of these days. It 's all to no use. Enter her for what stakes you like, she 'll be always disqualified. There 's only one thing carries these attempts through,—if you could give her a pot of money. Yes, Master Davis, there are fellows—and with good blood in their veins—that, for fifty or sixty thousand pounds, would marry even *your* daughter." With this last remark he finished all his reflections, and proceeded to prepare for bed.

Sleep, however, would not come; he was restless and uneasy; the incident in the theatre might get abroad, and his own name be mentioned; or it might be that Hamilton, knowing well who and what Davis was, would look to him, Beecher, for satisfaction. There was another pleasant eventuality,—to be drawn into a quarrel and shot for Grog Davis's daughter! To be the travelling-companion of such a man was bad enough; to risk being seen with him on railroads and steamboats was surely sufficient; but to be paraded in places of public amusement, to be dragged before the well-dressed world, not as his chance associate, but as a member of his domestic circle, chaperoning his daughter to the opera, was downright intolerable! And thus was it that this man, who had been dunned and insulted by creditors, hunted from place to place by sheriff's officers, browbeaten by bankruptcy practitioners, stigmatized by the press, haunted all the while by a conscience that whispered there was even worse hanging over him, yet did he feel more real terror from the thought of how he would be regarded by his own "order" for this unseemly intimacy, than shame for all his deeper and graver transgressions.

"No," said he, at last, springing from his bed, and lighting his candle, "I 'll be off. I 'll cut my lucky, Master Grog; and here goes to write you half a dozen lines to break the fact to you. I 'll call it a sudden thought—a notion—that I ought to see Lackington at once. I 'll say that I could n't think of subjecting Miss Davis to the inconvenience of that rapid mode of travelling I feel to be so imminently necessary. I 'll tell him that as I left the theatre, I saw one of Fordyce's clerks, that the fellow knew me and grinned, and that I know I shall be arrested if I stay here. I 'll hint that Hamilton, who is highly connected, will have the English Legation at us all. Confound it, he 'll believe none of these. I 'll just say"—Here he took his pen and wrote,—

> "Dear D.,—After we parted last night, a sudden caprice seized me that I 'd start off at once for Italy. Had you been alone, old fellow, I should never have thought of it; but seeing that I left you in such charming company, with one whose—['No, that won't do—I must strike out that; and so he murmured over the lines ending in 'company.' and then went on.]—I have no misgivings about being either missed or wanted.—['Better, perhaps, missed or regretted.'] We have been too long friends to—['No, we are too old pals, that's better—he does n't care much for friendship']—too old pals to make me suspect you will be displeased with this—this unforeseen—['That's a capital word!—unforeseen what? It's always calamity comes after unforeseen; but I can't call it calamity']— unforeseen 'bolt over the ropes,' and believe me as ever, or believe me 'close as wax,'
>
> "Yours, A. B."

"A regular diplomatic touch, I call that note," said he, as he reread it to himself with much complacency. "Lack-ington thinks me a 'flat;' then let any one read that, and say if the fellow that wrote it is a fool." And now he sealed and directed his epistle, having very nearly addressed it to Grog, instead of to Captain Davis. "His temper won't be angelic when he gets it," muttered he, "but I'll be close to Liege by that time." And with this very reassuring reflection he jumped into bed again, determining to remain awake till daybreak.

Wearied out at last with watching, Annesley Beecher fell off asleep, and so soundly, too, that it was not till twice spoken to he could arouse and awaken.

"Eh, what is it, Rivers?" cried he, as he saw the trim training-groom at his side. "Anything wrong with the horse?"

"No, sir, nothing; *he's* all right, anyhow."

"What is it, then; any one from town looking for us?"

"No, sir, nobody whatever. It's the Captain himself—"

"What of him? Is he ill?"

"Sound as a roach, sir; he's many a mile off by this. Says he to me, 'Rivers,' says he, 'when you gets back to the Tirlemont, give this note to Mr.

Beecher; he 'll tell you afterwards what's to be done. Only,' says he, 'don't forget to rub a little of the white oils on that near hock; very weak,' says he; 'be sure it's very weak, so as not to blister him.' Ain't he a wonderful man, sir, to be thinking o' that at such a moment?"

"Draw the curtain, there,—let me have more light," cried Beecher, eagerly, as he opened the small and crumpled piece of paper. The contents were in pencil, and very brief,—

> "I 'm off through the Ardennes towards Treves; come up
> to Aix with my daughter, and wait there till you hear from
> me. There 's a vacant 'troop' in the Horse Guards Blue this
> morning. Rivers can tell you all.—Yours, C. D."

"What has happened, Rivers?" cried he, in intense anxiety. "Tell me at once."

"Sir, it don't take long to tell. It did n't take very long to do. It was three, or maybe half-past, this morning, the Captain comes to my room, and says, 'Rivers, get up; be lively,' says he, 'dress yourself, and go over to Jonesse, that fellow as has the shooting-gallery, give him this note; he 'll just read it, and answer it at once; then run over to Burton's and order a coupé, with two smart horses, to be here at five; after that come back quickly, for I want a few things packed up.' He made a sign to me that all was to be 'dark,' and so away I went, and before three quarters of an hour was back here again. At five to the minute the carriage came to the corner of the park, and we stepped out quietly; and when we reached it, there was Jonesse inside, with a tidy little box on his knee. 'Oh, is that it?' said I, for I knowed what that box meant,—'is that it?'

"'Yes,' says the Captain, 'that's it; get up and make him drive briskly to Boitsfort.' We were a bit late, I think, for the others was there when we got up, and I heard them grumbling something about being behind time. 'Egad,' says the Captain, 'you 'll find we 've come early enough before we've done with you.' They were cruel words, sir, now that I think how he tumbled him over stone dead in a moment."

"Who dead?"

"That fine, handsome young man, with the light-brown beard,—Hamilton, they said his name was,—and a nicer fellow you could n't wish to see. I 'll never forget him as he lay there stretched on the grass, and the small blue hole in his forehead,—you 'd not believe it was ever half the size of a bullet,—and his glove in his left hand, all so natural as if he was alive. I believe I 'd have been standing there yet, looking at him, when the Captain called me, and said, 'Rivers, take these stirrups up a hole,'—for he had a saddle-horse all ready for him,—'and give this note to Mr. Beecher; he 'll give you his orders about Klepper,' says he, 'but mind you look to that hock.'"

"And Captain Hamilton was killed?" muttered Beecher, while he trembled from head to foot at the terrible tidings.

"Killed—dead—he never moved a finger after he fell!"

"What did his friend do? Did he say anything?—did he speak?"

"He dropped down on his knees beside him, and caught him by the hand, and cried out, 'George, my own dear fellow,—George, speak to me;' but George never spoke another word."

"And Davis,—Captain Davis,—what did he do?"

"He shook hands with Jones, and said something in French that made him laugh; and then going over to where the body lay, he said, 'Colonel Humphrey,' says he, 'you 're a witness that all was fair and honorable, and that if this unhappy affair ever comes to be—' and then the Colonel moved his hand for him to be off, and not speak to him. And so the Captain took his advice, and got into the saddle; but I heard him mutter something about 'teaching the Colonel better manners next time they met."

"And then he rode away?"

"Yes; he turned into the wood, at a walking pace, for he was lighting his cigar. I saw no more of him, after that, for they called me to help them with the body, and it was all we could do, four of us, to carry him to the road where the carriage was standing."

"Did you ever hear them mention my name amongst them?" asked Beecher, tremblingly.

"No, sir; nobody spoke of you but my master, when he handed me the note."

"What a sad business it has all been!" exclaimed Beecher, half aloud.

"I suppose it would go hard with the Captain, sir, if he was caught?" said Rivers, inquiringly.

Again Beecher read over the note, pondering every word as he went "What a sad business!" murmured he, "and all for nothing, or next to nothing!" Then, as if suddenly rousing himself to action, he said, "Rivers, we must get away at once. Take this passport to the police, and then look after a horse-box for the next train to Liege. We shall start at two o'clock."

"That's just what the Captain said, sir. 'Don't delay in Brussels,' says he; 'and don't you go a-talking about this morning's work. If they have you up for examination, mind that you saw nothing, you heard nothing, you know nothing.'"

"Send Miss Davis's maid here," said Beecher; "and then see about those things I 've mentioned to you."

Mademoiselle Annette was a French Swiss, who very soon apprehended that a "difficulty" had occurred somewhere, which was to be kept secret from her young mistress; and though she smiled with a peculiar significance at the notion of Miss Davis travelling under Beecher's protection, she did so with all the decorum of her gifted class.

"You 'll explain everything, Annette," said Beecher, who in his confusion was eager to throw any amount of burden or responsibility upon another; "you'll tell her whatever you like as to the cause of his going away, and I 'll swear to it."

"Monsieur need not give himself any trouble," was the ready answer; "all shall be cared for."

CHAPTER XXXI
EXPLANATIONS

What a sad pity it is that the great faculty of "making things comfortable," that gifted power which blends the announcement with the explanation of misfortune, should be almost limited to that narrow guild in life to which Mademoiselle Annette belonged! The happy knack of half-informing and all-mystifying would be invaluable on the Treasury benches; and great proficients as some of our public men are in this walk, how immeasurably do they fall short of the dexterity of the "soubrette"!

So neatly and so cleverly had Annette performed her task, that when Miss Davis met Beecher at breakfast, she felt that a species of reserve was necessary as to the reasons of her father's flight; that, as he had not directly communicated with herself, her duty was simply to accept of the guidance he had dictated to her. Besides this, let it be owned, she had not yet rallied from the overwhelming astonishment of her first meeting with her father, so utterly was he unlike all that her imagination had pictured him! Nothing could be more affectionate, nothing kinder, than his reception; a thoughtful anxiety for her comfort pervaded all he said. The gloomy old Tirlemont even caught up an air of home as she passed the threshold; but still he was neither in look, manner, nor appearance what she fancied. All his self-restraint could not gloss over his vulgarity, nor all his reserve conceal his defects in breeding. His short, dictatorial manner with the servants,—his ever-present readiness to confront nobody saw what peril,—a suspectful insistence upon this or that mark of deference as a right of which he might possibly be defrauded,—all gave to his bearing a tone of insolent defiance that at once terrified and repelled her.

To all her eager questionings as to their future life, where and how it was to be passed, he would only answer vaguely or evasively. He met her inquiries about the families and friends of her schoolfellows in the same way. Of her pleasures and pursuits, her love of music, and her skill in drawing, he could not even speak with those conventionalities that disguise ignorance or indifference. Of the great world—the "swells" he would have called them—he only knew such as were on the turf. Of the opera, he might possibly tell the price of a stall, but not the name of a singer; and as to his own future, what or where it should be, Grog no more knew than who would be first favorite for the Léger a century hence. To "fence off" any attempt "to pump him" in the ring, to dodge a clever cross-examiner in a court of justice, Davis would have proved himself second to none,—these were games of skill, which he could play with the best,—but it was a very different task to thread his way through the geography of a land he had not so much as heard of, and be asked to act as guide through regions whose very names were new to him.

The utmost that Lizzy could glean from that long first evening's talk was, that her father had few or no political ambitions, rather shunned the great world, cared little for dukes or duchesses, nor set any great store on mere intellectual successes. "Perhaps," thought she, "he has tried and found the hollowness of them all; perhaps he is weary of public life; perhaps he 'd like the quiet pleasures of a country house, and that calm existence described as the chateau life of England. Would that he were only more frank with me, and let us know each other better!"

We entreat our readers to forgive us this digression, necessary as it is to show that Lizzy, whatever her real doubts and anxieties, felt bound not to display them, but accept Beecher's counsel as her father's will.

"And so we start for Aix-la-Chapelle by two?" said she, calmly.

"Yes; and I represent papa," said Beecher. "I hope you feel impressed with a due reverence for my authority."

"Much will depend upon the way you exercise it," said she; "I could very easily be a rebel if I suspected the justice of the Crown."

"Come, come," said he, laughing, "don't threaten me! my viceroyship will be very short-lived,—he 'll perhaps be at Aix before us."

"And I suppose all my dreams of extravagance here are defeated," said she. "Annette and I have been plotting and planning such rare devices in 'toilette,' not exactly aware where or upon whom the captivations were to be exercised. I actually revelled in the thought of all the smart fineries my Pensionnat life has denied me hitherto."

There was that blending of levity with seriousness in her tone that totally puzzled Beecher; and so was it through all she said,—there ran the same half-mocking vein that left him quite unable even to fathom her meaning. He muttered out something about "dress" and "smart things" being to be found everywhere, and that most probably they should visit even more pretentious cities than Brussels erelong.

"Which means that you know perfectly well where we are going, but won't tell it. Well, I resign myself to my interesting part of 'Captive Princess' all the more submissively, since every place is new to me, every town an object of interest, every village a surprise."

"You 'd like to see the world,—the real, the great world, I mean?" asked Beecher.

"Oh, how much!" cried she, clasping her hands in eagerness, as she arose.

Beecher watched her as she walked up and down the room, every movement of her graceful figure displaying dignity and pride, her small and beautifully shaped head slightly thrown back, while, as her hand held the folds of her dress, her march had something almost stage-like in its sweeping haughtiness. "And how she would become it!" muttered he, below his breath, but yet leaving the murmured sounds half audible.

"What are you saying, sir? Any disparaging sentiment on school-girl conceit or curiosity?"

"Something very like the opposite," said Beecher. "I was whispering to myself that Grantley House and Rocksley Castle were the proper sphere for *you*."

"Are these very splendid?" asked she, calmly.

"The best houses in England. Of their owners, one is a Duke with two hundred thousand a year, the other an Earl with nearly as much."

"And what do they do with it?"

"Everything; all that money can have—and what is there it cannot?— is there. Gorgeous houses, horses, dress, dinners, pictures, plate, the best people to visit them, the best cook, the best deer-park, the fastest yacht at Cowes, the best hunting-stable at Melton."

"I should like that; it sounds very fascinating, all of it. How it submerges at once, too, all the petty cares and contrivances, perpetually asking, 'Can we do this?' 'Dare we do that?' It makes existence the grand, bold, free thing one dreams it ought to be."

"You 're right there; it does make life very jolly."

"Are *you* very rich?" asked she, abruptly.

"No, by Jove! poor as a church mouse," said he, laughing at the strangeness of the question, whose sincere simplicity excluded all notion of impertinence. "I'm what they call a younger son, which means one who arrives in the world when the feast is over. I have a brother with a very tidy fortune, if that were of any use to me."

"And is it not the same? You share your goods together, I suppose?"

"I should be charmed to share mine with him, on terms of reciprocity," said Beecher; "but I'm afraid he'd not like it."

"So that he is rich, and you poor?"

"Exactly so."

"And this is called brotherhood? I own I don't understand it."

"Well, it has often puzzled me too," said Beecher, laughingly; "but I believe, if I had been born first, I should have had no difficulty in it whatever."

"And papa?" asked she, suddenly,—"what was he,—an elder or a younger son?"

It was all that Beecher could do to maintain a decent gravity at this question. To be asked about Grog Davis's parentage seemed about the drollest of all possible subjects of inquiry; but, with an immense effort of self-restraint, he said,—

"I never exactly knew; I rather suspect, however, he was an only child."

"Then there is no title in our family?" said she, inquiringly.

"I believe not; but you are aware that this is very largely the case in England. We are not all 'marquises' and 'counts' and 'chevaliers,' like foreigners."

"I like a title; I like its distinctiveness: the sense of carrying out a destiny, transmitting certain traits of race and kindred, seems a fine and ennobling thing; and this one has not, one cannot have, who has no past. So that," said she, after a pause, "papa is only what you would call a 'gentleman.'"

"'Gentleman' is a very proud designation, believe me," said he, evading an answer.

"And how would they address me in England,—am I 'my Lady'?"

"No, you are Miss Davis."

"How meanly it sounds,—it might be a governess, a maid."

"When you are married, you take the rank and title of your husband,—a duchess, if he be a duke."

"A duchess be it, then," said she, in that light, volatile tone she was ever best pleased to employ, while, with a rattling gayety, she went on: "How I should love to be one of those great people you have described to me,—soaring away in all that ideal splendor which would come of a life of boundless cost, the actual and the present being only suggestive of a thousand fancied enjoyments! What glorious visions might one conjure up out of the sportiveness of an untrammelled will! Yes, Mr. Beecher, I have made up my mind,—I'll be a duchess!"

"But you might have all these as a marchioness, a countess—"

"No, I 'll be a duchess; you sha'n't cheat me out of my just claims."

"Will your Grace please to give orders about packing up, for we must be away soon after one o'clock," said he, laughing.

"If I were not humility itself, I'd say the train should await my convenience," said she, as she left the room with a proud and graceful dignity that would have become a queen.

For a few moments Beecher sat silent and thoughtful in his chair, and then burst out into a fit of immoderate laughing,—he laughed till his eyes ran over and his sides ached. "If this ain't going the pace, I 'd like to know what speed is!" cried he, aloud. "I wonder what old Grog would say if he heard her; and the best of the joke is, she is serious all the while. She is in the most perfect good faith about it all. And this comes of the absurdity of educating her out of her class. What a strange blunder for so clever a head to make! You might have guessed, Master Grog, that she never could be a 'plater.' Let her only enter for a grand match, and she 'll be 'scratched' from one end of England to the other. Ay, Davis, my boy, you fancy pedigrees are only cared for on the turf; but there *is* a Racing Calendar, edited by a certain Debrett, that you never heard of."

Again, he thought of Davis as a peer,—"Viscount Davis!" Baron Grog, as he muttered it, came across him, and he burst out once more into laughter; then suddenly checking himself, he said, "I must take right good care, though, that he never hears of this same conversation; he's just the fellow to say *I* led her on to laugh at and ridicule him; he 'd suspect in a moment that I took her that pleasant gallop,—and if he did—" A long, wailing whistle finished the sentence for him.

Other and not very agreeable reflections succeeded these. It was this very morning that he himself had determined on "levanting," and there he was, more securely moored than ever. He looked at his watch, and muttered, "Eleven o'clock; by this time I should have been at Verviers, and on the Rhine before midnight. In four days more, I 'd have had the Alps between us, and now here I am without the chance of escape; for if I bolted and left his daughter here, he'd follow me through the world to shoot me!"

He sat silent for some minutes, and then, suddenly springing up from his chair, he cried out,—

"Precious hard luck it is! but I can neither get on *with* this fellow nor *without* him;" and with this "summing up" he went off to his room to finish his preparations for the road.

CHAPTER XXXII
THE COUPÉ ON THE RAIL

Annesley Beecher felt it "deuced odd" to be the travelling companion and protector of a very beautiful girl of nineteen, to whose fresh youth every common object of the road was a thing of wonderment and curiosity; the country, the people, the scores of passengers arriving or departing, the chance incidents of the way all amused her. She possessed that power of deriving intense enjoyment from the mere aspect of life that characterizes certain minds, and while thus each little incident interested her, her gay and lively sallies animated one who without her companionship had smoked his cigar in half-sulky isolation, voting journey and fellow-travellers "most monstrous bores." As they traversed that picturesque tract between Chaude Fontaine and Verviers, her delight and enjoyment increased. Those wonderful little landscapes which open at the exit from each tunnel, and where to the darkness and the gloom succeed, as if by magic, those rapid glances at swelling lawns, deep-bosomed woods, and winding rivers, with peaceful homesteads dotting the banks, were so many surprises full of marvellous beauty.

"Ah! Mr. Beecher," said she, as they emerged upon one of these charming spots, "I'm half relenting about my decision in regard to greatness. I think that in those lovely valleys yonder, where the tall willows are hanging over the river, there might possibly be an existence I should like better than the life of even a duchess."

"It's a much easier ambition to gratify," said he, smiling.

"It was not of *that* I was thinking," said she, haughtily, "nor am I so certain you are right there. I take it people can generally be that they have set their heart on being."

"I should like to be convinced of your theory," cried he, "for I have been I can't say how many years wishing for fifty things I have never succeeded in attaining."

"What else have you done besides wishing?" asked she, abruptly.

"Well, that is a hard question," said he, in some confusion; "and after all, I don't see what remained to me to do but wish."

"If that were all, it is pretty clear you had no right to succeed. When I said that people can have what they set their heart on, I meant what they so longed for that no toil was too great, no sacrifice too painful to deter them; that with eyes upturned to the summit they could breast the mountain, not minding weariness, and even when, footsore and exhausted, they sank down, they arose to the same enterprise, unshaken in courage, unbroken in faith. Have you known this?"

"I can scarcely say I have; but as to the longing and pining after a good turn of fortune, I'll back myself against any one going."

"That's the old story of the child crying for the moon," said she, laughing. "Now, what was it you longed for so ardently?"

"Can't you guess?"

"You wanted to marry some one who would not have you, or who was beneath you, or too poor, or too some-thing-or-other for your grand relations?"

"No, not that."

"You aspired to some great distinction as a politician, or a soldier, or perhaps a sailor?"

"No, by Jove! never dreamed of it," burst he in, laughing at the very idea.

"You sighed for some advancement in rank, or perhaps it was great wealth?"

"There you have it! Plenty of money—lots of ready—with that all the rest comes easy."

"It must be very delightful, no doubt, to indulge every passing caprice, without ever counting the cost; but, after a while, what a spoilt-child weariness would come over one from all this cloying enjoyment,—how tiresome would it be to shorten the journey between will and accomplishment, and make of life a mere succession of 'tableaux'! I 'd rather strive and struggle and win."

"Ay, but one does n't always win," broke he in.

"I believe one does—if one deserves it; and even when one does not, the battle is a fine thing. How much sympathy, I ask you, have we for those classic heroes who are always helped out of their difficulties by some friendly deity? What do we feel for him who, in the thick of the fight, is sure to be rescued by a goddess in a cloud?"

"I confess I do like a good 'book,' 'hedged' well all round, and standing to win somewhere. I mean," added he, in an explanatory tone, "I like to be safe in this world."

"Stand on the bank of the stream, then, and let bolder hearts push across the river!"

"Well, but I'm rather out of patience," said he, in a tone of half irritation. "I've had many a venture in life, and too many of them unfortunate ones."

"How I do wonder," said she, after a pause, "that you and papa are such great friends; for I have rarely heard of two people who take such widely different notions of life. *You* seem to me all caution and reserve; *he*, all daring and energy."

"That's the reason, perhaps, we suit each other so well," said Beecher, laughing.

"It may be so," said she, thoughtfully; and now there was silence between them.

"Have you got sisters, Mr. Beecher?" said she, at length.

"No; except I may call my brother's wife one."

"Tell me of her. Is she young?—is she handsome?"

"She is not young, but she is still a very handsome woman."

"Dark or fair?"

"Very dark, almost Spanish in complexion; a great deal of haughtiness in her look, but great courtesy when she pleases."

"Would she like me?"

"Of course she would," said he, with a smile and a bow; but a flush covered his face at the bare thought of their meeting.

"I'm not so certain you are telling the truth there," said she, laughing; "and yet you know there can be no offence in telling me I should not suit some one I have never seen; do, then, be frank with me, and say what would she think of me."

"To begin," said he, laughing, "she'd say you were very beautiful—"

"'Exquisitely beautiful,' was the phrase of that old gentleman that got into the next carriage; and I like it better."

"Well, exquisitely beautiful,—the perfection of gracefulness,—and highly accomplished."

"She'd not say any such thing; she'd not describe me like a governess; she'd probably say I was too demonstrative,—that's a phrase in vogue just now,—and hint that I was a little vulgar. But I assure you," added she, seriously, "I'm not so when I speak French. It is a stupid attempt on my part to catch up what I imagine must be English frankness when I talk the language that betrays me into all these outspoken extravagances. Let us talk French now."

"You 'll have the conversation very nearly to yourself then," said Beecher, "for I'm a most indifferent linguist."

"Well, then, I must ask you to take my word for it, and believe that I 'm well bred when I can afford it. But your sister,—do tell me of her."

"She is 'très grande dame,' as you would call it," said Beecher; "very quiet, very cold, extremely simple in language, dresses splendidly, and never knows wrong people."

"Who are wrong people?"

"I don't exactly know how to define them; but they are such as are to be met with in society, not by claim of birth and standing, but because they are very rich, or very clever, in some way or other,—people, in fact, that one has to ask who they are."

"I understand. But that must apply to a pretty wide circle of this world's habitants."

"So it does. A great part of Europe, and *all* America," said Beecher, laughing.

"And papa and myself, how should we come through this formidable inquiry?"

"Well," said he, hesitating, "your father has always lived so much out of the world,—this kind of world, I mean,—so studiously retired, that the chances are that, in short—"

"In short, they 'd ask, 'Who are these Davises?'" She threw into her face, as she spoke, such an admirable mimicry of proud pretension that Beecher laughed immoderately at it "And when they 'd ask it," continued she, "I 'd be very grateful to you to tell me what to reply to them, since I own to you it is a most puzzling question to myself."

"Well," said Beecher, in some embarrassment, "it is strange enough; but though your father and I are very old friends,—as intimate as men can possibly be,—yet he has never spoken to me about his family or connections,—nay, so far has he carried his reserve, that, until yesterday, I was not aware he had a daughter."

"You don't mean to say he never spoke of me?"

"Never to *me*, at least; and, as I have told you, I believe no one possesses a larger share of his confidence than myself."

"That *was* strange," said she, in deep reflection. Then, after a few minutes, she resumed: "If I had a story of my life I 'd tell it you; but there is really none, or next to none. As a child, I was at school in Cornwall. Later on, papa came and fetched me away to a small cottage near Walmer, where I lived with a sort of governess, who treated me with great deference,—in short, observed towards me so much respect that I grew to believe I was something very exalted and distinguished, a sort of 'Man in the Iron Mask,' whose pretensions had only to be known to convulse half Europe. Thence I passed over to the Pensionnat at the Three Fountains, where I found, if not the same homage, all the indications of my being regarded as a privileged individual. I had my maid; I enjoyed innumerable little indulgences none others possessed. I 'm not sure whether the pony I rode at the riding-school was my own or not; I only know that none mounted him but myself. In fact, I was treated like one apart, and all papa's letters only reiterated the same order,—I was to want for nothing. Of course, these teachings could impress but one lesson,—that I was a person of high rank and great fortune; and of this I never entertained a doubt. Now," added she, with more energy, "so far as I understand its uses, I *do* like wealth, and so far as I can fancy its privileges, I love rank; but if the tidings came suddenly upon me that I had neither one nor the other, I feel a sort of self-confidence that tells me I should not be dispirited or discouraged."

Beecher gazed at her with such admiration that a deep blush rose to her face, as she said, "You may put this heroism of mine to the test at once, by telling me frankly what you know about my station. Am I a Princess in disguise, Mr. Beecher, or am I only an item in the terrible category of what you have just called 'wrong people'?"

If the dread and terror of Grog Davis had been removed from Annesley Beecher's mind, there is no saying to what excess of confidence the impulse of the moment might have carried him. He was capable of telling her any and every thing. For a few seconds, indeed, the thought of being her trusted friend so overcame his prudence that he actually took her hand between his own, as the prelude of the revelations he was about to open; when, suddenly, a vision of Davis swept before his mind,—Davis, in one of his moods of wrath, paroxysms of passion as they were, wherein he stopped at nothing. "He 'd send me to the dock as a felon; he 'd shoot me down like a dog," muttered he to himself, as, dropping her hand, he leaned back in the carriage.

She bent over and looked calmly into his face. Her own was now perfectly pale and colorless, and then, with a faint, sad smile, she said, —

"I see that you'd like to gratify me. It is through some sense of delicacy and reserve that you hesitate. Be it so. Let us be good friends now, and perhaps, in time, we may trust each other thoroughly."

Beecher took her hand once more, and, bending down, kissed it fervently. What a strange thrill was that that ran through his heart, and what an odd sense of desolation was it as he relinquished that fair, soft hand, as though it were that by its grasp he held on to life and hope together! "Oh," muttered he to himself, "why was not she — why was not he himself — twenty things that neither of them were?"

"I wish I could read your thoughts," said she, smiling gently at him.

"I wish to heaven you could!" cried he, with an honest energy that his nature had not known for many a day.

For the remainder of the way neither spoke, beyond some chance remark upon the country or the people. It was as though the bridge between them was yet too frail to cross, and that they trusted to time to establish that interchange of thought and confidence which each longed for.

"Here we are at the end of our journey!" said he, with a sigh, as they entered Aix.

"And the beginning of our friendship," said she, with a smile, while she held out her hand to pledge the contract.

So intently was Beecher gazing at her face that he did not notice the action.

"Won't you have it?" asked she, laughing.

"Which," cried he, — "the hand or the friendship?"

"I meant the friendship," said she, quietly.

"Tickets, sir!" said the guard, entering. "We are at the station."

Annesley Beecher was soon immersed in all those bustling cares which attend the close of a journey; and though Lizzy seemed to enjoy the confusion and turmoil that prevailed, he was far from happy amidst the anxieties about baggage and horse-boxes, the maid and the groom each tormenting him in the interests of their several departments. All was, however, safe; not a cap-case was missing; Klepper "never lost a hair;" and they drove off to the Hotel of the Four Nations in high spirits all.

CHAPTER XXXIII
THE "FOUR NATIONS" AT AIX

All the bustle of "settling down" in the hotel over, Annesley Beecher began to reflect a little on the singularity of his situation. The wondering admiration which had followed Lizzy Davis wherever she appeared on the journey seemed to have reached its climax now, and little knots and groups of lounging travellers were to be seen before the windows, curious to catch a glance at this surpassing beauty. Now, had she been his *bona fide* property, he was just the man to derive the most intense enjoyment from this homage at second hand; he 'd have exulted and triumphed in it. His position was, however, a very different one, and, as merely her companion, while it exposed her to very depreciating judgments, it also necessitated on his part a degree of haughty defiance and championship for which he had not the slightest fancy whatever.

Annesley Beecher dragged into a row for Grog Davis's daughter, Beecher fighting some confounded Count or other about Lizzy Davis, Annesley shot by some Zouave Captain who insisted on waltzing with his "friend,"—these were pleasant mind-pictures which he contemplated with the very reverse of enjoyment; and yet the question of her father's station away, he felt it was a cause wherein even one who had no more love for the "duello" than himself might well have perilled life. All her loveliness and grace had not been wasted when they could kindle up a little gleam of chivalry in the embers of that wasted heart!

He ran over in his mind all the Lady Julias and Georginasof the fashionable world. He bethought him of each of those who had been the queens of London seasons, and yet how vastly were they all her inferiors! It was not alone that in beauty she eclipsed them, but she possessed, besides, the thousand nameless attractions of manner and gesture, a certain blended dignity and youthful gayety that made her seem the very ideal of high-born loveliness. He had seen dukes' daughters who could not vie with her in these gifts; he had known countesses immeasurably beneath her. From these thoughts he went on to others as to her future, and the kind of fellow that might marry her; for, strangely enough, in all his homage there mingled the ever-present memory of Grog and his pursuits. Mountjoy Stubbs might marry her; he has fifty thousand a year, and his father was a pawnbroker. Lockwood Harris might marry her; he got all his money from the slave trade. There were three or four more,—all wealthy, and all equivocal in position: men to be seen in clubs, to be dined with and played with; fellows who had yachts at Cowes and grouse-lodges in Scotland, and yet in London were "nowhere." These men could within their own sphere do all they pleased,— they could afford any extravagance they fancied; and what a delightful extravagance it would be to marry Lizzy Davis! Often as he had envied these men, he never did so more than now. *They* had no responsibilities of station ever hanging over them; no brothers in the Peerage to bully them about this; no sisters in waiting to worry them about that. They could always, as he phrased it, "paint their coach their own color," without any fear of the Herald's Office; and what better existence could a man wish for than a prolific fancy and unlimited funds to indulge it. "If I were Stubbs, I 'd marry her." This he said fully a dozen times over, and even confirmed it with an oath. And what an amiable race of people are the Stubbses of this habitable globe! how loosely do responsibilities sit upon them! how generously are they permitted every measure of extravagance and every violation of good taste! What a painful contrast did his mind draw between Stubbs' condition and his own! There was a time, too, when the State repaired in some sort the injustice that younger sons groaned under,—the public service was full of the Lord Charleses and the Honorables, who looked up to a paternal Government for their support; but now there was actually a run against them. Beecher argued himself so warmly into this belief, that he said aloud, "If I asked for something to-morrow, they 'd refuse me, just because I 've a brother a Peer!"

The reader is already aware what a compensation he found for all his defeats and shortcomings in life by arraigning the injustice of the world. Downing Street, the turf, Lackington, Tattersall's, the Horse Guards, and "the little hell in St. James's Street" were all in a league to crush him; but he'd show them "a turn round the corner yet," he said; and with a saucy laugh of derision at all the malevolence of fortune, he set about dressing for dinner. Beecher was not only a very good-looking fellow, but he had that stamp of man of fashion on him which all the contamination of low habits and low associates had not effaced. His address was easy and unaffected, his voice pleasantly toned, his smile sufficiently ready; and his whole manner was an agreeable blending of deference with a sort of not ungraceful self-esteem. Negatives best describe the class of men he belonged to, and any real excellence he possessed was in not being a great number of things which form, unhappily, the social defects of a large section of humanity. He was never loud, never witty, never oracular, never anecdotic; and although the slang of the turf and its followers clung to him, he threw out its "dialectics" so laughingly that he even seemed to be himself ridiculing the quaint phraseology he employed.

We cannot venture to affirm that our readers might have liked his company, but we are safe in asserting that Lizzy Davis did so. He possessed that very experience of life—London life—that amused her greatly. She caught up with an instinctive quickness the meaning of those secret springs which move society, and where, though genius and wealth are suffered to exercise their influence, the real power is alone centred in those who are great by station and hereditary claims. She saw that the great Brahmins of fashion maintained a certain exclusiveness which no pretensions ever breached, and that to this consciousness of an unassailable position was greatly owing all the dignified repose and serenity of their manner. She made him recount to her the style of living in the country houses of England,—the crowds of visitors that came and went, the field-sports, the home resources that filled up the day, while intrigues of politics or fashion went silently on beneath the surface. She recognized that in this apparently easy and indolent existence a great game was ever being played, and that all the workings of ambition, all the passions of love and hate and fear and jealousy "were on the board."

They had dined sumptuously. The equivocal position in which they appeared, far from detracting from the deference of the hotel people, served but to increase their homage. Experience had shown that such persons as they were supposed to be spent most and paid best, and so they were served on the most splendid plate; waiters in full dress attended them; even to the bouquet of hothouse flowers left on "Mademoiselle's" napkin, all were little evidences of that consideration of which Annesley Beecher well knew the meaning.

"Will you please to enlighten my ignorance on one point, Mr. Beecher?" said she, as they sat over their coffee. "Is it customary in this rigid England, of which you have told me so many things, for a young unmarried lady to travel alone with a gentleman who is not even a relative?"

"When her father so orders it, I don't see that there can be much wrong in it," said he, with some hesitation.

"That is not exactly an answer to my question; although I may gather from it that the proceeding is, at least, unusual."

"I won't say it's quite customary," said Beecher; "but taking into account that I am a very old and intimate friend of your father's—"

"There must, then, have been some very pressing emergency to make papa adopt such a course," interrupted she.

"Why so?" asked he. "Is the arrangement so very distasteful to you?"

"Perhaps not; perhaps I like it very well. Perhaps I find you very agreeable, very amusing, very—What shall I say?"

"Respectful."

"If you like that epithet, I have no objection to put it in your character. Yet still do I come back to the thought that papa could scarcely have struck out this plan without some grave necessity. Now, I should like much to know what that is, or was." Beecher made no sign of reply, and she quickly asked, "Do you know his reasons?"

"Yes," said he, gravely; "but I prefer that you should not question me about them."

"I can't help that, Mr. Beecher," said she, in that half-careless tone she sometimes used. "Just listen to me for one moment," said she, earnestly, and fixing her eyes fully on him,—"just hear me attentively. From what I have gathered from your account of England and its habits, I am certainly now doing that which, to say the least, is most unusual and unwarrantable. Now, either there is a reason so grave for this that it makes a choice of evils imperative,—and, therefore, I ought to have my choice,—or there is another even worse interpretation—at least, a more painful one—to come."

"Which is?" cried he.

"That I am not of that station to which such propriety attaches of necessity."

She uttered these words with a cold sternness and determination that actually made Beecher tremble. "It was Davis's daughter spoke there," thought he. "They are the words of one who declares that, no matter what be the odds against her, she is ready to meet the whole world in arms. What a girl it is!" muttered he, with a sense of mingled fear and admiration.

"Well, Mr. Beecher," said she, at length, "I *do* think you owe me a little frankness; short as our acquaintance has been, I, at least, have talked in all the freedom of old friendship. Pray show me that I have not been indiscreet."

"Hang me, if I know what to say or do!" cried Beecher, in dire perplexity. "If I were to tell you why your father hurried away from Brussels, *he* 'd bring me to book very soon, I promise you."

"I do not ask that," interrupted she, eagerly. "It is upon the other point my interest is most engaged." He looked blankly at her, for he really did not catch to what she alluded. "I want you to tell me, in one word, who are the Davises? Who are we? If we are not recognizable by that high world you have told me of, who, then, are our equals? Remember that by an honest answer to my question you give guidance and direction to my future life. Do not shrink from fear of giving me pain,—there is no such pain as uncertainty; so be frank."

Beecher covered his face with his hands to think over his reply. He did not dare to look at her, so fearful was he of her reading his very embarrassment.

"I will spare you, sir," said she, smiling half superciliously; "but if you bad known me a little longer or a little better, you had seen how needless all this excessive caution on your part I have more of what you call 'pluck' than you give me credit for."

"No, by Jove! that you have n't," cried Beecher; "you have more real courage than all the men I ever knew."

"Show me, then, that you are not deficient in the quality, and give me a plain answer to a plain question. Who are we?"

"I have just told you," said Beecher, whose confusion now made him stammer and stutter at every word,—"I have just told you that your father never spoke to me about his relations. I really don't know his county, nor anything about his family."

"Then it only remains to ask, What are we? or, in easier words, Has my father any calling or profession? Come, sir, so much you can certainly tell me."

"Your father was a captain in a West India regiment, and, when I met him first, he was a man about town,—went to all the races, made his bets, won and lost, like the rest of us; always popular,—knew everybody."

"A 'sporting character,' in short,—is n't that the name newspapers give it?" said she, with a malicious twinkle of the eye.

"By Jove! how you hit a thing off at once!" exclaimed Beecher, in honest ecstasy at her shrewdness.

"So, then, I am at the end of the riddle at last," said she, musingly, as she arose and walked the room in deep meditation. "Far better to have told me so many a year ago; far better to have let me conform to this station when I might have done so easily and without a pang!" A bitter sigh escaped her at the last word, and Beecher arose and joined her.

"I hope you are not displeased with me, my dear Miss Davis," said he, with a trembling voice; "I don't know what I'd not rather suffer than offend you."

"You have *not* offended me," said she, coldly.

"Well, I mean, than I 'd pain you,—than I 'd say anything that should distress you. You know, after all, it was n't quite fair to push me so hard."

"Are you forgetting, sir," broke she in, haughtily, "that you have really told me next to nothing, and that I am left to gather from mere insinuations that there is something in our condition your delicacy shrinks from explaining?"

"Not a bit of it," chimed he in, quickly. "The best men in England are on the turf, and a good book on the Oaks is n't within reach of the income-tax. Your father's dealings are with all the swells in the Peerage."

"So there is a partnership in the business, sir," said she, with a quiet irony; "and is the Honorable Mr. Beecher one of the company?"

"Well—ha—I suppose—I ought to say yes," muttered he, in deep confusion. "We do a stroke of work together now and then—on the square, of course, I mean."

"Pray don't expose the secrets of the firm, sir. I am even more interested than yourself that they should be conducted with discretion. There is only one other question I have to ask; and as it purely concerns myself, you 'll not refuse me a reply. Knowing our station in life, as I now see you know it, by what presumption did you dare to trifle with my girlish ignorance, and lead me to fancy that I might yet move in a sphere which in your heart you knew I was excluded from?"

Overwhelmed with shame and confusion, and stunned by the embarrassment of a dull man in a difficulty, Beecher stood, unable to utter a word.

"To say the least, sir, there was levity in this," said she, in a tone of sorrowful meaning; "but, perhaps, you never meant it so."

"Never, upon my oath, never!" cried he, eagerly. "Whatever I said, I uttered in all frankness and sincerity. I know London town just as well as any man living, and I 'll stand five hundred to fifty there's not your equal in it,—and that's giving the whole field against the odds. All I say is, you shall go to the Queen's Drawing-room—"

"I am not likely to do so, sir," said she, with a haughty gesture, and left the room.

CHAPTER XXXIV
AIX-LA-CHAPELLE

Three days passed over,—three days varied with all the incidents that go to make up a longer existence,—and Beecher and his fair charge were still in Aix. If they forbore to speak to each other of the strange situation in which they found themselves, they were not the less full of it. Neither telegraph nor letter came from Davis, and Beecher's anxiety grew hourly greater. There was scarcely an eventuality his mind had not pictured. Davis was arrested and carried off to prison in Brussels,—was waylaid and murdered in the Ardennes,—was ill, dying in some unheard-of village,—involved in some other row, and obliged to keep secret,—arrested on some old charge; in fact, every mishap that a fertile fancy could devise had befallen him, and now only remained the question what was he himself to do with Lizzy Davis.

Whether it was that her present life was an agreeable change from the discipline of the Three Fountains, or that the new objects of interest about her engaged her to the exclusion of much thought, or that some higher philosophy of resignation supported her, but certain is it she neither complained of the delay nor exhibited any considerable impatience at her father's silence. She went about sightseeing, visited churches and galleries, strolled on the Promenade, before dinner, and finished with the theatre at night, frankly owning that it was a kind of do-nothing existence that she enjoyed greatly. Her extraordinary beauty was already a town talk; and the passages of the hotel were crowded as she went down to her carriage, and to her box at the opera were directed almost every glass in the house. This, however, is a homage not always respectful; and in the daring looks of the men, and the less equivocal glances of the women, Beecher read the judgment that had been pronounced upon her. Her manner, too, in public had a certain fearless gayety about it that was sure to be severely commented on, while the splendor of her dress was certain to be not more mercifully interpreted.

To have the charge of a casket of jewels through the thieves' quarter of London was the constant similitude that rose to Beecher's mind as he descended the stairs at her side. To be obliged to display her to the wondering gaze of some hundred idlers, the dissipated and debauched loungers of a watering-place, men of bad lives and worse tongues; to mark the staring insolence of some, and the quizzical impertinence of others; to see how narrowly each day they escaped some more overt outrage from that officious politeness that is tendered to those in equivocal positions, were tortures that half maddened him. Nor could he warn her of the peril they stood in, or dare to remonstrate about many little girlish ways which savored of levity. The scene of the theatre in Brussels was never off his mind, and the same one idea continually haunted him, that poor Hamilton's fate might be his own. The characterless men of the world are always cowards as to responsibility,—they feel that there is a flaw in their natures that must smash them if pressed upon; and so was it here. Beecher's life was actual misery, and each morning he awoke the day seemed full of menace and misfortune to him. In his heart, he knew that if an emergency arose he should be found wanting; he 'd either not think of the right thing, or have pluck for it if he even thought it; and then, whatever trouble or mishap he came through, there still remained worse behind,—the settlement with Grog himself at the end.

Like most persons who seek the small consolation of falling back on their own foresight, he called to mind how often he had said to himself that nothing but ill could come of journeying with Grog Davis,—he knew it, he was sure of it. A fellow to conspire with about a "plant"—a man to concert with on a race or a "safe thing with the cards"—was not exactly a meet travelling-companion, and he fretted over the fatal weakness that had induced his acceptance of him. They had only just started, and their troubles had already begun! Even if Davis himself were there, matters might not be so bad. Grog was always ready to "turn out" and have a shot with any one. It was a sort of pastime he rather liked when nothing else was stirring, it seemed like keeping his hand in; but, confound the fellow! he had gone off, and left in his place one who had a horror of hair-triggers, and shuddered at the very thought of a shot-wound.

He was far too conversant with the habits of *demi-monde* existence not to see that the plot was thickening, and fresh dangers clustering round him. The glances in the street were hourly growing more familiar,—the looks were half recognitions. Half a dozen times in the morning, well-dressed and well-bearded strangers had bolted into their sitting-room in mistake, and while apologizing for their blunder, delayed unnecessarily long over the explanation.

The waiter significantly mentioned that Prince Bottoffsky was then stopping at the hotel, with seven carriages and eighteen servants. The same intelligent domestic wondered they never went to see Count Czapto witch's camellias,—"he had sent a bouquet of them that very day to her Ladyship." And Beecher groaned in his spirit as the fellow produced it.

"I see how it's all to end," muttered he, as he paced the room, unable any longer to conceal the misery that was consuming him. "One of those confounded foreigners will come swaggering up to talk to her on the Promenade, and then I'm 'in for it.' It's all Davis's fault. It's all *her* fault. Why can't she look like other people,—dress like them,—walk like them? What stuff and nonsense it is for *her* to be going about the world like a Princess Royal! It was only last night she wore a Brussels lace shawl at the opera that cost five thousand francs; and when it caught on a nail in the box and was torn, she laughed, and said, 'Annette will be charmed with this disaster, for she was always coveting this lace, and wondering when she was to have it.' That's the fine 'bring-ing-up' old Grog is so proud of! If she were a Countess in her own right, with ten thousand a year, she 'd be a bad bargain!"

Ah, Beecher! your heart never went with you when you made this cruel speech; you uttered it in spleen and bitterness, but not in sincerity; for already in that small compartment of your nature where a few honest affections yet lingered *she was* treasured, and, had you known how to do it, you would have loved her. Poor devil as he was, Life was a hard battle to him,—always over head and ears in debt; protested bills meeting him at every moment; duns rising before him at every turn. Levity was to him, as to many, a mere mask over Fear, and he walked the world in the hourly terror that any moment might bring him to shame and ruin. If he were a few minutes alone, his melancholy was almost despair; and over and over had he pictured to his mind a scene in the police-court, where he was called on to find full and sufficient bail for his appearance on trial. From such sorrowing thoughts he made his escape to rush into society—anywhere, anyhow; and, by the revulsion of his mind, came that rattling and boisterous gayety that made him seem the most light-hearted fellow in existence. Such men are always making bonfires of their household gods, and have nothing to greet them when they are at home.

What a fascination must Lizzy Davis have exercised over such a mind! Her beauty and her gracefulness would not have been enough without her splendid dressing, and that indescribable elegance of manner which was native to her. Then how she amused him!—what droll caricatures did she sketch of the queer originals of the place,—the bearded old colonels, or the pretentious loungers that frequented the "Cursaal"! How witty the little epigrams by which she accompanied them, and how charmingly at a moment would she sit down at the piano and sing for him anything, from a difficult "scena" from Verdi to some floating barcarole of Venice! She could—let us tell it in one breath—make him laugh; and oh, dearly valued reader! what would you or I give for the company of any one who could do as much? The world is full of learned people and clever people. There are Bourse men, and pre-Raphaelite men, and Old-red-sandstone men, and Greek-particle men; but where are the pleasant people one used to chat with long ago, who, though talking of mere commonplaces, threw out little sparks of fun,—fireflies in the dark copses,—giving to what they said that smack of epigram that spiced talk but never over-seasoned it, whose genial sympathy sent a warm life-blood through every theme, and whose outspoken heartiness refreshed one after a cold bath of polite conventionalities? If they still exist upon this earth, they must be hiding themselves, wisely seeing it is not an age to suit them; they lie quiet under the ice, patiently hibernating till another summer may call them forth to vitality.

Now Lizzy Davis could make Beecher laugh in his lowest and gravest moments; droll situations and comical conceits came in showers over her mind, and she gave them forth with all the tact of a consummate actress. Her mimicry, too, was admirable; and thus he who rarely reflected and never read, found in her ready talents resources against all weariness and ennui. What a girl she was!—how perfectly she would become any—the very highest—station! what natural dignity in her manner!—and—Then, after a pause, he murmured, "What a fortune she'd make on the stage! Why, there's nothing to compare with her,—she's as much beyond them all in beauty as in genius!" And so he set about thinking how, by marrying her, a man might make a "deuced good thing of it." There's no saying what Webster wouldn't offer; and then there was America, always a "safe card;" not that it would do for himself to think of such a thing. Lackington would never speak to him again. All his family would cut him dead; he had n't an acquaintance would recognize him after such disgrace.

"Old Grog is *so* confoundedly well known," muttered he,—"the scoundrel is *so* notorious!" Still, there were fellows would n't mind that,—hard-up men, who had done everything, and found all failure. He knew—"Let us see," said he to himself, beginning to count on his fingers all the possible candidates for her hand. "There's Cranshaw Craven at Caen, on two hundred a year; *he'd* marry her, and never ask to see her if she 'd settle twenty thousand francs a year on him. Brownlow Gore would marry her, and for a mere five hundred too, for he wants to try that new martingale at Ems; he's certain he 'd break the bank with less. Foley would marry her; but, to be sure, he has a wife somewhere, and she might object to that! I'd lay an even fifty," cried he, in ecstasy at the bright thought, "Tom Beresford would marry her just to get out of the Fleet!"

"What does that wonderful calculation mean?" cried she, suddenly, as she saw him still reckoning on his fingers. "What deep process of reasoning is my learned guardian engaged in?"

"I 'd give you a long time to guess," said he, laughing.

"Am I personally concerned in it?" asked she.

"Yes, that you are!"

"Well," said she, after a pause, "you are counting over the days we have passed, or are still to pass here?"

"No, not *that!*"

"You are computing, perhaps, one by one, all your fashionable friends who would be shocked by my levity—that 's the phrase, I believe,—meaning those outspoken impertinences you encourage me to utter about everything and everybody!"

"Far from it. I was—"

"Oh! of course, you were charmed," broke she in; "and so you ought to be, when one performs so dangerous a trick to amuse you. The audience always applauds the rope-dancer that perils his neck; and you 'd be worse than ungrateful not to screen me when I 'm satirized. But it may relieve somewhat the load of obligation when I say that I utter these things just to please myself. I bear the world no ill-will, it is true; but I 'm very fond of laughing at it."

"In the name and on behalf of that respectable community, let me return you my thanks," said he, bowing.

"Remember," said she, "how little I really know of what I ridicule, and so let my ignorance atone for my ill-nature; and now, to come back, what was it that you were counting so patiently on your fingers? Not *my* faults, I'm certain, or you'd have had both hands."

"I'm afraid I could scarcely tell you," said he, "though somehow I feel that if I knew you a very little longer, I could tell you almost anything."

"I wish you could tell me that this pleasant time was coming. What is this?" asked she, as the waiter entered, and presented her with a visiting-card.

"Monsieur the Count desires to know if Mademoiselle will receive him," said the man.

"What, how? What does this mean?" exclaimed Beecher, in terror and astonishment.

"Yes," said she, turning to the waiter; "say, 'With pleasure.'"

"Gracious mercy!" exclaimed Beecher, "you don't know what you 're doing. Have you seen this person before?"

"Never!"

"Never heard of him!"

"Never," said she, with a faint smile, for the sight of his terror amused her.

"But who is he, then? How has he dared—"

"Nay," said she, holding behind her back the visiting-card, which he endeavored to snatch from her hand,—"this is *my* secret!"

"This is intolerable!" cried Beecher. "What is your father to think of your admitting a person to visit you,—an utter stranger,—a fellow Heaven knows—"

At this moment, as if to answer in the most palpable form the question he was propounding, a somewhat sprucely dressed man, middle-aged and comely, entered; and, passing Beecher by with the indifference he might have bestowed on a piece of furniture, advanced to where Lizzy was standing, and, taking her hand, pressed it reverently to his lips.

So far from resenting the liberty, she smiled most courteously on him, and motioned to him to take a seat on the sofa beside her.

"I can't stand this, by Jove!" said Beecher, aloud; while, with an assumption of courage his heart little responded to, he walked straight up to the stranger. "You understand English, I hope?" said he, in very indifferent French.

"Not a syllable," replied the other, in the same language.

"I only know 'All right';" and he laughed pleasantly as he uttered the words in an imitation of English.

"Come, I 'll not torture you any longer," said Lizzy, laughing; "read *that*." And she handed him the card, whereon, in her father's writing, there was, "See the Count; he'll tell you everything.—C. D."

"I have heard the name before.—Count Lienstahl," said Beecher to himself. "Has he seen your father? Where is he?" asked he, eagerly.

"He'll inform me on all, if you'll just give him time," said she; while the Count, with an easy volubility, was pouring out a flow of words perfectly unintelligible to poor Beecher.

Whether it was the pleasure of the tidings he brought, or the delicious enjoyment of once more hearing and replying in that charming tongue that she loved so dearly, but Lizzy ceased even to look at Beecher, and only occupied herself with her new acquaintance.

Now, while we leave her thus pleasantly engaged, let us present the visitor to our reader.

Nothing could be less like the traditional "Continental Count" than the plump, close-shaven, blue-eyed gentlemen who sat beside Lizzy Davis, with an expression of *bonhomie* in his face that might have graced a squire of Devon. He was neither frogged nor moustached; his countenance neither boded ill to the Holy Alliance, nor any close intimacy with billiards or dice-boxes. A pleasant, easy-tempered, soft-natured man he seemed, with a ready smile and a happy laugh, and an air of yielding good-humor about him that appeared to vouch for his being one none need ever dispute with. If there were few men less generally known throughout Europe, there was not one whose origin, family, fortune, and belonging were wrapped in more complete obscurity. Some said he was a Pomeranian, others called him a Swede; many believed him Russian, and a few, affecting deeper knowledge, declared he was from Dalmatia. He was a Count, however, of somewhere, and as certainly was he one who had the *entrée* to all the best circles of the Continent, member of its most exclusive clubs, and the intimate of those who prided themselves on being careful in their friendships. While his manners were sufficiently good to pass muster anywhere, there was about him a genial kindliness, a sort of perennial pleasantry, that was welcome everywhere; he brought to society that inestimable gift of adhesiveness by which cold people and stiff people are ultimately enabled to approximate and understand each other. No matter how dull and ungenial the salon, he was scarcely across the doorway when you saw that an element of social kindliness had just been added, and in his little caressing ways and coaxing inquiries you recognized one who would not let condescension crush nor coldness chill him. If young people were delighted to see one so much their senior indulging in all the gay and light frivolities of life, older folk were gratified to find themselves so favorably represented by one able to dance, sing, and play like the youngest in company. So artfully, too, did he contribute his talent to society, that no thought of personal display could ever attach to him. It was all good-nature; he played to amuse *you*,—he danced to gratify some one else; he was full of little attentions of a thousand kinds, and you no more thought of repayment than you'd have dreamed of thanking the blessed sun for his warmth or his daylight. Such men are the *bonbons* of humanity, and even they who do not care for sweet things are pleased to see them.

If his birth and origin were mysterious, far more so were his means of life. Nobody ever heard of his agent or his banker. He neither owned nor earned, and yet there he was, as well dressed, as well cared for, and as pleasant a gentleman as you could see. He played a little, but it was notorious that he was ever a loser. He was too constantly a winner in the great game of life to be fortunate as a gambler, and he could well afford to laugh at this one little mark of spitefulness in Fortune. Racing and races were a passion with him; but he loved sport for itself, not as a speculation,—so, at least, he said; and when he threw his arm over your shoulder, and said anything in that tone of genial simplicity that was special to him, I'd like to have seen the man—or, still more, the woman—who would n't have believed him.

The turf—like poverty—teaches one to know strange bed-fellows; and this will explain how the Count and Grog Davis became acquaintances, and something more.

The grand intelligence who discovered the great financial problem of France—the *Crédit Mobilier*—has proclaimed to the world that the secret lay in the simple fact that there were industrial energies which needed capital, and capital which needed industry, and that all he avowed to accomplish was to bring these two distant but all necessary elements into close union and co-operation. Now, something of the same kind moved Grog and the Count to cement their friendship; each saw that the other supplied some want of his own nature, and before they had passed an hour together they ratified an alliance. An instinct whispered to each, "We are going the same journey in life, let us travel together;" and some very profitable tours did they make in company!

His presence now was on a special mission from Davis, whom he just met at Treves, and who despatched him to request his daughter to come on to Carlsruhe, where he would await her. The Count was charged to explain, in some light easy way of his own, why her father had left Brussels so abruptly; and he was also instructed to take Annesley Beecher into his holy keeping, and not suffer him to fall into indiscretions, or adventure upon speculations of his own devising.

Lizzy thought him "charming,"—far more worldly-wise people than Lizzy had often thought the same. There was a bubbling fountain of good-humor about him that seemed inexhaustible. He was always ready for any plan that promised pleasure. Unlike Beecher, who knew nobody, the Count walked the street in a perpetual salutation,—bowing, hand-shaking, and sometimes kissing, as he went; and in that strange polyglot that he talked he murmured as he went, "Ah, lieber Freund!"—"Come sta?"—"Addio!"—"Mon meilleur ami!" to each that passed; so that veritably the world did seem only peopled with those who loved him.

As for Beecher, notwithstanding a certain distrust at the beginning, he soon fell captive to a manner that few resisted; and though the intercourse was limited to shaking hands and smiling at each other, the Count's pleasant exclamation of "All right!" with a jovial slap on the shoulder, made him feel that he was a "regular trump," and a man "to depend on."

One lurking thought alone disturbed this esteem,—he was jealous of his influence over Lizzy; he marked the pleasure with which she listened to him, the eager delight she showed when he came, her readiness to sing or play for him. Beecher saw all these in sorrow and bitterness; and though twenty times a day he asked himself, "What the deuce is it to me,—how can it possibly matter to *me* whom she cares for?" the haunting dread never left his mind, and became his very torturer. But why should he worry himself about it at all? The fellow did what he liked with every one. Rivers, the sulky training-groom, that would not have let a Royal Highness see "the horse," actually took Klepper out and galloped him for the Count. The austere landlady of the inn was smiles and courtesy to him; even to that unpolished class, the hackney coachmen, his blandishments extended, and they vied with each other who should serve him.

"We are to start for Wiesbaden to-morrow," said Lizzy to Beecher.

"Why so,—who says so?"

"The Count"

"Si, si, andiamo,—all right!" cried the Count, laughing; and the march was ordered.

CHAPTER XXXV
A FOREIGN COUNT

The announcement of Count Lienstahl's arrival at Wiesbaden was received with rejoicing. "Now we shall open the season in earnest. We shall have balls, picnics, races, hurdle-matches, gypsy parties, excursions by land and water. *He* 'll manage everything and everybody." Such were the exclamations that resounded along the Promenade as the party drove up to the hotel. Within less than an hour the Count had been to Beberich to visit the reigning Duke, he had kissed hands with half-a-dozen serene highnesses, made his bow to the chief minister and the Governor of Wiesbaden, and come back to dinner all smiles and delight at the condescension and kindness of the court and the capital.

If Lienstahl's popularity was great, he only shared a very humble portion of public attention when they appeared at the *table d'hote*. There Lizzy Davis attracted every look, and the fame of her beauty was already wide-spread. Such was the eagerness to obtain place at the table that the most extravagant bribes were offered for a seat, and a well-known elegant of Vienna actually paid a waiter five louis to cede his napkin to him and let him serve in his stead. Beecher was anything but gratified at these demonstrations. If his taste was offended, his fears were also excited. "Something bad must come of it," was his own muttered reflection; and as they retired after dinner to take their coffee, he showed very palpably his displeasure.

"Eh, *caro mio,*—all right?" said the Count, gayly, as he threw an arm over his shoulder.

"No, by Jove!—all wrong. I don't like it. It's not the style of thing I fancy." And here his confusion overwhelmed him, and he stopped abruptly; for the Count, seating himself at the piano, and rattling off a lively prelude, began a well-known air from a popular French vaudeville, of which the following is a rude version:—

> *"With a lovely face beside you,*
> *You can't walk this world far,*
> *But from those who 've closely eyed you,*
> *Comes the question, Who are you?*

And though Dowagers will send you
Cutting looks and glances keen,
The men will comprehend you
When you say, 'C'est ma cousine.'"

He was preparing for the second verse when Lizzy entered the room, and, turning at once to her, he poured forth some sentences with all that voluble rapidity he possessed.

"So," said she, addressing Beecher, "it seems that you are shocked or horrified, or your good taste is outraged, by certain demonstrations of admiration for me exhibited by the worthy public of this place; and, shall I own to you, I liked it I thought it very nice, and very flattering, and all that, until I thought it was a little—a very little, perhaps, but still a little—impertinent Was that your opinion?"

There was a blunt frankness about this question, uttered in such palpable honesty of intention that Beecher felt overwhelmed at once.

"I don't know the Continent like your friend there. I can't pretend to offer you advice and counsel like him; but if you really ask me, I'd say, 'Don't dine below any more; don't go to the rooms of an evening; don't frequent the Promenade—'"

"What would you say to my taking the veil, for I fancy I've some vocation that way?" And then, turning to the Count, she said something in French, at which he laughed immoderately.

Whether vexed with himself or with her, or, more probably still, annoyed by not being able to understand what passed in a foreign language, Beecher took his hat and left the room. Without his ever suspecting it, a new pang was just added to his former griefs, and he was jealous! It is very rare that a man begins by confessing a sense of jealousy to his own heart; he usually ascribes the dislike he feels to a rival to some defect or some blemish in his nature. He is a coarse fellow; rude, vulgar, a coxcomb, or, worst of all, a bore. In some such disposition as this Beecher quitted the town, and strolled away into the country. He felt he hated the Count, and yet he could not perceive why; Lienstahl possessed a vast number of the qualities he was generally disposed to like. He was gay, lively, light-hearted, never out of humor, never even thoughtful; his was that easy temperament that seemed to adapt itself to every phase of life. What was it, then? What could it be that he disliked about him? It was somewhat "cool," too, of Grog, to send this fellow over without even the courtesy of a line to himself. "Serve him right—serve them all right—if I were to cut my lucky;" and he ruminated long and anxiously over the thought. His present position was anything but pleasant or flattering to him. For aught *he* knew, the Count and Lizzy Davis passed their time laughing at his English ignorance of all things foreign. By dint of a good deal of such self-tormenting, he at last reached that point whereat the very slightest additional impulse would have determined him to decamp from his party, and set out all alone for Italy. The terror of a day of reckoning with Davis was, however, a dread that he could never shake off. Grog the unforgiving, the inexorable! Grog, whose greatest boast in his vainglorious moments was that, in the "long run," no man ever got the better of him, would assuredly bring him to book one day or other; and he knew the man's nature well enough to be aware that no fear of personal consequences would ever balk him on the road to a vengeance.

Sometimes the thought occurred to him that he would make a frank and full confession to Lackington of all his delinquencies, even to that terrible "count" by which the fame and fortune of his house might be blasted forever. If he could but string up his courage to this pitch, Lackington might "pull him through," Lackington would see that "there was nothing else for it," and so on. It is marvellous what an apparent strength of argument lies in those slang expressions familiar to certain orders of men. These conventionalities seem to settle at once questions which, if treated in more befitting phraseology, would present the gravest difficulties.

He walked on and on, and at last gained a pine wood which skirted the base of a mountain, and soon lost himself in its dark recesses. Gloomier than the place itself was the tone of his reflections. All that he might have been, all that lay so easily within his reach, all that life once offered him, contrasted bitterly with what he now saw himself. Conscience, it is true, suggested few of his present pangs; he believed—ay, sincerely believed—that he had been more "sinned against than sinning." Such a one had "let him in" here; such another "had sold him" there. In his reminiscences he saw himself trustful, generous, and confiding, while the world—the great globe that includes Tattersalls, Goodwood, Newmarket, and Ascot—was little better than a nest of knaves and vagabonds.

Why could n't Lackington get him something abroad,—in the Brazils or Lima, for instance? He was n't quite sure where they were; but they were far away, he thought,—places too remote for Grog Davis to hunt him out, and whence he could give the great Grog a haughty defiance. They—how it would have puzzled him to say who "they" were—they couldn't refuse Lackington if he asked. He was always voting and giving his proxies, and doing all manner of things for them; he made a speech, too, last year at Hoxton, and gave a lecture upon something that must have served them. Lackington would begin the old story about character; "but who had character nowadays?" "Take down the Court Guides," cried he, aloud, "and let *me* give you the private life and adventures of each as you read out the names. Talk of *me!* why, what have I done equal to what Lockwood, Hepton, Bulkleigh, Frank Melton, and fifty more have done? No, no; for public life, now, they must do as a sergeant of the Ninety-fifth told me t' other day, 'We 're obliged to take 'em little, sir, and glad to get 'em too!'"

It might be that there was something grateful to his feelings, reassuring to his heart, in this reflection, for he walked along now more briskly, and his head higher than before. Without being aware, he had already gone some miles from the town, and now found himself in one of those long grassy alleys which traversed the dense wood in various directions. As he looked down the narrow road which seemed like the vast aisle of some Gothic cathedral, he felt a sort of tremulous motion beneath his feet; and then, the moment after, he could detect the measured tramp of a horse at speed. A slight bend of the alley had hitherto shut out the view; but, suddenly, a dark object came sweeping round the turn and advancing towards him.

Half to secure a position, and half with the thought of watching what this might portend, Beecher stepped aside into the dense brushwood at the side of the alley, and which effectually hid him from view. He had barely time to make his retreat when a horse swept past him at full stride, and with one glance he recognized him as "Klepper." It was Rivers, too, who rode him, sitting high over the saddle and with his hands low, as if racing. Now, it was but that very morning Rivers had told him that the horse was not "quite right," — a bit heavy or so about the eyes, — "out of sorts" he called it; and there he was now, flying along at the top of his speed in full health and condition. It needed but the fortieth part of this to suggest a suspicion to such a mind as his, and with the speed of lightning there flashed across him the notion of a "cross." He, Annesley Beecher, was to be "put into the hole," to be "squared," and "nobbled," and all the rest of it! It did not, indeed, occur to him how very unprofitably such an enterprise would reward its votaries, that it would be a most gratuitous iniquity to "push him to the wall," that all the ingenious malevolence in the world could never make the venture "pay;" his self-conceit smothered these reasonings, and he determined to watch and to see how the scheme was to be developed. He had not to wait long in suspense; at the bend of the alley where the horse had disappeared, two horsemen were now seen slowly approaching him. As they drew nearer, Beecher could mark that they were in close, and what seemed confidential conversation. One he quickly recognized to be the Count; the other, to his amazement, was Spicer, of whose arrival at Aix he had not heard anything. They moved so slowly past the spot where he was standing that he could gather some of the words that escaped them, although being in French. The sound of his own name quickly caught his ear. It was the Count spoke as they came up,—

"He is a *pauvre sire*, this Beecher, and I don't yet see what use he can be to us."

"Davis likes him, or, at least, he wants him," replied Spicer, "and that's enough for us. Depend upon it, Grog makes no mistakes." The other laughed; but what he replied was lost in the distance?

It was some time ere Beecher could summon resolution to leave the place of his concealment and set out towards the town. Of all the sentiments that swayed and controlled him, none had such a perfect mastery over his nature as distrust. It was, in fact, the solitary lesson his life's experience had taught him. He fancied that he could trace every mistake he had ever made, every failure he had ever incurred, to some unlucky movement of credulity on his own part, and that "believing" was the one great error of his whole life. He had long been of opinion that high station and character had no greater privileges than the power they possessed of imposing a certain trustfulness in their pledges, and that the great "pull" a duke had over a "leg" was that his Grace would be believed in preference. But it also appeared to him that rogues were generally true to each other; now, if this last hope were to be taken away, what was there left in life to cling to? Spicer had said, "Davis wants him." What did that mean?—what could it mean? Simply that Grog found him, not an associate or colleague, but a convenient tool. What an intolerable insult, that he, the Honorable Annesley Beecher, whose great connections rambled through half Debrett, was to be accounted a mere outpost sentry in the corps of Grog Davis!

His anger increased as he went along. The wound to his self-esteem was in the very tenderest spot of his nature. Had any man ever sacrificed so much to be a sharp fellow as he had? Who had, like him, given up friends, station, career, and prospects? Who had voluntarily surrendered the society of his equals, and gone down to the very dregs of mankind, just to learn that one great secret? And was it to be all in vain? Was all his training and teaching to go for nothing? Was he, after descending to the ranks, to discover that he never could learn the manual exercise? How often, in the gloomiest hours of his disappointment, had he hugged the consolation to his heart, that Grog Davis knew and valued him! "Ask G. D. if I'm a flat," was the proud rejoinder he would hurl at any attempt to depreciate his shrewdness. What was to become of him, then, if the bank that held all his fortune were to fail? If Beecher deemed a sharp fellow the most enviable of all mortals, so he regarded a dupe as the meanest and most miserable, and the very thought of such a fate was almost maddening. "No, confound me! they sha'n't have it to say that they 'landed' A. B.; they shall never boast they nobbled me," cried he, warming with the indignation that worked within him. "I 'm off, and this time without beat of drum. Davis may do his worst. I'll lie by snug for a year or two. There must be many a safe spot in Germany or Italy, where a man may defy detection." And then he ran over in his mind all the successful devices he had seen adopted for disguising a man's appearance. Howard Vane had a wig and whiskers that left him unrecognized by his own mother; Crofton Campbell travelled with Inspector Field in search of himself, all by means of a nose. It was wonderful what science was accomplishing every day for the happiness and welfare of mankind!

The plan of escape was not without its difficulties, however. First of all, he had no money. Davis had given him merely enough to pay railroad fares and the charges incidental to the road, and he was living at the hotel on credit. This was a serious obstacle, but it was also one which had so often before occurred in Beecher's experience that he was not so much dismayed by it as many another might have been. "Money was always to be had somehow," was a golden rule of his philosophy, the somehow meaning that it resolved itself into a simple question of skill and address of the individual in want of it Aix was a considerable town, much frequented by strangers, and must, doubtless, possess all the civilizing attributes of other cities,—namely, Jews, money-lenders, and discounters. Then, the landlord of the inn; it was always customary to give him the preference in these cases. *He 'd* surely not refuse an advance of a few hundred francs to a man who came accompanied as he was. Klepper alone was good security for ten times more than he needed. Must it be confessed that he felt elevated in his own esteem when he had resolved upon this scheme? It savored of shrewdness,—that great touchstone of capacity which he revered so highly. "They shall see if I'm a flat, this time," chuckled he to himself as he went along; and he stepped out briskly in the excitement of self-approval. Then he went over in his mind all the angry commentaries that would be passed upon his flight,—the passionate fury of Grog, the amazement of Spicer, the almost incredulous surprise of the Count,—till at last he came to Lizzy; and then, for the first time in all his calculations, a sense of shame sent the color to his cheek, and he blushed till his face grew crimson. "Ay, by Jove! what will *she* think!" muttered he, in a voice of honest truthfulness. How he should appear to her—how he should stand in her estimation—after such an ignoble desertion, was a thought not to be encountered by self-praises of his cunning. What would her "pluck" say to his "cowardice," was a terrible query.

CHAPTER XXXVI
A COUNTRY VISIT

Let us now return to the Hermitage, and the quiet lives of those who dwelt there. Truly, to the traveller gazing down from some lofty point of the Glengariff road upon that lowly cottage deep buried in its beech wood, and only showing rare glimpses of its trellised walls, nothing could better convey the idea of estrangement from the world and its ambitions. From the little bay, where the long low waves swept in measured cadence on the sands, to the purple-clad mountains behind, the scene was eminently calm and peaceful. The spot was precisely one to suggest the wisdom of that choice which prefers tranquil obscurity to the struggle and conflict of the great world. What a happy existence would you say was theirs, who could drop down the stream of a life surrounded with objects of such beauty, free to indulge each rising fancy, and safe from all the collisions of mankind!—how would one be disposed to envy the unbroken peacefulness that no ambitions ruffled, no rude disappointments disturbed! And yet such speculations as these are ever faulty, and wherever the human heart throbs, there will be found its passions, its hopes and fears. Beneath that quiet roof there dwelt all the elements that make the battle of life; and high aspirings and ignoble wishes, and love and fear, and jealousy, and wealth-seeking lived there, as though the spot were amidst the thundering crash of crowded streets and the din of passing thousands!

Sybella Kellett had been domesticated there about two months, and between Lady Augusta and herself there had grown a sort of intimacy,— short, indeed, of friendship, but in which each recognized good qualities in the other.

Had Miss Kellett been older, less good-looking, less grace-ful in manner, or generally less attractive, it is just possible that—we say it with all doubt and deference—Lady Augusta might have been equally disposed to feel satisfied. She suspected "Mr. Dunn must have somewhat mistaken the object of her note," or "overlooked the requirements they sought for." Personal attractions were not amongst the essentials she had mentioned. "My Lord," too, was amazed at his recommending a "mere girl,"—she couldn't be more than "twenty,"—and, consequently, "totally deficient in the class of knowledge he desired."

Two months,—no very long period,—however, sufficed to show both father and daughter that they had been, to some extent, mistaken. Not only had she addressed herself to the task of an immense correspondence, but she had drawn out reports, arranged prospectuses, and entered into most complicated financial details with a degree of clearness that elicited marked compliment from the different bodies with whom this intercourse was maintained. The Glengariff Joint Stock Company, with its half-million capital, figured largely in the public journals. Landscapes of the place appeared in the various illustrated papers, and cleverly written magazine articles drew attention to a scheme that promised to make Ireland a favored portion of the empire. Her interest once excited, Sybella Kellett's zeal was untiring.

Already she anticipated the time when the population of that poor village—now barely subsisting in direst poverty—should become thriving and happy. The coast-fisheries—once a prolific source of wealth—were to be revived; fishing-craft and tackle and curing-houses were all to be provided; means of transporting the proceeds to the rich markets of England procured; she had also discovered traces of lead in the neighborhood; and Dunn was written to, to send down a competent person to investigate the matter. In fact, great as was her industry, it seemed only second to an intelligence that adapted itself to every fresh demand and every new exigency, without a moment's interruption. To the old Lord her resources appeared inexhaustible, and gradually he abandoned the lead and guidance he had formerly given to his plans, and submitted everything to her will and dictation. It did not, indeed, escape his shrewdness that her zeal was more warmly engaged by the philanthropy than by the profit of these projects. It was to the advancement of the people, the relief of their misery, the education of their children, the care of their sick, that she looked as the great reward of all that they proposed. "What a lesson we shall teach the rest of Ireland if we 'succeed'!" was the constant exclamation she uttered. "How we shall be sought after to explain this and reveal that! What a proud day for us will it be when Glengariff shall be visited as the model school of the empire!"

Thus fed and fostered by her hopes, her imagination knew no bounds, and the day seemed even too short for the duties it exacted. Even Lady Augusta could not avoid catching some of the enthusiasm that animated her, only restraining her expectations, however, by the cautious remark, "I wonder what Mr. Dunn will say. I am curious to know how he will pronounce upon it all."

The day at last came when this fact was to be ascertained, and the post brought the brief but interesting intelligence that Mr. Davenport Dunn would reach the Hermitage for dinner.

Lord Glengariff would have felt excessively offended could any one have supposed him anxious or uneasy on the score of Dunn's coming. That a great personage like himself should be compelled occasionally in life to descend to the agencies of such people was bad enough, but that he should have any misgivings about his co-operation or assistance, was really intolerable; and yet, we blush to confess, these were precisely the thoughts which troubled his Lordship throughout the whole of that long day.

"Not that Dunn has ever forgotten himself with *me*,—not that he has ever shown himself unmindful of our respective stations,—so much I must say," were the little scraps of consolation that he repeated over and over to himself, while grave doubts really oppressed him that we had fallen upon evil days, when men of that stamp usurped almost all the influence that swayed society. No easy matter was it, either, to resolve what precise manner to assume towards him. A cold and dignified bearing might possibly repel all confidence, and an easy familiarity be just as dangerous as surrendering the one great superiority his position conferred. It was true his Lordship had never yet experienced any difficulty on such a score,—of all men, he possessed a consummate sense of his own dignity, and suffered none to infringe it; but "this fellow Dunn had been spoiled." Great men— greater men than Lord Glengariff himself—had asked him to dinner. He had passed the thresholds of certain fine houses in Piccadilly, and well-powdered lackeys in Park Lane had called "Mr. Dunn's carriage." Now, the Irishman that has soared to the realm of whitebait with a minister, or even a Star and Garter luncheon with a Secretary of State, becomes, to the eyes of his home-bred countrymen, a very different person from the celebrity of mere Castle attentions and Phoenix Park civilities. Dunn was this, and more. He lounged into the Irish Office as into his own lodgings, and he walked into the most private chambers of Downing Street as if by right. Consulted or not, he had the reputation of holding the patronage of all Ireland in his hands; and assuredly they who attained promotion were not slow in testifying to what quarter they owed their gratitude. Some of that mysterious grandeur that clung to the old religions of the Greeks seems to hover round the acts of a great Government, till the Ministers, like Priests or Augurs, appear less equals and fellow-men than stewards and dispensers of immense bounties intrusted to their keeping. There was about Dunn's manner much to foster this illusion. He was a blending of mystery with the deepest humility, but with a very evident desire that you should neither believe one nor the other. It was the same conscious power looming through the affected modesty of his pretensions that offended Lord Glengariff, and made him irritable in all his intercourse with him.

Let us take a passing glance at Lady Augusta. And why, may we ask, has she taken such pains about her toilette to-day? Not that her dress is unusually rich or costly, but she has evidently made a study of the "becoming," and looks positively handsome. She remembered something of a fuchsia in her hair, long, long ago; and now, by mere caprice of course, she has interwoven one in those dark clusters, never glossier nor more silky. Her calm, cold features, too, have caught up a gentler expression, and her voice is softer and lower. Her maid can make nothing of it. Lady Augusta has been so gracious and so thoughtful, and asked about her poor old sick grandmother. Well, these sunlights are meant to show what the coldest landscapes may become when smiled on by brighter skies!

And Sybella. Pale and melancholy, and in mourning, she, too, has caught up a sense of pleasure at the coming visit, and a faint line of color tinges her white cheek. She is very glad that Mr. Dunn is expected. "She has to thank him for many kindnesses; his prompt replies to her letters; his good nature to poor Jack, for whom he has repeatedly written to the Horse Guards; not to speak of the words of encouragement and hope he has addressed to herself. Yes, he is, indeed, her friend; perhaps her only friend in the world."

And now they are met in the drawing-room, waiting with anxiety for some sounds that may denote the great man's coming. The three windows open to the ground; the rich sward, spangled here and there with carnations or rich-scented stocks, slopes down towards a little river, from the bridge over which a view is caught of the Glen-gariff road; and to this spot each as silently loitered, and as listlessly turned back again without a word.

"We are waiting for Mr. Dunn, Augusta, ain't we?" asked Lord Glengariff, as if the thought had just suddenly struck him for the first time.

"Yes," replied she, gravely; "he promised us his company to-day at dinner."

"Are you quite sure it was to-day he mentioned?" said he, with an affected indifference in his tone.

"Miss Kellett can inform us with certainty."

"He said Thursday, and in time for dinner," said Sybella, not a little puzzled by this by-play of assumed forgetfulness.

"The man who makes his own appointments ought to keep them. I am five minutes beyond the half-hour," said Lord Glengariff, as he looked at his watch.

"I suspect you are a little fast," observed Lady Augusta.

"There!—I think I heard the crack of a postilion's whip," cried Sybella, as she went outside the window to listen. Lady Augusta followed, and was soon at her side.

"You appear anxious for Mr. Dunn's coming. Is he a *very* intimate friend of yours, Miss Kellett?" said she, with a keen, quick glance of her dark eyes.

"He was the kind friend of my father, when he lived, and, since his death, he has shown himself not less mindful of me. There—I hear the horses plainly! Can't you hear them now, Lady Augusta?"

"And how was this kindness evidenced,—in your own case I mean?" said Lady Augusta, not heeding her question.

"By advice, by counsel, by the generous interference which procured for me my present station here, not to speak of the spirit of his letters to me."

"So then you correspond with him?" asked she, reddening suddenly.

"Yes," said she, turning her eyes fully on the other. And thus they stood for some seconds, when, with a slight, but very slight, motion of impatience, Lady Augusta said,—

"I was not aware—I mean, I don't remember your having mentioned this circumstance to me."

"I should have done so if I thought it could have had any interest for you," said Sybella, calmly. "Oh, there is the carriage coming up the drive; I knew I was not mistaken."

Lady Augusta made no reply, but returned hastily to the house. Bella paused for a few seconds, and followed her.

No sooner was Mr. Dunn's carriage seen approaching the little bridge over the stream than Lord Glengariff rang to order dinner.

"It will be a rebuke he well merits," said he, "to find the soup on the table as he drives up."

There was something more than a mere movement of irritation in this; his Lordship regarded it as a fine stroke of policy, by which Dunn's arrival, tinged with constraint and awkwardness, should place that gentleman at a disadvantage during the time he stayed, Lord Glengariff's favorite theory being that "these people were insufferable when at their ease."

Ah, my Lord, your memory was picturing the poor tutor of twenty years before, snubbed and scoffed at for his ungainly ways and ill-made garments,—the man heavy in gait and awkward in address, sulky when forgotten, and shy when spoken to,—this was the Davenport Dunn of your thoughts; there the very door *he* used to creep through in bashful confusion, yonder the side-table where he dined in a mockery of consideration. Little, indeed, were you prepared for him whose assured voice was already heard outside giving orders to his servant, and who now entered the drawing-room with all the ease of a man of the world.

"Ah, Dunn, most happy to see you here. No accident, I trust, occurred to detain you," said Lord Glengariff, meeting him with a well-assumed cordiality, and then, not waiting for his reply, went on: "My daughter, Lady Augusta, an old acquaintance—if you have not forgotten her. Miss Kellett you are acquainted with."

Mr. Dunn bowed twice, and deeply, before Lady Augusta, and then, passing across the room, shook hands warmly with Sybella.

"How did you find the roads, Dunn?" asked his Lordship, still fishing about for some stray word of apology; "rather heavy, I fear, at this season."

"Capital roads, my Lord, and excellent horses. We came along at a rate which would have astonished the lumbering posts of the Continent."

"Dinner, my Lord," said the butler, throwing wide the folding-doors.

"Will you give Lady Augusta your arm, Dunn?" said Lord Glengariff, as he offered his own to Miss Kellett.

"We have changed our dinner-room, Mr. Dunn," said Lady Augusta, as they walked along; thus by a mere word suggesting "bygones and long ago."

"And with advantage, I should say," replied he, easily, as he surveyed the spacious and lofty apartment into which they had just entered. "The old dinner-room was low-ceilinged and gloomy."

"Do you really remember it?" asked she, with a pleasant smile.

"An over-good memory has accompanied me through life, Lady Augusta," said he. And then, as he remarked the rising color of her cheek, quickly added, "It is rarely that the faculty treats me to such grateful recollections as the present."

Lord Glengariffs table was a good specimen of country-house living. All the materials were excellent, and the cookery reasonably good; his wine was exquisite,—the years and epochs connoisseurship loves to dwell upon; but Mr. Dunn ate sparingly and drank little. He had passed forty without gourmand tastes, and no man takes to epicurism after that. His Lordship beheld, not without secret dissatisfaction, his curdiest salmon declined, his wonderful "south-down" sent away scarcely tasted, and, horror of horrors! saw water mixed with his 1815 claret as if it were a "little Bordeaux wine" at a Swiss *table d'hôte*.

"Mr. Dunn has no appetite for our coarse country fare, Augusta," said Lord Glengariff; "you must take him over the cliffs, to-morrow, and let him feel the sharp Glengariff air. There's nothing but hunger for it."

"Pardon me, my Lord, if I say that I accept with gratitude the proposed remedy, though I don't acknowledge a just cause for it. I am always a poor eater."

"Tell him of Beverley, Augusta, tell him of Beverley," said my Lord.

"Oh, it was simply a case similar to your own," said she, hesitatingly, "and, in all probability, incurred in the same way. The Duke of Beverley, a very hard-worked man, as you know, always at Downing Street at ten, and never leaving it till night, came here two years ago, to pass a few weeks with us, and although hale and stout, to look at, could eat nothing,—that is, he cared for nothing. It was in vain we put in requisition all our little culinary devices to tempt him; he sat down with us, and, like yourself, would fain persuade us that he dined, but he really touched nothing; and, in utter despair, I determined to try what a course of open air and exercise would do."

"She means eight hours a day hard walking, Dunn," chimed in Lord Glengariff; "a good grouse-shooter's pace, too, and cross country."

"Well, confess that my remedy succeeded," said she, triumphantly.

"That it did. The Duke went back to town fifteen years younger. No one knew him; the Queen did not know him. And to this day he says, 'Whenever I'm hipped or out of sorts, I know what a resource I have in the Glengariff heather.'"

It is possible that Davenport Dunn listened with more of interest to this little incident because the hero of it was a Duke and a Cabinet Minister.

Assuredly the minor ills of life, the petty stomachic miseries, and such like, are borne with a more becoming patience when we know that they are shared by peers and great folk. Not by *you*, valued reader, nor even by *me*,—we have no such weaknesses,—but by the Davenport Dunns of this world, one of whom we are now treating. It was pleasant, too, to feel that he not only had a ducal ailment, but that he was to be cured like his Grace! And so he listened eagerly, as Lady Augusta went on to tell of the various localities, strange and unpronounceable, that they used to visit, and how his Grace loved to row across such an arm of the lake, and what delight he took in the ascent of such a mountain. "But you shall judge for yourself, Mr. Dunn," said she, smiling, "and I now engage you for to-morrow, after breakfast." And with that she rose, and, accompanied by Sybella, passed into the drawing-room. Dunn was about to follow, when Lord Glengariff called out, "I'm of the old school, Dunn, and must have half an hour with my bottle before I join the ladies."

We do not stop to explain—perhaps we should not succeed to our wishes if we tried—why it was that Dunn was more genial, better satisfied, and more at his ease than when the dinner began; but so it was that as he filled the one glass of claret be meant to indulge in, he felt that he had been exaggerating to his own mind the disagreeables of this visit, and that everybody was kinder, pleasanter, and more natural than he had expected.

"Jesting apart, Dunn," said his Lordship, "Augusta is right. What you require is rest,—perfect repose; never to read or write a letter for three weeks, not look at a newspaper, nor receive a telegraphic despatch. Let us try if Glengariff cannot set you up. The fact is, we can't spare you."

"Your opinion is too flattering by half, my Lord; but really, any one—I mean any one whose views are honest, and whose intentions are upright— can complete the work I have begun. There is no secret,—no mystery in it."

"Come, come, this is over-modest. We all know that your head alone could carry on the vast number of these great schemes which are now in operation amongst us. Could you really tell the exact number of companies of which you are Director?"

"I 'm afraid to say that I could," said Dunn, smiling.

"Of course you could n't. It is marvellous, downright marvellous, how you get through it. You rise early, of course?"

"Yes, my Lord, at five, summer and winter; light my own fire, and sit down to the desk till eight; by that time I have finished my correspondence on business topics. I then take a cup of tea and a little dry toast. This is my preparation for questions of politics, which usually occupy me till eleven. From that hour till three I receive deputations,—heads of companies, and such like. I then take my ride, weather permitting, and usually contrive to call at the Lodge, till nigh dinner-hour. If alone, my meal is a frugal one, and soon despatched; and then begins the real work of the day. A short nap of twenty minutes refreshes me, and I address myself with energy to my task. In these quiet hours, undisturbed and uninterrupted,—for I admit none, not one, at such seasons,—my mind is clear and unclouded, and I can work, without a sense of fatigue, till past midnight; it has even happened that morning has broke upon me without my being aware of it."

"No health, no constitution, could stand that, Dunn," said Lord Glengariff, with a voice artfully modulated to imply deep interest.

"Men are mere relays on the road of life; when one sinks, wearied or worn out, a fresh one comes forth ready to take his place in the traces."

"That may be—that may be, in the mass of cases; but there are exceptional men, Dunn,—men who—men, in fact, whose faculties have such an adaptiveness to the age we live in—do you perceive my meaning?—men of the situation, as the French say." Here his Lordship began to feel that he was getting upon very ticklish ground, and by no means sure how he was to get safely back again, when, with a violent plunge, he said, "That fellow Washington was one of those men, Louis Napoleon is another, and you—I don't hesitate to say it—you are also an instance of what I mean."

Dunn's pale face flushed up as he muttered some broken words of depreciating meaning.

"The circumstances, I am aware, are different. You have not to revolutionize a country, but you have undertaken just as hard a task: to remodel its social state,—to construct out of the ruined materials of a bankrupt people the elements of national wealth and greatness. Let no man tell me, sir, that this is not a bolder effort than the other. Horse, foot, and dragoons, as poor Grattan used to say, won't aid you here. To your own clear head and your own keen intellect must you trust."

"My dear Lord," broke in Dunn, in a voice not devoid of emotion, "you exaggerate both my labor and my capacity. I saw that the holders of Irish property were not the owners, and I determined that they should be so. I saw that the people were improvident, less from choice than necessity, and I gave them banks. I saw land unproductive for want of capital, and I established the principle of loans for drainage and other improvements. I perceived that our soil and our climate favor certain species of cultivation, and as certainly deny some others. I popularized this knowledge."

"And you call this nothing! Why, sir, where's the statesman can point to such a list of legislative acts? Peel himself has left no such legacy behind him."

"Ah, my Lord, this is too flattering,—too flattering by half." And Dunn sipped his wine and looked down. "By the way, my Lord," said he, after a pause, "how has my recommendation in the person of Miss Kellett succeeded?"

"A very remarkable young woman,—a singularly gifted person indeed," said the old Lord, pompously. "Some of her ideas are tinctured, it is true, with that canting philanthropy we are just now infected with,—that tendency to discover all the virtue in rags and all the vice in purple; but, with this abatement to her utility, I must say she possesses a very high order of mind. She comes of a good family, doesn't she?"

"None better. The Kelletts of Kellett's Court were equal to any gentry in this county."

"And left totally destitute?"

"A mere wreck of the property remains, and even that is so cumbered with claims and so involved in law that I scarcely dare to say that they have an acre they can call their own."

"Poor girl! A hard case,—a very hard case. We like her much, Dunn. My daughter finds her very companionable; her services, in a business point of view, are inestimable. All those reports you have seen are hers, all those drawings made by her hand."

"I am aware, my Lord, how much zeal and intelligence she has displayed," said Dunn, who had no desire to let the conversation glide into the great Glengariff scheme, "and I am also aware how gratefully she feels the kindness she has met with under this roof."

"That is as it should be, Dunn, and I am rejoiced to hear it. It is in no spirit of self-praise I say it, but in simple justice,—we do—my daughter and myself, both of us—do endeavor to make her feel that her position is less that of dependant than—than—companion."

"I should have expected nothing less from your Lordship nor Lady Augusta," said Dunn, gravely.

"Yes, yes; you knew Augusta formerly; you can appreciate her high-minded and generous character, though I think she was a mere child when you saw her first."

"Very young indeed, my Lord," said Dunn, coloring faintly.

"She is exactly, however, what she then promised to be,—an Arden, a genuine Arden, sir; no deceit, no double; frank, outspoken; too much so, perhaps, for our age of mock courtesy, but a noble-hearted girl, and one fit to adorn any station."

There was an honest, earnest sincerity in the old Lord's manner that made Dunn listen with respect to the sentiments be uttered, though in his heart the epithet "girl," as applied to Lady Augusta, seemed somewhat ill chosen.

"I see you take no wine, so that, if you have no objection, we'll join the ladies."

"Your Lordship was good enough to tell me that I was to make myself perfectly at home here; may I begin at once to avail myself of your kindness, and say that for this evening I beg to retire early? I have a number of letters to read, and some to answer."

"Really, Lady Augusta will feel quite offended if you slight her tea-table."

"Nay, my Lord. It is only for this evening, and I am sure you will make my excuses becomingly."

"It shall be as you please," said the old Lord, with a rather stiff courtesy.

"Thank you, my Lord; thank you. I assure you it is very rarely the sacrifice to duty costs me so keenly. Goodnight."

CHAPTER XXXVII
"A MAN IN REQUEST"

The bountifully spread breakfast-table of the following morning was not destined to be graced by Mr. Dunn's presence. A clerk had arrived early in the morning with a mass of correspondence from Dublin, and a Government messenger, armed with an ominous-looking red box, came post-haste about an hour later, while a request for a cup of tea in his own room explained that Mr. Dunn was not to make his appearance in public.

"This savors of downright slavery," said Lady Augusta, whose morning toilette was admirably devised.

"To me it savors of downright humbug," said Lord Glengariff, pettishly. "No one shall tell me that a man has not time to eat his meals like a gentleman. A Secretary of State does n't give himself such airs. Why, I protest, here comes another courier! what can this fellow be?"

"A messenger from the Home Office has just arrived for Mr. Dunn," said Miss Kellett, entering the room.

"Our little cottage is become like a house in Whitehall Gardens," said Lord Glengariff, angrily. "I have no doubt we ought to feel excessively flattered by the notoriety the newspapers are certain to accord us."

"Mr. Dunn is more to be pitied than any of us," said Lady Augusta, compassionately.

"I suspect he'd not agree with you," said his Lordship, bitterly. "I rather opine that Mr. Dunn has another and a very different estimate of his present position."

"Such a life is certainly not enviable. Perhaps I'm wrong, though," said she, quickly; "Miss Kellett does not seem of *my* mind."

Sybella blushed slightly, and in some embarrassment said, "Certain minds find their best happiness in great labor; Mr. Dunn's may be one of these."

"Pulteney found time for a cast with the hounds, and Charles Fox had leisure for his rubber of whist. It is these modern fellows have introduced the notion that 'the House' is like a 'mill at Manchester.' There goes one with his despatches," cried he, as a mounted messenger rode off from the door. "I 'd wager a trifle that if they never came to hand the world would just jog on its course as pleasantly, and no one the worse for the mishap."

"With Mr. Dunn's compliments, my Lord," said a servant, placing several open letters on the table; "he thought your Lordship would like to see the latest news from the Crimea."

While Lord Glengariff took out his spectacles, his face grew crimson, and he seemed barely able to restrain a burst of passionate indignation. As the servant closed the door, he could no longer contain himself, but broke out: "Just fancy their sending off these despatches to this fellow Dunn. Here am I, an Irish peer, of as good blood and ancient family as any in my country, and I might as well expect to hear Buckingham Palace was fitted up for my town residence when next I went to London, as look for an attention of this sort. If I had n't it here under my own eyes, and saw the address, 'Davenport Dunn, Esq.,' 'on her Majesty's service,' I 'd say flatly it was impossible."

"May I read some of them?" asked Lady Augusta, wishing by any means to arrest this torrent of angry attack.

"Yes, read away," cried he, laying down his spectacles. "Miss Kellett, too, may indulge her curiosity, if she has any, about the war."

"I have a dearer interest at stake there," said Sybella, blushing.

"I see little here we have not already read in the 'Times,'" said Lady Augusta, perusing the paper before her. "The old story of rifle-pits, sorties against working parties, the severity of the duty, and the badness of the commissariat."

"This is interesting," broke in Sybella. "It is an extract from a private letter of some one high in command. It says: 'The discontent of our allies increases every day; and as every post from France only repeats how unpopular the war is in that country, I foresee that nothing short of some great *fait d'armes*, in which the French shall have all the glory, will induce the Imperial Government to continue the struggle. The satisfaction felt in France at the attacks of the English journals on our own army, its generalship, and its organization, are already wearing out, and they look now for some higher stimulant to the national vanity.'"

"Who writes this?" cried Lord Glengariff, eagerly.

"The name is not given," said she. "The despatch goes on merely to say, 'Your Lordship would do well to give these words the consideration they seem to deserve.' But here again, 'the coolness of the Marshal increases, and our intercourse is neither frank nor confidential.'"

"All this sounds badly," said Lord Glengariff. "Our only progress would seem to be in ill-will with our ally. I suppose the end of it will be, we shall be left to continue the struggle alone."

"Would that it were so!" burst in Sybella. "A great orator said t' other day in the House, that coalitions were fatal; Englishmen never liked them. He only spoke of those alliances where parties agree to merge their differences and unite for some common object; but far more perilous are the coalitions where nations combine, the very contest that they wage being a field to evoke ancient rivalries and smouldering jealousies. I 'd rather see our little army alone, with its face to the foe and its back to the sea, than I 'd read of our entrance into Sebastopol side by side with the legions of France."

The passionate enthusiasm of the moment had carried her away, and she grew pale and heart-sick at her unwonted boldness as she finished.

"I hope Mr. Dunn may be able to benefit by your opinions on strategy," said Lady Augusta, as she rose from the table.

"What was it Lady Augusta said?" cried Lord Glengariff, as she left the room.

"I scarcely heard her aright, my Lord," said Sybella, whose face was now crimson.

It was the first moment in her life in which dependence had exposed her to insult, and she could not collect her faculties, or know what to do.

"These things," said Lord Glengariff, pushing the despatches contemptuously away, "add nothing to our knowledge. That writer in the 'Times' gives us everything we want to know, and gives it better too. Send them back to Dunn, and ascertain, if you can, when we are likely to see him. I want him to come down to the bay; he ought to see the harbor and the coast. Manage this, Miss Kellett,—not from me, of course, but in your own way,—and let me know."

Lord Glengariff now left the room, and Sybella was once more deep in the despatches.

Dry and guarded as they were,—formal, with all the stamp of official accuracy,—they yet told of the greatest and grandest struggle of our age. It was a true war of Titans, with the whole world for spectators. The splendid heroism of our army seemed even eclipsed by the unbroken endurance of daily hardship,—that stern and uncomplaining courage that faced death in cold blood, and marched to the fatal trenches with the steadfast tramp of a forlorn hope.

"No conscript soldiers ever bore themselves thus," cried she, in ecstasy. "These are the traits of personal gallantry, not the disciplined bravery that comes of the serried file and the roll of the drum."

With all her anxieties for his fate, she gloried to think "dear Jack" was there,—that he was bearing his share of their hardships, and reaping his share of their glory. And oh! if she could but read mention of his name; if she could hear of him quoted for some act of gallantry, or, better still, some trait of humanity and kindness,—that he had rescued a wounded comrade, or succored some poor maimed and forlorn enemy!

How hard was it for her on that morning, full of these themes, to address herself to the daily routine of her work! The grand panorama of war continued to unroll itself before her eyes, and the splendid spectacle of the contending armies revealed itself like a picture before her. The wondrous achievements she had read of reminded her of those old histories which had been the delight of her childhood, and she gloried to think that the English race was the same in daring and chivalry as it had shown itself centuries back!

She tried hard to persuade herself that the peaceful triumphs of art, the great discoveries of science, were finer and grander developments of human nature; but with all her ingenuity they seemed inglorious and poor beside the splendid displays of heroism.

"And now to my task," said she, with a sigh, as she folded up the map of the Crimea, on which she was tracing the events of the war.

Her work of that morning was the completion of a little "Memoir" of Glengariff and its vicinity, written in that easy and popular style which finds acceptance in our periodicals, and meant to draw attention to the great scheme for whose accomplishment a company was to be formed. Lord Glengariff wished this sketch should be completed while Dunn was still there, so that it might be shown him, and his opinion be obtained upon it.

Never had her task seemed so difficult, never so uncongenial; and though she labored hard to summon up all her former interest in the great enterprise, her thoughts would stray away, in spite of her, to the indented shores of the Crimea, and the wild and swelling plains around Sebastopol. Determined to see if change of place might not effect some change of thought, she carried her papers to a little summer-house on the river-side, and once more addressed herself resolutely to her work. With an energy that rarely failed her, she soon overcame the little distraction, and wrote away rapidly and with ease. She at last reached that stage in her essay where, having enumerated all the advantages of the locality, she desired to show how nothing was wanting to complete its celebrity and recognition but the touch of some of those great financial magicians whose great privilege it is to develop the wealth and augment the resources of their fellow-men. She dwelt earnestly and, indeed, eloquently on the beauty of the scenery. She knew it in every varying aspect of its coloring, and she lingered over a description of which the reality had so often captivated her. Still, even here, the fostering hand of taste might yet contribute much. The stone pine and the ilex would blend favorably with the lighter foliage of the ash and the hazel, and many a fine point of view was still all but inaccessible for want of a footpath. How beautifully, too, would the tasteful cottage of some true lover of the picturesque peep from amidst the evergreen oaks that grew down to the very shore. While she wrote, a shadow fell over her paper. She looked up, and saw Mr. Dunn. He had strolled by accident to the spot, and entered unperceived by her.

"What a charming place you have chosen for your study, Miss Kellett!" said he, seating himself at the table. "Not but I believe," continued he, "that when once deeply engaged in a pursuit, one takes little account of surrounding objects. Pastorals have been composed in garrets, and our greatest romancer wrote some of his most thrilling scenes amid the noise and commonplace interruptions of a Court of Sessions."

"Such labors as mine," said she, smiling, "neither require nor deserve the benefit of a chosen spot."

"You are engaged upon Glengariff," said he; "am I at liberty to look?" And he took the paper from the table as he spoke. At first he glanced half carelessly at the lines; but as he read on he became more attentive, and at last, turning to the opening pages, he read with marked earnestness and care.

"You have done this very well,—admirably well," said he, as he laid it down; "but shall I be forgiven if I make an ungracious speech?"

"Say on," said she, smiling good-naturedly.

"Well, then," said he, drawing a long breath, "you are pleading an impossible cause. They who suggested it were moved by the success of those great enterprises which every day develops around us, and which, by the magic word 'Company,' assume vitality and consistence; they speculated on immense profits just as they could compute a problem in arithmetic. It demanded so much skill and no more. *You*—I have no need that you should tell me so—were actuated by very different motives. You wanted to benefit a poor and neglected peasantry, to disseminate amongst them the blessings of comfort and civilization; *you* were eager for the philanthropy of the project, *they* for its gain."

"But why, as a mere speculation, should it be a failure?" broke she in.

"There are too many reasons for such a result," said he, with a melancholy smile. "Suffice it if I give you only one. We Irish are not in favor just now. While we were troublesome and rebellious, there was an interest attached to us,—we were dangerous; and even in the sarcasms of the English press there lurked a secret terror of some great convulsion here which should shake the entire empire. We are prosperous now, and no longer picturesque. Our better fortune has robbed us of the two claims we used to have on English sympathy; we are neither droll nor ragged, and so they can neither laugh at our humor nor sneer at our wretchedness. Will not these things show you that we are not likely to be fashionable? I say this to you; to Lord Glengariff I will speak another language. I will tell him that his scheme will not attract speculators. I myself cannot advocate it. I never link my name with defeats. He will be, of course, indignant, and we shall part on bad terms. He is not the first I have refused to make rich."

There was a tone of haughty assumption in the way he spoke these words that astonished Sybella, who gazed at him without speaking.

"Are you happy here?" asked he, abruptly.

"Yes,—that is, I have been so up to this—"

"In short, until I had robbed you of an illusion," said he, interrupting her. "Ah, how many a pang do these 'awakenings' cost us in life!" muttered he, half to himself. "Every one has his ambitions of one sort or other, and fancies his goal the true one; but, his faith once disturbed, how hard it is to address himself earnestly to another creed!"

"If it be duty," broke she in, "and if we have the consciousness of an honest breast and a right intention—"

"That is to say, if we gain a verdict in the court where we ourselves sit as judge," said he, with a suddenness that surprised her. "I, for instance, have my own sense of what is right and just; am I quite sure it is *yours?* I see certain anomalies in our social condition, great hardships, heavy wrongs; if I address myself to correct them, am I so certain that others will concur with me? The battle of life, like every other conflict, is one in which to sustain the true cause one must do many a cruel thing. It is only at last, when success has crowned all your efforts, that the world condescends to say you have done well."

"You, of all men, can afford to await this judgment patiently."

"Why do you say that of *me*?" asked he, eagerly.

"Because, so long as I can remember, I have seen your name associated with objects of charity and benevolence; and not these alone, but with every great enterprise that might stimulate the efforts and develop the resources of the country."

"Some might say that personal objects alone influenced me," said he, in a low voice.

"How poor and narrow-minded would be such a judgment!" replied she, warmly. "There is an earnestness in high purpose no self-seeking could ever counterfeit."

"That is true,—quite true," said he; "but are you so certain that the world makes the distinction? Does not the vulgar estimate confound the philanthropist with the speculator? I say this with sorrow." said he, painfully, "for I myself am the victim of this very injustice." He paused for a few seconds, and then rising, he said, "Let us stroll along the river-side; we have both worked enough for the day." She arose at once, and followed him. "It is ever an ungracious theme,—one's self," said he, as they walked along; "but, somehow, I am compelled to talk to you, and, if you will allow me, confidentially." He did not wait for a reply, but went on: "There was, in the time of the French Regency, a man named Law, who, by dint of deep study and much labor, arrived at the discovery of a great financial scheme; so vast, so comprehensive, and so complete was it, that not only was it able to rescue the condition of the State from bankruptcy, but it disseminated through the trading-classes of the nation the sound principles of credit on which alone commerce can be based. Now, this man—a man of unquestionable genius and, if benefits to one's species gave a just title to the name, a philanthropist—lived to see the great discovery he had made prostituted to the basest arts of scheming speculators. From the Prince, who was his patron, to the humblest agent of the Bourse, he met nothing but duplicity, falsehood, and treachery, and he ended in being driven in shame and ignominy from the land he had succeeded in rescuing from impending rain! You will say that the people and the age explain much of this base ingratitude; but, believe me, nations and eras are wonderfully alike. The good and evil of this world go on repeating themselves in cycles with a marvellous regularity. The fate which befell Law may overtake any who will endeavor to imitate him; there is but one condition which can avert this catastrophe, and that is success. Law had too long deferred to provide for his own security. Too much occupied with his grand problem, he had made himself neither rich nor great, so that when the hour of adversity came no barriers of wealth or power stood between him and his enemies. Had he foreseen this catastrophe,—had he anticipated it,—he might have so dovetailed his own interests with those of the State that attack upon one involved the fate of the other. But Law did nothing of the kind; he made friends of Princes, and with the fortune that attaches to such friendships, he fell!" For some minutes he walked along at her side without speaking, and then resumed: "With all these facts before me, I, too, see that Law's fate may be my own!"

"But have you—" When she had gone thus far, Sybella stopped, and blushed deeply, unable to continue.

"Yes," said he, answering what might have been her words,—"yes, it was my ambition to have been to Ireland what Law was to France,—not what calumny and injustice have pictured him, remember, but the great reformer, the great financier, the great philanthropist,—to make this faction-torn land a great and united nation. To develop the resources of the richest country in Europe was no mean ambition, and he who even aspired to it was worthy of a better recompense than attack and insult."

"I have seen none of these," broke she in. "Indeed, so long as I remember, I can call to mind only eulogies of your zeal, praises of your intelligence, and the grandeur of your designs."

"There are such, however," said he, gloomily; "they are the first low murmurings, too, of a storm that will come in full force hereafter! Let it come," muttered he, below his breath. "If I am to fall, it shall be like Samson, and the temple shall fall with me."

Sybella did not catch his words, but the look of his features as he spoke them made her almost shudder with terror.

"Let us turn back," said she; "it is growing late."

Without speaking, Dunn turned his steps towards the cottage, and walked along in deep thought.

"Mr. Hankes has come, sir," said Dunn's servant, as he reached the door. And without even a word, Dunn hastened to his own room.

CHAPTER XXXVIII
MR. DAVENPORT DUNN IN
MORE MOODS THAN ONE

Although Mr. Hankes performs no very conspicuous part in our story, he makes his appearance at the Hermitage with a degree of pomp and circumstance which demand mention. With our reader's kind leave, therefore, we mean to devote a very brief chapter to that gentleman and his visit.

As in great theatres there is a class of persons to whose peculiar skill and ability are confided all the details of "spectacle," all those grand effects of panoramic splendor which in a measure make the action of the drama subordinate to the charms of what, more properly, ought to be mere accessories; so modern speculation has called to its aid its own special machinists and decorators,—a gifted order of men, capable of surrounding the dryest and least promising of enterprises with all the pictorial attractions and attractive graces of the "ballet"

If it be a question of a harbor or dock company, the prospectus is headed with a colored print, wherein tall three-deckers mingle with close-reefed cutters, their gay buntings fluttering in the breeze as the light waves dance around the bows; from the sea beneath to the clouds above, all is motion and activity,—meet emblems of the busy shore where commerce lives and thrives. If it be a building speculation, the architecture is but the background of a brilliant "mall," where splendid equipages and caracoling riders figure, with gay parasols and sleek poodles intermixed.

One "buys in" to these stocks with feelings far above "five percent." A sense of the happiness diffused amongst thousands of our fellow-creatures—the "blessings of civilization," as we like to call the extension of cotton prints—cheer and animate us; and while laying out our money advantageously, we are crediting our hearts with a large balance on the score of philanthropy. To foster this commendable tendency, to feed the tastes of those who love, so to say, to "shoot at Fortune with both barrels," an order of men arose, cunning in all the devices of advertisement, learned in the skill of capitals, and adroit in illustrations.

Of these was Mr. Hankes. Originally brought up at the feet of George Robins, he was imported into Ireland by Mr. Davenport Dunn as his chief man at business,—the Grand Vizier of Joint Stock Companies and all industrial speculations.

If Dr. Pangloss was a good man for knowing what wickedness was, Mr. Hankes might equally pretend to skill in all enterprises, since he had experienced, for a number of years, every species of failure and defeat The description of his residences would fill half a column of a newspaper. They ranged from Brompton to Boulogne, and took in everything from Wilton Crescent to St John's Wood. He had done a little of everything, too, from "Chief Commissioner to the Isthmus"—we never heard of what isthmus—to Parliamentary Agent for the friends of Jewish emancipation. With a quickness that rarely deceived him, Dunn saw his capabilities. He regarded him as fighting fortune so bravely with all the odds against him, that he ventured to calculate what such a man might be, if favorably placed in the world. The fellow who could bring down his bird with a battered old flint musket might reasonably enough distinguish himself if armed with an Enfield rifle. The venture was not, however, entirely successful; for though Hankes proved himself a very clever fellow, he was only really great under difficulties. It was with the crash of falling fortunes around him—amidst debt, bankruptcy, executions, writs, and arrests—Hankes rose above his fellows, and displayed all the varied resources of his fertile genius. The Spartan vigor of his mind assorted but badly with prosperity, and Hankes waxed fat and indolent, affected gorgeous waistcoats and chains, and imperceptibly sank down to the level of those decorative arts we have just alluded to.

The change was curious: it was as though Gerard or Gordon Cumming should have given up lion-hunting and taken to teach piping bullfinches!

Every venture of Davenport Dunn was prosperous. All his argosies were borne on favoring winds, and Hankes saw his great defensive armor hung up to rust and to rot. Driven in some measure, therefore, to cut out his path in life, he invented that grand and gorgeous school of enterprise whose rashness and splendor crush into insignificance all the puny attempts of commonplace speculators. He only talked millions; thousands he ignored. He would accept of no names on the direction of his schemes save the very highest in rank. If he crossed the Channel, his haste required a special steamer. If he went by rail, a special train awaited him. The ordinary world, moving along at its tortoise pace, was shocked at the meteor course that every now and then shot across the hemisphere, and felt humiliated in their own hearts by the comparison.

Four smoking posters, harnessed to the neatest and lightest of travelling-carriages, had just deposited Mr. Hankes at the Hermitage; and he now sat in Mr. Dunn's dressing-room, arranging papers and assorting documents in preparation for his arrival.

It was easy to perceive that as Dunn entered the room he was very far from feeling pleased at his lieutenant's presence there.

"What was there so very pressing, Mr. Hankes," said he, "that could not have awaited my return to town?"

"A stormy meeting of the Lough Allen Tin Company yesterday, sir, — a very stormy meeting indeed. Shares down to twenty-seven and an eighth, — unfavorable report on the ore, and a rumor — mere rumor, of course — that the last dividend was paid out of capital."

"Who says this?" asked Dunn, angrily.

"The 'True Blue,' sir, hinted as much in the evening edition, and the suggestion was at once caught up by the Tory Press."

"Macken — isn't that the man's name — edits the 'True Blue'?"

"Yes, sir; Michael Macken."

"What answer shall I give him, then?" asked Hankes.

"Tell him — explain to him that the exigencies of party — No, that won't do. Send down Harte to conduct his election, let him be returned for the borough, and tell Joe Harte to take care to provide a case that will unseat him on a petition; before the petition comes on, we shall have the sale completed. The Colonel shall be taught that our tactics are somewhat sharper than his own."

Hankes smiled approvingly at this stratagem of his chief, and really for the moment felt proud of serving such a leader. Once more, however, did he turn to his dreary note-book and its inexorable bead-roll of difficulties; but Dunn no longer heard him, for he was deep in his private correspondence, tearing open and reading letter after letter with impatient haste. "What of the Crimea — what did you say, there?" cried Dunn, stopping suddenly, and catching at the sound of that one word.

"That report of the 'Morning Post' would require a prompt contradiction."

"What report?" asked Dunn, quickly.

"Here's the paragraph." And the other read from a newspaper before him: "'Our readers, we feel assured, will learn with satisfaction that the Government is at this moment in negotiation for the services of Mr.

Davenport Dunn in the Crimea. To any one who has followed the sad story of our Commissariat blunders and shortcomings, the employment of this— the first administrative mind of our day—will be matter for just gratification. We have only to turn our eyes to the sister country, and see what success has attended his great exertions there, to anticipate what will follow his labors in the still more rugged field of the Crimea.'

"This is from the 'Examiner': 'We are sorry to hear, and upon the authority that assumes to be indisputable, that a grave difficulty has suspended, for the time at least, the negotiation between the Government and Mr. Daren-port Dunn; the insistence on the part of that gentleman of such a recognition for his services as no Administration could dare to promise being the obstacle.'

"'Punch' has also his say: 'Mr. Davenport Dunn's scheme is now before the cabinet It resolves itself into this: The Anglo-French alliance to be conducted on the principles of a Limited Liability Company. For preference shares, address Count Morny in Paris, or Dowb at Balaklava.'"

"So much for official secrecy and discretion. This morning brings me the offer from the Minister of this appointment; and here is the whole press of England speculating, criticising, and ridiculing it, forty-eight hours before the proposal is made me! What says the great leading journal?" added he, opening a broad sheet before him. "Very brief, and very vague," muttered he. "'No one knows better than the accomplished individual alluded to, how little the highest honors in the power of the Crown to bestow could add to the efficiency of that zeal, or the purpose of that guidance he has so strenuously and successfully devoted to the advancement of his country.' Psha!" cried he, angrily, as he threw down the paper, and walked to the window.

Hankes proceeded to read aloud one of those glowing panegyrics certain popular journals loved to indulge in, on the superior virtue, capacity, and attainments of the middle classes. "Of these," said the writer, "Mr. Dunn is a good specimen. Sprung from what may be called the very humblest rank—"

"Who writes that? What paper is it?"

"The 'Daily Tidings.'"

"You affect to know all these fellows of the press. It is your pride to have been their associate and boon companion. I charge you, then, no matter for the means or the cost, get that man discharged; follow him up too; have an eye upon him wherever he goes, and wherever he obtains employment. He shall learn that a hungry stomach is a sorry recompense for the pleasure of pointing a paragraph. Let me see that you make a note of this, Mr. Hankes, and that you execute it also."

It was something so new for Hankes to see Dunn manifest any the slightest emotion on the score of the press, whether its comments took the shape of praise or blame, that he actually stared at him with a sort of incredulous astonishment.

"If I were born a Frenchman, an Italian, or even a German," said Dunn, with a savage energy of voice, "should I be taunted in the midst of my labors that my origin was plebeian? Would the society in which I move be reminded that they accept me on sufferance? Would the cheer that greeted my success be mingled with the cry, 'Remember whence you came'? I tell you, sir," and here he spoke with the thickened utterance of intense passion, — "I tell you, sir, that with all the boasted liberty of our institutions, we cultivate a social slavery in these islands, to which the life of a negro is freedom in comparison!"

A sharp tap at the door interrupted him, and he cried, "Come in." It was a servant to say dinner was on the table, and his Lordship was waiting.

"Please to say I am indisposed, — a severe headache. I hope his Lordship will excuse my not appearing to-day," said he, with evident confusion; and then, when the servant withdrew, added: "You may go down to the inn. I suppose there is one in the village. I shall want horses to-morrow, and relays ready on the road to Killarney. Give the orders, and if anything else occurs to my recollection, I 'll send you word in the evening."

Whether it was that Mr. Hankes had been speculating on the possible chances of dining with "my Lord" himself, or that the prospect of the inn at Glengariff was little to his taste, but he assuredly gathered up his papers in a mood that indicated no peculiar satisfaction, and withdrew without a word.

A second message now came to inquire what Mr. Dunn would like to take for his dinner, and conveying Lord Glengariffs regrets for his indisposition.

"A little soup—some fish, if there be any—nothing else," said Dunn, while he opened his writing-desk and prepared for work. Not noticing the interruption of the servant as he laid the table, he wrote away rapidly; at last he arose, and, having eaten a few mouthfuls, reseated himself at his desk. His letter was to the Minister, in answer to the offer of that morning's post. There was a degree of dexterity in the way that he conveyed his refusal, accompanying it by certain suggestive hints, vague and shadowy of course, of what the services of such a man as himself might possibly accomplish, so as to indicate how great was the loss to the State by not being fortunate enough to secure such high acquirements. The whole wound up with a half-ambiguous regret that, while the Ministry should accept newspaper dictation for their appointments, they could not also perceive that popular will should be consulted in the rewards extended to those who deserted their private and personal objects to devote their energies to the cause of the empire.

"Whenever such a Government shall arise," wrote he, "the Ministry will find few refusals to the offers of employment, and men will alike consult their patriotism and their self-esteem in taking office under the Crown; nor will there be found, in the record of replies to a Ministerial proffer, one such letter as now bears the signature of your Lordship's

"Very devoted and very obedient servant,

"Davenport Dunn."

This history does not profess to say how Mr. Dunn's apology was received by his noble host. Perhaps, however, we are not unwarranted in supposing that Lord Glengariffs temper was sorely and severely tested; one thing is certain, the dinner passed off with scarcely a word uttered at the table, and a perfect stillness prevailed throughout the cottage.

After some hours of hard labor, Dunn opened his window to enjoy the fresh air of the night, tempered slightly as it was with a gentle sea-breeze. If our western moonlights have not the silver lustre of Greece, of which old Homer himself sings, they have, in compensation, a mellow radiance of wondrous softness and beauty. Objects are less sharply defined and picked out, it is true, but the picture gains in warmth of color, and those blended effects where light and shadow alternate. The influences of Nature—the calm, still moonlight; the measured march of the long, sweeping waves upon the strand; those brilliant stars, "so still above, so restless in the water"— have a marvellous power over the hard-worked men of the world. They are amidst the few appeals to the heart which they can neither spurn nor reject.

Half hidden by the trees, but still visible from where he sat, Dunn could mark the little window of his humble bedroom twenty years ago! Ay! there was the little den to which he crept at night, his heart full of many a sorrow; the "proud man's contumely" had eaten deep into him, and each day brought some new grievance, some new trial to be endured, while the sight of her he loved—the young and haughty girl—goaded him almost to madness.

One after another came all the little incidents of that long-forgotten time crowding to his memory; and now he bethought him how noiselessly he used to glide down those stairs, and, stealing into the wood, meet her in her morning's walk, and how, as with uncovered head, he bowed to her, she would bestow upon him one of her own half-saucy smiles,—more mockery than kindness. He called to mind the day, too, he had climbed the mountain to gather a bouquet of the purple heath,—she said she liked it,—and how, after a great effort of courage, he ventured to offer it to her. She took it half laughingly from his hand, and then, turning to her pet goat beside her, gave it him to eat. He could have shot himself that morning, and yet there he was now, to smile over the incident!

As he sat, the sounds of music floated up from the open window of the room beneath. It was the piano, the same he used to hear long ago, when the Poet himself of the Melodies came down to pass a few days at the Hermitage. A low, soft voice was now singing, and as he bent down he could hear the words of poor Griffin's beautiful song:—

"*A place in thy memory, dearest,*
Is all that I claim;
To pause and look back as thou nearest
The sound of my name."

What a strange thrill did the words send through him! They came, as it were, to fill up the whole story of the past, embodying the unspoken prayer his love-sick heart once was filled with. For that "smile and kind word when we meet," had he once pined and longed, and where was the spirit now that had once so yearned for love? A cold shudder passed over him, and he felt ill. He sat for a long while so deep in reflection that he did not notice the music had ceased, and now all was still and silent around. From the balcony outside his window a little winding stair led down to the lawn beneath; and down this he now took his way, resolving to stroll for half an hour or so before bedtime.

Walking carelessly along, he at last found himself on the banks of the river, close to the spot where he had met Miss Kellett that same morning. How glad he would have been to find her there again! That long morning's ramble had filled him with many a hopeful thought—he knew, with the instinct that in such men as himself rarely deceives—that he had inspired her with a sort of interest in him, and it warmed his self-esteem to think that he could be valued for something besides "success." The flutter of a white dress crossing the little rustic bridge caught his eye at this moment, and he hurried along the path. He soon gained sufficiently upon the retiring figure to see it was a lady. She was strolling quietly along, stopping at times to catch the effects of the moonlight on the landscape.

Dunn walked so as to make his footsteps heard approaching, and she turned suddenly and exclaimed, "Oh, Mr. Dunn, who would have thought to see you here?"

"A question I might almost have the hardihood to retort, Lady Augusta," said he, completely taken by surprise.

"As for me," said she, carelessly, "it is my usual walk every evening. I stroll down to the shore round by that rocky headland, and rarely return before midnight; but *you*," added she, throwing a livelier interest into her tone, "they said you were poorly, and so overwhelmed with business it was hopeless to expect to see you."

"Work follows such men as myself like a destiny," said he, sighing; "and as the gambler goes on to wager stake after stake on fortune, so do we hazard leisure, taste, happiness, all, to gain—I know not what in the end."

"Your simile points to the losing gamester," said she, quickly; "but he who has won, and won largely, may surely quit the table when he pleases."

"It is true," said he, after a pause,—"it is true, I have had luck with me. The very trees under whose branches we are walking, could they but speak, might bear witness to a time when I strolled here as poor and as hopeless as the meanest outcast that walks the high-road. I had not one living soul to say, 'Be of good cheer, your time will come yet.' My case had even more than the ordinary obstacles to success; for fate had placed me where every day, every hour of my life, should show me the disparity between myself and those high-born great to whose station I aspired. If you only knew, Lady Augusta," added he, in a tone tremulous with emotion, "what store I laid on any passing kindness,—the simplest word, the merest look,—how even a gesture or a glance lighted hope within my heart, or made it cold and dreary within me, you 'd wonder that a creature such as this could nerve itself to the stern work of life."

"I was but a child at the time you speak of," said she, looking down bashfully; "but I remember you perfectly."

"Indeed!" said he, with an accent that implied pleasure.

"So well," continued she, "that there is not a spot in the wood where we used to take our lesson-books in summer, but lives still associated in my mind with those hours, so happy they were!"

"I always feared that I had left very different memories behind me here," said he, in a low voice.

"You were unjust, then," said she, in a tone still lower,—"unjust to yourself and to us."

They walked on without speaking, a strange mysterious consciousness that each was in the other's thoughts standing in place of converse between them. At length, stopping suddenly in front of a little rocky cavern, over which aquatic plants were drooped, she said, "Do you remember calling that 'Calypso's grotto'? It bears no other name still."

"I remember more," said he; and then stopped in some confusion.

"Some girlish folly of mine, perhaps," broke she in hurriedly; "but once for all, let me ask forgiveness for many a thoughtless word, many a childish wrong. You, who know all tempers and moods of men as few know them, can well make allowances for natures spoiled as ours were,—pampered and flattered by those about us, living in a little world of our own here. And yet, do not think me silly when I own that I would it were all back again. The childish wrong. You, who know all tempers and moods of men as few know them, can well make allowances for natures spoiled as ours were— pampered and nattered by those about us, living in a little world of our own here. And yet, do not think me silly when I own that I would it were all back again. The childhood and the lessons, ay, the dreary Telemachus, that gave me many a headache, and the tiresome hours at the piano, and the rest of it." She glanced a covert glance at Dunn, and saw that his features were a shade darker and gloomier than before. "Mind," said she, quickly, "I don't ask you to join in this wish. You have lived to achieve great successes—to be courted, and sought after, and caressed. I don't expect you to care to live over again hours which perhaps you look back to with a sort of horror."

"I dare not well tell you how I look back to them," said he, in a half-irresolute manner.

Had there been any to mark it, he would have seen that her cheek flushed and her dark eyes grew darker as he spoke these words. She was far too skilful a tactician to disturb, even by a syllable, the thoughts she knew his words indicated; and again they sauntered along in silence, till they found themselves standing on the shore of the sea.

"How is it that the sea, like the sky, seems ever to inspire the wish that says, 'What lies beyond that?'" said Dunn, dreamily.

"It comes of that longing, perhaps, for some imaginary existence out of the life of daily care and struggle—"

"I believe so," said he, interrupting. "One is so apt to forget that another horizon is sure to rise to view,—another bourne to be passed!" Then suddenly, as if with a rapid change of thought, he said, "What a charming spot this is to pass one's days in,—so calm, so peaceful, so undisturbed!"

"I love it!" said she, in a low, murmuring voice, as though speaking to herself.

"And I could love it too," said he, ardently, "if fortune would but leave me to a life of repose and quiet."

"It is so strange to hear men like yourself—men who in a measure make their own fate,—always accuse Destiny. Who is there, let me ask," said she, with a boldness the stronger that she saw an influence followed her words,—"who is there who could with more of graceful pride retire from the busy cares of life than he who has worked so long, so successfully, for his fellow-men? Who is there who, having achieved fortune, friends, station—Why do you shake your head?" cried she, suddenly.

"You estimate my position too flatteringly, Lady Augusta," said he, slowly, and like one laboring with some painful reflection. "Of fortune—if that mean wealth—I have more than I need. Friends—what the world calls such—I suppose I may safely say I possess my share of. But as to station, by which I would imply the rank which stamps a certain grade in society, and carries with it a prestige—"

"It is your own whenever you care to demand it," broke she in. "It is not when the soldier mounts the breach that his country showers its honours on him—it is when, victory achieved, he comes back great and triumphant. You have but to declare that your labours are completed, your campaign finished, to meet any, the proudest, recognition your services could claim. You know my father," said she, suddenly changing her voice to a tone at once confidential and intimate—"you know how instinctively, as it were, he surrounds himself with all the prejudices of his order. Well, even he, as late as last night, said to me, 'Dunn ought to be one of us, Augusta. We want men of his stamp. The lawyers overbear us just now. It is men of wider sympathies lets technical less narrowed, that we need. He ought to be one of us.' Knowing what a great admission that was for one like him, I ventured to ask how this was to be accomplished. 'Ministers are often the last to ratify the judgment the public' he pronounced."

"Well, and what said you to that," asked Dunn, eagerly.

"Let him only open his mind to Lady Augusta," said she. "If he but have the will I promise to show him the way."

Dunn uttered no reply, but with bent-down head walked along, deep in thought.

"May I ask you to lend me your arm, Mr. Dunn?" said Lady Augusta, in her gentlest of voices; and Dunn's heart beat with a strange, proud significance as he gave it.

They spoke but little as they returned to the cottage.

CHAPTER XXXIX
"A LETTER TO JACK"

Long after the other inhabitants of the Hermitage were fast locked in sleep, Sybella Kellett sat at her writing-desk. It was the time—the only time—she called her own, and she was devoting it to a letter to her brother. Mr. Dunn had told her on that morning that an opportunity offered to send anything she might have for him, and she had arranged a little packet—some few things, mostly worked by her own hands—for the poor soldier in the Crimea.

As one by one she placed the humble articles in the box, her tears fell upon them—tears half pleasure and half sorrow—for she thought how "poor dear Jack" would feel as each new object came before him, reminding him of some thoughtful care, some anticipation of this or that casualty; and when at last all seemed packed and nothing forgotten, she arose and crossed the room towards a little shelf, from which she took a small volume, and, kissing it twice fervently, laid it in the box. This done, she knelt down, and with her head between her hands, close pressed and hidden, prayed long and fervently. If her features wore a look of sadness as she arose, it was of sadness not without hope; indeed, her face was like one of those fair Madonnas which Raphael has left us,—faces where trustfulness is more eminently the characteristic than any other quality.

Her long letter was nearly completed, and she sat down to add the last lines to it. It had grown into a sort of Journal of her daily life, its cares and occupations, and she was half shocked at the length to which it extended. "I am not," wrote she, "so unreasonable as to ask you to write as I have done, but it would be an unspeakable pleasure if you would let me give the public some short extracts from the letters you send me, they are so unlike those our papers teem with. The tone of complaint is, I know, the popular one. Some clever correspondents have struck the key-note with success, and the public only listen with eagerness where the tale is of sufferings which might have been spared, and hardships that need not have been borne. But you, dear Jack, have taken another view of events, and one which, I own, pleases me infinitely more. You say truly, besides, that these narratives, interesting as no doubt they are to all at home here, exercise a baneful influence on the military spirit of our army. Men grow to care too much for newspaper distinction, too little for that noble *esprit de camaraderie* which is the finest enthusiasm of the service. I could not help feeling as if I heard your voice as I read, 'I wish they would n't go on telling us about muddy roads, raw coffee, wet canvas, and short rations; we don't talk of these things so much amongst ourselves; we came out here to thrash the Russians, and none of us ever dreamed it was to be done without rough usage.' What you add about the evil effects of the soldier appealing to the civilian public for any redress of his grievances, real or imaginary, is perfectly correct. It is a great mistake.

"You must forgive my having shown your last letter to Mr. Davenport Dunn, who cordially joins me in desiring that you will let me send it to the papers. He remarks truly, that the Irish temperament of making the ludicrous repay the disagreeable is wanting in all this controversy, and that the public mind would experience a great relief if one writer would come forth to show that the bivouac fire is not wanting in pleasant stories, nor even the wet night in the trenches without its burst of light-hearted gayety.

"Mr. Dunn fully approves of your determination not to 'purchase.' It would be too hard if you could not obtain your promotion from the ranks after such services as yours; so he says, and so, I suppose, I ought to concur with him; but as this seven hundred pounds lies sleeping at the banker's while your hard life goes on, I own I half doubt if he be right. I say this to show you, once for all, that I will accept nothing of it I am provided for amply, and I meet with a kindness and consideration for which I was quite unprepared. Of course, I endeavor to make my services requite this treatment, and do my best to merit the good-will shown me.

"I often wonder, dear Jack, when we are to meet, and where. Two more isolated creatures there can scarcely be on earth than ourselves, and we ought, at least, to cling to each other. Not but I feel that, in thus struggling alone with fortune, we are storing up knowledge of ourselves, and experiences of life that will serve us hereafter. When I read in your letters how by many a little trait of character you can endear yourself to your poor comrades, softening the hardship of their lot by charms and graces acquired in another sphere from theirs, I feel doubly strong in going forth amongst the poor families of our neighborhood, and doubly hopeful that even I may carry my share of comfort to some poorer and more neglected.

"The last object I have placed in your box, dearest Jack,—it will be the first to reach your hands,—is my prayer-book. You have often held it with me, long, long ago! Oh, if I dared to wish, it would be for that time again, when we were children, with one heart between us. Let us pray, my dear brother, that we may live to meet and be happy as we then were; but if that is not to be,—if one be destined to remain alone a wanderer here,—pray, my dearest brother, that the lot fall not to me, who am weak-hearted and dependent.

"The day is already beginning to break, and I must close this. My heartfelt prayer and blessings go with it over the seas. Again and again, God bless you."

Why was it that still she could not seal that letter, but sat gazing sadly on it, while at times she turned to the open pages of poor Jack's last epistle to her?

CHAPTER XL
SCHEMES AND PROJECTS

The post-horses ordered for Mr. Dunn's carriage arrived, duly, at break of day; but from some change of purpose, of whose motive this veracious history can offer no explanation, that gentleman did not take his departure, but merely despatched a messenger to desire Mr. Hankes would come over to the Hermitage.

"I shall remain here to-day, Hankes," said he, carelessly, "and not impossibly to-morrow also. There's something in the air here suits me, and I have not felt quite well latterly."

Mr. Hankes bowed; but not even his long-practised reserve could conceal the surprise he felt at this allusion to health or well-being. Positive illness he could understand,—a fever or a broken leg were intelligible ills; but the slighter casualties of passing indispositions were weaknesses that he could not imagine a business mind could descend to, no more than he could fancy a man's being turned from pursuing his course because some one had accidentally jostled him in the streets.

Dunn was too acute a reader of men's thoughts not to perceive the impression his words had produced; but with the indifference he ever bestowed upon inferiors, he went on:—

"Forward my letters here till you hear from me; there's nothing so very pressing at this moment that cannot wait my return to town. Stay—I was to have had a dinner on Saturday; you'll have to put them off. Clowes will show you the list; and let some of the evening papers mention my being unavoidably detained in the south,—say nothing about indisposition."

"Of course not, sir," said Hankes, quite shocked at such an indiscretion being deemed possible.

"And why, 'of course,' Mr. Hankes?" said Dunn, slowly. "I never knew it was amongst the prerogatives of active minds to be exempt from ailment."

"A bad thing to speak about, sir,—a very bad thing, indeed," said Hankes, solemnly. "You constantly hear people remark, 'He was never the same man since that last attack.'"

"Psha!" said Dunn, contemptuously.

"I assure you, sir, I speak the sense of the community. The old adage says, 'Two removes are as bad as a fire,' and in the same spirit I would say, 'Two gouty seizures are equal to a retirement'."

"Absurdity!" said Dunn, angrily. "I never have acknowledged—I never will acknowledge—any such accountability to the world."

"They bring us 'to book' whether we will or not," said Hankes, sturdily.

Dunn started at the words, and turned away to hide his face; and well was it he did so, for it was pale as ashes, even to the lips, which were actually livid.

"You may expect me by Sunday morning, Hankes,"—he spoke without turning round,—"and let me have the balance-sheet of the Ossory Bank to look over. We must make no more advances to the gentry down there; we must restrict our discounts."

"Impossible, sir, impossible! There must be no discontent—for the present, at least," said Hankes; and his voice sunk to a whisper.

Dunn wheeled round till he stood full before him, and thus they remained for several seconds, each staring steadfastly at the other.

"You don't mean to say, Hankes—" He stopped.

"I do, sir," said the other, slowly, "and I say it advisedly."

"Then there must be some gross mismanagement, sir," said Dunn, haughtily. "This must be looked to! Except that loan of forty-seven thousand pounds to Lord Lacking-ton, secured by mortgage on the estate it went to purchase, with what has this Bank supplied us?"

"Remember, sir," whispered Hankes, cautiously glancing around the room as he spoke, "the loan to the Viscount was advanced by ourselves at six per cent, and the estate was bought in under your own name; so that, in fact, it is to us the Bank have to look as their security."

"And am I not sufficient for such an amount, Mr. Hankes?" said he, sneeringly.

"I trust you are, sir, and for ten times the sum. Time is everything in these affairs. The ship that would float over the bar at high water would stick fast at half-flood."

"The 'Time' I am anxious for is a very different one," said Dunn, reflectively. "It is the time when I shall no longer be harassed with these anxieties. Life is not worth the name when it excludes the thought of all enjoyment."

"Business is business, sir," said Mr. Hankes, with all the solemnity with which such men deliver platitudes as wisdom.

"Call it slavery, and you 'll be nearer the mark," broke in Dunn. "For what or for whom, let me ask you, do I undergo all this laborious toil? For a world that at the first check or stumble will overwhelm me with slanders. Let me but afford them a pretext, and they will debit me with every disaster their own recklessness has caused, and forget to credit me with all the blessings my wearisome life has conferred upon them."

"The way of the world, sir," sighed Hankes, with the same stereotyped philosophy.

"I know well," continued Dunn, not heeding the other's commonplace, "that there are men who would utilize the station which I have acquired; they'd soon convert into sterling capital the unprofitable gains that I am content with. They 'd be cabinet ministers, peers, ambassadors, colonial governors. It's only men like myself work without wages."

"'The laborer is worthy of his hire,' says the old proverb." Mr. Hankes was not aware of the authority, but quoted what he believed a popular saying.

"Others there are," continued Dunn, still deep in his own thoughts, "that would consult their own ease, and, throwing off this drudgery, devote what remained to them of life to the calm enjoyments of a home."

Mr. Hankes was disposed to add, "Home, sweet home;" but he coughed down the impulse, and was silent.

Dunn walked the room with his arms crossed on his breast and his head bent down, deep in his own reflections, while his lips moved, as if speaking to himself. Meanwhile Mr. Hankes busied himself gathering together his papers, preparatory to departure.

"They 've taken that fellow Redlines. I suppose you 've heard it?" said he, still sorting and arranging the letters.

"No," said Dunn, stopping suddenly in his walk; "where was he apprehended?"

"In Liverpool. He was to have sailed in the 'Persia,' and had his place taken as a German watchmaker going to Boston."

"What was it he did? I forget," said Dunn, carelessly.

"He did, as one may say, a little of everything; issued false scrip on the Great Coast Railway, sold and pocketed the price of some thirty thousand pounds' worth of their plant, mortgaged their securities, and cooked their annual accounts so cleverly that for four years nobody had the slightest suspicion of any mischief."

"What was it attracted the first attention to these frauds, Hankes?" said Dunn, apparently curious to hear an interesting story.

"The merest accident in the world. He had sent a few lines to the Duke of Wycombe to inquire the character and capacity of a French cook. Pollard, the Duke's man of business, happened to be in the room when the note came, and his Grace begged he would answer it for him. Pollard, as you are aware, is Chairman of the Coast Line; and when he saw the name 'Lionel Redlines,' he was off in a jiffy to the Board room with the news."

"One would have thought a little foresight might have saved him from such a stupid mistake as this," said Dunn, gravely. "A mode of living so disproportioned to his well-known means must inevitably have elicited remark."

"At any other moment, so it would," said Hankes; "but we live in a gambling age, and no one can say where, when, the remedy be curative or poisonous." Then, with a quick start round, he said, "Hankes, do you remember that terrific accident which occurred a few years ago in France, — at Angers, I think the place was called? A regiment in marching order had to cross a suspension-bridge, and coming on with the measured tramp of the march, the united force was too much for the strength of the structure; the iron beams gave way, and all were precipitated into the stream below. This is an apt illustration of what we call credit. It will bear, and with success, considerable pressure if it be irregular, dropping, and incidental. Let the forces, however, be at once consentaneous and united, — let the men keep step, — and down comes the bridge! Ah, Hankes, am I not right?"

"I believe you are, sir," said Hankes, who was not quite certain that he comprehended the illustration.

"His Lordship is waiting breakfast, sir," said a smartly dressed footman at the door.

"I will be down in a moment. I believe, Hankes, we have not forgotten anything? The Cloyne and Carrick Company had better be wound up; and that waste-land project—let me have the papers to look over. You think we ought to discount those bills of Barrington's?"

"I'm sure of it, sir. The people at the Royal Bank would take them to-morrow."

"The credit of the Bank must be upheld, Hankes. The libellous articles of those newspapers are doing us great damage, timid shareholders assail us with letters, and some have actually demanded back their deposits. I have it, Hankes!" cried he, as a sudden thought struck him,—"I have it! Take a special train at once for town, and fetch me the balance-sheet and the list of all convertible securities. You can be back here—let us see—by to-morrow at noon, or, at latest, to-morrow evening. By that time I shall have matured my plan."

"I should like to hear some hint of what you intend," said Hankes.

"You shall know all to-morrow," said he, as he nodded a good-bye, and descended to the breakfast-room. He turned short, however, at the foot of the stairs, and returned to his chamber, where Hankes was still packing up his papers. "On second thoughts, Hankes, I believe I had better tell you now," said he. "Sit down."

And they both eat down at the table, end never moved from it for an hour. Twice—even thrice—there cane messages from below, requesting Mr. Dunn's presence at the breakfast-table, but a hurried "Yes, immediately," was his reply, and he came not.

At last they rose? Hankes the first, saying, as he looked at his watch, "I shall just be in time. It is a great idea, a very great idea indeed, and does you infinite credit."

"It ought to have success, Hankes," said he, calmly.

"Ought, Sir! It will succeed. It is as fine a piece of tactics as I ever heard of. Trust me to carry it out, that's all."

"Remember, Hankes, time is everything. Goodby!"

CHAPTER XLI
"A COUNTRY WALK"

What a charming day was that at the Hermitage,—every one pleased, happy, and good-humored! With a frankness that gave universal satisfaction, Mr. Dunn declared he could not tear himself away. Engagements the most pressing, business appointments of the deepest moment, awaited him on every side, but, "No matter what it cost," said he, "I will have my holiday!" Few flatteries are more successful than those little appeals to the charms and fascinations of a quiet home circle; and when some hard-worked man of the world, some eminent leader at the Bar, or some much-sought physician condescends to tell us that the world of clients must wait while he lingers in our society, the assurance never fails to be pleasing. It is, indeed, complimentary to feel that we are, in all the easy indolence of leisure, enjoying the hours of one whose minutes are valued as guineas; our own value insensibly rises at the thought, and we associate ourselves in our estimate of the great man. When Mr. Davenport Dunn had made this graceful declaration, he added another, not less gratifying, that he was completely at his Lordship's and Lady Augusta's orders, as regarded the great project on which they desired to have his opinion.

"The best way is to come down and see the spot yourself, Dunn. We 'll walk over there together, and Augusta will acquaint you with our notions as we go along."

"I ought to mention," said Dunn, "that yesterday, by the merest chance, I had the opportunity of looking over a little sketch of your project."

"Oh, Miss Kellett's!" broke in Lady Augusta, coloring slightly. "It is very clever, very prettily written, but scarcely practical, scarcely business-like enough for a prosaic person like myself. A question of this kind is a great financial problem, not a philanthropic experiment. Don't you agree with me?"

"Perfectly," said he, bowing.

"And its merits are to be tested by figures, and not by Utopian dreams of felicity. Don't you think so?"

He bowed again, and smiled approvingly.

"I am aware," said she, in a sort of half confusion, "what rashness it would be in me to say this to any one less largely minded than yourself; how I should expose myself to the censure of being narrow-hearted and worldly, and so forth; but I am not afraid of such judgments from you."

"Nor have you need to dread them," said he, in a voice a little above a whisper.

"Young ladies, like Miss Kellett, are often possessed by the ambition—a very laudable sentiment, no doubt—of distinguishing themselves by these opinions. It is, as it were, a 'trick of the time' we live in, and, with those who do not move in 'society,' has its success too."

The peculiar intonation of that one word "society" gave the whole point and direction of this speech. There was in it that which seemed to say, "*This* is the real tribunal! Here is the one true court where claims are recognized and shams nonsuited." Nor was it lost upon Mr. Davenport Dunn. More than once—ay, many a time before—had he been struck by the reference to that Star Chamber of the well-bred world. He had even heard a noble lord on the Treasury benches sneer down a sturdy champion of Manchesterism, by suggesting that in a certain circle, where the honorable gentleman never came, very different opinions prevailed from those announced by him.

While Dunn was yet pondering over this mystic word, Lord Glengariff came to say that, as Miss Kellett required his presence to look over some papers in the library, they might stroll slowly along till he overtook them.

As they sauntered along under the heavy shade of the great beech-trees, the sun streaking at intervals the velvety sward beneath their feet, while the odor of the fresh hay was wafted by on a faint light breeze, Dunn was unconsciously brought back in memory to the "long, long ago," when he walked the self-same spot in a gloom only short of despair. Who could have predicted the day when he should stroll there, with *her* at his side, *her* arm within his own, *her* voice appealing in tones of confidence and friendship? His great ambitions had grown with his successes, and as he rose higher and higher, his aims continued to mount upwards; but here was a sentiment that dated from the time of his obscurity, here a day-dream that had filled his imagination when from imagination alone could be derived the luxury of triumph, and now it was realized, and now—

Who is to say what strange wild conflict went on within that heart where worldliness felt its sway for once disputed? Did there yet linger there, in the midst of high ambitions, some trait of boyish love, or was it that he felt this hour to be the crowning triumph of his long life of toil?

"If I were not half ashamed to disturb your revery," said Lady Augusta, smiling, "I'd tell you to look at that view yonder. See where the coast stretches along there, broken by cliff and headland, with those rocky islands breaking the calm sea-line, and say if you saw anything finer in your travels abroad?"

"Was I in a revery? have I been dreaming?" cried he, suddenly, not regarding the scene, but turning his eyes fully upon herself. "And yet you 'd forgive me were I to confess to you of what it was I was thinking."

"Then tell it directly, for I own your silence piqued me, and I stopped speaking when I perceived I was not listened to."

"Perhaps I am too confident when I say you would forgive me?"

"You have it in your power to learn, at all events," said she, laughingly.

"But not to recall my words if they should have been uttered rashly," said he, slowly.

"Shall I tell you a great fault you have,—perhaps your greatest?" asked she, quickly.

"Do, I entreat of you."

"And you pledge yourself to take my candor well, and bear me no malice afterwards?"

"It is a coldness,—a reserve almost amounting to distrust, which seems actually to dominate in your temper. Be frank with me, now, and say fairly, was not this long alley reylying all the thoughts of long ago, and were you not summing up the fifty-one little grudges you had against that poor silly child who used to torment and fret you, and, instead of honestly owning all this, you fell back upon that stern dignity of manner I have just complained of? Besides," added she, as though hurried away by some strong impulse, "if it would quiet your spirit to know you were avenged, you may feel satisfied."

"As how?" asked he, eagerly, and not comprehending to what she pointed.

"Simply thus," resumed she. "As I continued to mark and read of your great career in life, the marvellous successes which met you in each new enterprise, how with advancing fortune you ever showed yourself equal to the demand made upon your genius, I thought with shame and humiliation over even my childish follies, how often I must have grieved—have hurt you! Over and over have I said, 'Does he ever remember? Can he forgive me?' And yet there was a sense of exquisite pleasure in the midst of all my sorrow as I thought over all these childish vanities, and said to myself, 'This man, whom all are now flattering and fawning upon, was the same I used to irritate with my caprices, and worry with my whims!'"

"I never dreamed that you remembered me," said he, in a voice tremulous with delight.

"Your career made a romance for me," said she, eagerly. "I could repeat many of those vigorous speeches you made,—those spirited addresses. One, in particular, I remember well; it was when refusing the offer of the Athlone burgesses to represent their town; you alluded so happily to the cares which occupied you,—less striking than legislative duties, but not less important,—or, as you phrased it, yours was like the part of those 'who sound the depth and buoy the course that thundering three-deckers are to follow.' Do you remember the passage? And again, that proud humility with which, alluding to the wants of the poor, you said, 'I, who have carried my musket in the ranks of the people!' Let me tell you, sir," added she, playfully, "these are very haughty avowals, after all, and savor just as much of personal pride as the insolent declarations of many a pampered courtier!"

Dunn's face grew crimson, and his chest swelled with an emotion of intense delight.

"Shall I own to you," continued she, still running on with what seemed an irrepressible freedom, "that it appears scarcely real to me to be here talking to you about yourself, and your grand enterprises, and your immense speculations. You have been so long to my mind the great genius of wondrous achievements, that I cannot yet comprehend the condescension of your strolling along here as if this world could spare you."

If Dunn did not speak, it was that his heart was too full for words; but he pressed the round arm that leaned upon him closer to his side, and felt a thrill of happiness through him.

"By the way," said she, after a pause, "I have a favor to ask of you: papa would be charmed to have a cast of Marochetti's bust of you, and yet does not like to ask for it. May I venture—"

"Too great an honor to me," muttered Dunn. "Would you—I mean, would he—accept—"

"Yes, I will, and with gratitude; not but I think the likeness hard and harsh. It is, very probably, what you are to that marvellous world of politicians and financiers you live amongst, but not such as your friends recognize you,—what you are to-day, for instance."

"And what may that be," asked he, playfully.

"I was going to say an impudence, and I only caught myself in time."

"Do, then, let me hear it," said he, eagerly, "for I am quite ready to cap it with another."

"Yours be the first, then," said she, laughing. "Is it not customary to put the amendment before the original motion?"

Both Mr. Dunn and his fair companion were destined to be rescued from the impending indiscretion by the arrival of Lord Glengariff, who, mounted on his pony, suddenly appeared beside them.

"Well, Dunn," cried he, as he came up, "has she made a convert of you? Are you going to advocate the great project here?"

Dunn looked sideways towards Lady Augusta, who, seeing his difficulty, at once said, "Indeed, papa, we never spoke of the scheme. I doubt if either of us as much as remembered there was such a thing."

"Well, I'm charmed to find that your society could prove so fascinating, Augusta," said Lord Glengariff, with some slight irritation of manner, "but I must ask of Mr. Dunn to bear with me while I descend to the very commonplace topic which has such interest for me. The very spot we stand on is admirably suited to take a panoramic view of our little bay, the village, and the background. Carry your eyes along towards the rocky promontory on which the stone pines are standing; we begin there."

Now, most worthy reader, although the noble Lord pledged himself to be brief, and really meant to keep his word, and although he fancied himself to be graphic,—truth is truth,—he was lamentably prolix and confused beyond all endurance. As for Dunn, he listened with an exemplary patience; perhaps his thoughts were rambling away elsewhere,—perhaps he was compensated for the weariness by the occasional glances which met him from eyes now downcast, now bent softly upon him. Meanwhile the old Lord floundered on, amidst crescents and bathing-lodges, yacht stations and fisheries, aiding his memory occasionally with little notes, which, as he contrived to mistake, only served to make the description less intelligible. At length he had got so far as to conjure up a busy, thriving, well-to-do watering-place, sought after by the fashionable world that once had loved Brighton or Dieppe. He had peopled the shore with loungers, and the hotels with visitors; equipages were seen flocking in, and a hissing steamer in the harbor was already sounding the note of departure for Liverpool or Holyhead, when Dunn, suddenly rousing himself from what might have been a revery, said, "And the money, my Lord,—the means to do all this?"

"The money—the means—we look to *you*, Dunn, to answer that question. Our scheme is a great shareholding company of five thousand—no, fifty—nay, I'm wrong. What is it, Augusta?"

"The exact amount scarcely signifies much, my Lord. The excellence of the project once proved, money can always be had. What I desired to know was, if you already possessed the confidence of some great capitalist favorable to the undertaking, or is it simply its intrinsic merits which recommend it?"

"Its own merits, of course," broke in Lord Glengariff, hastily. "Are they not sufficient?"

"I am not in a position to affirm or deny that opinion," said Dunn, gravely. "Let me see," added he, to himself, while he drew a pencil from his pocket, and on the back of a letter proceeded to scratch certain figures. He continued to calculate thus for some minutes, when at last he said: "If you like to try it, my Lord, with an advance of say twenty thousand pounds, there will be no great difficulty in raising the money. Once afloat, you will be in a position to enlist shareholders easily enough." He spoke with all the cool indifference of one discussing the weather.

"I must say, Dunn," cried Lord Glengariff, with warmth, "this is a very noble—a very generous offer. I conclude my personal security—"

"We can talk over all this at another time, my Lord," broke in Dunn, smiling. "Lady Augusta will leave us if we go into questions of bonds and parchments. My first care will be to send you down Mr. Steadman, a very competent person, who will make the necessary surveys; his report, too, will be important in the share market."

"So that the scheme enlists your co-operation, Dunn,—so that we have *you* with us," cried the old Lord, rubbing his hands, "I have no fears as to success."

"May we reckon upon so much?" whispered Lady Augusta, while a long, soft, meaning glance stole from her eyes.

Dunn bent his head in assent, while his face grew crimson.

"I say, Augusta," whispered Lord Glengariff, "we have made a capital morning's work of it—eh?"

"I hope so, too," said she. And her eyes sparkled with an expression of triumph.

"There is only one condition I would bespeak, my Lord. It is this: the money market at this precise moment is unsettled, over-speculation has already created a sort of panic, so that you will kindly give me a little time—very little will do—to arrange the advance. Three weeks ago we were actually glutted with money, and now there are signs of what is called tightness in discounts."

"Consult your own convenience in every respect," said the old Lord, courteously.

"Nothing would surprise me less than a financial crisis over here," said Dunn, solemnly. "Our people have been rash in their investments latterly, and there is always a retribution upon inordinate gain!"

Whether it was the topic itself warmed him, or the gentle pressure of Lady Augusta's arm as in encouragement of his sentiments, but Dunn continued to "improve the occasion" as they strolled along homeward, inveighing in very choice terms against speculative gambling, and deploring the injury done to honest, patient industry by those examples of wealth acquired without toil and accumulated without thrift. He really treated the question well and wisely, and when he passed from the mere financial consideration to the higher one of "morals" and the influence exerted upon national character, he actually grew eloquent.

Let us acknowledge that the noble Lord did not participate in all his daughter's admiration of this high-sounding harangue, nor was he without a sort of lurking suspicion that he was listening to a lecture upon his, own greed and covetousness; he, however, contrived to throw in at intervals certain little words of concurrence, and in this way occupied they arrived at the Hermitage.

It is not always that the day which dawns happily continues bright and unclouded to its close; yet this was such a one. The dinner passed off most agreeably, the evening in the drawing-room was delightful. Lady Augusta sang prettily enough to please even a more critical ear than Mr. Dunn's, and she had a tact, often wanting in better performers, to select the class of music likely to prove agreeable to her hearers. There is a very considerable number of people who like pictures for the story and music for the sentiment, and for these high art is less required than something which shall appeal to their peculiar taste. But, while we are confessing, let us own that if Mr. Dunn liked "the melodies," it assuredly added to their charm to hear them sung by a peer's daughter; and as he lay back in his well-cushioned chair, and drank in the sweet sounds, it seemed to him that he was passing a very charming evening.

Like many other vulgar men in similar circumstances, he wondered at the ease and unconstraint he felt in such choice company! He could not help contrasting the tranquil beatitude of his sensations with what he had fancied must be the coldness and reserve of such society. He was, as he muttered to himself, as much at home as in his own house; and truly, as with one hand in his breast, while with the fingers of the other he beat time,—and all falsely,—he looked the very ideal of his order.

"Confound the fellow!" muttered the old peer, as he glanced at him over his newspaper, "he is insufferably at his ease amongst us!"

And Sybella Kellett, where was she all this time—or have we forgotten her? Poor Sybella! she had been scarcely noticed at dinner, scarcely spoken to in the drawing-room, and she had slipped unperceived away to her own room.

They never missed her.

CHAPTER XLII
THE GERM OF A BOLD STROKE

If Mr. Davenport Dunn had passed a day of unusual happiness and ease, the night which followed was destined to be one of intense labor and toil. Scarcely had the quiet of repose settled down upon the Hermitage, than the quick tramp of horses, urged to their sharpest trot, was heard approaching, and soon after Mr. Hankes descended from his travelling-carriage at the door.

Dunn had been standing at his open window gazing into the still obscurity of the night, and wondering at what time he might expect him, when he arrived.

"You have made haste, Hankes," said he, not wasting a word in salutation. "I scarcely looked to see you before daybreak."

"Yes, sir; the special train behaved well, and the posters did their part as creditably. I had about four hours altogether in Dublin, but they were quite sufficient for everything."

"For everything?" repeated Dunn.

"Yes; you'll find nothing has been forgotten. Before leaving Cork, I telegraphed to Meekins of the 'Post,' and to Browne of the 'Banner,' to meet me on my arrival at Henrietta Street. Strange enough, they both were anxiously waiting for some instructions on the very question at issue. They came armed with piles of provincial papers, all written in the same threatening style. One in particular, the 'Upper Ossory Beacon,' had an article headed, 'Who is our Dionysius?'"

"Never mind that," broke in Dunn, impatiently. "You explained to them the line to be taken?"

"Fully, sir. I told them that they were to answer the attacks weakly, feebly, deprecating in general terms the use of personalities, and throwing out little appeals for forbearance, and so on. On the question of the Bank, I said, 'Be somewhat more resolute; hint that certain aspersions might be deemed actionable; that wantonly to assail credit is an offence punishable at law; and then dwell upon the benefits already diffused by these establishments, and implore all who have the interest of Ireland at heart not to suffer a spirit of faction to triumph over their patriotism.'"

"Will they understand the part?" asked Dunn, more impatiently than before.

"Thoroughly; Browne, indeed, has a leader already 'set up'—"

"What do I care for all these?" broke in Dunn, peevishly. "Surely no man knows better than yourself that these fellows are only the feathers that show where the wind blows. As to any influence they wield over public opinion, you might as well tell me that the man who sweats a guinea can sway the Stock Exchange."

Hankes shook his head dissentingly, but made no reply.

"You have brought the Bank accounts and the balance-sheet?"

"Yes, they are all here."

"Have you made any rough calculation as to the amount—" He stopped.

"Fifty thousand ought to cover it easily—I mean with what they have themselves in hand. The first day will be a heavy one, but I don't suspect the second will, particularly when it is known that we are discounting freely as ever."

"And now as to the main point?" said Dunn.

"All right, sir. Etheridge's securities give us seventeen thousand; we have a balance of about eleven on that account of Lord Lackington; I drew out the twelve hundred of Kellett's at once; and several other small sums, which are all ready."

"It *is* a bold stroke!" muttered Dunn, musingly.

"None but an original mind could have hit upon it, sir. I used to think the late Mr. Robins a very great man, sir,—and he *was* a great man,—but this is a cut above him."

"Let us say so when it has succeeded, Hankes," said Dunn, with a half-smile.

As he spoke, he seated himself at the table, and, opening a massive account-book, was soon deep in its details. Hankes took a place beside him, and they both continued to con over the long column of figures together.

"We stand in a safer position than I thought, Hankes," said Dunn, leaning back in his chair.

"Yes, sir; we have been nursing this Ossory Bank for some time. You remember, some time ago, saying to me, 'Hankes, put condition on that horse, we'll have to ride him hard before the season is over'?"

"Well, you have done it cleverly, I must say," resumed Dunn. "This concern is almost solvent."

"Almost, sir," echoed Hankes.

"What a shake it will give them all, Hankes," said Dunn, gleefully, "when it once sets in, as it will and must, powerfully! The Provincial will stand easily enough."

"To be sure, sir."

"And the Royal, also; but the 'Tyrawley'—"

"And the 'Four Counties,'" added Hankes. "Driscoll is ready with four thousand of the notes 'to open the ball,' as he says, and when Terry's name gets abroad it will be worse to them than a placard on the walls."

"I shall not be sorry for the 'Four Counties.' It was Mr. Morris, the chairman, had the insolence to allude to me in the House, and ask if it were true that the Ministry had recommended Mr. Davenport Dunn as a fit object for the favors of the Crown? That question, sir, placed my claim in abeyance ever since. The Minister, pledged solemnly to me, had to rise in his place and say 'No.' Of course he added the stereotyped sarcasm, 'Not that, if such a decision had been come to, need the Cabinet have shrunk from the responsibility through any fears of the honorable gentleman's indignation.'"

"Well, Mr. Morris will have to pay for his joke now," said Hankes. "I 'm told his whole estate is liable to the Bank."

"Every shilling of it. Driscoll has got me all the details."

"Lushington will be the great sufferer by the 'Tyrawley,'" continued Hankes.

"Another of them, Hankes,—another of them," cried Dunn, rubbing his hands joyfully. "Tom Lushington—the Honorable Tom, as they called him—blackballed me at 'Brookes's. They told me his very words: 'It's bad enough to be "Dunned," as we are, out of doors, but let us, at least, be safe from the infliction at our Clubs.' A sorry jest, but witty enough for those who heard it."

"I don't think he has sixpence."

"No, sir; nor can he remain a Treasury Lord with a fiat of bankruptcy against him. So much, then, for Tom Lushington! I tell you, Hankes," said he, spiritedly, "next week will have its catalogue of shipwrecks. There's a storm about to break that none have yet suspected."

"There will be some heavy sufferers," said Hankes gravely.

"No doubt, no doubt," muttered Dunn. "I never heard of a battle without killed and wounded. I tell you, sir, again," said he, raising his voice, "before the week ends the shore will be strewn with fragments; we alone will ride through the gale unharmed. It is not fully a month since I showed the Chief Secretary here—ay, and his Excellency, also—the insolent but insidious system of attack the Government journals maintain against me, the half-covert insinuations, the impertinent queries, pretended inquiries for mere information's sake. Of course, I got for answer the usual cant about 'freedom of the press,' 'liberty of public discussion,' with the accustomed assurance that the Government had not, in reality, any recognized organ; and, to wind up, there was the laughing question, 'And what do you care, after all, for these fellows?' But now I will show what I *do* care,—that I have good and sufficient reason to care,—that the calumnies which assail me are directed against my material interests; that it is not Davenport Dunn is 'in cause,' but all the great enterprises associated with his name; that it is not an individual, but the industry of a nation, is at stake; and I will say to them, 'Protect me, or—' You remember the significant legend inscribed on the cannon of the Irish Volunteers, 'Independence or—' Take my word for it, I may not speak as loudly as the nine-pounder, but my fire will be to the full as fatal!"

Never before had Hankes seen his chief carried away by any sense of personal injury; he had even remarked, amongst the traits of his great business capacity, that a calm contempt for mere passing opinion was his characteristic, and he was sorely grieved to find that such equanimity could be disturbed. With his own especial quickness Dunn saw what was passing in his lieutenant's mind, and he added hastily,—

"Not that, of all men, I need care for such assaults; powerful even to tyranny as the press has become amongst us, there is one thing more powerful still, and that is—Prosperity! Ay, sir, there may be cavil and controversy as to your abilities; some may condemn your speech, or carp at your book, they may cry down your statecraft, or deny your diplomacy; but there is a test that all can appreciate, all comprehend, and that is—Success. Have only *that*, Hankes, and the world is with you."

"There's no denying that," said Hankes, solemnly.

"It is the gauge of every man," resumed Dunn,—"from him that presides over a Railway Board to him that sways an Empire. And justly so, too," added he, rapidly. "A man must be a consummate judge of horseflesh that could pick out the winner of the Oaks in a stable; but the scrubbiest varlet on the field can *see* who comes in first on the day of the race! Have you ever been in America, Hankes?" asked he, suddenly.

"Yes; all over the States. I think I know Cousin Jonathan as well as I know old John himself."

"You know a very shrewd fellow, then," muttered Dunn; "over-shrewd, mayhap."

"What led you to think of that country now?" asked the other, curiously.

"I scarcely know," said Dunn, carelessly, as he walked the room in thoughtfulness; then added, "If no recognition were to come of these services of mine, I 'd just as soon live there as here. I should, at least, be on the level of the best above me. Well," cried he, in a higher tone, "we have some trumps to play out ere it come to that."

Once more they turned to the account books and the papers before them, for Hankes had many things to explain and various difficulties to unravel. The vast number of those enterprises in which Dunn engaged had eventually blended and mingled all their interests together. Estates and shipping, and banks, mines, railroads, and dock companies had so often interchanged their securities, each bolstering up the credit of the other in turn, that the whole resembled some immense fortress, where the garrison, too weak for a general defence, was always hastening to some one point or other,—the seat of immediate attack. And thus an Irish draining-fund was one day called upon to liquidate the demands upon a sub-Alpine railroad, while a Mexican tin-mine flew to the rescue of a hosiery scheme in Balbriggan! To have ever a force ready on the point assailed was Dunn's remarkable talent, and he handled his masses like a great master of war.

Partly out of that indolent insolence which power begets, he had latterly been less mindful of the press, less alive to the strictures of journalism, and attacks were made upon him which, directed as they were against his solvency, threatened at any moment to assume a dangerous shape. Roused at last by the peril, he had determined on playing a bold game for fortune; and this it was which now engaged his thoughts, and whose details the dawning day saw him deeply considering. His now great theory was that a recognized station amongst the nobles of the land was the one only security against disaster. "Once amongst them," said he, "they will defend me as one of their order." How to effect this grand object had been the long study of his life. But it was more,—it was also his secret! They who fancied they knew the man, thoroughly understood the habits of his mind, his passions, his prejudices, and his hopes, never as much as suspected what lay at the bottom of them all. He assumed a sort of manner that in a measure disarmed their suspicion; he affected pride in that middle station of life he occupied, and seemed to glory in those glowing eulogies of commercial ability and capacity which it was the good pleasure of leading journalists just then to deliver. On public occasions he made an even ostentatious display of these sentiments, and Davenport Dunn was often quoted as a dangerous man for an hereditary aristocracy to have against them.

Such was he who now pored over complicated details of figures, intricate and tangled schemes of finance; and yet, while his mind embraced them, with other thoughts was he picturing to himself a time when, proud amongst the proudest, he would take his place with the great nobles of the land. It was evident that another had not regarded this ambition as fanciful or extravagant. Lady Augusta—the haughty daughter of one of the haughtiest in the peerage—as much as said, "It was a fair and reasonable object of hope; then none could deny the claims he preferred, nor any affect to undervalue the vast benefits he had conferred on his country." There was something so truly kind, so touching too, in the generous tone she assumed, that Dunn dwelt upon it again and again. Knowing all the secret instincts of that mysterious brotherhood as she did, Dunn imagined to himself all the advantage her advice and counsels could render him. "She can direct me in many ways, teaching me how to treat these mysterious high-priests as I ought What shall I do to secure her favor? How enlist it in my cause? Could I make her partner in the enterprise?" As the thought flashed across him, his cheek burned as if with a flame, and he rose abruptly from the table and walked to the window, fearful lest his agitation might be observed. "That were success, indeed!" muttered he. "What a strong bail-bond would it be when I called two English peers my brothers-in-law, and an earl for my wife's father! This would at once lead me to the very step of the 'Order.' How many noble families would it interest in my elevation! The Ardens are the best blood of the south, connected widely with the highest in both countries. Is it possible that this could succeed?" He thought of the old Earl and his intense pride of birth, and his heart misgave him; but then, Lady Augusta's gentle tones and gentler looks came to his mind, and he remembered that though a peer's daughter, she was penniless, and—we shame to write it— not young. The Lady Augusta Arden marries the millionnaire Mr. Dunn, and the world understands the compact There are many such matches every season.

"What age would you guess me to be, Hankes?" said he, suddenly turning round.

"I should call you—let me see—a matter of forty-five or forty-six, sir."

"Older, Hankes,—older," said he, with a smile of half-pleasure.

"You don't look it, sir, I protest you don't. Sitting up all night and working over these accounts, one might, perhaps, call you forty-six; but seeing you as you come down to breakfast after your natural rest, you don't seem forty."

"This same life is too laborious; a man may follow it for the ten or twelve years of his prime, but it becomes downright slavery after that."

"But what is an active mind like yours to do, sir?" asked Hankes.

"Take his ease and rest himself."

"Ease!—rest! All a mistake, sir. Great business men can't exist in that lethargy called leisure."

"You are quite wrong, Hankes; if I were the master of some venerable old demesne, like this, for instance, with its timber of centuries' growth, and its charms of scenery, such as we see around us here, I 'd ask no better existence than to pass my days in calm retirement, invite a stray friend or two to come and see me, and with books and other resources hold myself aloof from stocks and statecraft, and not so much as ask how are the Funds or who is the Minister."

"I 'd be sorry to see you come to that, sir, I declare I should," said Hankes, earnestly.

"You may live to see it, notwithstanding," said Dunn, with a placid smile.

"Ah, sir," said Hankes, "it's not the man who has just conceived such a grand idea as this "—and he touched the books before him—"ought to talk about turning hermit."

"We'll see, Hankes,—we'll see," said Dunn, calmly. "There come the post-horses—I suppose for you."

"Yes, sir; I ordered them to be here at six. I thought I should have had a couple of hours in bed by that time; but it does n't signify, I can sleep anywhere."

"Let me see," said Dunn, calculating. "This is Tuesday; now, Friday ought to be the day, the news to reach me on Thursday afternoon; you can send a telegraphic message and then send on a clerk. Of course, you will know how to make these communications properly. It is better I should remain here in the interval; it looks like security."

"Do you mean to come over yourself, sir?"

"Of course I do. You must meet me there on Friday morning. Let Mrs. Hailes have the house in readiness in case I might invite any one."

"All shall be attended to ir," said Hankes. "I think I'll despatch Wilkins to you with the news; he's an awful fellow to exaggerate evil tidings."

"Very well," said Dunn. "Good-night, or, I opine, rather, good-morning." And he turned away into his bedroom.

CHAPTER XLIII
THE GARDEN

From the moment that Mr. Davenport Dunn announced he would still continue to enjoy the hospitality of the Hermitage, a feeling of intimacy grew up between himself and his host that almost savored of old friendship. Lord Glengariff already saw in the distance wealth and affluence; he had secured a co-operation that never knew failure,—the one man whose energies could always guarantee success.

It was true, Dunn had not directly pledged himself to anything; he had listened and questioned and inquired and reflected, but given nothing like a definite opinion, far less a promise. But, as the old Lord said, "These fellows are always cautious, always reserved; and whenever they do not oppose, it may be assumed that they concur. At all events, we must manage with delicacy; there must be no haste, no importunity; the best advocacy we can offer to our plans is to make his visit here as agreeable as possible." Such was the wise counsel he gave his daughter as they strolled through the garden after breakfast, talking over the character and the temperament of their guest.

"By George, Gusty!" cried Lord Glengariff, after a moment's silence, "I cannot yet persuade myself that this is 'Old Davy,' as you and the girls used to call him long ago. Of all the miraculous transformations I have ever witnessed, none of them approaches this!"

"It is wonderful, indeed!" said she, slowly.

"It is not that he has acquired or increased his stock of knowledge,— that would not have puzzled me so much, seeing the life of labor he has led,—but I go on asking myself what has become of his former self, of which not a trace nor vestige remains? Where is his shy, hesitating manner, his pedantry, his suspicion,—where the intense eagerness to learn what was going on in the house? You remember how his prying disposition used to worry us?"

"I remember," said she, in a low voice.

"There is something, now, in his calm, quiet deportment very like dignity. I protest I should—seeing him for the first time—call him a well-bred man."

"Certainly," said she, in the same tone.

"As little was I prepared for the frank and open manner in which he spoke to me of himself."

"Has he done so?" asked she, with some animation.

"Yes; with much candor, and much good sense too. He sees the obstacles he has surmounted in life, and he just as plainly perceives those that are not to be overcome."

"What may these latter be?" asked she, cautiously.

"It is pretty obvious what they are," said he, half pettishly,—"his family; his connections; his station, in fact."

"How did he speak of these,—in what terms, I mean?"

"Modestly and fairly. He did not conceal what he owned to feel as certain hardships, but he was just enough to acknowledge that our social system was a sound one, and worked well."

"It was a great admission," said she, with a very faint smile.

"The Radical crept out only once," said the old Lord, laughing at the recollection. "It was when I remarked that an ancient nobility, like a diamond, required centuries of crystallization to give it lustre and coherence. 'It were well to bear in mind, my Lord,' said he, 'that it began by being only charcoal.'"

She gave a low, quiet laugh, but said nothing.

"He has very sound notions in many things,—very sound, indeed. I wish, with all my heart, that more of the class he belongs to were animated with *his* sentiments. He is no advocate for pulling down; moderate, reasonable changes,—changes in conformity with the spirit of the age, in fact,—these he advocates. As I have already said, Gusty, these men are only dangerous when our own exclusiveness has made them so. Treat them fairly, admit them to your society, listen to their arguments, refute them, show them where they have mistaken us, and they are *not* dangerous."

"I suppose you are right," said she, musingly.

"Another thing astonishes me: he has no pride of purse about him; at least, I cannot detect it. He talks of money reasonably and fairly, acknowledges what it can and what it cannot do—"

"And what, pray, is that?" broke she in, hastily.

"I don't think there can be much dispute on *that* score!" said he, in a voice of pique. "The sturdiest advocate for the power of wealth never presumed to say it could make a man,—one of us!" said he, after a pause, that sent the blood to his face.

"But it can, and does, every day," said she, resolutely. "Our peerage is invigorated by the wealth as well as by the talent of the class beneath it; and if Mr. Dunn be the millionnaire that common report proclaims him, I should like to know why that wealth, and all the influence that it wields, should not be associated with the institutions to which we owe our stability."

"The wealth and the influence if you like, only not himself," said the Earl, with a saucy laugh. "My dear Augusta," he added, in a gentle tone, "he is a most excellent and a very useful man—where he is. The age suits him, and he suits the age. We live in stirring times, when these sharp intellects have an especial value."

"You talk as if these men were *your* tools. Is it not just possible you may be *theirs?*" said she, impatiently.

"What monstrous absurdity is this, child!" replied he, angrily. "It is—it is downright—" he grew purple in the endeavor to find the right word,— "downright Chartism!"

"If so, the Chartists have more of my sympathy than I was aware of."

Fortunately for both, the sudden appearance of Dunn himself put an end to a discussion which each moment threatened to become perilous, and whose unpleasant effects were yet visible on their faces. Lord Glengariff had not sufficiently recovered his composure to do more than salute Mr. Dunn; while Lady Augusta's confusion was even yet more marked. They had not walked many steps in company, when Lord Glengariff was recalled to the cottage by the visit of a neighboring magistrate, and Lady Augusta found herself alone with Mr. Dunn.

"I am afraid, Lady Augusta," said he, timidly, "my coming up was inopportune. I suspect I must have interrupted some confidential conversation."

"No, nothing of the kind," said she, frankly. "My father and I were discussing what we can never agree upon, and what every day seems to widen the breach of opinion between us, and I am well pleased that your arrival should have closed the subject."

"I never meant to play eavesdropper, Lady Augusta," said he, earnestly; "but as I came up the grass alley I heard my own name mentioned twice.

Am I indiscreet in asking to what circumstance I owe the honor of engaging your attention?"

"I don't exactly know how to tell you," said she, blushing. "Not, indeed, but that the subject was one on which your own sentiments would be far more interesting than our speculations; but in repeating what passed between us, I might, perhaps, give an undue weight to opinions which merely came out in the course of conversation. In fact, Mr. Dunn," said she, hastily, "my father and I differ as to what should constitute the aristocracy of this kingdom, and from what sources it should be enlisted."

"And was used as an illustration?" said Dunn, bowing low, but without the slightest trace of irritation.

"You were," said she, in a low but distinct voice.

"And," continued he, in the same quiet tone, "Lady Augusta Arden condescended to think and to speak more favorably of the class I belong to than the Earl her father. Well," cried he, with more energy of manner, "it is gratifying to me that I found the advocacy in the quarter that I wished it. I can well understand the noble Lord's prejudices; they are not very unreasonable; the very fact that they have taken centuries to mature, and that centuries have acquiesced in them, would give them no mean value. But I am also proud to think that you, Lady Augusta, can regard with generosity the claims of those beneath you. Remember, too," added he, "what a homage we render to your order when men like myself confess that wealth, power, and influence are all little compared with recognition by you and yours."

"Perhaps," said she, hesitatingly, "you affix a higher value on these distinctions than they merit."

"If you mean so far as they conduce to human happiness, I agree with you; but I was addressing myself solely to what are called the ambitions of life."

"I have the very greatest curiosity to know what are yours," said she, abruptly.

"Mine! mine!" said Dunn, stammering, and in deep confusion. "I have but one."

"Shall I guess it? Will you tell me, if I guess rightly?

"I will, most faithfully."

"Your desire is, then, to be a Cabinet Minister; you want to be where the administrative talents you possess will have their fitting influence and exercise."

"No, not that!" sighed he, heavily.

"Mere title could never satisfy an ambition such as yours; of that I am certain," resumed she. "You wouldn't care for such an empty prize."

"And yet there is a title, Lady Augusta," said he, dropping his voice, which now faltered in every word,—"there is a title to win which has been the guiding spirit of my whole life. In the days of my poverty and obscurity, as well as in the full noon of my success, it never ceased to be the goal of all my hopes. If I tremble at the presumption of even approaching this confession, I also feel the sort of desperate courage that animates him who has but one throw for fortune. Yes, Lady Augusta, such a moment as this may not again occur. I know you sufficiently well to feel that when one, even humble as I am, dares to avow—"

A quick step in the walk adjoining startled both, and they looked up. It was Sybella Eellett, who came up with a sealed packet in her hand.

"A despatch, Mr. Dunn," said she; "I have been in search of you all over the garden." He took it with a muttered "Thanks," and placed it unread in his pocket Miss Eellett quickly saw that her presence was not desired, and with a hurried allusion to engagements, was moving away, when Lady Augusta said,—

"Wait for me, Miss Kellett; Mr. Dunn must be given time for his letters, or he will begin to rebel against his captivity." And with this she moved away.

"Pray don't go, Lady Augusta," said he. "I 'm proof against business appeals to-day." But she was already out of hearing.

Amongst the secrets which Davenport Dunn had never succeeded in unravelling, the female heart was pre-eminently distinguished. The veriest young lady fresh from her governess or the boarding-school would have proved a greater puzzle to him than the most intricate statement of a finance minister. Whether Lady Augusta had fully comprehended his allusion, or whether, having understood it, she wished to evade the subject, and spare both herself and him the pain of any mortifying rejoinder, were now the difficult questions which he revolved over and over in his mind. In his utter ignorance of the sex, he endeavored to solve the problem by the ordinary guidance of his reason, taking no account of womanly reserve and delicacy, still less of that "finesse" of intelligence which, with all the certainty of an instinct, can divine at once in what channel feelings will run, and how their course can be most safely directed.

"She must have seen to what I pointed," said he; "I spoke out plainly enough,—perhaps too plainly. Was that the mistake I made? Was my declaration too abrupt? and if so, was it likely she would not have uttered something like reproof? Her sudden departure might have this signification, as though to say, 'I will spare you any comment; I will seem even not to have apprehended you.' In the rank to which she pertains, I have heard, a chief study is, how much can be avoided of those rough allusions which grate upon inferior existences; how to make life calm and peaceful, divesting it so far as may be of the irritations that spring out of hasty words and heated tempers. In her high-bred nature, therefore, how possible is it that she would reason thus, and say, 'I will not hurt him by a direct refusal; I will not rebuke the presumption of his wishes. He will have tact enough to appreciate my conduct, and return to the topic no more!' And yet, how patiently she had heard me up to the very moment of that unlucky interruption. Without a conscious sense of encouragement I had never dared to speak as I did. Yes, assuredly, she led me on to talk of myself and my ambitions as I am not wont to do. She went even further. She overcame objections which, to myself, had seemed insurmountable. She spoke to me like one taking a deep, sincere interest in my success; and was this feigned? or, if real, what meant it? After all, might not her manner be but another phase of that condescension with which her 'Order' listen to the plots and projects of inferior beings,— something begotten of curiosity as much as of interest?"

In this fashion did he guess and speculate and question on a difficulty where even wiser heads have guessed and speculated and questioned just as vaguely.

At last he was reminded of the circumstance which had interrupted their converse,—the despatch. He took it from his pocket and looked at the address and the seal, but never opened it, and with a kind of half-smile replaced it in his pocket.